One Wilde Ride
Book Three

What Should Never Be

LM Foster

ISBN-10: 0692389067
ISBN-13: 978-0692389065

Cover
The Birthplace of Herbert Hoover,
West Branch, Iowa, 1931
By American painter Grant Wood (1891–1942)
Oil on Masonite
Minneapolis Institute of Arts

Design by
Ravenna Young
www.ravennayoung.blogspot.ca

9th Street Press
www.9thstreetpress.com

And the wild regrets, and the bloody sweats,
  None knew so well as I:
For he who lives more lives than one
  More deaths than one must die.
       – Oscar Wilde, *The Ballad of Reading Gaol*

ONE

Leo Adrian Wilde, aged twelve, sat in an uncomfortable plastic chair in a hospital waiting room, all by himself. He was scared. His mother was in surgery. She was gonna be okay. Gil had already told him that. They were just putting a pin in her broken leg. She'd lost the baby, but she was gonna be okay.

Leo wasn't scared for his mom. He was scared for himself. His mom . . . The miscarriage, the surgery . . . Gil was gonna say it was all his fault. It was really Gil's fault, but he was the adult, as he never failed to remind Leo. Gil was bigger, stronger, in charge of Leo's life. He was going to say it was all Leo's fault, and then he'd proceed to take it out on him.

Leo lived in a world where everything changed on a daily basis, as if all the rooms he occupied were connected to giant pulleys. They'd switch around, up and down, back and forth, on end, without warning.

Today, his mom would be happy and joyful and loving. She'd hug him, kiss him, tell him how proud she was of him. She'd tell him what a great big brother he was going to be.

Then the next day, she'd be quiet and sad. She wouldn't hug him, she wouldn't even look at him. She'd say how she wasn't sure if it was the best idea to be bringing a new life into the world. She'd be annoyed. She'd tell him not to piss Gil off.

Leo believed that his mother loved him, most days, except those times when she chose to placate Gil instead of accommodating Leo's wants or needs. Those were the days when she said, "Gil won't like that," and then Leo knew that he wouldn't get to play soccer or he wouldn't be getting that new computer game. Leo realized that this was for the best – Gil in his normal surly mode was better than Gil angry, for both of them – but Leo hated his mom a little bit when she did it.

His stepfather's moods were similarly erratic. Leo learned the signs and symptoms of Gil's dark days: perhaps a whiff of alcohol on his breath, or silence when he entered a room, followed by a hate-filled glare. From about the age of five or so, Leo had learned to make himself scarce immediately at these times, if it was at all possible.

Gil did have some good days. There were never any hugs and kisses, or praise, although on the best days, Gil would be almost friendly to his stepson. He might say hello, offer Leo the slight upturning of his mouth that passed for a smile. He might ask Leo what he was up to, how his life was going. Gil wouldn't listen to the boy's replies, because he didn't care what his stepson was up to. Gil didn't care about how Leo's life was going, and Leo knew it. But at least he asked every now and again.

Still, Leo had learned to be wary of his stepfather's good days also, because they could quickly turn sour. Sometimes his cheer was the result of tossing back a couple with his buddies from the job. If those buddies were around, then it was all right. Gil didn't deride Leo, or insult him, he didn't tell him that he was as worthless as his ol' man, if his friends were at the house. Gil didn't backhand Leo in front of his buddies.

Gil never said that oldie but goodie in front of Leo's mom, either: *you're as worthless as your ol' man.* That one was Gil's special expression of love for his stepson, held in reserve for those unfortunate times when they found themselves alone. If Leo failed at some task, or said the wrong thing, and no one else was around, that was Gil's go to comment: *you're as worthless as your ol' man.*

That saying the wrong thing problem? That was the funny thing, except it wasn't funny at all. It was another portal into the shifting-of-rooms feeling for Leo. He was never sure, from one day to the next, what the wrong thing was going to be. Some days, when his stepfather was in a black mood, if Leo just said hi, it was enough for Gil to reply, "Hey, how 'bout you shut the fuck up?"

Sometimes, a question answered, a simple comment made, would get Leo that familiar glare, but on other days, Gil would be almost conversational. He might even ask Leo's opinion – what color should we paint the bathroom? Or, how 'bout dem Raiders?

Even then, Leo was never sure what to expect. If he suggested white for the bathroom, Gil might think that was a good idea, or he might tell Leo that he lacked imagination. Win or lose, if he praised the Raiders, one day Gil might agree. The next he might say Leo was a band-wagoner if they were winning, or a hater if they were losing.

This constant eddying state of flux of his parents' moods caused Leo to become vigilant, cagey. He became a pathological liar, at least when he was dealing with them. The simplest answer was always the best, regardless if it was true or not.

"Did you go up to the store yet?"

2

A simple enough question. But was he gonna get yelled at if he said he'd already gone, because something new was to be added to the list? Or was he gonna get screamed at for being lazy for still being here?

Leo would stare keenly at Gil or his mom, trying to read his or her mind. He'd become almost preternaturally observant, far beyond his years, as if he was a psychologist, bound to discover his parents' deepest motivations. What was the answer they wanted today? Which answer would be the safest?

Leo became adept at reading their moods, if not their minds, and he'd supply the answer that would allow his life to go on in the smoothest manner possible, whether it was the truth or not. Whether he'd already visited the market or hadn't, he manufactured a lie based on what he thought they wanted to hear. Whatever would get them to shut up and leave him alone the quickest.

The mindless uncertainty to his parents' moods, as well as the definite certainty of his stepfather's dislike, was the way of Leo's life. He was able to hate it – he was able to hate Gil – because he knew things didn't have to be this way. When he was with his grandparents or his aunts – and especially when he was with his Uncle Nick – Leo experienced what a normal, loving family was like. From the time he could cross the street by himself, from the time he could go up the hill without getting lost and frightened on the path through the trees, he tried to spend as much time with his extended family as he could.

But they were only his extended family, after all. Leo lived under Gil's roof. Gil supported him, housed him, clothed him, fed him – his stepfather never let him forget all that – so Leo (and his always appeasing mother) were therefore subject to Gil's strict rules, his whims.

Since he knew that there was another way, since he realized that the other adults in his family were kind and fair, loving and just, Leo didn't act out. He didn't rebel against the many unfairnesses of his life. He appeared for all the world to be a quiet, thoughtful, well-adjusted boy. But just like anyone else who lived with a viper in his midst, Leo was also sneaky and scheming. He woke up in a brave new world every day. What kind of fanciful stories would he have to invent to help him get through it unscathed?

To his constant and appalled amazement, Leo saw proof that his mother loved Gil. She wished that her husband was nicer to her boy, but . . . Leo thought that she was just waiting out the time until Leo

3

was a grown-up and would be gone. He thought that his mother loved him only when it was convenient for her, when it wouldn't piss Gil off for some unfathomable reason. Leo could see that she was frequently torn between her love for her boy and her love for her husband, but since she almost always picked her husband – her son would be gone someday – Leo thought his mother was weak. He loved her, but he also hated that weakness in her. He lied to her as effortlessly as he lied to Gil. There was no need to keep multiple stories straight that way, and since she most often sided with Gil anyway, a lie was easier. Safer.

Gil loved no one but himself, Leo was sure of that. He unfailingly took his own needs into consideration first, way before those of his wife and stepson. Gil wouldn't want to drive Leo to soccer practice, or stand around on the sidelines while he played, so soccer was out. No computer game this month, because Gil didn't think there was any point to them, and he could use the money for something for himself, such as putting gas in Leo's grandfather's boat.

Gil didn't take *One Wilde Ride* out very often, but anytime he did, he'd invariably be gone for the whole weekend, and that was fine with Leo. His mother didn't care for the activity, and Leo hated the water, so Gil went by himself.

When he was little, Leo's aversion to water had disconcerted his grandfather. Leo loved Grandpa Ian, so he'd tried to please him and enjoy boating, but it was just not possible. The brown waters of Lake Perris and the green ones of Elsinore always felt slimy and unclean on Leo's skin. His imagination peopled them with sea monsters, waiting for the first opportunity to drag him to their depths, to his doom.

Even if Leo couldn't be persuaded to enjoy boating, his grandfather had insisted that the boy learn to swim. It was something everybody needed to know how to do, Ian contended. It was an integral part of life. So Grandpa Ian and Uncle Nick faithfully took Leo to swim lessons every Saturday at the YMCA. He still didn't take to the life aquatic. Leo just didn't like to be in the water. But at least at the Y's big blue pool, the water was clean and he could see the bottom.

Leo received his certificate at the age of six. He knew how to swim. His grandfather was proud of this simple achievement, undertaken by the boy just to please him. Leo could swim, his grandfather was satisfied, and boat rides were never brought up again. Grandpa Ian didn't use his boat anymore, anyway.

Gil would pack up *One Wilde Ride* and head off to the lake by himself, or with a couple of his buddies. Leo relished these weekends, rare though they were, because he got to spend them alone with his mom. She'd be pleasant and attentive then. She'd show Leo a motherly devotion, assure him that he was the most important thing in her life. And Leo would believe it, at least until Gil came back home.

TWO

Leo didn't have to lie to the rest of his family. Their moods were always relevant to the situation; an answer to a question posed yesterday would garner the same reaction today. All the rooms in their houses stayed put. His grandparents loved each other, and they loved him, and the two little old ladies that he called his aunts, they loved him, too.

But all these members of Leo's family were old, and they always struck Leo as unusually watchful – especially Daina, his grandmother. *Like she's waiting for something,* Leo had thought for his entire life. *What is she waiting for?*

But Leo's Uncle Nick wasn't watchful. He wasn't that much older than the boy – a little more than fifteen years – so he was too young to be Leo's father. Nick had always treated Leo like a favorite little brother; he'd always been Leo's best friend. More or less, Nick was his only friend. Gil didn't like it if his stepson invited his peers over to the house, and kids Leo's own age didn't like his stepfather's menacing stares.

But Nick didn't care about Gil's hard looks. Leo knew that his stepfather and his uncle didn't get along. From little on, Leo had noticed that they avoided each other. That was also fine with Leo.

Nick's parents had gifted him with Marta's red 1986 BMW as a Christmas present in 1992. The DMV was closed the next day, on his sixteenth birthday, but when he passed his driver's test the following Monday, the first place he drove was out to see his eight-month-old-cousin. From then on, it was Uncle Nick that did all the kid things with Leo. Nick took him to the Festival of Lights downtown during the holidays, Nick took him to the mall to sit on Santa's knee. Gil had been the one to tell Leo that there really was no Santa Claus, but Leo had asked Nick for confirmation.

Nick took Leo to Disneyland and Knott's Berry Farm. Nick took him to the movies, played games with him on his computer. Nick would've taken him to soccer practice, but Gil put his foot down. "That asshole Wilde kid doesn't need another excuse to be hanging around here. He's here too much as it is."

Nick covertly encouraged Leo's dislike for his stepdad. "I know he's an asshole, Leo. You just gotta put up with it for now. When you get old enough, you can tell him to fuck off and come live with me." Nick would smile and slap his cousin on the back. "But don't tell him I said that. It'll only make things worse now."

Things had been bad enough his whole life. Now, at twelve, Leo knew that they were about to get much worse.

Leo took his flip-phone out of his pocket and called Nick again. He glanced furtively out the window of the waiting room as he did so. The phone had been a gift from his uncle – Gil thought it was ridiculous that a twelve-year-old kid had something as expensive and delicate, as complicated, as a cellphone – and he didn't like to see Leo on it. He didn't even have one himself, although he was always talking about getting one.

Come on, answer! Leo thought as the phone rang. He'd already left two messages.

Nick picked up at last. "I'm on my way, Leo. How's she doing?"

"Gil says she's gonna be okay. She's in surgery, for her leg. Gil says she lost the baby."

"I'm sorry, Leo. What happened?"

Leo opened his mouth to speak. A lie didn't spring immediately to his mind. He didn't lie to his uncle or his grandparents. It was impossible to lie to his aunts: *they knew things.* Nick and the rest of his family took explanations (good or bad) for what they were. They didn't punish Leo for the truth, like his parents did, if the truth wasn't to their liking.

But at that moment, Gil looked in through the window and skewered Leo with a hateful stare.

"It's a long story, Nick." Leo had dropped the *Uncle* from about the age of ten. Nick wasn't his father's brother; they were actually cousins, and they'd always been more like brothers themselves, anyway. "I'll tell you when you get here. Did you tell –"

"Yeah. We'll be there soon."

Leo said okay and hung up. Gil looked at him with that *you're as worthless as your ol' man* glare for another moment and then turned to ask something of a nurse that was walking by. Leo relaxed a little bit. His family would be here soon, Nick and his aunts and his grandparents. His uncle had relayed the news of his mother's accident to them. Leo knew that Gil wouldn't have done it.

THREE

Randi awakened in a bright, unfamiliar room. There were noises, voices around her. She tried to move, but her limbs didn't answer. All she could feel was a vague achiness all over. A smiling young woman in nurses' scrubs came up to the side of her bed. The bed had a railing on it, and Randi realized that she was in the hospital.

But she couldn't be in the hospital. Not yet. The baby wasn't due for another four months . . .

The nurse answered the question in Randi's eyes. "You're in Recovery, honey."

Randi opened her mouth to speak, but she discovered that her throat was dry, and no sound came out. She swallowed and tried again. "My baby?"

The nurse's face clouded. Her smile fled. She shook her head. "I'm sorry, honey. But I'm sure you can have another one. Just as soon as your leg heals . . ."

"What happened to me?" Randi asked the nurse. She felt like she should be alarmed, but somehow the emotion couldn't quite assert itself through the lingering anesthesia.

The nurse consulted her chart. "It was an accident. You've got a broken leg. The doctor will be right in, honey. He'll tell you all about it. How's your pain?"

"I feel . . . numb. No pain. Where's my husband?"

"We'll go find him. As soon as the doctor talks to you, we'll get you to a room, and you can see your family. He'll be in soon." The nurse patted Randi on the shoulder, smiled, then moved away to see to her other patients.

Randi tried to remember . . . It was Saturday. Was it still Saturday? There were no windows in the Recovery Room. Randi couldn't see a clock. What day was it?

What happened? How did I get here? Randi concentrated, tried to bring up the day's events.

It was Saturday, or it had been. She'd had an appointment to see her obstetrician, her regularly monthly appointment. That had been scheduled for 12:30. Randi remembered being in the car with Gil and Leo. They were taking her to the doctor's office.

Now it all played out in Randi's mind. They were in the car . . . Gil stopped at the end of the street, looked both ways. But he didn't pull out onto Jurupa, because . . . the flag was up on the mailbox . . .

The little cul-de-sac on which Gil, Randi and Leo, Ian and Daina, and Penny and Bellona lived was called Parcay Street. The mailman delivered Gil and Randi's mail and Ian and Daina's to their doors. But because their house had been there before the other two dwellings had been constructed, and because it was only reached by a footpath, Penny and Bellona's mailbox was located out on the curb on Jurupa Road.

Jurupa was the main thoroughfare through the neighborhood. Wide and busy, it ran in front of the long front yard to Ian and Daina's house, and past Allan Coleman's old shop, and past Hilltop Market. It was a dangerous street: traffic was plentiful and moved fast. There were frequent accidents. Many of Penny and Bellona's long string of cats had met its demise trying to cross Jurupa Road.

Her husband had seen the flag up on Penny and Bellona's mailbox . . . It was all coming back to Randi now.

Gil put his arm behind her headrest, looked over his shoulder at Leo. Gil was angry . . .

He yelled, "Goddamn it! Don't you ever do anything you're told? Why didn't you take your aunts' mail up to them?"

It was one of Leo's many chores. Besides cutting the grass and taking the garbage cans in and out at his own house, Gil had made Leo into a veritable slave on Parcay Street. He cut his grandparents' lawn; he carried his aunts' garbage from their house to their cans at the bottom of the hill, took the cans to and from the curb. He took Ian and Daina's cans back in, if Ian didn't get to them first.

And another one of Leo's assigned tasks was to take Penny and Bellona's mail up to them, if he saw that the flag was up. The boy didn't mind helping out his relatives. He didn't see these little duties as the punishments Gil had intended them to be.

But Leo had missed his aunts' mail today, Randi remembered. He'd just –

"I forgot," Leo said.

"You always forget," Gil said irritably over his shoulder. "You've always got some excuse."

It wasn't true. Her son was a good boy. Leo always did what he was told, without complaint . . .

"I'll do it right now," he'd said. He was a good boy.

But after he undid his seatbelt, as he leaned forward, about to get out of the car . . . Randi remembered that Gil grabbed Leo by the back of the neck and slammed his head into the back of her headrest.

9

Randi remembered feeling the vibration, remembered looking anxiously in the rearview mirror . . .

Leo wasn't hurt. It wasn't a damaging action on Gil's part, just a humiliating one. Leo had bounced back into the seat. Gil said, "Not now, stupid. You'll make us late."

Leo glared at Gil. "That's all right. You guys go. I wouldn't want to make anybody late." Leo opened the car door, got out.

And that would've all been okay, if Gil, furious, hadn't also jumped out of the car. Leo wasn't going to defy him. He yelled at him to get the fuck back in the car . . .

Leo glanced up Jurupa Road, then down, then back at Gil. Then he made a break for it . . . He dashed across the street. As he crossed the yellow line, he stumbled, fell . . . He slid into the dirt shoulder.

Randi remembered screaming, *"Leo!"* She remembered struggling with her seat belt for a second, throwing open the car door. Leo was trying to get up, but wasn't doing a good job of it. Randi remembered the fear . . . *Oh my God, my baby's hurt!* She remembered stepping out into the street . . . She had to get to him . . .

Randi remembered nothing after that.

FOUR

The doctor came in and told Randi that she'd sustained a broken left femur, that her tibia had been shattered. When she stepped out in front of the surprised man in the little pickup, he'd swerved to miss her, but his bumper had struck her in the left leg. It could've been a lot worse.

The doctor had installed pins into her bones. It would be a long road to recovery, maybe four to six months. A hospital stay, physical therapy, a walker, crutches . . . The doctor smiled. "You're very lucky, Mrs. Hogan. You'll eventually be as good as new."

"Where's my son?" Randi asked.

The doctor looked at his nurse. She shrugged. Was it her job to keep track of family members now, too? She said, "I'm sure he'll be right in to see you. We're going to move you to your room now."

"I'll look in on you again later, Mrs. Hogan," the doctor assured Randi, as they wheeled her bed out of Recovery.

As soon as the hospital staff had her situated in her room, they let Gil in to see her. He looked pale, worried. He took her hand, the one that didn't have an IV attached to it. He said, "How ya doin', baby? I guess you didn't see that truck coming. Why did you have to –"

"Where's Leo?" All Randi could see was the picture of her son, lying dazed in the dirt on the shoulder. "Is he okay?"

Gil frowned. All she ever thought about was that brat. She'd stepped out in front of a truck, got herself all busted up . . . She'd killed his baby . . . All because Leo had run away like a little girl, and had tripped over his own clumsy feet.

Gil paused, allowing Randi to stew in her fear for a second. Then he said, "Leo's fine. Not a scratch on him."

Not yet, Gil thought. *But I'm gonna beat his ass this time, maybe black his eye for him. I was finally going to get to have a kid of my own, a kid that looks like me, but Randi had to run after Leo . . .*

"Where is he?" Randi insisted.

"Oh, for Christ's sake, Randi! He's out in the hall. They'll only let us in one at a time! You don't even care about . . . ." Gil saw the tears well up in her eyes and he stopped. He squeezed her hand. "We'll try again, baby. Just as soon as you're better."

Randi wept, and Gil kissed her dry lips gently. He brushed the hair out of her eyes. He was surprised to see a few strands of gray among the black.

Randi had turned thirty-four back in May. She was still of childbearing age, but this pregnancy had been a complete surprise. Gil was thirty-nine, and he considered it a little old to be just starting out on fatherhood. Now it would probably be a year or more before they could try again.

Gil wondered if, after getting hit by a truck, after having a miscarriage . . . He wondered if Randi *could* conceive again. He wondered if she'd want to.

FIVE

Gil left Randi's room to find a crowd of people waiting anxiously for news.

There was Mrs. Green, looking dumpy and worn-out as usual. Gil wondered who'd called her. Randi didn't talk to her mother too much, but Grandma Green always remembered Leo on his birthday and at Christmas, so Gil figured that he'd called her. Randi's brothers and sister weren't there. Her youngest brother might be in jail again for all Gil knew – he had a bit of a methamphetamine problem – and her oldest brother and older sister had long ago moved out of town.

Gil gave Mrs. Green a comforting hug and she went in to see her daughter.

Randi's son and *his* family stood in a circle: his grandfather and his grandmother – Gil noted that she still looked good, even at fifty-seven. Seeing Mrs. Wilde made Gil remember that he hadn't yet called to tell Nadine about the accident (she also still looked good at fifty-seven, too, and was still just as passionate as she'd ever been).

Gil saw that the two little old ladies were also present, looking concerned. And there was Nick Wilde, that perennial pain-in-the-ass, standing next to Leo.

Gil frowned and decided that he'd just by-pass this little gathering and go on down the hall, find a payphone and call Nadine. He thought, not for the first time, that maybe he should invest in one of those cellphones, like the one that shithead Nick had given to Leo.

But Gil wasn't so sure. He'd looked at Leo's, had noted that the thing kept a record of who called and who was called. Having lived the equivalent of a double-life for a very long time, Gil recognized that such a thing could be used as evidence against him. Gil knew that you could probably erase the call records . . . But he'd never been much good with electronic stuff, so why risk it?

Mrs. Green came back out of Randi's room. "She wants to see Leo."

Of course she does. Gil gritted his teeth. *The apple of her eye,* Gil thought, *just like Grandma used to say. She lost the baby because of him, and now she wants to see if her surviving kid is okay . . .*

Leo skirted past Gil, avoiding his gaze, and went into his mother's room.

The old man, Ian, made eye contact with Gil, started to walk over to him. Ian had always been polite to him, kind, even – Leo's grandfather let him use his boat whenever he wanted to. But Gil wasn't in the mood to commiserate with the old guy right now. Before Ian could get within speaking distance, Gil held his hand up to the side of his head – *I have to make a phone call* – Ian nodded and turned back to his family. Gil strode off down the hall to call Nadine.

SIX

Leo was worried about his mom, and he was sorry that she'd lost the baby, but there was a silver lining to the tragedy: he got to stay with Nick until she got out of the hospital.

Leo had taken Nick aside and whispered the tale to him: there'd been an argument with Gil, so Leo decided that he didn't want to go to the doctor's with them. He'd gotten out of the car, dashed across the street, slipped. His mom had seen him fall, she'd tried to run to him. She got hit by a truck, lost the baby . . . And Gil was going to blame it all on him.

Nick could tell that the kid was frightened. He knew that Gil was an asshole to Leo, that he backhanded him on occasion. But Nick had no concept of child abuse – neither of his parents had ever raised a hand to him or Bobby – so Nick didn't completely understand the nightmare in which Adrian's son daily lived.

"He's gonna beat my ass," Leo whispered fearfully.

Nick thought that the kid was a little old for a spanking, but he believed Leo when he said Gil would blame the whole sad episode on him. Gil was a bastard, a cheating, murdering son of a bitch; he never took responsibility for anything. Randi wasn't going to be there to intercede between her son and his stepfather's rage for a while, so Nick wasn't going to leave Leo alone with him.

Gil had acquiesced without argument, just like Nick knew he would. Gil didn't care about Adrian's son, not in the least. It was July – Adrian would've been thirty-four, just last week – so it wasn't like Leo had to be in school.

Gil wouldn't miss Leo. In fact it would be a pleasure to not to have to look at him. And he'd be able to spend his evenings with Nadine, for as long as Randi was in the hospital.

SEVEN

Like his Uncle Rob, Nick had remained a bachelor. Like his uncle, Nick had just never found the right woman. He never wanted for a date, but . . . Although he'd never admit it, the torch he'd carried for Randi when he was a teenager had burnt Nick. *Scorched him.*

Randi had once seemed so perfect . . .

But she refused to see that Gil had murdered Adrian. That fact had destroyed Nick's love for her, and if the woman he'd once found to be so perfect could turn out to be so black-hearted, so weak as to take back the man who'd murdered Adrian, whom she'd once loved so much . . .

Frailty, thy name is woman, his father's poetic twin had said one time, after one of his more contentious break-ups. Uncle Ian had nodded sagely. Nick agreed, but he didn't know why Ian was agreeing. He had a perfect relationship, a perfect marriage. Nick remembered how much Adrian had admired his parents' love, how much he'd sought to find a girl that he'd love as much as his dad loved his mom. In his short twenty-one years, Adrian hadn't found her.

Not for lack of trying, Nick would recall with a grin. Then his grin would fade. The last one Adrian tried had turned out to be the worst one of all. The last one had gotten him killed.

And Nick had once considered Randi to be so wonderful. If she could turn out to be such a traitor . . . And the thoughts would circle back upon themselves in his mind. His disillusionment with Randi had caused Nick to distrust all women. And after a while, the ones he dated sensed his distrust, and left him. What had any of them ever done to him? Why was he always so suspicious?

Nick didn't mourn them when they said goodbye. Women were like buses: if you missed one, another one would arrive shortly. And maybe the next one would be more trustworthy than the last . . .

Nick would be twenty-nine in December. Sometimes he thought that life was getting away from him, that he might remain single like his Uncle Rob forever, that he might never find that bus that he could believe in. But he had a lot of fun looking for her.

Nick was a software engineer for a firm that wrote programs for small businesses. This job paid the bills, and rather well. But Nick's passion, his avocation, as it'd been all his life, was playing and writing music. Still, it was 2004, and Nick Wilde couldn't be bothered with writing it out longhand.

Leo often stood and gazed over his cousin's shoulder while he composed. The notes onscreen always looked like chicken scratch to Leo. He had no interest whatsoever in music.

But Nick's computer was state of the art.

Leo didn't have a Nintendo or a PlayStation, because Gil wouldn't allow it. So Nick had bought him a modest computer, and he liked to play games on it and surf the web. But because his cousin wrote music on his, the sound on Nick's rig was exponentially better than Leo's little PC speakers at home.

Whenever he visited his cousin, Leo would wait patiently until Nick finished whatever gobbledygook he was writing and closed the program – Leo wouldn't dare disturb it while it was running because what it produced looked so foreign to him – then he'd go online and lose himself in cyberspace. In surround-sound.

Nick also had several guitars, sitting on stands in the living room of his bachelor pad. They were mostly to impress the ladies – Nick had never found another band in which to play.

"Women love a guitar player," Nick frequently told Leo. Then he'd regale the kid with a story about his dad from their Urban Equinox days.

But Leo was too young to be aware of women yet, and he showed no interest whatsoever in Nick's instruments. Nick had hung Adrian's beloved guitar, his yellow and black 1982 Charvel EVH Graphic, up on the wall behind his computer. When he told Leo that seeing his dad's axe served as an inspiration for his songwriting, Leo would gaze solemnly up at it as if it was some kind of incomprehensible striped talisman.

Then he'd look at the picture of his dad and the rest of the band that Nick kept on a little shelf nearby, and Nick would tell him again what a great guy his dad had been, and how much fun they'd had in the old days, and how much he missed Adrian. Every day.

EIGHT

Leo got to spend two glorious weeks at Nick's apartment.

When his mother returned home, her leg was still encased in bulky plaster. She hobbled around painfully on crutches. Leo became the shadow at her side for the remainder of the summer, waiting on her hand and foot. Without complaint, he made her sandwiches, fetched a pillow for her, dutifully retrieved her pain pills whenever she asked for them.

Before his stepfather was due home from work each day, Leo made sure his mother was comfortable, that she had the remote to the TV nearby, that she had her pills and a glass of water within reach. As soon as he'd hear Gil's car in the driveway, Leo would retire to his room to play on his computer, or he'd invent a reason to visit his grandparents or his aunts. Or he'd call his cousin, and if Nick wasn't busy, Leo would walk down to the corner and wait for him there. Anything to avoid his stepdad.

The slight upturning of his mouth that passed for a smile was completely absent when Gil looked at Leo now. His hatred and disgust for the boy were always on display. Leo didn't think that his mom noticed the change, maybe because she was still in pain. Or maybe it was because she was more or less always zoned out on her painkillers.

NINE

A year after the accident, Randi was still in pain. Twin orthopedists, Robert and William Wilde, were consulted. They examined Randi, watched her limp across the room. They studied how the fractures looked on the original x-rays. They ordered new x-rays and studied them. They met with Doctor Reed, who'd performed Randi's surgery. He was a colleague. They complimented the work of their brother in Hippocrates: according to the x-rays, Randi's injuries had healed flawlessly.

There was no medical reason why she limped, why she was still in pain, why she still *needed* at least one or two Vicodin every day.

"It's all in your head," Doctor William Wilde told her.

"You should try to wean yourself off of the pain medication," Doctor Robert Wilde advised.

"I'll do that," Randi told her son's relatives. They'd come at his cousin's request, because Nick was concerned that Randi was still in pain. His father and his uncle were the best orthopedists in town. If anyone could make Randi's pain go away, Nick knew it was them.

"Thanks so much for coming out to see me," Randi said.

Will and Rob told her that it was no trouble at all – she was family – and took their leave.

They don't understand, Randi thought as she watched them get into Will's Benz and drive away. *They're not the ones with pins and screws and wires and God only knows what else in their bones.*

They want to take my medicine away! she realized suddenly.

Some days, the Vicodin was the only thing that helped Randi make it through. Some days, she needed it for the pain. But on other days, there was no pain. Some days, Randi just popped a Vicodin because it helped her to ignore Gil's constant belittling of Leo. Some days, the narcotic helped her ignore Gil altogether. He'd never gotten over the miscarriage. He blamed Leo for it, and she thought that he blamed her, too, because she hadn't conceived again. Randi thought that somehow Gil knew that she hadn't really wanted to try again . . .

Gil warned her not to take too many of the pills. He wasn't worried about an overdose. He knew that if she used them up too quickly, Doctor Reed wouldn't refill the prescription anymore.

"He'll think you're getting addicted and cut you off," Gil told her. "Cold turkey," he'd added with a malicious little grin.

Randi became petrified of this idea, that one day, she wouldn't be allowed to have any more of the fat, white pills. They were her little friends. They helped her to sleep, to forget, to ignore the things in life that she didn't want to face. So when she visited the doctor, Randi made sure not to appear to be *a med-seeking patient* as Gil had termed it.

A year and a half after her surgery, Doctor Reed pronounced her completely healed, as good as new. He told her that she didn't have to come to see him anymore, because there was nothing else he could do for her. He at last expressed concern that she was still on pain medication. He gave her the same advice that the Doctors Wilde had given her six months earlier: she should try to wean herself off from them.

"I'll do that," Randi told him. "Thanks so much for all you've done for me. I'll miss you." Randi gave Doctor Reed a hug and left his office.

When her orthopedic surgeon's last prescription for Vicodin ran out, Randi simply made an appointment with another doctor. "They don't talk to each other," Gil told her. "Just tell him that you fell or something. He'll give you another prescription."

Gil found that he liked Randi better when she'd taken a pill or two. He didn't think she was addicted: she only took one or two a week now. He liked to have one every now and then himself. Randi seemed a little livelier, a little happier when she took her pills. She didn't mope around the house as much. She didn't constantly bitch about her leg hurting her.

As if all that was my fault.

Time passed, and Gil came to see Randi as a feeling-sorry-for-herself whiner more and more. She didn't do anything but sit around the house. He hadn't been able to persuade her to go back to work at Mohini's. She claimed that she was in too much pain to work all day.

Yet Gil never failed to notice that Randi never blamed Leo for wrecking her life, for killing her baby, however. She was always just as kind and loving to her boy as she'd always been, would get all sentimental and talk baby-talk to him as if he was five again, if she was on a good Vicodin bender.

No, Randi never blamed Leo for the fact that he'd crippled her, that it was his fault that she didn't have a baby to raise. It was Leo's fault that his mother's life was empty. *And mine as well,* Gil told himself. *It's all Leo's fault. It's always been Leo's fault.*

TEN

Nick Wilde had been not quite eleven years old on the 5th of July, 1986 – the DMV was closed on the 4th – when he and Bobby, Ian, and a solemn and silent Daina, had accompanied Adrian to take his driver's test. Nick had been happy for his cousin when he passed, and gleefully thankful that someone besides their parents would now be available to drive him to guitar lessons.

And Nick was as proud as any papa on April 8th, 2008, when he drove his cousin's son to the same DMV to take *his* driver's test.

Leo used Nick's brand new, quick little Civic for this rite of passage. While the momentous date was still in the future, Nick had taught Leo to drive, and more particularly, how to drive a stick-shift, in an empty parking lot. A spot of dolor clouded Nick's mood when he recalled that he'd had to learn the same skills on his own. Adrian had always promised to teach him how to drive, but Adrian was gone long before Nick had turned sixteen.

Leo passed his driver's exam with a nearly perfect score. Nick quipped that he would've expected nothing else, seeing as how his cousin had been playing *Grand Theft Auto* on his computer for years.

"Where do you want to go first?" the elder Wilde asked.

Leo shrugged. "Back to your house, I guess."

Nick was appalled. The vistas of Leo's life had just expanded, even if he didn't have a car waiting for him at home. Randi and that son of a bitch that she was married to hadn't been parents enough to buy him one yet, but still . . . Leo was footloose and fancy-free. He didn't have a fatherless, eight-month-old cousin to go to visit, like Nick had had at the same age.

"Look," Nick told him. "You can borrow my car. Don't you have some girl you'd like to go see?"

Leo squinted, as if he was considering it. "Maybe . . ." Then he shook his head. "Nah. No one in particular."

Nick blinked in surprise. Leo had his father's looks, if not his charm, and by the time Adrian was sixteen . . . "Don't you like girls, Leo?"

Leo grinned. "What're ya trying to say, Nick? I like girls. I just don't trust 'em very much."

Nick reflected that perhaps his own attitudes had rubbed off on his cousin's son. But Nick was almost thirty-two. He figured that he had considerably more experience with women than did his sixteen-year-old cousin: by this late date, Nick had plenty of reasons to be suspicious of them.

But Leo was just a kid. He had access to a new car; he should be more than ready to take some pretty young thing out for a ride . . .

Nick asked, "What don't you trust about them?"

The new driver shrugged again. "I don't trust anybody, my brutha."

It was a bittersweet pang to Nick to hear Adrian's expression come out of his son's mouth. Since he'd never known his dad, Nick realized that the kid had to have learned it from him. It wasn't like Bobby ever visited him. Leo didn't know his father's other cousin.

"Except you, of course," Leo continued. He shrugged a third time. "I wonder about girls' motivations. What do they want from me?"

Nick made an obscene gesture.

Leo grinned. "That's usually it."

Nick thought that Leo was the spitting image of Adrian: the same black hair, the same blue eyes. But there were also startling differences. Where Adrian had always worn his hair long and feathered – a little bit calmer of a 'do than his idol Eddie Van Halen had sported in his heyday – Leo kept his hair close-cropped. Like a gladiator or a Marine, Leo wore it that way so his stepfather couldn't grab him by it. But Nick didn't know that.

Adrian had always been outgoing, daring, fearless, a perennial smart-ass. He always had a quick, easy, friendly smile. Leo had the same smile, but he was slow to display it. Leo was watchful, careful, reticent, fearful. He could be a smart-ass, too, but he was subtle about it. Leo was one of those people who'd pronounce a witty one every now and then, but if you weren't paying careful attention to his restrained words, you'd miss it.

Leo had some of his dad in him, however, Nick decided with satisfaction. At sixteen, he already knew what girls wanted, even if it seemed that he was hesitant to give it them.

"They can be so moody. *Sometimey,*" Leo said. "Up one day, down the next. They didn't like you yesterday, but they like you today. And who knows about tomorrow?"

Nick realized with a start that the kid could be describing Randi. If anybody was *sometimey,* it was Leo's mother.

"Lemme put it this way," Leo continued with a philosophical air. "I like to get to know a girl a little bit first. To find out –"

"What she wants?"

22

Leo nodded.

"You wait too long, they go get what they want from someone else, Cuz."

Again Leo shrugged. "I can't miss what I never had. And if they can't wait 'til I get around to asking for it, then maybe that's all they wanted anyway, and it'll do from anybody." Leo paused, then said, "I just don't like to rush into things."

"Leap and the net will appear," Nick suggested.

"Or not." Leo grinned, and his smile looked so much like Adrian's that it hurt Nick's heart.

ELEVEN

During the year between his sixteenth and seventeenth birthdays, Leo Wilde worked on becoming an adult. His first step was to get a job. He bagged groceries at Hilltop Market, so he could save up enough money for the next step: buying himself a car.

"If you're old enough to get a job, then maybe you're old enough to start paying rent," Gil said.

Randi laughed out loud at the ridiculousness of that: Leo should pay rent at a house that the three of them lived in for practically nothing. Since he'd been half-kidding, Gil let the idea go. He knew why Leo had found a job. What sixteen-year-old kid, even one as stupid and useless as Leo, didn't want a car? Gil didn't know who'd taught him how to drive – he suspected that it was Leo's equally-as-worthless cousin – but Gil didn't begrudge him the desire to be like other kids.

Hell, if I'm lucky, the little bastard'll go out and wreck whatever he buys and get himself killed, and then I'll finally be rid of him.

After he bought a car, Leo's lies to his parents expanded. It was almost as if he lived a double life. Gil would've appreciated that, perhaps, if he'd ever found out about it.

As far as Randi and his stepfather knew, Leo remained a studious, hard-working boy. He remained quiet and shy, as always. He never went out anywhere in the car he'd bought, just to school and to visit his cousin.

But reality was a little more complicated than that. Leo still visited Nick, but it wasn't as often as he told his parents.

Though he seemed introverted to the casual observer, Leo wasn't really shy. He'd witnessed his smart-ass and often off-color cousin's big mouth for his entire life: no one would ever mistake Nick Wilde for being shy. Leo would speak up if spoken to, whether it was a masculine challenge or a feminine flirt. But since he never sought to be the center of attention, the challenges were few – Leo had never been in any fights. And since he was never standing on tiptoe looking, waiting eagerly for the flirts, the young ladies had to go out of their way to make sure they had his attention.

Leo had led rather a sheltered life. He hadn't had any playmates as a kid, because he was the only kid in the neighborhood, and anyone he brought over, once he'd started school, didn't come back because Leo's stepfather was an asshole. Nick had always been his best friend. Since he had a way to get out into the world now, he'd taken Nick's advice and socialized when the opportunity presented itself.

Leo liked to go to parties, and he knew Nick wasn't going to attend any high school get-togethers with him. That was all right. Leo liked to go by himself. He liked to watch the people, to guess their motivations. Why was this guy such a blowhard? Why was that girl trying to get drunk already? What did they hope to achieve by their actions?

If they chose to interact with him, Leo sometimes tried to manipulate his contemporaries with an appropriate lie, by telling them what he thought they wanted to hear. He enjoyed their reactions, liked to see if he could guess what they wanted from him before they said it.

Everybody always wanted something. The guys often wanted a wingman or a drinking buddy, but by this time in their life, most of them already had their own little cliques. They recognized Leo as a quiet loner and didn't recruit his friendship too much, because he didn't recruit theirs.

His apparent shyness put them off. Leo Wilde didn't talk much. He'd always kept his thoughts to himself, his feelings, his emotions. It was easier that way.

"How are you today?" his mother might ask.

He was always fine. He might be hurt or seething or joyful, but he never let it show. He'd never been rewarded for expressing an opinion, so the simplest answer was always the best. If he said what he thought or felt, then he'd have to deal with others' reactions to what he'd said. At home that reaction could never be predicted. It was easier to agree, to demur, to remain silent. To lie.

His mother didn't know him. Leo believed that she didn't really want to know him. His thoughts and feelings, his opinions, wants, needs, aspirations – they might not coincide with Gil's mood at the moment. Leo didn't want to listen to his mother tell him that he had to think about what Gil wanted first, in order to keep the peace. He kept the peace by keeping his thoughts to himself.

The girls Leo met at parties wanted him to go out with them, wanted him to immediately be their boyfriend. This fascinated Leo, so he went to the movies with them, out to dinner, even to a couple of concerts. He was curious to find out what it was that they seemed to like about him so much, and before too long, he discovered that it was just his looks. None of them wanted to get to know him as a

25

person too much. They were teenage girls: flighty, self-absorbed, and he didn't get to know any of them intimately, no matter how much they hinted that that was their intention.

Leo lied to them, too, once he discovered that their interest in him was only passing, superficial, physical. He'd claim he was sick, or that he had extra chores to do around the house. Then he'd wait to see if they texted him again the next day or the day after that. When they lost interest, found more accommodating partners, Leo would just chalk it up to what he'd suspected all along: girls were *sometimey*. They didn't want him in particular, Leo Wilde, quiet, good-looking, observant young man that he was. They just wanted *somebody*, and anybody would do. They wanted a way to kill an evening. They just wanted to have a good time.

Some of the girls Leo went out with were willing to bare all to him immediately, both physically and emotionally. It never ceased to amaze him. *You don't even know me*, he'd think, *yet you're willing to let me . . .* It was always too soon for him. They didn't know him, and he didn't know them, so the eternal speculation that whatever they were willing to do with him – they must be willing to do it with anybody – was always uppermost in his mind.

Leo tended almost toward prudishness. The concept that the girls were young (as he was) and were happy to give in to the fire in their blood, that it was all in good fun, that none of it meant anything, that in a hundred years, no one would remember a little tumble in the back seat of a car – all that was lost on him. They were too eager to get drunk, to do drugs. They were all too trusting. For all they knew, he could be an ax murderer, just waiting until they were incapacitated to strike.

Leo had no interest in getting sloppy drunk or stupid high. He had no desire to lose himself, even for a little while. But he didn't mind that others did it. He liked to watch how they changed when they were under the influence.

Leo trusted no one, so he wasn't going to let his guard down by drinking or smoking pot. He suspected these girls' friendliness when they started to get a little slurry or glassy-eyed. Or even when they were stone sober: Leo suspected that the girls that showed an interest in him had already made it up in their minds what he was supposed to be. They assumed that he was just like them, out for a good time, ready to go. The prospect of casual sex appalled him – these girls didn't even know him. He wasn't like them.

26

As he approached seventeen, Leo reflected that the good times in his life had been few and far between. His stepfather had always attempted to make him feel like he was a burden, a pain in the ass. Worthless. His mother had always given him the impression that while she loved him, she couldn't wait until he was gone.

Leo had never taken his parents' treatment to heart. He didn't feel that he was worthless. His grandparents and his aunts and his uncle loved him, and he loved them. They didn't *want* anything from him. They were just happy that he was alive.

And some day, when he was grown and free of his parents . . . Leo was sure that he'd love and be loved, he'd have a normal, respectful, give and take kind of relationship with other people, just like the rest of his family had. But in the meantime . . . Leo's parents *wanted* him gone, and the girls he met . . . They *wanted* him for something else. But he reckoned that their desire was just as transitory as his parents'. If he gave these girls what they wanted, then they'd eventually want him gone, too.

Except for Sheryl. She didn't seem to want anything from him. She was just as shy as Leo made the world think that he was. She'd stared at him in study hall for about a week before ever daring to speak to him, then she just said *hi,* and scuttled away.

Leo thought Sheryl was exceptionally pretty, and he took the initiative the next time he saw her: he said *hi* first. After a while, it just seemed natural that they'd sit together in study hall. After a while, it just seemed natural that he wanted to hold her hand and that she'd let him.

They talked about things that didn't matter: the weather, school gossip, current events. They talked about everything except the attraction that existed between them. Leo liked it better that way. He liked holding her hand, and when they discovered that if they sat behind one of the large pillars in the cafeteria during study hall, no one could see them – Leo found that he liked kissing Sheryl.

Leo liked Sheryl well enough, because she didn't ask him how he felt all the time, didn't ask him what he was thinking about. And she didn't talk about what she felt or what she was thinking. They talked about not much at all.

Sheryl didn't demand that he text her or call her, she didn't pout or bitch if they didn't see each other every day after school. Leo didn't have to lie to her, because she didn't ask him too many questions. She'd just smile and say *hi,* and they'd kiss for a while. Leo didn't think she wanted anything more from him than that, and

27

that was fine with him. He didn't want anything more than that from her.

After he bought a car, Leo's next step toward adulthood was to check out colleges. He'd graduate from high school in June. He'd always excelled in school, and was looking forward to higher learning. He planned on going into computer tech, like his cousin Nick.

Nick was proud of Leo, and he knew that Adrian would've been proud of him, too. Despite a whiny, *sometimey,* pill-popping mother, and a cheating, murdering, low-life, asshole stepfather, Leo had turned out all right. On his seventeenth birthday, to demonstrate to the kid just exactly how proud he was, Nick told Leo that he'd pay his way through college.

Leo had told him that Gil had laughed when the subject had come up. "You'd better go find yourself another job," he'd told Leo. "I'm not paying for shit."

Nick was more than happy to put Adrian's son through school, just to spite Gil, and also because Nick was thrilled that the kid even wanted to go. In that way, Leo differed enormously from his father. Adrian had always been too cool for school, Nick remembered, sometimes literally. He'd just barely squeaked by enough to graduate, and had never been in any way inclined to go to college.

Leo smiled gratefully at Nick's generosity. "And as soon as I'm eighteen . . ."

"As soon as you're eighteen, you can come and live with me."

"All I gotta do is make it through one more year," Leo said. "One more year, then bye-bye Gil." Leo grinned from ear-to-ear, and again Nick saw Adrian in him.

TWELVE

Now, a month into that year, Nick came home to find his cousin sitting on his couch. A girl was with him.

In the year since he'd started to drive, Nick believed that Leo had backed off a little bit on his distrust of women. He looked enough like his dad that he had no trouble attracting girls, despite his subdued demeanor, and had dated more than his share. He never took them home to meet his parents, however. If he liked a girl enough, if she allowed him to take his careful time and get to know her first, Leo would bring her over to meet Nick.

The one with him today, Sheryl, was cute, sandy-haired and curvy. If Nick was ten years younger . . . But, he thought, even then, she'd still be too young for him. Nick liked his women to be of an age with him, or even a few years older. They seemed likely to be more mature then, more settled, more . . . honest.

Leo had a key to Nick's apartment. He'd had it since he was old enough to have keys. Nick knew that he'd never come home to a houseful of Leo's friends, drinking or doing drugs. Leo didn't bring any friends to Nick's place, only the occasional girl.

And if there was any hanky-panky going on with Sheryl – Leo had admitted that she was sort of his girlfriend – then Nick knew that the kid would be safe and discreet. Leo had grown up having to watch every word he said, every move he made. If that was going on – and Nick suspected that it might be – he knew that Leo would have any such activities concluded long before he might even remotely get caught in the act. The kid planned ahead. Nick knew he'd never walk in and surprise any scenes of young love when he got home from work. Leo hated surprises.

Sheryl was as quiet and unassuming as her sort-of boyfriend. She smiled shyly at Nick when he came into his apartment. But Leo frowned, *scowled*, at his cousin. Now Sheryl just looked fearfully from one to the other and remained silent.

"'Sup, my brutha?" Nick asked cheerfully.

But Leo's glower remained. "I always trusted you Nick. I always believed that you were the one person in my life that I could always depend on."

Nick's eyebrows went up. "How has that changed?"

Leo angrily leapt up from the couch. But even pissed off, he was graceful, and as always, Nick was reminded of Adrian. At this unusual show of anger, Nick realized that Leo wasn't really a kid anymore. He was as tall as Adrian had been. He was grown.

Leo snatched two pieces of paper out of the printer beside the computer and held one of them out to Nick. His blue eyes – so much like Adrian's, Nick noted again – narrowed accusingly.

Nick took the first paper, silently read the headline: *Second Shotgun Slaying – Police Seek Witnesses, Suspects.* The article was from the *Riverside Press-Enterprise*, dated July 10th, 1991.

Nick had Googled Adrian's name before, but he hadn't gotten anything but birth and death records, and just the date was mentioned on that. No cause. Leo must've signed up on the *Press-Enterprise's* website, specifically to search their archives . . .

Ah, the internet. Nothing ever stays a secret anymore . . .

Nick scanned the old clipping. *Riverside County Sheriffs are asking for the public's assistance in identifying a suspect in two July shootings that killed a 21 and a 25-year-old man.*

At 9:15 on July 4th, sheriffs responding to a call from a residence in the vicinity of the 9600 block of Jurupa Road found Adrian Robert Wilde, 21, dead at the scene. It was determined that the murder weapon was a shotgun.

On July 8th, Kenneth "Sonny" Moore, 25, was gunned down by a similar weapon at approximately 2:30 am, while he worked at a liquor store in the 8900 block of Limonite Avenue, less than three miles away from the first shooting.

The assailant stole several hundred dollars from the store's cash register. Robbery is also suspected as the motive for the earlier homicide.

Anyone with information is asked to call Sheriff's Detective Clancy Chalmers or Deputy Alex West or, to remain anonymous, call the We Tip hotline.

Nick looked up, met Leo's stare. His cousin was hurt, angry, betrayed.

"Leo –"

Leo shook his head and handed the second paper to him. It was another article from the *Press-Enterprise,* dated July 6th, 1991.

Sheriffs Investigating 4th of July Homicide

The Riverside County Sheriff's Department is investigating a homicide that took place in the vicinity of the 9600 block of Jurupa Road at approximately 9:15 pm on Thursday, July 4th.

According to Detective Clancy Chalmers, Adrian Robert Wilde, 21, was shot and killed inside his home by a masked assailant. Police are looking for a single male suspect.

Robbery is suspected as the motive for the crime.

Anyone with information is asked to call Detective Chalmers or Deputy Alex West or, to remain anonymous . . .

Again, Nick looked up at Adrian's son.

"Why didn't you tell me, Nick? *Why?* For my whole life, you let me think it was a car accident, when you knew . . ."

"I thought about telling you, Leo. Then I thought about not telling you . . . What good would it do?"

"I deserved to know!" Leo shouted. Sheryl jumped.

"In my defense, it wasn't entirely up to me to tell you, Leo. Your mom thought the car wreck story was –"

"Fuck my mom!" Leo thundered. "I always trusted you, Nick. I always believed –"

"I planned to tell you someday," Nick said quietly.

"When?" Leo's eyes still blazed in betrayed agony.

Nick sighed. "How about right now?"

"No better time." Leo plopped down on the couch. He leaned forward and stared attentively at his cousin. He waited.

Nick said something that he didn't say very often: "I need a drink."

He'd never been a big drinker, had always been disgusted with careless drunks and stupid stoners. But he wanted something now. A dose of liquid courage, a shot to steady his nerves.

Leo had discovered the truth about his father's death, and now Nick was going to have to take a difficult walk down a sad and sordid Memory Lane. And he was going to have to take Leo with him.

He'd dreaded this moment for his cousin's entire existence, but he'd always known that it would come one day. Nick had hoped that it wouldn't be for a few more years, but Leo wanted to know now, and Nick supposed he was grown enough.

Nick went out to the kitchen, and opened and closed cabinets until he found the Johnnie Walker. He made himself a quick whisky highball, then, as a postscript, he made one for Leo, too.

Leo took his drink without comment and set it down on the coffee table in front of him.

31

"I'm sorry I never told you, Leo. But you're right. You deserve to know, and I guess you're old enough now to hear about what really happened.

"You might want to pull that whisky a little closer to you, though." Nick took a belt of his own drink, shuddered at the burn. "It's bad, Cuz. It's not a pleasant tale."

"Leo? I think I . . . I think I should go," Sheryl said softly. "This is family stuff. Personal. None of my business."

Nick could tell that Sheryl wanted Leo to tell her to stay. She wanted him to tell her that it was okay, that she was his girlfriend, so that made her almost family. Now, at this crucial moment in his life, Sheryl wanted Leo to reaffirm – or affirm in the first place – their relationship.

Leo looked at her as if he'd forgotten she was there. Maybe he had. "Okay." He arose and crossed the room. "I'll call you later." He opened the door.

I'll bet she won't answer, Nick thought, observing Sheryl's crestfallen face. *Oh, well, another one'll be along shortly . . .* Nick didn't have time to worry about Sheryl's hurt feelings. As Adrian's Aunt Penny always said, he had bigger fish to fry at the moment. Leo had discovered that his father had been murdered, and he wanted to know all the details. The time had come at last.

Leo shut the door and returned to the couch. Sheryl was forgotten.

Nick considered making comment on Leo's coarse treatment of his girlfriend, but decided it was not the time. His cousin wanted to hear what had happened – *what had really happened.* Nick shrugged. He forgot about Sheryl, too.

"Once upon a time, we had a band. Me and my brother and his girlfriend, and your dad. We played parties. People came to see us. They said we were good.

"People liked to hear your dad sing. Especially the young ladies. Bobby called them *groupies,* and he found them annoying, but that was because he and Tracy had been joined at the hip since they were fourteen. Your dad, on the other hand, wasn't averse to entertaining an adoring fan. Or two."

Leo smiled, despite the gravity of the situation. He'd heard some of the groupie tales already.

Nick did not smile.

"One of these adoring fans was your mom."

This didn't seem like bad news to Leo. He reached for his drink, took a small sip, coughed. Eyes watering, he waited for Nick to continue.

"I once had a huge crush on your mom, Leo," Nick admitted.

The kid's eyes widened. Here was something that he never would've suspected. Nick was always cool to his mom, sometimes downright cold. It'd always seemed that Nick didn't care for Randi too much at all. It never would've crossed Leo's mind that Nick could've *loved* her once . . .

Nick sipped his whisky, waved his hand dismissively. "I was just a kid, and your mom . . . The closest I ever got was a kiss on New Year's Eve. Right after I turned fifteen. Gil made a big stink about it, dragged her out of the party . . ."

Leo's mouth dropped open in stunned surprise.

"Yeah. That." Nick took another pull on his whisky. "I imagine that Gil hasn't sat you down for any heartwarming, how-I-met-your-mother stories, seeing how he's not your father."

"Seeing how he hates me." Leo took a swig from his own drink. The whiskey still burned, but he was prepared for it this time. His eyes still watered, but he didn't cough.

"What I've got to tell you will go a long way toward explaining why Gil hates you, Leo, as well as why he hates me. There's really no delicate way to tell you. You already know what a son of a bitch he is, so what I have to say probably won't come as too much of a surprise . . . But it's still not pretty. And it gets *really* ugly at the end.

"So here goes. Your mom had been living with Gil since she was sixteen."

Leo had always been under the impression that his mom hadn't met Gil until after he was born, until after his dad died. His eyes didn't even water when he hit his whisky this time.

"She must've been almost eighteen when she met your dad. She worked at Mohini's, and Adrian dropped off some candles there for your grandma. After they met, Randi started coming to our shows.

"I thought your mom was beautiful, Leo, but like I say, she only had eyes for Adrian. I was just a kid," Nick repeated. "She never noticed me.

"After two or three parties, Randi brought her boyfriend with her to the next one. It'd always been obvious that she had a thing for Adrian, so . . ." Nick stared intensely at his cousin for a moment, then looked away. He spoke quickly. "So it shouldn't have surprised

Adrian when Gil came up to him after our set, and told him that if he ever touched Randi . . . Gil would kill him."

Nick paused to let that sink in. "But it did surprise Adrian. He wasn't interested in her . . ."

She was just too fucking adoring, Nick thought. *Jesus, the way she used to look at him . . . Why did you break your own rule, Adrian?*

"He didn't want someone else's girlfriend," Nick continued. "But she hung around, came to every party we played, stared at Adrian. I threw her a surprise birthday party when she turned twenty-one, at your aunts' house. She was surprised. I think she was a little disappointed when she found out that I'd cooked it up and not Adrian . . . But that's neither here nor there.

"It was at this surprise party . . ." *That I got surprised,* Nick thought. "That the shit hit the fan. You're gonna find this next part a little hard to believe, Leo." Nick stood. "How's your drink?"

Leo's glass was half empty. He handed it silently to his cousin.

Nick went out to the kitchen, freshened their highballs and returned. He sat back in his chair, sighed again. "We played *Happy Birthday.* Your mom blew out her candles. After a few minutes, I lost track of her in the crowd. I went around to the back of the house, looking for her. She was down on the path. I called to her, and she told me she was going to run up to the store to buy a disposable camera –"

"A what?"

"I don't know if they even make 'em anymore. It was a little plastic box. It had a lens, and film in it, and you took your pictures, then you took it to the store to have 'em developed." Nick gestured at the picture of Urban Equinox on the shelf beside Adrian's guitar. "Your mother took that with a disposable camera."

Leo shook his head. "I've never heard of –"

"Your mom loved 'em. They were very popular." Nick sipped his new drink. "Anyway, Randi said she was going to run up to the store and buy one of these cameras –"

"You just bought 'em at the store? Were they expensive?"

"No. Maybe five bucks." Nick felt a flare of annoyance. He was about to drop the bomb here, and Leo wanted to talk about obsolete photography devices.

"Anyway," he repeated, "she said she'd be right back, so I turned to go back to the party. I glanced through the window to the spare bedroom and I saw Gil. With Nadine." Nick paused significantly.

"Who?" The name didn't immediately register with Leo. The only person he knew named *Nadine* was an old lady, a friend of his grandmother's. He'd seen her around most of his life, whenever she'd been up at his aunts' house visiting.

Nick gazed steadily at him. Leo had studied people's expressions all his life, in an attempt to figure out what they wanted from him, so he gleaned immediately that Nick wanted him to realize that he wasn't talking about some person that was unknown to him. Or else he would've said, "I saw Gil with some woman you don't know." But he hadn't said that, had he?

Again Leo's mouth dropped open. "You don't mean . . . The old lady? Grandma's friend?"

Nick grinned humorlessly. "That's exactly what your dad said when I told him. *She's old enough to be his mother.* It was disgusting –"

"What did you see?" Leo asked in horror.

"They were making out. Enthusiastically." Nick grimaced in revulsion. Leo mirrored his expression.

"But . . . she's so old!"

"She was old even then, Cuz. She's like eighteen years older than Gil. But he didn't care. It was obvious that he liked it." Nick shook his head.

"I was furious at the thought that this bastard was cheating on your mom. I went around the corner of the house and told Adrian about it. He didn't believe me – like you say, it was just too vile to think about.

"I didn't care if he believed me or not. I told him I was gonna tell Randi, the moment she came back. I thought that she should know what a son of a bitch Gil really was, and I thought that maybe she might . . ." Nick looked sheepishly down at the floor, reliving the hope he'd felt as a fifteen-year-old boy.

"I thought that maybe if I told her, that she'd dump Gil, and maybe she'd . . . see me." Nick quickly shook his head again to make the feeling go away.

Leo remained expressionless at this reaffirmation of his cousin's one-time love for his mom. He hadn't quite processed that part yet. He hadn't quite processed *any of it* yet.

"Adrian didn't believe me, and he said that even if it was true – I shouldn't tell Randi, because it would break her heart. It would make her hate me. I didn't want that, so I kept my mouth shut.

"Later, at this same party, Nadine announces that she's going to be moving her mom up the coast in a U-Haul at the end of the month. And guess who's volunteered to go along and help the two little old ladies out? Just because he's a big-hearted, humanitarian kind of guy?

"Adrian started to believe me then, but he still wouldn't let me tell Randi. But after Gil and Nadine left town together . . ."

Nick sighed. "I let the cat out of the bag, anyway, Leo. Your mom called the hotel where Gil was staying, and a woman answered. I told her it was Nadine, that they had to be staying in the same room.

"She didn't believe me, said there had to be some other explanation. I didn't see her again . . . I only talked to her once, before . . ." Nick took a large swallow of whiskey. "I went to Europe with my family. When we got back, your dad . . ."

"What happened, Nick?"

Nick paused, sighed heavily, then quickly told the rest of the story. "Sometime, while Gil was still out of town, Randi decided that I was telling the truth. She went to your dad, on the 4th of July. On his birthday. Gil was supposedly in Bakersfield, but your mom called him and told him she was leaving him.

"Then she went to see your dad, Leo. It was the only time they were ever together. You were . . . conceived that night. They were together . . ." Nick put his face in his hands. "And then someone kicked in the door and shot him."

After a moment, Nick looked up at his cousin.

Leo saw Nick's tears, unshed, but Leo himself remained dry-eyed. Nick mourned. He missed Leo's father every day. But Leo felt no pain at the loss of someone he'd never known – he'd always enjoyed Nick's stories, and once he found out that his dad had been murdered, he wanted to know about that – but this whole deal was just incredible.

Leo went over the startling revelations in his head: his mom knew Gil from when she was just a teenager. Nick had a crush on his mom. His mom had a crush on his dad, but he wasn't interested, because Gil had jealously threatened to kill him. Gil had an affair with that old lady. Mom found out about it, and ran to his dad.

36

They went to bed together and conceived him, then someone shot him, on the very same night.

It was all too much to digest all at once.

Gil was supposedly in Bakersfield, but your mom called him and told him she was leaving him . . . It'd always been obvious that she had a thing for Adrian . . . so it shouldn't have surprised Adrian when Gil came up and told him that if he ever touched Randi, Gil would kill him . . . But it did surprise him.

Nick saw the pieces click together in Leo's nimble mind.

"I went to the cops, Leo. I told the detective that Gil was jealous, but he just laughed at me. I was just a kid. He said that Gil was in Bakersfield, that there were witnesses that placed him there."

"Bakersfield is only a couple hours away," Leo whispered.

"That's what I told the cops. I said he could've drove here, then went back. But Nadine alibied him. I was just a kid, Leo. The cops wouldn't believe me."

Leo took another hit from his glass, then set it on the table. He decided that he didn't want any more of it. The whiskey was beginning to make him feel fuzzy, and he had to think. He had to sort through all the outrageous shit that his cousin had just said . . .

"So what you're telling me . . ."

Now Nick waited silently. He'd allow Adrian's son to figure it out for himself the rest of the way. He was old enough. Leo didn't trust girls. He'd seen his own mother's inconsistent moods, her *sometimeyness,* and he was old enough to be cognizant of the power of jealousy. He'd experienced first-hand Gil's hatred, his violence . . .

"So you're telling me . . . You think Gil killed my dad?"

Nick nodded. "I don't see how it could've been anyone else."

"And my mom? Does she know?"

Nick hesitated a split-second, then shook his head, looked at the floor. What Randi knew or didn't know, what she chose to believe . . . Nick couldn't prove any of that.

"But . . . the other guy, at the liquor store . . ." Leo gestured at the newspaper articles on the coffee table, the keys that had unlocked the truth of his father's death for him.

Nick shook his head. "A coincidence."

Leo stared at his cousin in silence for a moment. At last he stammered, "I dunno, Nick . . . It all seems so . . . If that old lady said Gil was in Bakersfield with her . . . If there were witnesses, then maybe . . ."

Well, I'll be damned! Nick said to himself, amazed. *He doesn't believe me, either.*

"You wanted to hear the story. Now you've heard it."

Nick thought that perhaps it was a good thing that Leo didn't believe that his stepfather had murdered his father. Then he wouldn't lie awake nights and agonize about it, the way Nick had done, frequently, over the years . . .

The actors in this drama were known to Leo – his mother and Gil, anyway – but he knew them now, when they were old, sedate. Gil had mellowed, and Randi was practically comatose sometimes. The sparkling, fire-cracker of a girl that Nick had once loved was long gone. The flaming motivations of their youth – desire unrequited, then at last fulfilled; jealousy insurmountable, lethally discharged . . .

Leo didn't know these people like Nick did. He hadn't flashed to the truth in a second, the way Nick had, the moment that Ian told him that Randi had been in bed with Adrian . . .

Leo was just a kid, far more of a kid than Nick had been at his age. Of course he didn't believe it.

And Nick thought that maybe it was for the best. It wasn't as if Leo could do a damn thing about it, any more than he could.

THIRTEEN

Nick called Leo a cab. Sheryl had brought him over, and just as Nick had guessed, she didn't answer the phone when Leo called her for a ride home.

Nick stumbled into his bedroom and collapsed in a heap on his bed. The Johnnie Walker had gone straight to his head. He dreamed of Randi, when she was young and beautiful. When he'd been in love with her. He dreamed of that New Year's Eve, when she'd let him kiss her . . .

But Leo wasn't drunk, and he couldn't sleep. He stared up into the darkness and thought about what Nick had told him. It hadn't been a car wreck at all. It had been a home invasion. His parents hadn't had a long and happy relationship, as he'd always imagined. They had been together for the first time, the only time . . . Then someone had broken in and shot his dad.

And Nick thought Gil had done it, in a jealous rage.

But that was so . . . *rash.* Reckless. Leo couldn't imagining killing someone over a woman. Leo couldn't even imagine killing someone over his mom. Leo couldn't imagine killing anyone for any reason.

California's a death penalty state . . . Gil's a chickenshit. He wouldn't risk going to the chair over something as meaningless as . . .

But it hadn't been meaningless, had it? It had produced him, had it not? *Way to go, Dad . . . thanks.*

But if Nick was right, the cops would've agreed with him. They would've investigated. If Gil had done it, they would've found hair and fibers, fingerprints, DNA. They would've tested his hands for gunpowder residue. If Gil had done it, forensics would've convicted him. Just like on *CSI.*

But Bakersfield wasn't that far away . . . Maybe that old lady would've lied for Gil . . .

Leo finally drifted off to sleep, undecided about his cousin's unbelievable allegations.

FOURTEEN

Leo was able to avoid his stepfather the next morning, because he'd volunteered to drive his mother to the airport. Randi was flying up to Oakland to see her sister. Her sister – Leo's Aunt Beth, whom he'd met exactly once – had just had a baby. She already had three: Leo's other cousins, whom he'd never met at all. Aunt Beth had requested Randi's help with the new arrival. It would only be for a few days, a week at the most.

Randi didn't talk to her sister very often. They hadn't gotten along well as kids, she'd told Leo. But Aunt Beth had apparently buried the hatchet, because she needed the help. Randi was delighted to go on a little surprise trip, and besides, "What else have I got to do?" she'd said to Gil.

Leo had silently agreed. What else did she have to do? She didn't do anything. It wasn't like she had a job. Randi hadn't worked since her accident, five years before.

So Leo drove her out to the airport, kissed her goodbye at the gate, and returned to Parcay Street.

But he didn't go home. It was Saturday. Gil had said something about going to the lake, but his car was still in the driveway. If Leo went home, his stepfather would just think up some menial work for him to do. Maybe digging holes and filling them back in again. It was one of Gil's favorite threats.

Leo wasn't in the mood for Gil's bullshit this morning. But he didn't want to visit his grandparents or his aunts or Nick, either. He wanted to be alone, to think further about what Nick had told him the night before.

So Leo left his car parked in front of the old, abandoned auto repair shop up the street, and walked back to his grandparents' house. He went into the garage and shut the door behind him.

Leo had often hid out in this place when he was a kid. It was quiet and cool there, and he could think. When he was little, he'd dream about when he'd be old enough to go and live with his cousin. Now that day was less than eleven months away.

Leo liked to sit on the bow of *One Wilde Ride* and lie back against the windshield. He didn't like the water, didn't like boating. The idea of swimming or – *yikes! waterskiing* – horrified him. But he liked to lie on the boat's cool, slick fiberglass while it was in the garage.

It was quiet here. He could think about what his cousin had told him.

After some rumination, Leo came to the conclusion that it just couldn't be true. Nick had been a grief-stricken fifteen-year-old boy at the time of his father's death. His senseless murder. Nick had just lashed out, blamed the person he hated the most, the guy who possessed the woman he loved . . .

Sure, Gil's a bastard, Leo thought. *He's a small-minded, controlling son of a bitch. I'm not his kid, so he naturally hates me, and I hate him. But just like they say on TV, being an ill-mannered asshole doesn't make him a murderer . . .*

Leo decided that Nick had to be mistaken. He thought that maybe he'd go over to the Sheriff's Office and ask to see the case files on his father's murder someday. Leo was sure that they'd let him look at them. He was the decedent's son, after all. He had a right to look at them. People did stuff like that on TV all the time. The police were always helpful and sympathetic, and sometimes a friend or family member would see some detail in the file that allowed the police to solve the crime . . .

Leo took out his phone. Maybe Sheryl had forgiven him for giving her the bum's rush last night. He'd been surprised when she didn't answer to come back and give him a ride home. Nick hadn't been surprised. He'd told Leo that it had been obvious that Sheryl had wanted him to ask her to stay.

But if she'd wanted to stay and listen to Nick's story, why had she volunteered to leave? Saying one thing but secretly wanting something else . . . She'd never acted that way before.

Leo shrugged. Whatever. Maybe she was over her uncharacteristic displeasure by now.

Hi, Leo's text said. But before he could hit *Send,* the side door to the garage opened and Gil walked in.

Shit, Leo thought. *Yeah, he's not a murderer. But I still hate him.*

FIFTEEN

"I thought I told you not to sit on my boat. You're gonna scratch it."

Leo purposely didn't look up from his phone. He sent his text to Sheryl. "It's not your boat. It's my grandpa's boat."

Gil felt a weird stirring at that moment. He heard his father's voice in his head: *I thought I told you to be home before midnight.* Gil had hated Ritchie. He'd replied, *Fuck you, Dad,* and Ritchie had taken a swing at him. Seconds later, the ol' man was dead, and Gil's life had gotten exponentially better after that.

Gil had hated Ritchie, and *Christ, how I hate this kid!*

It wasn't like he hadn't tried. *The good Lord knows, I tried.*

Gil had even believed that he loved Leo once, as much as he could love any kid that wasn't his, that didn't look anything like him. Strangers would often comment on it, how much Leo looked like his mom, with the same black hair and blue eyes. Gil thought he looked like Randi, too, but Gill also knew who else he looked like.

Gil had tried to disregard all that, for the longest time. He'd tried to be a father to the boy. Maybe things would've been different if he and Randi had been able to move away, if they'd been able to forget the past, if they'd been able to truly start fresh, somewhere where a bunch of people didn't know that Leo wasn't Gil's son. If they'd been able to escape the Wilde family. Especially Nick.

At first, Gil had believed that Nick constantly hung around because he wanted to get at Randi. That had amused Gil, because he knew that Randi had never considered the kid once, nonetheless twice. Nick didn't look anything like his dead cousin, even if he did play the guitar. But after a while, Gil realized that Nick's ardor for his woman had cooled. Nick had his own girls, girls his own age. None of them seemed to stick around long, but he'd brought two or three of them out to meet Leo when he was a kid.

That was the reason that Nick still visited, to this day. It wasn't Randi. It was Leo, his asshole cousin's illegitimate offspring, conceived by a stroke of some kind of incredible bad luck – to Gil's way of thinking, anyway – at the moment of his death. Nick loved the boy, like the little brother he'd never had, almost like Leo was his own son.

And every time he saw his cousin, Nick talked to him about his father. *His real father.*

Even that annoyance hadn't been too much for Gil to take at first. Leo had lived an insular life. He didn't attend pre-school, because his aunts took care of him. He didn't see other children, because there weren't any families with children nearby. When he was little, Leo didn't have cause to wonder why other kids called their mothers' husbands *Daddy,* while he called his *Gil.*

Gil never heard Randi speak to her son about his father. Gil was convinced that Randi had forgotten all about Adrian Wilde.

But all Gil's perceptions changed, and rudely, when Leo started kindergarten. The child's mind immediately grasped the way the rest of the world worked: his schoolmates had daddies, but he did not. There was a man at home, a man that loved his mommy, the only man that he'd ever known. But because of Nick Wilde, little Leo knew that that man was not his father.

It had been decided that the family would tell Leo that Adrian had *gone to heaven.* Penny had frowned at that, but had reluctantly agreed that it was a good enough story until the boy was old enough to grasp more grown-up concepts. The *hows* and *whys* of Adrian's trip to the pearly gates would be worked out later. The family decided that they'd construct that bridge when they came to it: when Leo asked for specifics, then a more specific story would be manufactured.

Nick arranged to have his afternoons free, so that he could pick Leo up from kindergarten, so he could continue to *bond* with him, so he could continue his eternal campaign to make sure that Leo always remembered and never forgot that Gil was not his dad. Leo's dad was in heaven.

Leo had been attending kindergarten for a few weeks, and he loved it. All the new sights and sounds and people, the arts and crafts and rules. He observed the other kids with their parents, and as Gil had always knew it would, it struck the little boy that things were different in his family.

Nick brought Leo home from school one afternoon, and the moment the two of them walked into the house, after Leo had hugged and kissed Randi hello, Nick said, "Your son wants to ask you something."

Randi looked at Nick uneasily. He'd grown cold to her over the five and a half years of Leo's life. She sometimes caught him frowning at her, as if his polite aloofness wasn't just the result of maturity, of reality setting in, of Nick's finally accepting that the two of them would never, ever be together. Sometimes Randi thought that Nick actively hated her.

"Go ahead, Champ. Ask your mom what you asked me in the car."

Leo looked up at Randi. "Why did my daddy have to go to heaven, Mommy?"

Randi blinked in surprise at her son, then she looked back at Nick. "What did you tell him?"

Nick stared steadily at her. "I told him to ask you."

Randi looked down at Leo again. He waited patiently for her response. To buy a moment, Randi picked him up, sat down with him on her lap on the couch.

"Sometimes these things just happen, Leo. Mommies and daddies . . . Sometimes they're called to heaven. It's not that they want to go, but sometimes . . . God calls them away."

Nick frowned. The concept of God was not something that anyone had explained too thoroughly to Leo. None of the Wilde clan was religious, so Leo had never seen the inside of a church. But Randi had told Leo just enough about God so that she could trot out the all-seeing deity to round out her tale of how sometimes He called mommies and daddies home.

"But God is not mean, Leo. He took . . . Your daddy went to heaven, but God sent . . . God gave Gil to us. So he could be your daddy."

"Gil's not my daddy."

Nick grinned. He'd given Leo a little plastic play-guitar for his fifth birthday; Leo had ignored it. Nick had reckoned that Leo was an individual, that maybe a lot of Adrian wasn't natively inherent in him, at least not yet.

But Leo knew this fact, just like he knew that Santa would be there on Christmas Eve, like he knew not to pull the tail of his aunts' old black cat. He knew it because Nick had made sure he knew it: Gil wasn't his daddy.

Randi frowned at Nick; his grin widened. She turned back to her boy. "But Gil loves us, Leo."

The idea of love was immaterial to Leo. No one he'd met had ever showed him anything but love. Leo still thought everybody loved him. "I wish my daddy wasn't in heaven. Uncle Nick says he misses him. He says he misses him every day. But you never talk about him. Do you miss my daddy, Mommy?"

Tears welled up in Randi's eyes when she looked guiltily at Nick's cold, accusing face. It was true: she didn't talk to Leo about Adrian. She thought about Adrian, occasionally, usually late at night, when she couldn't sleep. But besides that . . . Randi's life was with Gil.

"I don't talk about your daddy too much because it makes me sad, Leo. Because he isn't here to see you grow up."

Leo was only five and a half years old, and he'd never known his father. The concept of missing someone he'd never met was not yet within his understanding. "Uncle Nick's not sad when he talks about him."

Nick grinned humorlessly.

Randi ignored him. "But just like you said, your Uncle Nick still misses your daddy, honey. He just tries not to show that he's sad because Daddy's not here with us anymore."

This point had been established for Leo. Uncle Nick missed his dad, and maybe he was sad about it, but his mother hadn't answered his question. Leo wanted to know: "Do *you* miss him, Mommy?"

"Yes, Leo. Yes, I do." She wiped the tears away before they could fall and looked at Nick. "Every day. And whenever I look at you . . ."

"You look just like your daddy, Leo," Uncle Nick reminded him.

And that might've been the end of a poignant chapter in the life of a little boy whose father had died before he was born. Life might've gone on as it had before for Leo, if it wasn't for the fact that Gil had come in through the back door and had heard it all. Randi and Nick and Leo hadn't noticed him standing in the kitchen doorway. He went out the way he'd come in, being careful to close the back door quietly, so they wouldn't know that he'd overheard.

Gil was furious. Randi missed *Leo's real daddy* every day, did she? Gil wouldn't have believed it, if he hadn't heard the words come right out of her mouth, if he hadn't seen her wipe away the tears.

Randi had never spoken of Adrian. Up until that moment, Gil had been confident in his belief that she'd forgotten all about him. But apparently he'd been mistaken. Apparently he didn't know Randi as well as he thought he did.

Gil reflected that maybe it was impossible to ever completely know another person. Randi had always been an open book to him: her desires and motivations had always been as plain to Gil as the nose on her face. But everybody had secrets. Didn't Gil have enough of them? There was the one about his pivotal role in sending Leo's *real daddy* to heaven; there was the one about his uninterrupted relationship with Nadine.

Now Gil knew Randi's secret: she'd never forgotten about Adrian Wilde.

All the declarations of her love for Gil over the past five years – they'd all been lies. It was just as that little bitch Nick had said, that day when he'd somehow managed to get the jump on Gil, that day when he'd threatened to tell Randi that Gil had never given up Nadine. The day Nick had rather forcefully suggested that Gil make sure that Leo knew he wasn't his father.

Nick had said it then, and Gil realized now that it was true: *You're only here 'cause Adrian's not, and Randi decided to give you sloppy seconds. She decided to* settle for you, *since the better man's gone.*

Randi still loved Adrian Wilde. Even though he was dead, gone, never coming back, Randi still missed him, *longed for him.* Every day. *I bet she still gets that faraway look in her eyes when she thinks about him –*

Now Adrian's ghost came home to roost in Gil's mind. Whatever love he'd tried to foster for Leo slowly drained away. Sure, Wilde's cousin had put it in the little brat's mind from Day One that Gil wasn't actually his father, but who cared what the kid thought? Gil had tried to be a father to him, regardless.

The reason that Gil came to loathe Leo didn't really have anything to do with the kid's non-existent memories of Wilde. It was the contemplation of *Randi's* memories that turned Gil against her son.

Wilde was dead, and Gil had once believed that Randi's memory of him had faded. Randi *should've* forgotten him. They'd shared only moments together. Randi's thoughts and heart and mind and will should've returned to Gil, as they'd belonged to Gil before she'd ever met the talentless guitar player.

But on that day when Leo was five and a half, fresh home from kindergarten, Gil discovered that things hadn't gone that way. Because their fatally interrupted tryst had produced issue, Randi hadn't forgotten Adrian. She'd said it to the boy: *whenever I look at you . . .*

From that day forward, Gil could see the memory of that smug bastard Wilde in Randi's eyes, each and every time she looked at his worthless kid.

So Leo had become a memento to Gil, too, of Adrian.

Gil was constantly reminded of what he'd seen on that 4th of July. The scene played over and over in his mind. It became inescapable.

He'd peeped in the window first, just to make sure that his guess had been correct. He hadn't wanted to just burst in, guns a'blazin', if nothing was going on, if Randi and Wilde were just sitting around having a beer.

But Gil's guess had been correct. In spades. The scene he'd glimpsed through the window had enraged him. Randi's head was thrown back, her black hair fanned out, stark against the whiteness of the pillow in the moonlight. Then Gil saw her smile up at Wilde and he smiled back. The *intimacy* of it sent a bolt of fury through Gil's mind, so real and complete that he was blinded for a second.

Then Wilde kissed her mouth, her neck . . . Randi threw her head back again, cried out, her face the very picture of ecstasy.

Gil had seen her make similar faces, but never quite that one – neither before nor since. With Adrian Wilde, she'd achieved ultimate pleasure.

But it had only been for a second, hadn't it? Gil and Richie's shotgun had put the kibosh on *all that,* hadn't they? And because it had been so momentary, because it had ended quite so badly, Gil had always believed that Randi had put it from her mind. Gil had always told himself that he'd put it from *his* mind.

But from the day that Gil heard Randi confess to her son that she missed his father, *every day*, Gil knew the truth. Because that single moment of ultimate pleasure had produced Leo, Randi was reminded of Wilde and the rhapsody she'd shared with him, every time she looked at his little brat.

Randi still loved Wilde, and for all these years, since he was five and a half years old, Gil had hated Leo because of it.

Gil knew Leo reminded Randi of his dead father, but Gil had only seen Randi in him: Leo had always been just a black-haired, chickenshit, snot-nosed, sniveling little nuisance to Gil, nothing at all like his asshole father. Leo would never get girls the way his father had – the kid was too backward, too shy, too afraid of his own shadow. Too gutless. Girlish.

So girlish was Leo to Gil, in fact, that from about the time he turned thirteen, Leo had started to remind Gil of Randi, from when he'd first met her, when she was just a pretty, dumb little sixteen-year-old girl, before the witchcraft, before Adrian. The boy had begun to remind Gil of his happy life with Randi, from before he'd met Nadine or any of the hated Wilde clan. The impression had grown as Leo grew.

And he really looked like Randi now, frightened, but still a little defiant. Gil felt that stirring again, because he realized that he wanted to hurt Leo, because he was a pain in the ass, because he reminded Randi of Adrian, even though Adrian was long dead.

Gil wanted to hurt him because, thereby, Leo reminded *Gil* of Adrian, and the one thing that he'd wanted to do for all these years was *to forget Adrian,* to forget the way he'd smiled at Randi that night, the way she'd smiled back at him, that look of pleasure on her face . . .

Gil wanted to hurt Leo, and there was *no better time than . . . Right now!* In one smooth, lightning quick, animal motion, Gil reached out and grabbed Leo by the scruff of his neck. So fast was Gil's strike that Leo dropped his phone. It shattered into plastic and glass chunks on the concrete floor of the garage.

Gil dragged Leo off the boat, spun him around, bent him over the side and slammed his head down onto the bow. Gil kept his hand on Leo's neck, pinning him there.

Dazed, Leo didn't immediately struggle to get up. Gil had enough time to take the big Buck knife out of his back pocket. Still holding Leo down with his left hand, Gil opened the blade with his right hand and his teeth. He took a second to admire the knife. It'd been a gift from Nadine. Gil had told Randi that he'd won it at the Christmas raffle at work.

"I'm just about through with your shit, son."

"I'm not your son!" Leo yelled in impotent hatred, his cheek mashed against the fiberglass.

"No. You killed my son." The baby that Randi had miscarried because of this sniveling little bastard . . . He would've been Gil's son. Due to the continuing complications of her injuries, the injuries that Leo had caused, she hadn't wanted to try again.

"No, you're not my son, but I've still had to put up with your shit, nonetheless." Gil caressed Leo's neck with the blade. "But I'm done, kid, done with putting up with you *and* your shit. Just like I was done with putting up with your daddy's shit, once upon a time."

Right through the temple, Gil thought, his bloodlust rising. *I'll get Nadine to vouch for me again. I'll tell Randi that I ran into her at the store, that we just went and had a cup of coffee together for old time's sake. She'll be pissed, but then someone'll find Leo, and she'll be too broken up about her worthless son to worry about me and Nadine . . .*

She'll come back to me, just like she did after I killed Adrian. Nadine'll vouch for me. She'll be happy to see that I put another Wilde in the ground. I'll skate on this one, too . . . Randi and I'll move away – no reason to stay here, after Leo's gone . . . Too many bad memories . . . Murdered, just like his daddy. At last I'll be free of all the Wildes . . .

Gil deftly flipped the knife over in his hand, prepared to make the downward thrust . . .

But before he had a chance to murder his stepson, Gil heard the door to the garage slam open. He looked over his shoulder to see Ian standing there, open-mouthed, stunned.

"What the fuck, Gil?" he sputtered.

"Back off, old man."

Gil knew he couldn't kill Leo now. Still looking over his shoulder, he crossed his arm in front of his chest, set the knife down on the boat to his left, where Ian wouldn't see it. But he kept his hand on Leo's neck. Gil couldn't kill the worthless brat now, or he'd have to kill Ian, too.

But that didn't mean Gil couldn't discipline him, maybe slam his head into the boat again. What was the old man gonna do about that?

"This isn't any of your –"

Leo reached out and felt around for the knife. His left hand closed around the handle. Gil had relaxed his grip on his neck a little when Ian had burst in the garage, and Leo used the opportunity to push off the bow of the boat with his right hand. At the same time, he spun around and buried the big pocketknife in the side of Gil's neck.

Gil's mouth worked soundlessly. He scrabbled at the knife, at Leo's hand. Their eyes locked, and Gil's widened in surprise. Leo put his right hand on the side of Gil's head and wrenched the knife loose. Blood gouted, and Leo stepped back to avoid getting any more of it on him. He watched Gil slide bonelessly to the floor, his hands flapping at the wound in his neck.

Leo looked down, watched as his stepfather's eyes glazed over, as they stared unseeing at the ceiling. He watched Gil's blood trace the short path across the concrete until it dripped into the grate in the floor.

Then his eyes flickered up to Ian. "He was gonna kill me, Dad. He was gonna kill me . . . *again*. Just like Nick said. It was self-defense."

Ian had just witnessed a brutal murder, but that was . . . He'd just worry about that later . . . Leo had called him *Dad*. He looked into his grandson's eyes, saw something familiar there, something he'd never seen before, the same thing Gil had seen . . .

"ADRIAN?"

The teenager shook his head and nodded at the same time, and Ian's heart leapt to his throat. It was a gesture Adrian had frequently made, but not Leo . . .

The boy looked down at the corpse again, then at the knife in his hand. He took off his shirt. The left arm of it was soaked to the elbow with Gil's blood, but his undershirt was unsullied. He wadded up his shirt and wiped the knife on it, then went over to the sink and matter-of-factly washed the blood from his hand and arm. He dried off on the part of his shirt that wasn't soaked through. As an afterthought, he stuffed the shirt and the knife into the cabinet under the sink, then turned to look at Ian again.

"I guess I'm gonna have to do something about this." He smiled, more of a grimace, really, and Ian felt a tightening in his chest. It wasn't his grandson smiling at him. *It was Adrian.* "I'm sure that Aunt Penny will know what to do —"

They heard a car door slam on the other side of the garage door. The door was windowless, as was the rest of the garage — *Thank Christ!* Ian thought hysterically — but someone was definitely here.

"Come on, Dad," the boy said. He stepped gingerly over Gil's body. "We'll deal with this in a minute. Let's see who's here."

He slapped Ian on the back and took a step toward the door. Ian grabbed him by the arms, searched his face. The tightening in his chest had become painful, and he could only whisper one word: "Adrian?"

The same gesture again: nodding and head-shaking at the same time. They heard footsteps on the sidewalk beside the garage. They stepped quickly through the side door, and Ian pulled it closed.

The unexpected visitor was Nadine. Ian hadn't seen her in months. She didn't visit very often any more, yet here she was now, at the most inopportune of moments imaginable. A feeling of impending doom seized Ian. He felt like an elephant was sitting on his chest.

Leo . . . No! Ian told himself. *Adrian, returned from the dead, just like Daina has always believed he would someday . . . Adrian just stabbed Gil . . .*

And who should appear out of the blue but Nadine. Ian saw it all at once – what Nick had told them, all those years ago – Ian had never thought about it because it was just too sordid . . .

But now he knew it was true. Nadine wasn't here to see Daina, or Penny or Bellona, or even him. Ian knew that Randi was out of town . . . Nadine was here to see Gil.

Nadine hadn't found Gil at home, so she'd come over here looking for him. Maybe he was planning on taking her out for a boat ride . . .

A panic-stricken giggle almost escaped from Ian, but he held it in. *No, Nadine didn't find Gil at home, and he's never gonna take a boat ride again.* Ian broke out in a sweat. *He's lying dead on the floor on the other side of the wall, because Leo . . . no, not Leo!* Adrian *just murdered him.*

"Are you all right?" Nadine asked Ian. "You look a little pale."

"I'm fine." Ian glanced at Leo. Adrian looked out from his grandson's face. "Let's go in the house."

Ian took a few steps away from the garage – *from the scene of the crime,* he thought – and a cramp seized him through the midsection. He stopped, grabbed his stomach. "I think I might've eaten something bad. There's some Pepto in the house."

Ian took a few more steps toward the back door, stumbled, and collapsed on the sidewalk.

Leo dropped to one knee beside him. "What's wrong, Dad?" Ian's eyes fluttered. *"Dad?"*

Nadine also squatted beside her soulmate. Her mind panicked. "Are you okay, Ian?"

"Chest . . . hurts . . ." Ian said.

"Help him, AnTeen!" Leo cried. "He's having . . . Hold on, Dad! I'll call an ambulance."

Leo dashed into the house. Nadine sat on the ground, cradled Ian's head in her lap. His eyelids fluttered again, then remained open. He smiled weakly up at her. "Hurts . . ."

Nadine brushed the hair out of his eyes. The lustrous, chocolate brown color that she'd so loved when they were younger was long gone. Ian was sixty-three, and he was gray now, but he still wore his hair in the same shaggy style of his youth.

This was the closest, the most intimate Nadine had ever been with him, except for random hugs over the years, except for that Hallowe'en when he'd danced with her. She felt the tears well up in her eyes.

Leo stepped through the back door. "Hold on, Dad. They're coming." He shared a glance with Nadine and she saw the worry, the fear . . . But there was also something else. "I'll be right back," Leo said, and scampered up the path behind the garage.

Leo ran up the steps, barreled across the deck. He burst into the house. Daina and Penny and Bellona were sitting at the kitchen table. They looked up in surprise at his breathless entrance. "Dad's – *Grandpa's* having a heart attack! He's behind the house! I called an ambulance . . ."

Daina was already gone, out the door, but Penny and Bellona sat motionless, staring at Leo.

After a heartbeat, Penny smiled. "Welcome home, Capo."

"I have to go help Dad," he replied, and turned to go. Then he stopped. "I . . . there's a mess in the garage," he said to them over his shoulder.

"Go to the hospital with Ian," Bellona advised. She looked at her sister. "We'll see to the mess."

"There's a . . . Under the sink . . ."

"We'll handle it," Bellona repeated. "Go see to your father."

The boy nodded and ran out of the house.

SIXTEEN

Nadine had only cried once since her destiny had been so cruelly turned aside. That had been at Ian and Daina's wedding, when she'd allowed herself one soul-wracking sob, when she'd allowed the tears to flow unhindered for a moment, when she'd vowed her revenge.

Never again, in all the ensuing years, had Nadine ever cried. There'd been endings aplenty: Chuck and Charlie, and Anthony, and a legion more, all the myriad men with whom she'd wasted her life. She'd only taken up with them because there was something about each that had reminded her of Ian. There'd been good times. Nadine could've settled down with any of them. But none of them were Ian. And because none of them were, she'd never shed a tear when things ended with them, because Nadine had always been the one that had brought about the endings. Because none of them were Ian.

Nadine had shed false tears when the detective had questioned her after Adrian's murder. She'd been the very picture of woe at Adrian's funeral. But now Nadine cried for real. Silently, piteously. The tears dripped off her chin, stained her black suit. It was the same one that she'd worn to Daina's detested brat's memorial service, eighteen years before.

The memory of Ian's collapse replayed in her mind. She'd sat on the sidewalk, cradled his head in her lap, forcing her tears to remain unshed. Ian looked up at her, tried to laugh at the fear she couldn't hide. But it had turned into a wince as another pain squeezed him. He said, "I guess I'm getting old, 'Deen. Wearing out."

Nadine had tried to smile. She whispered, *"To me, fair friend, you never can be old. For as you were when first your eye I eyed, such seems your beauty still."* She'd dared to kiss his brow.

Nadine had not heard his confession, as a priest would, but had instead offered her own. *"I love you, Ian! I've always loved you!"* And Ian had just smiled kindly at her and asked for his wife.

Daina arrived then and took her husband into her arms. She took him away from Nadine. Daina cooed, and rocked Ian, the way she'd once rocked Adrian, and Leo. "You're gonna be okay, baby," she assured him.

Nadine saw Ian look up at his wife with love, and Daina smiled back at him with her own love. No further words were necessary between them.

Nadine had waited to receive such a look from Ian since the night when she'd first read their fate in the Tarot, since the moment when she'd first heard his voice, when she'd first beheld him and had known that he was her soulmate. Nadine had seen that look in the eyes of most of the men with whom she'd peopled her life. But coming from them, it had meant nothing to her. She'd only ever wanted to see that love in Ian's eyes.

And Nadine had seen it again, at the last, as they loaded him into the ambulance. But it hadn't been for her. It hadn't ever been for her. Ian hadn't even glanced in her direction. To the end, all his love was for Daina.

Ian had expired en route to the hospital.

SEVENTEEN

Nadine lingered at the funeral home. She didn't feel as though she had the strength to leave just yet. Her sorrow was abject.

Ian had never been permitted to realize what the two of them had been meant to have, and Gil . . . Gil had been the only man that Nadine had ever wanted that hadn't reminded her in the least of Ian. She sobbed again. Gil had loved her, as Ian never had.

It had almost been a week now. No one had seen him, no one had heard from him. It was as if Gilbert Hogan, her lover, her *paramour* for twenty years, had simply fallen off the earth. As if he'd simply ceased to exist.

Nadine missed him. Even though she'd never wanted Gil around full time, now that he'd disappeared, she missed him. They'd shared so many secrets. She took great relish in the fact that he'd carried her revenge (and his own) onto a second generation by making Leo's life miserable. Gil and Nadine had despised the Wildes, *pater et fils*. This mutual hatred was a topic that they'd seldom discussed, but it was something that they'd shared, nonetheless.

Recalling her thirst for vengeance, Nadine was reminded of its source. Daina had stolen Ian from her, and fate had repaid her for that theft by taking her son from her at his majority, at the ripe old age of twenty-one. Nadine had prided herself that she'd aided fate – had she not goaded Gil into his irreversible move?

Adrian had deserved to die. It was decreed by the forces of the universe long before he was born. It was just desserts for Daina's treachery. And his mother had lived in sorrow for the past eighteen years, but her love for her husband had never faltered, nor his for her. Ian had never seen that he'd been duped by a thieving whore.

Nadine had become fate's warrior, had dealt her enemy a near fatal blow by helping to dispatch her son. But the universe had again shifted, and once more, Nadine was the loser.

Adrian Robert Wilde was returned. Nadine had never been so sure of anything in her life.

The personality that had looked out from behind Leo's normally fearful eyes had still been fearful, but Leo had never in his life heard the word *AnTeen*. That annoying garbling of her name had died with his father on the night he'd been conceived.

The voice that had said, "Help him, AnTeen!" had been fearful, but it hadn't been Leo's. It was Adrian. No one had ever called her

AnTeen but Daina's despicable monkey, and he was afraid because his father – not his *grandfather*, but his father: *What's wrong, Dad?* – had collapsed in front of him.

Leo hadn't reached into his pocket to call for the life squad on his cellphone, the thing that had grown attached to his hand since Nick had gifted him with one when he was twelve. Adrian had died in 1991. There'd been no cellphones then. He'd run into the house to use the landline, the only kind of phone he knew about. And he'd run up the hill to fetch his mother. Adrian didn't know that Daina had a little phone in her pocket, too, a futuristic-looking device like a communicator from *Star Trek*. Because Adrian, dead since 1991 but now returned, was not yet aware that such a marvel existed.

Adrian's return must've just then occurred. Right before Ian collapsed.

The penalty for Daina's theft had been the death of her son. Nadine wondered suddenly if Daina had sacrificed Ian to get Adrian back. That was not generally how such things worked, but Nadine knew that there were more things in heaven and earth than were dreamt of in her philosophy. And if such a thing could be accomplished, Nadine believed that a cold whore like Daina would be more than willing to do it. Sacrifice the father to have the son returned . . .

And if such was the case, Daina and her deathless brat had again robbed Nadine. Daina had stolen Ian from her once, and now she'd stolen him again by sacrificing him for Adrian's return. Ian was gone, Leo was gone. But Adrian was back, and now Gil was gone, vanished the same day Ian suffered his heart attack, the same day Nadine had witnessed Adrian's personality eclipse his son's.

Ian was gone, but his son was back, and Nadine was convinced that Daina, and Penny and Bellona and probably Lily – they must know it as unequivocally as she did. In fact, Penny and Bellona had no doubt had a hand in it. Daina was not witch enough to accomplish a supernatural feat so marvelous by herself.

Penny and Bellona had foreseen Adrian's death, and Ian had never been anything more than a pawn to them. Adrian had been a *solitaire*. Penny and Bellona would have been happy to help Daina sacrifice Ian to help continue their witches' dynasty. A great, wonderful, duped man, sacrificed to have a young sorcerer returned. It made perfect sense.

Nadine wondered if Randi, schooled in the ancient arts, also knew that her once lover – it had only been *once* – had come back from the other side.

Nadine reckoned that the surprise of Adrian's return had engendered Ian's heart attack. Perhaps that had been part of the plan. Ian knew that Adrian was back – *it must've* just then *occurred!* – and the shock had killed him. Even in the middle of a cardiac arrest, Ian would've started at Leo's calling him *Dad,* had he not already known that it was Adrian that spoke.

It seemed to Nadine that fate was not entirely unfair: it might return her beloved son to her, but Daina would not be permitted to have both her men with her again in this life. But she'd obviously been willing to trade one for the other.

Nadine sat in the empty funeral home and recalled the events of the last week, the worst week of her life.

Three days after Ian died, her doorbell had chimed. Joy seized her: it had to be Gil. No one else visited. All the anger at his silent absence vanished. Wherever he'd been . . . Maybe a phone wasn't readily available. He'd never gotten a cellphone. Maybe Randi was breathing down his neck the whole time.

Nadine leapt up, threw the door open with a beaming smile. But it wasn't Gil upon her doorstep. It was his wife.

"Is he here?"

"Well, hello, Randi. Long time, no see –"

"Cut the bullshit," Randi sobbed. "Is Gil here?"

"I have no idea what you're talking about, Randi." Nadine feigned offense at the younger woman's tone. "I haven't seen Gil *for years.* Not since he broke it off with me and married you."

"I know that's not true." Randi sobbed again.

"You know nothing of the kind, dear," Nadine said kindly.

Randi didn't know, because Nadine and Gil had been more than discreet. Since they'd been found out, all those years ago, Gil had behaved as if he thought himself to be under constant surveillance. He only visited Nadine in the afternoons, when his wife thought he was still at work. And even then, he didn't park at her apartment, but left his car in the hospital lot a couple of blocks away.

Randi had been out of town on the one occasion that Nadine had dared to go to Gil's house to see him. They were supposed to take Ian's boat to the lake that day. But Gil wasn't home when Nadine knocked on the door. Then Ian died . . .

Nadine had not seen nor heard from Gil since he'd called her that morning. And apparently, neither had Randi.

"Come inside, Randi. Tell me what's going on."

Randi peered at Nadine, this woman that she'd hated in her heart for eighteen years. She hadn't wanted to believe that maybe Gil had returned to this old tramp, that maybe Gil had been seeing her all along. But even such a heart-wrenching thought had given Randi some hope.

"Gil's gone," she told Nadine. "I was at my sister's when Leo called to tell me about his grandfather."

When Randi mentioned her son, Nadine looked keenly at her. She sought some expression of inexplicable wonder – Adrian was returned! But all Nadine kenned was Randi's fear and worry over her missing husband. They consumed her. She harbored no other emotions at the moment. Randi was unaware that her son was her son no longer.

"I took the next flight back. In all the sadness over Ian's passing, none of them seemed to notice that Gil was missing." Randi sobbed again, bordering on hysteria. "His wallet and his keys were gone, but his car was in the driveway! Where could he have gone? Leo said that he wasn't home when he got back from taking me to the airport.

"I called his mom, his brothers. Nobody's seen him. I waited the twenty-four hours, then called the police. They came out, made a report . . . Then I thought of you."

Nadine's first inclination was to suggest to Randi that perhaps Gil had gone off with some *other* woman. When he'd failed to call, the thought had occurred to Nadine: maybe she'd grown too old for him. The passion of their earlier days had relaxed. They still made love when he visited, sometimes, but mostly they just held each other and talked. He'd bitch about what a lifeless lump his wife had become, about how much he loathed his useless stepson . . .

Nadine hadn't really believed that Gil had found someone else. They were comfortable together, satisfied with each other, as familiar as a pair of old shoes. But Randi didn't know any of that, and at first, Nadine thought of implanting the idea of a new infidelity into her mind just to be mean, just to get Randi off of her doorstep.

But Nadine saw her own pain reflected in the younger woman's eyes. Poor, dumb, crippled, gullible Randi. She loved Gil far more than Nadine ever had. There was no need to be cruel to her.

"I haven't seen him, Randi. Did the police . . ."

"The police say they've done whatever it is that they do," she replied bitterly. "I hate the police. They talked to Leo. They talked to Penny and Bellona. Daina's in seclusion. They say that they talked to Gil's family. They say they checked at his job. Nothing. No one's seen him."

Nadine felt pity for Gil's wife. She felt pity for herself. "I'm so sorry, Randi. I hope he turns up. But I haven't seen him. Not for years."

Nadine saw the bright, hard spark of hope die in Randi's eyes, and she felt a similar hope die in herself. If Gil wasn't with his wife, and he wasn't with his mistress, then Gil was gone.

Randi nodded, wiped the tears from her face. She turned and left Nadine's doorstep.

EIGHTEEN

Nadine was convinced that Adrian, newly returned from the oblivion to which Gil had sent him, had something to do with his murderer's disappearance. And she'd pursue the matter with all the fury of a harpy. She'd go to the police, she'd tell them . . . What would she tell them? That this family had taken Ian from her, not once, but twice, and now Daina's abominable brat had returned from the other side and taken Gil from her? They'd lock her up.

Making an insane nuisance of herself to the authorities wouldn't bring Gil back.

Feeling sorry for herself, Nadine sobbed again. With Ian gone, what was the point of living? She was an orphan. She had neither husband nor child, neither lover nor friend . . .

But then Nadine sniffed back her tears, got a grip on herself, banished the maudlin self-pity. She wasn't ready to move on just yet. The child that should have been hers, despised though he was, was returned from the grave, a grave to which she'd indirectly sent him. That was an interesting development.

Nadine didn't believe that death was *the undiscover'd country from whose bourn no traveler returns*. Nadine knew that she'd live again. It was something that she'd believed all her life. Had not Penny told her that she'd known Ian before, in previous lives, that she'd know him again in future ones? Had Adrian not returned? So Nadine wasn't ready to die just yet.

She ruminated upon Ian's memorial service, just passed. The most bereft members of his family had sat in the front row, before the table and the urn that held his earthly remains.

Doctor Robert Wilde, retired, was ashen. Normally so jaunty in appearance, the perennial bachelor seemed to have aged irrevocably overnight. Rob looked as though he had one foot in the grave himself. He'd ignored Nadine as he walked up the aisle. Perhaps he hadn't even recognized her.

Nadine had managed to never speak to her former flame. Not once in all the ensuing years, not since they'd all stood around in the hallway at Community Hospital and congratulated Ian on the birth of his son. She'd heard talk of him and his life from Ian and Daina, had seen pictures of him with a cavalcade of women. But fate had smiled on Nadine. She'd been able to avoid the eminent doctor for forty years. For a lifetime.

On his arm, Rob supported the black-clad, grieving widow. Nadine would've liked to see Daina's face, to gauge the depth of her grief. Nadine would've liked to study her manner, to try to ascertain from her expression if her enemy had indeed sacrificed Ian in order to facilitate Adrian's return. But like a proper widow, like a good witch, Daina had been veiled for her husband's service. Nadine couldn't read her features through the gauzy black netting.

Leo sat on his grandmother's other side, his face tear-streaked, his eyes swollen, his entire countenance positively tragic with loss. If Nadine hadn't known the reason, she would've found it odd that Ian's grandson had taken a place among the most bereft in the first row.

As the years passed, Nadine had succeeded in the loathsome necessity of remaining friends with Daina and her aunts. She was well aware that the scarlet letter upon her breast was known to the entire clan, so she avoided the major holidays, because Randi and her son, and of course, her husband, were always present for those gatherings. Nadine's presence at the Thanksgiving feast, beside the Christmas tree, would've been awkward. There might've been a scene.

But Nadine still visited Parcay Street as frequently as she could stand to make small talk with the hated witches, because always, when she visited, there was a chance that she might also get to share a few words with Ian. He might drop a couple of lines of verse to her, their meaning and beauty perennially lost on his ignorant, thieving whore of a wife. He might put his arm around Nadine's shoulders, give her a friendly squeeze. Eternally, Nadine had been willing to put up with Daina and Penny and Bellona, to endure their happy, insipid conversation. She'd been willing to risk running into Randi, just on the off-chance that she might also be permitted a glimpse, a fleeting moment with Ian.

On these visits, Nadine had also frequently seen and observed the watchful, quiet boy that was now no longer Daina's grandson. So Nadine knew that Leo had never been overly attached to his grandfather. There were the generational differences, of course, but more importantly, Leo and Ian had never shared any common interests.

Leo enjoyed cyberspace and computer games. He was constantly looking down at his cellphone, as was the wont of his generation. He had no interest in poetry and literature, no time to listen to the ramblings of his schoolteacher grandfather. Ian's chief joy in life – before righteous fate had deprived him of his son – had been the lake, the river, the boat. Waterskiing had once been more than a hobby to Ian: it'd been a *lifestyle, what he did.*

Nadine had heard him say on more than one occasion, and sadly, what a shame it was that Leo was afraid of the water. The fact had appalled him, mystified him. Nadine thought that Ian took the boy's aversion personally, that it hurt his feelings just a little bit.

Grandfather and grandson had shared nothing in common. They were never close. Yet here was Leo, *weeping,* among the first row of mourners. *Sir John, thy tender lambkin now is king,* Nadine thought. The grandson embodied the grief that would've befitted the son. And that was because the grandson was gone, the son returned. Leo sat beside Daina in Adrian's place, because *Leo was Adrian.*

Randi hadn't been present at Ian's service to comfort her devastated son. *Thank Christ for small favors,* Nadine had thought. She was no doubt *in seclusion* herself, still distraught at her husband's disappearance.

In the next row of mourners had been Will and Marta. Nadine had managed to never speak to them, either, in the last four decades. Will ignored her, but Marta had offered a sad glance of recognition. Beside them were their grown sons, and Bobby's wife. Nadine watched Nick lean forward and put his hand on Leo's shoulder in condolence. Leo turned, acknowledged his cousin, but he didn't speak, Nadine noticed.

Behind Will's family sat Penny and Bellona and Lily. Lily turned once, searched the sad faces behind her until she found Nadine in the last row. She nodded, acknowledging Nadine's grief, which was more than Penny and Bellona had done. They'd glided past her like two black birds, without even a glance. Nadine hoped that the next time she was among this gathering of witches, veiled, it would be for one of their funerals.

Ian's friends and colleagues spoke a few words of tribute. Nadine caught a glimpse of a tiny, past middle-aged woman in the crowd of mourners that might have been Sissy, grown-up, grown old. Nadine wasn't positive it was her, as it'd been a million years since she'd seen Sissy, since she'd even thought of her. Nadine didn't care, regardless. She had her own grief, and didn't pause to consider the sadness of another, never-requited aspirant to Ian's affections.

The ceremony wore on. At last, the funeral director observed a moment of silence, and it was over.

Daina, Leo; Penny and Bellona and Lilly; Rob and Will and Marta; Bobby and Tracy and Nick. All the friends and co-workers, maybe-Sissy and all those whose lives had been touched enough by Ian Wilde that they mourned his passing. They'd all gone home already. His widow had taken his ashes with her.

Nadine sat in an empty room and cried.

NINETEEN

"I knew she'd still be here," Penny said to her sister. "Mourning her *soulmate.*"

Nadine looked up to find the ancient witches standing beside her chair. She hadn't heard them enter the room, and wondered how long they'd been watching her. At first they seemed smaller to Nadine, shrunken, elderly. She reasoned that they had to be at least in their late eighties by now, possibly older. Penny and Bellona no longer seemed the powerful sorceresses that Nadine had once loved but had later come to revile.

But the impression of the witches' vast age only lasted for a moment. The beldames' eyes were alive, sparkling. They were filled with menace, almost hatred, Nadine saw with surprise.

"Here." Penny flung an index card at Nadine. Having little mass, it fluttered end over end to the floor. "I return your curse to you."

Nadine picked it up and read the words she'd spoken at Adrian's funeral, eighteen years before. She looked at them in astonishment. "Wherever did you get this?"

"You left it on the table beside Adrian's urn. Don't you remember? Is age making its inevitable pathways into your mind, 'Deen?" Penny sneered. She nodded at the table at the front of the room, which had so recently held Ian's own urn. "But there are some things you'll never forget, aren't there?"

"But . . . How? We all went home . . ."

"There was a public service for Adrian after we left," Bellona reminded her. "The young people left cards and notes. Remembrances."

"Randi gathered them all into an envelope. It's been sitting beside Adrian's ashes in the cabinet, for all these years. Just this morning, when we were making room for Ian's urn, we found the envelope, read all the tributes left behind by Adrian's sorrowful friends."

"Why would you curse Adrian, 'Deen?" Bellona asked, her voice small, soft with stunned amazement.

Nadine blinked. "It's . . . It's a prayer."

"It's a curse!" Penny roared, and snatched the card from Nadine's fingers. Her shrill words echoed in the empty room. "When we rediscovered it this morning, we again recalled your little awkward haiku from Adrian's service –"

"It's not a haiku, Penn," Bellona said absently. "There are too many syllables, too many lines . . ."

Penny glared at her sister for a moment, then returned her icy countenance to Nadine. "We remembered your weird little tribute from Adrian's service, recalled that it had struck us as odd at the time. 'Nadine's usually so poetic,' Bell had commented.

"'I would've thought she would've chosen a passage from the Bard,' I said. 'Even something as worn and overused as *good night sweet prince: and flights of angels sing thee to thy rest!* would've been better than what she offered,' I said."

"Then it was forgotten," Bellona remarked. "Until we found it again this morning."

Nadine frowned. "I'm sorry if you found a blessing of my own devising inappropriate."

"Of your own devising – true," Penny hissed. "But not a blessing." She read from the card. "A heartfelt prayer: Musician sheer, always in memory. Now dreamers wince, but will endure. Parting for a while; saddened never."

Nadine shrugged. "Maybe it is a little . . . cumbersome. But it was from the heart. How is it not a blessing? A prayer?"

"They have a new thing, 'Deen," Penny said. "My sister has always attempted to be abreast with modern times, to eternally be *with it,* as they say."

"Nobody says that anymore, Penn."

Penny fluttered her hands in annoyance. "Lily is also a modern girl, so last Christmas, she gifted Bell with a modern device. A computer. Upon this device, one may find the international web –"

"The *worldwide* web, Penn," Bellona corrected. "The *internet.*"

Again Penny glared at her sister. "Whatever you call it, there are plenty of places on it for English majors. Places to help with theses, places for poetry, literature . . . *anagrams.*"

Nadine was expressionless. Penny continued. "It was actually Lily that first suggested it. She found your *prayer* odd, too. *Cumbersome,* just like you said. So this morning, before Ian's service, she typed it onto Bell's electronic screen. Even with the help of the . . ."

"*Program,*" Bellona supplied.

"Even with the help of the program, it took us a little while –"

"Much scratching out – extra words and letters . . ."

"But with the computer's assistance, when all the letters are used, what remains is not a prayer. Read it to her, Bell."

"I don't want to, Penn," Bellona said in whispered alarm. "A curse unspoken –"

"– is a curse unheard." Penny smiled without humor. "It's already been spoken, yet it still went unheard. Unheeded. Unanswered. Go ahead, Bell. Remind this black witch of her poisonous, useless words."

Bellona shook her head resolutely. She removed a scrap of notebook paper from her pocket and handed it to her sister.

Penny read the spidery script: "Hereafter, raptly, I curse his name. A womanly misery; crime answered, won. Debut well, Ruin. A forepart timing, an end deserved." Penny flung paper and index card at Nadine. Again, both drifted to the floor. "As a curse, it's just as cumbersome. And to think, you had to scribble out that evil drivel all on your own. Without assistance from the international –"

"The internet, Penn," Bellona insisted. Then she turned sad, somber eyes upon Nadine. "Why would you curse Adrian, 'Deen?"

"I will not stand accused by a machine. It's a blessing." Now Nadine smiled without humor. "Regardless, I didn't have to curse Adrian. He was cursed before he was born. Fate just ran its course."

Penny's eyes narrowed. "After discovering this . . ." She gestured at the papers on the floor. "I suspect that perhaps you were an instrument of his fate."

Nadine's eyebrows rose. Had she not been thinking that only moments ago? "And how is that?"

"Perhaps through your relationship with the unfortunate Mr. Hogan?"

Nadine didn't miss the word *unfortunate.* Her hated once-aunts knew what had happened to Gil. But still the denial leapt to her lips. "I don't know what you're –"

"Young Nicholas told us all about your adulterous affair with Randi's husband, Nadine," Penny said.

He told everybody, Nadine thought. *Randi, every single living Wilde, the law . . .*

"He also told us how he suspected that Mr. Hogan was the perpetrator of Adrian's murder. His arguments were persuasive. He was angry that no one believed him."

"Like Cassandra," Bellona added.

Penny sighed. "I tried to comfort Nicholas. I told him that all the sins and goodnesses of our hearts are weighed against the feather of truth in the end. And if the balance skews, oblivion awaits."

"But perhaps fate has already stepped in . . ." Bellona looked steadily at Nadine. "Taken its course sooner rather than later in Mr. Hogan's case."

"Perhaps," Penny agreed. "Perhaps the universe has timely punished him. If not for Adrian's murder . . . But no one ever proved he did it, did they? Nobody even suspected, except for Nicholas. Because Mr. Hogan was in Bakersfield at the time, if memory serves. With you." Penny smiled. "If fate didn't serve Mr. Hogan for Adrian's death, then maybe he didn't do it. Perhaps fate exercised its outrage for Mr. Hogan's unspeakable treatment of poor, fatherless Leo all these years."

"That was something you allowed to happen," Nadine said noncommittally. Then she scowled. *"Poor, fatherless Leo!* He had a father. Fate chose Gil to be his father."

"And his influence made Leo into a shy, fearful, reticent child," Bellona said.

"Yet you permitted it," Nadine reiterated.

Penny shrugged. *"Into each life some rain must fall.* Shy, fearful, maybe . . . But Leo was always tough enough. And since Mr. Hogan's influence has . . . been removed, Leo has emerged from his chrysalis. He is still watchful, for the moment, but he is neither fearful nor shy, anymore." Penny grinned brilliantly and winked at her sister. "Perhaps his father has at last come out in him!"

Bellona returned her lavish smile, then sobered again when she looked at Nadine. "We leave you with our pity, 'Deen." She nodded at the empty table at the front of the room. "And our sorrow for your loss."

"If you love something, set it free. If it comes back, it was, and always will be yours. If it never returns, it was never yours to begin with." Penny sighed. "We all grieve at Ian's loss. *He was a man, take him for all in all, I shall not look upon his like again.*

"But I suspect you grieve the most, 'Deen, as Ian has now moved on, without ever having an inkling that he was your . . . *soulmate."* Penny's giggle was cruel.

Bellona did not join in it. She said sadly, "You wasted your life in that pursuit, 'Deen. It's my most fervent hope that, before it's too late, you can throw off your hatreds, your disappointments, your curses —"

"Very doubtful," Penny said to her sister. "What did I tell you when you were just a child, Nadine? A curse is a weapon of the

67

powerless. Ian and Daina found true love, and you cursed them for it, every day of your life. You attempted to curse their son.

"But a curse takes something from its sender, just like I warned you." Penny raised her arms to encompass the empty room, let them fall again. "You're an old, bitter, friendless witch, 'Deen. Your curse has taken everything from you."

Bellona would not be so harsh. "It need not be so, 'Deen. There's always time for atonement. There's always hope for your soul."

"Repent, the end is near!" Penny said sarcastically. *"My sources say no."* She sighed again. "I guess this is farewell, Nadine. I don't see any cause for you to darken our doorway again.

"Come, Bell. We must be off home, to comfort Ian's wife, and his myriad cousins, and his . . . *grandson."* Penny winked at her sister, and walked out of the room.

"Goodbye, Nadine," Bellona said softly, sadly, finally. Then she left after her sister.

Every subject's duty is the king's, but every subject's soul is his own, Nadine thought. *There's always hope for my soul. Right.* By her own measure, Nadine's soul was spotless.

She'd been robbed, and had fought back and triumphed for a while over the thief. Now Daina's treasure was returned to her, but at the price of her husband's life.

Nadine knew she'd see Ian again, and the next time, he'd be hers. Fate would not allow another such injustice to turn it from its rightful path a second time. She only had to continue to be as she'd always been: patient.

But that didn't mean that Nadine had to forgive Daina her trespass, nor Adrian, nor Penny, nor Bellona, no matter how much the last *hoped for her soul.*

Now that Gil was gone, it would be Nadine's hatred alone that would keep her warm at night. It had been her rock for the greater part of her life, the mountaintop to which she'd climbed, rising above despair. Her hatred had sustained her so far, and Nadine was convinced that it would continue to do so.

Only the good die young, she thought.

TWENTY

Leo graduated from high school the month after his grandfather's sudden death. His school chums, and Sheryl, too, attempted to console him in that brief month, but Leo was withdrawn, silent, inconsolable. After the caps and gowns and congratulations were put up, Leo retired completely into mourning.

Leo saw little of his grandmother, past the occasional brief, wordless hug if their paths crossed. She was also in mourning. Daina had lost everything she'd ever loved, and the bleak prospect of the empty life that remained to her was reflected in her slack, almost drugged expression. Her grief enveloped her like a fog. Leo felt deeply for her, but he was unable to verbalize any condolences. Not yet.

Randi was also in mourning. It was not for Ian, but for her vanished husband. Leo saw Randi even less frequently than he did Daina, and he spoke to her not at all. Randi seldom left her room. Leo only saw her if she roused herself enough to come out and sit at the kitchen table, where she'd then commence to stare at the wall.

Like Daina, her expression was slack, but Leo knew that the drugged look in her eyes was more from actual drugs than from grief. Randi had prevailed on the latest quack Doctor Feelgood to write her a prescription for tranquilizers. Leo knew this because he'd gone to the pharmacy to pick them up for her. Randi couldn't be persuaded to leave the house, not even to retrieve this chemical surcease from her sorrows.

Penny and Bellona took care of the grieving women. They cooked for them, and made sure that what had been prepared was eaten. They laundered their clothes, though neither changed what they wore very often. Throughout the long and sweltering summer after Ian's death and Gil's disappearance, Penny and Bellona made sure the bills were paid on Parcay Street. They watched over these husbandless women as if they were children.

Leo was old enough to look after himself, although Penny and Bellona always made sure he had walking around money in his pocket. He spent a lot of time with his aunts, the only women in his life that weren't practically ghosts. He also took long walks around the neighborhood, long drives.

Leo shunned the company of the few friends he had. Sheryl broke up with him via an unreturned text message and started seeing someone else.

Leo visited Nick, but they didn't talk much. Leo would be online when Nick walked in after work, then he'd say *hi* and conclude whatever he was doing. Then he'd turn on the big screen television that Nick had just bought, and stare at it for a while. Then he'd go home.

By the middle of August, Nick decided it was time to take the bull by the horns. He never would've believed that Leo would be so saddened by his grandfather's passing: Nick had never realized that they'd been that close. But the kid hadn't spoken a hundred words since Ian died. Nick thought that at least Leo should be glad that Gil had taken off, but he couldn't be compelled to speak of that marvel, either.

On Friday, the 14th of August, Nick decided that something had to be done. Leo was too young to be this low, for this long.

When he got home from work, Leo was there, and he tried to enact his usual routine. Nick sat in a chair and watched him go through the familiar motions: Leo logged off the internet and flopped down on the couch. But when he reached for the television remote, Nick said, "Leave the TV for a minute, Cuz. We need to talk."

Leo set the remote back on the coffee table and regarded his cousin expressionlessly.

"I know you've been sad, Leo. I know you haven't signed up for school yet, but it's not too late. You could –"

Leo shook his head. "Maybe next year." He tapped the side of his head. "My mind's not really ready for school right now."

Nick considered his cousin. Leo looked unkempt, for Leo – almost immodest. It was obvious that he hadn't had a haircut since his grandfather passed; he was starting to look a little shaggy. And Leo always wore undershirts and collared shirts – short-sleeved in the summer and long-sleeved in the winter. And he always wore jeans, regardless of the season, and running shoes. *In case I have to run from Gil,* he'd told Nick once. Nick had never realized that he was only half-kidding.

But Leo had abandoned his conservative dress in favor of comfort for the season. He wore a tank top and a pair of board-shorts; flip-flops. Nick was again reminded of Adrian – but this kind of casual attire had been part of his cousin's laid-back, easygoing nature. On slightly uptight Leo it signaled depression to Nick: the kid just didn't care enough to get all the way dressed anymore.

"All right," Nick said. "Next year's good enough." Leo didn't comment. Nick noticed that he was studying his father's guitar on the wall. "Look, Leo. I know you've had a rough couple of months. Your grandfather . . . And then Gil taking off . . ."

Leo looked back at Nick. "Fuck Gil."

At least that's some reaction, Nick thought. "But you gotta snap out of this, Leo. I'm worried about you. I know you miss Ian." *I didn't know you'd miss him this much . . .* "We all miss him. But all this moping around, it's not healthy. It's –"

" *'Tis unmanly grief.* " A faint smile touched Leo's lips at Nick's look of surprise. "Something I heard . . . Grandpa say."

Nick had heard Ian recite the lines from *Hamlet* to Adrian once, when he was just about Leo's age. Adrian had always been fond of his aunts' cats. Old ones were always disappearing and new ones were always arriving. Nick didn't know where the new ones came from, but he knew Jurupa Road took most of the old ones.

An ancient, decrepit old tom named Holt had been missing for a few days, and Adrian, even at sixteen or seventeen, was quite broken up about it.

"It's just a cat, son," Ian had said.

"It's not just a cat, Dad. It's Holt. I've known him all my life."

"To persever in obstinate condolement is a course of impious stubbornness; 'tis unmanly grief," Ian had pronounced. "Let's go get another cat."

And Ian had loaded Adrian and his aunts into the car – his wife drove Nick and Bobby and Tracy in her car – and they'd all convoyed to the animal shelter and picked out another cat.

Ian was a good man, Nick thought. *But he's gone, and Leo's gotta get over it.*

Nick tried again. "I know you're sad, Leo, but –"

"I gotta get over it." That faint smile again. "I know. I'm working on it."

TWENTY-ONE

Hallowe'en was on a Saturday in 2009, and even though he was getting a little old for such things – he'd be thirty-four in December – Nick went to a party.

There was a new programmer at work. He'd seen her standing in the break room on Monday. She was cute, with dark hair and big brown eyes, and no wedding ring. So Nick had switched on the ol' Wilde charm and said, "Hi. Welcome. I'm Nick." He reflected that perhaps the ol' Wilde charm was a little rusty.

But she smiled. "I'm Zelda, just like the game."

"Really?" Nick opened the refrigerator and took out his lunch sack. *"It's dangerous to go alone! Take this."*

Zelda giggled prettily. "Wow! I've never heard that one before. Especially not from someone who writes code."

But she *had* giggled, and Nick was charmed.

They went out to lunch the next day, and on Wednesday, she invited him to go to this Hallowe'en party with her on Saturday. "Costumes are optional," she assured him.

The old programmer and the new programmer had lunch again on Friday, then went out to dinner and a movie that night.

Nick was breaking two of his own rules: dating someone from work, and dating someone younger – Zelda was only twenty-six. But she was cute and bubbly. She knew her job. She smiled and flirted with him in the office. She laughed at his jokes. Why the hell not?

Zelda didn't invite him in when he dropped her off at her apartment after the movie.

Nick feigned disappointment. "Did I tell you I play guitar?" It was okay that she didn't invite him in. That would be rushing it.

"Yes, you did. And I can't wait to hear you play." She kissed him quickly, playfully on the nose. "But I've gotta get my costume ready. I'll see you tomorrow. At eight. Don't be late!" Zelda giggled, eyes sparkling, and scooted into her apartment.

Nick was a little disconcerted when Zelda opened the door the next evening, dressed as her Nintendo namesake, right down to the pointy ears and tiara.

She twirled in the long white gown and asked Nick what he thought.

"It's very . . . authentic." He'd gone with the no-costume option.

But it was Hallowe'en and she did look cute. Nick didn't remember Zelda's bodice being quite so tight in the game. Never did

Zelda the princess's bosom seem to being trying to escape from its purple confines either, as Zelda the programmer's did.

She insisted that they stop at the liquor store and pick up a six-pack for the party, and Nick had another second thought. What were they, still in college? But the kid behind the counter had stared appreciatively at Nick's princess, and that put him in a good mood again.

Nick wasn't the only one at the party that wasn't costumed, but almost. There were the normal coterie of pirates and witches and vampires; the miner from *My Bloody Valentine*. Officer Naughty winked at him. A few of the Watchmen were there, beers in hand, chatting with no less than two Wolverines, and a fat Mr. Spock. There were also several video game characters: Zelda air-kissed with Harley Quinn, gave Mario a hug.

Nick sighed. He *was* back in college.

But it was all right. Zelda sat next to him on the couch. After one beer, she squeezed his hand. After a couple more, she whispered in his ear that she might like to go back to his place after the party and watch him *play his instrument.* "I might even help," she said and giggled.

That sounded like a plan to Nick, and even if she was a little young for his tastes (in temperament if not in years), even if they did work together, he might've just gone right ahead and done it, because her bosom was just crying out to him to free it from that purple bodice.

Nick was down, and it had appeared that Zelda was down. Until Link showed up.

He was as young as the princess, if not younger, with the character's shaggy blonde hair, and he arrived fully decked out in the green hat and tunic, knee-high boots, and plastic sword. This Link had foregone the pointy ears, however.

Nick watched him look hopefully at Zelda when he walked in the door. She ignored him with an elaborate toss of her head. Ten minutes later, they were yelling at each other in the kitchen. Nick sat on the couch morosely and told himself that if he didn't want to go back to college, he shouldn't be going to costume parties with girls named *Zelda, just like the game.*

He heard her voice, raised, shrill, from the kitchen: "You never listen!"

Perhaps his princess needed a hero. Perhaps he should just stomp out there like Donkey Kong and rescue the fair maiden from

73

her tormentor, take her back to his apartment. Maybe she'd show her gratitude by unzipping that horrible dress . . .

Nick peeked in the kitchen, found it empty save for Zelda and Link. Nick caught her eye.

"You just stay right there!" she said to Link and strode across to him. "I'm sorry, Nick," she whispered. "Apparently, we still have issues. I'm sorry. I have to talk to him. You don't have to stay if you don't want to. I can find a ride home."

"Ah . . . okay." Nick was disappointed about not getting to see Zelda's bosom unencumbered, but he figured he was dodging a major bullet otherwise. He should've known that someone pushing thirty would have baggage. Everyone did. Except for him. "I'll see you at work on Monday."

Zelda said that she was sorry again, and gave him a kiss on the cheek. Then in a twirl of white gown, she rounded on Link again. "You never gave back my Lady Gaga CD!"

"It's in the car," Link said.

In his rush to get out of there, Nick bumped into Mario at the door.

"After you," Mario said with a wiggle of his black mustache. He gestured at the door with one white-gloved hand.

"Thank you, Mario, but our princess is in another castle. After you."

Mario grinned and went out the door first.

TWENTY-TWO

Nick got into his car and looked at his watch. It was only nine-thirty. He sighed, started the car and drove home. Where else was he gonna go?

Nick smelled marijuana as he went to put the key into his apartment door. He paused. He could hear the television. Leo must be here. *Wait 'til he hears about Zelda,* Nick said to himself, at the same time thinking that the pot smell must be coming from the college kids' apartment down the hall.

The living room was dark except for the glow of the television. *Pirates of the Caribbean* was playing on the big screen, and lending a proper ghostly atmosphere, smoke eddied in lazy strata in front of it.

Leo said, "Oh, shit! Turn on the light, Sasha!"

Nick blinked in astonishment at the scene revealed by the lamp beside the couch. A Playboy bunny sat closest to the light. This must be Sasha. A redheaded female football player, wearing smeared eye-black to protect her enormous hazel eyes from the non-existent glare, sat on the other end of the couch. She was wearing shoulder pads and skin-tight football pants, and a very short black mesh jersey. Her number was 69, Nick noted.

Leo, shirtless, with a Caspar the Friendly Ghost mask pushed back on his head, sat between them. Officer Naughty, complete with Aviator shades – it was not the same one from the party: she'd been plump all around and this one was only plump in the right places – sat in the chair across from them. She absently twirled a pair of handcuffs.

Beer cans littered the coffee table. A bag of pot and a small but impressive bong sat in their midst.

"I thought you were going to a party, Nick," Leo said innocently.

"Party's over," quoth Officer Naughty.

When silence reigned for a heartbeat, Leo quickly broke it. "These are my friends. The cop is Chrissy. She's not really a cop." Leo giggled, and Nick was amazed to see that he was stoned. The girls, also stoned, also giggled. "My guest from the Playboy mansion is Sasha, and our little Heisman trophy hopeful is . . ." Leo looked at the girl and she smiled adoringly at him. "I'm sorry, honey. I've forgotten your name."

"It's Ada, Leo. I'll make sure you'll remember it the next time."

"Well, that sounds like a plan. Ladies, this is my cousin, Nick. Do you want a beer, my brutha?"

"A –? Where'd you get . . . You're not old enough to buy –"

"Relax, Grandpa," Office Naughty said. "We're old enough." She winked at Nick, but he just stared at her, nonplussed. She sighed and said to Leo, "It looks like our party's over, too, darlin'. Unless you want to come back to our place."

"By all means." Leo looked at Nick, took in his dumbstruck expression. "Let me clean up this mess really quick."

"We'll wait for you in the car," Officer Naughty said.

"Don't be too long," the football player added.

"It was nice meeting you, Nick," the bunny said. She retrieved the bong and the bag of pot from the table and stuffed them quickly into her purse. Then the three of them sashayed out the door. It was the only word that fit. They *sashayed.*

Nick turned back to find that Leo was gone. He'd dashed out to the kitchen to retrieve a trash bag. He returned, and began stuffing the beer cans into it. Leo was singing quietly to himself. Nick caught the lyrics: *She said, that ain't the way to have fun, son . . .*

"Leo . . ." Nick's voice failed him, and he had to begin again. "Leo . . . Those girls. They're not . . . You didn't . . . pay them . . ."

Leo looked at the door, then back at Nick. *"Pay them?* What are you talking about? Oh . . . The costumes." Leo laughed. "It's Hallowe'en, Nick, for Christ's sake! You remember Hallowe'en, don'tcha? Girls like to let the inner tramp out on Hallowe'en." Leo wiggled his black eyebrows. "Trick or treat." When Nick didn't look convinced, he added. "They're just college girls."

"You don't go to –"

"No. No, I do not." Leo grinned. "But what is it that you always say? *I know a couple people. Up the street. Down the block. I know them."* He set the trash bag down and retrieved a flannel shirt off the arm of the couch. He shrugged into it, but didn't bother to button it. Nick again thought that Leo had grown slovenly since his grandpa died. But he obviously wasn't depressed any more.

Leo picked the trash bag up again and smiled. "I gotta go, Cuz. Can't keep the ladies waiting. I'll toss this in the dumpster on my way out." He walked to the door.

"Leo . . ."

"Yes, my brutha?" Leo grinned and he looked so much like Adrian that Nick's heart skipped a beat. Leo looked just like Adrian, on the make, on his way out to meet an adoring groupie. Or two. In this case, *three.*

Nick was worried that the kid might be overdoing it, making up for all the years he'd had to put up with his oppressive stepfather. But Nick was also glad to see Leo come out of his shell. Nick remembered being seventeen. He was glad that his young cousin wasn't sad anymore.

"You're not driving are you?"

"Nope."

Nick grinned back. "Have fun."

"You may rely on it. I'll text you later. Or maybe –"

"Tomorrow."

Leo nodded and went out the door.

Nick sighed and sat on the couch. He killed *Pirates of the Caribbean,* and wondered for a moment when he'd gotten so old. He looked over at the wall above his computer. Adrian's guitar was gone.

Nick started to get angry, thinking that one of Leo's college-girl *friends* had stolen it. One of them had probably kept Leo *occupied,* while the other two just reached up and took it down, ran it out to the car. In the dark, Leo hadn't even noticed that it was gone.

It wasn't like it was valuable, not overly, not unless you were some kind of rabid Eddie Van Halen fan, like Adrian had been. Even then, it wasn't an expensive axe, not like his Stratocaster . . . Nick looked in alarm at the three stands in front of his computer: all his guitars were there.

Why would they bother to climb up and take Adrian's old Charvel? Nick had always thought it was an ugly guitar, but it was the only thing that he had to remind him of Adrian, and three slutty college girls weren't going to get away with stealing it.

Nick took out his phone. It lit up in his hand.

Borrowed Dad's guitar, Leo's text said. *Sasha's dad's a big VH fan. I'll bring it back soon.*

Ok. Wipe the dust off of it b4 u show it 2 him.

☺

Nick supposed it was all right. It wasn't like Leo was going to break the strings playing *Mama Told Me Not To Come* on it. He was no musician, but his dad had been one, and Leo was trying to impress a girl by borrowing a little of that long-ago glory. It was all right for Leo to show off Adrian's ugly yellow and black Charvel. As long as he brought it back.

77

TWENTY-THREE

Thanksgiving dinner was more or less cancelled on Parcay Street in 2009. The thought of creating her traditional green bean casserole had sent Daina into a torrent of fresh tears, and like most days, Randi stayed in bed. The old witches were confident that the widows would come back to themselves eventually, but they didn't want to push their recovery with meaningless festivities too soon.

Penny and Bellona also felt for Leo in his loneliness, even though they knew he was Leo no longer.

"See what Nick's up to, Capo," Bellona advised. "Young men shouldn't be alone on Thanksgiving."

"I'm going to Bobby and Tracy's," Nick said on the phone. "Come with me. I'm sure they'd like to see you."

"All right," his cousin said slowly. "I'll be there in half an hour."

"And bring your dad's —" but Leo had already hung up.

Nick looked at his phone and debated whether or not he should call his brother and let him know that he was bringing Adrian's son along for Thanksgiving dinner. After a moment, Nick decided that he'd just surprise Bobby, and Tracy, as well.

Nick's former bandmates, his bass player and his drummer, his brother and sister-in-law, had never been a part of Leo's life. They remembered him on his birthday and at Christmas, of course. They always sent him a birthday card and a Christmas card full of best wishes and a generous amount of cash. But that was it.

Nick knew that they were ashamed of the fact that they never saw the kid. But their shame couldn't overcome the reason that they shunned Leo: Bobby, and to a lesser extent, Tracy, had never gotten over Adrian's murder.

Nick had always loved Adrian, looked up to him. They'd shared a telepathic bond. But Nick had been nearly six years younger than his cousin. He hadn't even been old enough to drive yet when Adrian died.

Nick had always *watched* Adrian, observed his foibles and habits, his mannerisms, his way with the ladies. Nick had always wanted to be just like Adrian when he grew up, when he grew into a man's body to match his man's perceptions. Adrian knew Nick's mind, his temperament, his burning desire to be an adult in appearance as well as mind, and being the smart-ass that he was,

Adrian had always teased Nick about being just a kid. But Adrian had loved Nick, despite his teasing.

Scarcely more than two years had separated Bobby and Adrian in age, however. They'd grown up together. They were like brothers. They were as close, if not closer, than Rob and Will. Bobby and Nick's father and his twin had differing opinions on life and its meanings: Rob had remained a fun-seeking bachelor, while Will had resigned himself to the role of responsible family man.

But Bobby and Adrian had been simpatico. To them, life had been all about playing music. It was about looking for love – Adrian looked a lot – and finally finding it. Adrian had always admired Bobby and Tracy's success in that endeavor.

Their lifelong love had never produced offspring, however, and Nick had always marveled at the fact that everyone seemed to notice it but them. His mother still harped on her dearth of grandchildren. But Bobby and Tracy's love for each other had always been enough. Nothing else was necessary.

As with Ian and Daina, the only thing that had sustained Bobby and Tracy in the devastating aftermath of Adrian's death had been that love. Still, Nick believed that Bobby had never fully recovered.

His memories of his cousin and their band were just too painful to bear. Along with his bass, and Tracy's drums, along with the amps and mikes and pedals, Bobby had stored all the photo albums crammed full of his life with Adrian. Nick had never seen a single picture of their cousin at Bobby and Tracy's house.

To cope, Bobby had stopped playing music altogether. Where once he'd planned on a career as a music teacher, like their beloved Mr. Johnson, after Adrian's death, Bobby switched majors. He'd gotten a generic degree in Business Administration. He was a mid-level manager at a company that sold respirators to hospitals now. To everybody's surprise, Tracy became a pediatric nurse. Nick had always figured that her chosen field offered her children enough, so she hadn't had to have any of her own.

When he was younger, his brother's actions had infuriated Nick. It seemed as if Bobby was trying to bury Adrian twice, to pretend as if he'd never existed. But as Nick matured, as he watched Leo grow up, it slowly dawned on him that Bobby wasn't trying to forget his cousin, his best friend. Bobby had never been either as stubborn or as tough as his little brother. Bobby was just not in control of his grief.

It had been difficult for Nick to stick it out and stay in Leo's life: the pain of Adrian's loss always remained fresh, the monumental unfairness that this great kid had had his father taken from him before he was even born was ever in the back of Nick's mind. But he'd persevered through his pain. Nick had loved Adrian, and now he'd love his son.

He'd never let Leo forget his dad, would always remind him of what a great guy he'd been. And Nick had been rewarded for his efforts: Leo was his best friend, as Adrian had been Bobby's best friend. Despite the age difference, Nick felt that he and Leo, too, were like brothers. Nick had seen glimpses, flashes of Adrian in Leo all his life – a repeated phrase here, a certain expression there – and lately, over the summer and fall, since Leo had thrown off his grief and come into his young manhood, Nick had found the resemblance to be striking.

Nick thought it was time that Bobby got to know Adrian's son. It'd been painfully impossible for his brother to watch Leo grow up, and Nick strove to understand that, but Leo was an adult now, and Bobby should see how proud the kid had done his dad. Bobby should be proud of him, as Nick was.

It wasn't Leo's fault that Adrian was gone, nor was it Leo's fault that Bobby had never been able to master his loss. Yet, to Nick, it'd always seemed that Bobby had taken it out on Leo by shunning him.

'Tis unmanly grief, Nick thought. Adrian was gone, a part of the past. But Leo was here. He was the future that Adrian had never been permitted to have. It was time that Bobby got to know him.

Leo had resumed his conservative dress for dinner. He even wore a tie, albeit loosely. He'd never gotten around to getting a haircut, however, and his nearly shoulder-length locks, parted in the middle like his father used to wear them, again underlined Leo's resemblance to Adrian. *Bobby's in for quite a surprise,* Nick thought.

"You didn't bring your dad's Charvel back," Nick stated when Leo walked into his apartment, empty-handed.

"I thought my mom might like to see it. If she ever comes out of her room."

"Don't let your grandma see it," Nick warned. Leo had told him about Daina's crying jag over the green bean casserole. "I think it would just make her sad."

"Sadder," Leo said and shook his head, sad himself. "Grandma's still in seclusion, Nick. Just like my mom. I want to talk to her, to tell her that everything's gonna be all right. But I just haven't found the right words yet."

80

Nick wasn't sure that anything Leo could say could ever make up for Daina's losses. And Randi . . . Daina was aware of her son and husband's endings, tragic though they were, but Randi hadn't been afforded even so painful a closure. The fact that her husband had just fallen off the planet . . . *Randi's son is still here, but the loss of her worthless husband has made her neglect him,* Nick thought.

"Mom's gonna need more than words," Leo was saying. "Mom's gonna need a 12-step program to get over that asshole."

"What?"

Leo laughed. "Nothing." He dismissed his mother's lingering melancholy with a wave of his hand. "Dad's guitar is safe. I wouldn't let anything happen to it. I know how much it means to you. I've just been looking at it, thinking . . . Maybe I should take lessons. Somebody told me that the ladies always love a guitar player."

Nick blinked back sudden tears. "I'll teach you, Leo," he said softly. It was something he'd always wanted to do, if Leo had ever shown as much as a moment's interest. Nothing would please Nick more than to teach Adrian's son how to play the guitar.

Leo laughed, oblivious to his cousin's emotions. "Is it hard?"

"Nothing in life worth doing is easy, my brutha."

"Shit, Cuz. You sound like Aunt Penny."

Nick smiled wryly. Maybe preachiness was a part of this getting old phenomenon that he'd noticed in himself lately . . .

Nick got the impression that Leo wasn't really serious about learning to play the guitar, at least not today. But he'd mentioned it, and that was a start.

"I've got one more request before we go," Leo said. "You still got that video camera? Sasha wants me to –"

"No, Leo." Nick shook his head firmly. "You're not making any amateur –"

"What a filthy mind you have, Cuz! I am shocked. Shocked and appalled. That thought never crossed my mind, but now that you mention it . . ." Leo wiggled his eyebrows. "I guess her dad's *getting the band back together,*" he continued, rolling his eyes. "She wanted to know if I could tape their first rehearsal."

"Okay," Nick said, relieved.

"Show me how to use it again, really quick. Before we go."

"What?" Nick exclaimed in surprise. "Mr. *Dragon Ball Z* doesn't remember how to use a video camera?"

Leo shrugged. "Just run me through it again once. I don't want to look like an idiot."

TWENTY-FOUR

"I wish I would've thought to have a camera ready," Nick said.

Bobby had answered his front door at his brother's knock, and when he beheld Leo standing there beside Nick, his mouth fell open. His color drained away; he was paper white.

"The look on your face." Nick slapped Leo on the back. "But there's no need to scare up the monkey's paw and make that final wish, Bob. This isn't Adrian returned from the grave." Bobby flinched at the word *grave*. "You remember Leo, don'tcha?"

Nick had decided that the forthright approach would be the best. No use standing around avoiding each other's eyes. No use trying to sidestep the sad truth: the only memory Bobby harbored of Leo was the fact that his best friend had died the night he'd been conceived. Nick decided to rip the Band-Aid right on off. This wound had lain unexamined for too long.

Leo considered his older cousin expressionlessly. "Hello . . . Uncle Bobby," he said and extended his hand.

Christ! He looks so much like Adrian! Bobby remained motionless for another second, then he remembered himself and shook Leo's hand. "Of course I remember you! It has been a long time, though."

"Like all his life," Nick said. When his brother looked sharply at him, Nick sighed. "You think we could come in now? I'm sure Tracy would like to see Leo, too."

Bobby nodded wordlessly and let them into his house.

Tracy was as shocked to see Adrian's son as was her husband, but she recovered her composure better. She stated the obvious: "You look so much like your dad!" and gave Leo a big hug.

Leo sat at the foot of the small table, with Nick to his right. Tracy and Bobby brought out the food. The man of the house carved the turkey, and the Wildes, one and all, served themselves. In silence. The happy family reunion between his brother and his cousin's son for which Nick had hoped did not materialize.

The clinking of silverware amidst the lack of conversation at last became noticeable to Tracy. "How's your mom, Leo?"

Leo glanced over at Nick in surprise, then said to Tracy, "She's . . . Uh . . . She's in seclusion."

Now Tracy waited for an explanation from Nick, since Leo was looking at him.

"Her husband disappeared," he replied nonchalantly, as if he was talking about a missing family pet. "The same day Ian passed. May he rest in peace."

Nick tucked into his turkey and stuffing. He wasn't going to dwell on Ian's death, wasn't going to observe a moment of silence. Ian was gone, and Leo had just recently gotten over it. Just in the past month or so, he'd gotten back to the business of being a young man. Nick wasn't going to talk about Ian and how much he was missed. He wasn't going to resurrect Leo's grief.

Tracy stared wide-eyed at Nick. Why hadn't he said anything?

"Her husband . . . *disappeared?*"

She looked at Leo. He gazed back at her, still expressionless. Nick was cutting up his turkey. Tracy turned to her husband. Bobby returned her that look that married couples share, the one that said, *How the hell was I supposed to know? You brought it up. You deal with it.*

Nick looked up from his plate and said, "Yep. Gone. Like the wind."

Tracy was speechless at Nick's glibness. She'd never been friends with Randi, not really, even back in the band days. Randi had been just another one of Adrian's adoring groupies to Tracy. There'd been hundreds of them. And Randi's boyfriend – *Gil; that was his name* – he'd just been another asshole to Tracy. She'd avoided talking to him whenever possible, because he'd always leered at her if she did.

Leo hadn't been a part of Tracy's life because of Bobby's grief, and they certainly hadn't kept up on the lives of his mother and her husband. Now the guy was *missing. Jesus!* Tracy didn't know what to say.

"Maybe he ran off with some other woman, eh, Bobby?" Nick said and grinned at his brother. Bobby didn't return his grin. "Maybe ol' Nadine was getting a little creaky for him, maybe she couldn't quite . . ."

Nick started to make an obscene gesture, but Bobby cut him off. "How's work, Nick?" Bobby had been cutting off Nick's obscene gestures at the dinner table since his smart-ass brother had been about ten years old.

Nick's grin widened. "Work's fine, Bob. How's work with you?"

Bobby didn't want to dredge up the past, didn't want to discuss Gil's long ago affair with Nadine. *He doesn't want to go there,* Nick thought. *Not anywhere* near *there. Why, if we go there, he thinks the next thing I'll bring up is how, while Gil was supposed to be out of town with his mistress, he really high-tailed it back to Riverside and murdered Adrian. And then the topic'll go on to when Adrian died, and what he was doing at the time, and what his activities produced . . .*

While Bobby talked about work, Nick glanced over at his cousin. Leo smiled faintly at him.

Tracy talked about what was going on at the hospital, then Nick told the story about Zelda and the Hallowe'en party, with big eyes and large hand gestures. Zelda's purple bodice was a central theme to his narrative. Bobby and Tracy and Leo laughed politely at the end of the story, and then silence fell again, like a guillotine.

Nick reflected that there really wasn't a lot for his sister-in-law and his brother and his young cousin to talk about. *How's your grandma, Leo?* That was out. They didn't want to hear him say that his grandmother was *in seclusion,* just like his mother, mourning her husband.

So, how ya been all your life, Leo? That was out, too.

Bobby and Tracy knew nothing about Adrian's son. They didn't know what hobbies he enjoyed, that he liked computer games and the internet; they didn't know if he had a girlfriend; they didn't know if he was in school. Bobby just looked down at his plate and shoveled Thanksgiving dinner into his face in silence. Tracy smiled at Leo every now and then, but she didn't speak either.

All they've ever done is send him money, Nick thought. *Picking out a present for a little boy – that was beyond them. What did they know about gifts for little boys? What did I know about gifts for little boys? But I cared enough to find out.*

He was never a little boy to them, anyway. He was always just the embodiment of their grief. They never wanted to know him. They just wanted to forget. But that's not fair . . .

Nick's anger at his brother's weakness grew. He caught Tracy's eye and frowned. She looked at her husband, and so did Nick. Bobby was aware of their eyes, but didn't look up from his plate.

The quietness grew tense. At last, Nick said, "You know what? This is bullshit. You guys have never even –"

"Who wants pie?" Bobby said.

"I do," Leo replied immediately, seeking to avoid a scene.

"Great!" Bobby smiled blandly. "We've got apple and pumpkin."

"Pumpkin for me," Leo said. He looked steadily at his older cousin, but Bobby couldn't meet his eye.

"Great," Bobby repeated. He stood.

"Let me help you," Nick said, and the brothers Wilde went out to the kitchen.

"What the fuck is wrong with you?" Nick whispered furiously.

"Why didn't you tell me you were bringing him? Give me a little warning? Christ, Nick! He looks so much like Adrian!" Bobby put his face in his hands.

"But he's not Adrian, Bobby. Adrian's dead." Again Bobby winced. "He's Adrian's son. You owe it to –"

"Don't tell me what I owe, Nick."

"He's a great kid. If you'd just talk to him –"

"Talk to him? What are we gonna talk about? *Gee, Leo, it's great to see you all grown up. You look just like your dad. Your dad was my best friend, and somebody murdered him, shot him down in cold blood like a dog. . ."*

Bobby looked wonderingly at his brother. "Does he even know? That somebody killed Adrian? That they got away with it?" Nick nodded. "Who told him? *You?"*

Nick nodded and shook his head at the same time, a quirk he'd unknowingly picked up from Adrian while still just a boy. "He found the newspaper article on the internet. He asked me about it, so I told him."

Bobby's eyes narrowed suspiciously. "What exactly did you tell him?"

"I told him Gil did it."

"Oh, Christ, Nick!" Bobby put his face in his hands again, then looked up in alarm. "You said Gil's missing. You don't think he . . ."

Nick barked laughter. "Leo? Leo wouldn't hurt anybody. He's a lover, not a fighter. Just like his dad. At least he is lately. He didn't believe me, anyway." Nick smiled and put his hand on his brother's shoulder. "I'm telling you, Bobby. He's a great kid. If you'd just talk to him –"

"You want me to talk to him? I can't even look at him."

Nick's face hardened again. He took his hand back. "It would be a lot easier to look at him now, if you'd been around for any part of his life. I was always –"

"Yeah, *you were always.* You're a fucking saint, Nick. It was easier for you. Adrian wasn't your best friend. He always made fun of you –"

86

"Don't make me punch you on Thanksgiving, Bobby." He wasn't kidding.

"I'm sorry, Nick. I just . . . I just can't."

Nick was amazed to see his brother's sorrow, still fresh after all these years. But he remained unmoved. *'Tis unmanly grief.* Bobby had penalized Leo for his entire life, just because he was too weak to get over Adrian's death.

"You're a pussy, Bob. I'm ashamed of you." Nick turned away from his brother in disgust. Bobby grabbed his arm and Nick turned back. "What?"

Bobby was crying. "I'm sorry, Nick. Tell him . . . Tell him . . . I'm sorry. I just can't."

Nick flinched out of Bobby's grasp. "Fuck *you're sorry,* Bobby. You're not sorry. You're weak. Leo might forgive you. But I never will." He picked up one of the desserts from the counter. "Come on. *Let's have pie.*"

TWENTY-FIVE

Nick begged off from Christmas dinner with his parents. He told them that he had the flu, but the truth was that he didn't want to see his brother again so soon.

Christmas on Parcay Street also promised to be a somber affair this year, so Leo went to Nick's place. They decided on dinner at Paul's – one of the few Riverside eateries open on Christmas Day – then went back home and watched movies. They had a few drinks to toast our Savior's birth. They toasted their bachelorhood – Sasha and Leo had called it quits right around Thanksgiving – and they expressed hopes for better prospects in the coming new year.

Leo wished his cousin *Merry Christmas* and *Happy Birthday.* Nick called him a cab and Leo arrived back home around midnight.

The next morning, Nick was awakened by someone pounding on his front door. He had no idea who it could be. It was eight o'clock, he had a hangover, and besides, who'd be pounding on his door the day after Christmas?

It was Bobby. He had his hands balled into fists. He was pissed.

"I suppose you think this is funny?"

"Hi, Nick, my only brother," Nick said. "Happy birthday!"

"Fuck you, Nick. I don't care if it's your birthday. I want you to take it down. It's not funny. It's disrespectful. It's sick."

Nick considered his brother: he was furious about something, red-faced, almost panting. Nick decided that he didn't particularly care what Bobby was so wound up about. He'd lost a lot of respect for him lately.

"I have no idea what you're talking about, but whatever it is, it can wait until after I have some coffee."

"Fuck you, Nick," Bobby repeated. "I know you're in on it. He couldn't have done it without –"

"Uh-uh." Nick wagged his finger. "Coffee."

Nick took his time in the kitchen. Maybe a little wait would calm his brother's temper down a few degrees. Nick wasn't really in the mood for Bobby and whatever he was mad about at the moment. He could just hold on a few minutes until Nick had his coffee, or he could hit the road.

At last Nick returned to the living room and flopped onto the couch.

"You're gonna wanna come over here," Bobby said. He was seated in front of the computer.

Nick waved his hand dismissively. "It's uncomfortable over there. The couch is soft. I have a headache. I can see it from here."

"You've already seen it," Bobby accused. "I want you to take it down."

"Whatever. I haven't the foggiest what you're talking about." Nick waved his hand again, sipped his coffee. "Proceed."

Bobby right-clicked and a YouTube video box opened. Nick heard a low hiss, and thought that whatever this was going to be, the sound quality was going to be minimal.

"This goes out to my cousins, Bobby and Nick. It's a compilation of a few of my favorite riffs."

Bobby stopped the video and glared at his brother.

Nick smiled in tender amazement. Adrian had appeared in the small box. He was wearing a black tank top – *good ol' Adrian,* Nick thought, *gotta show off those guns* – and he was seated, holding his beloved, ugly EVH Charvel in his lap. He smiled into the camera. Nick recognized the bookcase and part of the bright yellow of Penny and Bellona's living room wall behind him.

"Wow, Bobby!" Nick marveled. "Where'd you find *this?"*

"Did you think I wouldn't find it?"

"What –"

"Rob brought some woman about half his age with him to dinner last night. He said they're just friends, said he met her at the supermarket . . ." Bobby shook his head. "Whatever. It doesn't matter. We all get to talking. She says her son plays drums in some band. Mom says, 'Tracy used to play the drums.'

"'Oh, really?' the woman says, and the conversation goes on. Rob tells her that we used to have a band. She asks if anyone ever taped us. I guess her daughter is in film school. A regular MTV family are they, rock star son, videographer daughter.

"I said I didn't think so, it was a long time ago, and video technology wasn't what it was today, and so on. But Tracy says she thinks she remembers a guy with a camera at some frat party we played. You remember how big and bulky video cameras used to be?"

Nick nodded.

"I said that I didn't remember any guy with a camera, and anyway, what difference would it make? It was a long time ago. And this woman says, 'You never know, someone might've put it up on YouTube.' And she types *Urban Equinox* into the search box on mom's Apple. No frat party video. Nothing at all, except for your sick little joke."

"What are you talking about, Bobby? Adrian obviously knew someone with a camera, and he got them to –"

"Fuck you, Nick," Bobby growled a third time. "That's not Adrian. And you know it."

"What?" Nick snatched the remote to the big screen television off the coffee table. He pushed a couple of buttons and the image from the computer appeared. "Make it full screen." Bobby complied and the image of Adrian filled the large TV. "Okay, start it over."

"This goes out to my cousins, Bobby and Nick. It's a compilation of a few of my favorite riffs."

Adrian looked down at the Charvel for a second, then played the opening to *Johnny B. Goode.* He smiled into the camera. Instinctively, Nick smiled back. Adrian segued into *Day Tripper,* then *(I Can't Get No) Satisfaction.* The Stones' anthem had always been one of Nick's favorites.

Nick remembered the parties, the shows, the way Adrian's banter made the crowd laugh; how they'd play portions of songs that they didn't plan to play in their entirety. Adrian had always liked to play just the good parts, anyway. Some chick must've had access to a camera, and he'd had her tape him doing just that. Playing just the good parts.

Adrian played *Purple Haze,* then a quick bit of *Crossroads.* Then *Paranoid,* and *Smoke on the Water.* He played the timeless intro to *Don't Fear the Reaper,* and *Walk This Way.*

Nick started to get into it. Whatever other talents Adrian may or may not have possessed – Nick knew he could waterski (as could Bobby), and that he was legendary with the ladies (as Bobby was not) – he could certainly play the guitar. Adrian mostly looked down as he played, but would shoot a quick grin at the camera every now and then, like when he played *Cult of Personality,* and when he rolled into that Van Halen standard, *Hot for Teacher.*

Nick grinned at his brother and said, *"I don't feel tardy."*

Bobby threw a HTTP manual at him. Nick dodged it. Bobby stopped the video, closed the page. He was still furious. "I want you to take it down, Nick."

Nick started to get a little angry himself. "What the fuck is wrong with you, Bobby? It's great! Jesus, getting to hear Adrian play again . . ."

"It's not Adrian, Nick, and you know it. It's Leo."

Nick laughed. "You're outta your mind, Bobby. Leo doesn't play guitar."

Bobby narrowed his eyes. "But you do. I figure, you must've turned his amp off or something. You were playing in the background.

"How did it go, Nick? 'Hey, let's dress you up like your dad? Let's pretend you're your dad and make a guitar video?' I want you to take it down, Nick. Just like you told me, he's not Adrian. Adrian's dead.

"And if someone looks up our band on YouTube, this is all they're gonna get – some kid playing rock-star dress-up while his cousin plays in the background. It's not Adrian and I don't want anyone to think it is. I want you to take it down."

"I don't know what you're –"

"Where's Adrian's axe, Nick?" Bobby glanced behind him at the empty wall. "Leo's got it, doesn't he?"

"Yes, but –"

"It's disrespectful, Nick. It's mocking the dead."

"Mocking the –? You don't know what you're talking about, Bobby. That was Adrian. Leo doesn't know how to play, and I wouldn't . . ." Now Nick's own anger, long held, simmered. "I bet you don't even remember what Adrian looked like, Bobby. You don't have any pictures of him, you don't –" Nick sprang off the couch and grabbed the photo of the band off the shelf.

Bobby snatched it away from him, gestured at it. "This is Adrian. That was his son."

Nick took the picture back, studied it. A doubt crossed his mind. "Maybe he looked a little different than this, but . . . Leo doesn't play, Bobby."

"I want you to take it down, Nick. You . . . Or Leo, whichever one of you posted it. The last part's the most disrespectful of all."

"The last part? What –"

"That's how I knew you were behind it. Leo looks at the camera and says, 'And in conclusion, here's a little vintage Urban Equinox.' Then he plays *One More Time Today.*"

"*One More Time Today?* That's not possible, Bobby. Leo couldn't have ever even *heard* that! Adrian never even wrote it down!"

"But you wrote it down, didn't you? You wrote it down in that old ratty notebook you used to carry around.'"

"Jesus, Bobby! I haven't had that notebook in years, I . . ." A thought struck Nick.

Bobby scowled. "'This is gonna be a hit,' you said. 'We'll get Mr. Johnson to help us record it, as soon as we get back from Europe.' But when we got back from Europe, Adrian was dead. And I'm not going to let you let his kid masquerade as –"

"I think I know what's going on, Bobby." Nick set the picture of Urban Equinox back on its shelf. *No, it wasn't Adrian in the video. Leo looks a lot like him – especially because I haven't seen him in eighteen years. Leo doesn't play, so I just naturally assumed . . . But that wasn't Adrian. Bobby's right. Somehow . . . It's Leo.*

Nick called up his copy of Sibelius. He searched around for a moment, then retrieved the sheet music to *One More Time Today*. Bobby grinned humorlessly in vindication.

"I don't know how . . ." Nick stammered. "I don't know who he got to play it –"

"Right," Bobby said. "Take it down."

"I didn't post it, Bobby. Leo must've –"

"Then you get *him* to take it down."

TWENTY-SIX

After his brother stomped off in his offended huff, still insisting that Nick and Leo were mocking the dead, Nick watched the video again, all the way through this time.

Sunshine of Your Love, Back in Black, Crazy Train, Owner of a Lonely Heart, Thunderstruck, Aqualung, Pretty Woman, Ain't Talkin' 'Bout Love, Sweet Child o' Mine. The video went on for thirteen minutes. At the end, just like Bobby said, Leo not only played but sang the last song Adrian ever wrote. Nick wouldn't have been able to recall all the lyrics – he'd only written down the music – but when he heard Leo sing the words, he remembered enough. It was his father's tune. *One More Time Today.*

This is just bizarre.

Adrian had played guitar more or less every day for fifteen years, three quarters of his life. After listening to something a couple of times, Adrian could replicate it. He could read and write music; he could write lyrics. Adrian Wilde had been a musician.

His son was not.

Nick texted Leo: *Where u at, Cuz?*

I'm sleeping off last night's Xmas cheer. Happy bday.

Thanks. U gonna b around 4 awhile?

I'm gonna b sleepin 4 awhile, lol. Then . . . where do I have to go?

I'm gonna come out & see u.

Don't make it 2 soon. Beauty sleep.

Ok.

Nick watched the video again. Bobby was right. Leo was dressed like his dad used to dress; he *seemed* to be playing. Nick looked closely at the bookcase in the background, and he saw the four books of *The Twilight Saga* by Stephenie Meyer. Nick was not much of a reader, but he knew that Penny and Bellona loved all that supernatural shit. More importantly, he knew that the vampire books had just come out in the last couple of years. If he'd still harbored any doubts – this video was just the oddest thing – the books' presence confirmed that it wasn't Adrian in it. It was modern, new.

It was Leo.

The sound quality was okay, although there was that hiss . . . Nick realized that Leo had to have taped it on his cheap little video camera. He hadn't borrowed it to record Sasha's ol' man's band. Leo and Sasha had broken up. He'd borrowed it to make this weird little clip.

Nick couldn't even form full questions in his mind. All he could string together were the interrogatives: how . . .? *Why . . .?*

Nick tried to watch *Quantum of Solace,* the last movie that he and Leo had rented from the Redbox the night before. He wanted to kill some time, to let Leo sleep. But the *how* and the *why* of the guitar video kept asking for answers in his head. They wouldn't allow him to concentrate on James Bond. Nick's mind was full of question marks. It was just the weirdest thing.

So Nick put the DVDs back in their cases. Almost without thinking about it, he took his Stratocaster and a small practice amp and stuck them in the back of his Civic. He deposited the movies in the Redbox, then headed out to Parcay Street. Leo could catch up on his beauty sleep later. Nick had to find out how this thing had come to exist.

It seemed like he was actually playing, Nick said to himself. His hands moved, he hit the whammy when the tune called for it, but someone could've showed him how to fake that. Maybe Leo had taken a few lessons . . . But why would they teach him how to fake it instead of how to actually play? Who did he find in the month since Thanksgiving to show him? Maybe one of his college friends from *up the street. Down the block.*

But what was the point? Somebody else had to be doing the actual playing. There was no possible way that Leo could've learned all those riffs. There was just no way. He'd played enough like Adrian that Nick had thought that it *was Adrian playing.* So someone who knew what they were doing had to be playing in the background while Leo just moved his hands and pretended to play. And whoever it was, they had to be able to read music – Leo must've printed out *One More Time Today,* and the man in the shadows must've learned it – but how did Leo know the words?

Today was Nick's thirty-fourth birthday, and he reckoned that, in a not entirely unadventurous life, this was the strangest thing that he'd yet encountered. How had Leo faked thirteen minutes of famous rock and roll? Why had he recorded it and posted it on the internet?

Nick rang the doorbell at Leo's house. *Adrian's house,* he thought again, as he'd always thought, every time he'd rung the bell for the last eighteen years. But Adrian was gone . . .

And his son didn't know how to play the guitar!

No one came to the door. Leo's car was there, so he had to be home. Nick sidled around the back of the house and peeped in Leo's window, found his bed empty. Where the hell was he?

Nick decided to cross the street and look for his cousin in Daina and Ian's garage. He knew that the kid liked to go in there and sit on the boat. Nick heard faint music as he approached the door, but when he turned the knob, he discovered that it was locked. Annoyed, he knocked.

The music died abruptly. There was silence for a second. Then Leo's voice: "Who is it?"

"It's Nick. Open the fucking door."

Nick heard a whisper, a giggle, then the door opened. A cloud of marijuana smoke wafted out.

"Jesus Christ, Leo! It's ten o'clock in the morning!"

Leo and two girls were sitting in folding chairs. An old wooden cable spool served as a table between them. A bag of pot was in the middle of it, along with a couple of Budweiser cans.

"Since you woke me up, I decided to walk up to Hilltop and get some groceries." Leo indicated a paper bag on the concrete floor beside the spool. "I ran into Angie and . . .?"

"Deidre."

Leo smiled at Deidre, then looked back at his cousin. "I ran into Angie and Deidre, and they invited me to a little wake and bake." He looked at the table. "The beers are from a couple days ago. I think." Leo grinned.

Nick was not amused. The kid was becoming a stoner. "Where's your dad's axe, Leo?"

Angie giggled at the unfamiliar term.

"Nobody says *axe* anymore, Cuz."

Nick found that his annoyance was increasing. He'd always had little patience with sloppy drunks and giggling potheads, and he was concerned with the fact that Leo was smoking weed at ten o'clock in the morning on the day after Christmas with two slatternly locals. And he wanted to get to the bottom of this video.

He gritted his teeth. "Where's your dad's guitar, Leo?" he asked evenly.

"It's at the house. In my room. Safe."

When it became evident that Leo was not going to speak further, Nick said, "I saw your video."

"Of course you did. I sent you an email. What did ya think of it?"

95

Nick shook his head. "I didn't get any email, Leo. Bobby came over this morning, having a fit –"

"You didn't get an email?" Leo blinked in confusion, but he wasn't stoned, Nick noticed. *Not yet, anyway.*

"I thought sure I sent you one. Maybe I forgot." Leo looked at the girls and abruptly clapped his hands, making them jump. "That's it, ladies. You're leading me astray." Leo winked at his cousin. "Your influence is making me forgetful. I'm going to have to send you on home."

"But, Leo! We just got here!" Angie protested.

"Call me later. I have to have a few words with my cousin right now." When they didn't move immediately, Leo flapped his hands at them. "Go on, now."

Reluctantly, the girls arose. Nick noticed that these two were fresher than Leo's college friends: they were his age, or maybe younger. *Yikes!* Nick thought. Deidre snatched up the baggie and stuck it in her pocket, and they slowly crossed the garage.

"Close the door, will ya?" Leo requested. They complied, and he looked expectedly at Nick.

"It's never yours, is it?"

"What?"

"The pot. It's never yours."

"It doesn't have to be." Leo grinned.

Nick grinned back, despite his concern. He thought again that maybe he was getting old. It was just pot. He'd never smoked it, but he'd certainly supplied enough of it to Adrian and Bobby, once upon a time. And it hadn't hurt them.

"I meant to send you an email, Nick, with the link. Penny and Bellona helped me make it and post it. Bellona's damn internet savvy for an old gal. I wanted you to see it first. Now that you have . . . Tell me what you thought of it."

Nick's smile faltered. He shook his head, sat down in one of the folding chairs across from Leo. He considered his cousin closely for a minute, then said, "What did you want me to think of it?"

Leo hesitated. Then he sighed and said, "I'm not the man I used to be, Nick."

Nick barked a short laugh. He gestured at the beer cans, looked over his shoulder at the door through which the girls had just exited. "You can say that again."

"Them? They're just girls. Someone to occupy my time for a minute." Leo paused again, then repeated, "What did you think of my clip?"

Again, Nick said, "What did you want me to think of it?"

"Like I say, I'm not the man I used to be, my brutha. You might say that I'm an entirely new man. But not really. I'm . . ." Leo looked at his cousin steadily. "When you first saw the clip, who did you think it was? Playing the Charvel?"

Nick answered immediately. "I thought it was your dad."

Leo paused for effect. What he had to say next was life-altering, something that may never have been said before in all of history. At least he'd never heard of anybody ever saying it, so he was going to milk it for all the suspense that he could. He gazed at Nick mysteriously for a moment, then at last he said, "And you were right."

Nick blinked, then took out his phone and started hitting numbers.

"Who are you calling?"

"I'm calling the men in the white coats, Leo." Nick considered him mildly. He put his phone back into his pocket. "Just what exactly is it that you're trying to tell me?"

"When you saw me play, you thought I was –"

"You look a lot like your dad, Leo. Especially lately, since your hair's getting long. Bobby called the video up. I was sitting across the room. When I saw the Charvel, and you said, 'This goes out to my cousins,' I just naturally assumed that Bobby had unearthed some lost clip your dad had made.

"He was freaking out, saying that you were mocking the dead."

"Really?"

Nick nodded. "You saw how he is. At Thanksgiving."

"I did. He can't stand to look at me."

Nick frowned. "And I told him that he was weak because of that."

He searched Leo's face for resentment – it wasn't the kid's fault that Adrian was dead – but the impression that Nick got was that Leo didn't slight Bobby for being unable to overcome the shock of his best friend's murder.

"Bobby knew all along that it was you."

"But I can't play the guitar."

"That's why I'm here. I want to know how you did it."

Leo grinned craftily. "How do you think I did it?"

97

"I figure you found somebody to help you. Somebody showed you how to move your fingers. Somebody was playing in the background. Somebody –"

"That all sounds pretty far-fetched, Nick."

"There's no other explanation."

"Unless I'm Adrian Wilde."

Nick continued to frown. "Bobby said it was a sick joke. I didn't think that, but . . . What the fuck are you talking about, Leo? *Is* this some kind of a sick joke? Are you delusional? Have you lost your mind? Are you going to claim to be Napoleon next?"

"How else could I play like that, Nick?"

"You're not Adrian, Leo. Adrian is dead. You're . . . You're a great kid, even if you aren't a musician. You're you."

Nick studied his cousin, trying to figure out what his game was. Nick didn't want to think that Leo had suddenly lost his mind and believed that he was his father. Nick didn't want to think that people just went absolutely insane at the drop of a hat like that.

There had to be some angle. Leo was clever. He'd always observed people. He'd just begun to come out of his shell since he'd been so inexplicably, so fortunately, relieved of the burden of Gil's tyranny. Nick had always talked Adrian up to his son, so perhaps Leo wanted to show Nick that he could be like his dad, now that Gil was gone. It had to be some kind of game.

So Nick decided to play along. "You're going to have to explain this to me, Cuz. How can you be . . .?" He couldn't even say it. He shook his head and began again. "If you're suddenly Adrian, what happened to Leo?"

"Leo's here, too. But he's fading, Nick. I can remember everything that happened in Leo's life, but it's like a story that somebody told me. I can tell you everything that ever happened to him.

"I can tell you about how surprised he was the first time Gil ever backhanded him. You and me, we would've been pissed – but Leo was just surprised. After that . . . He always wanted to get by more than fight back."

Leo frowned, and Nick thought that perhaps here was the angle. Now that Gil was gone, Leo wanted to be someone else. Someone cool, like his dad . . .

"I can tell you about the first girl he ever kissed, the first girl he ever . . ." Leo grinned. "There was just the one, actually, some little mousy thing from study hall . . ." His grin faded. "But it's like somebody told me about it. None of it happened to me. Leo's gone, Nick. I'm back."

Nick squinted. "Where have you been?"

"That I don't know."

"How did you . . . return?"

"There was . . . a trigger. Something happened to Leo . . . Then . . . Here I am."

"Maybe Leo's got multiple personality disorder," Nick suggested. "Maybe there's two or three more people in there with you guys. Jerry Garcia. Elvis."

"Jerry Garcia's dead?"

Nick looked steadily at his cousin. *Maybe Leo* is *crazy,* he thought with dismay. *Maybe he's developed a split personality . . . Part of him's decided that he wants to be Adrian. But still: who taught "Adrian" how to play the guitar?*

"I was Leo, Nick. But then . . . something happened. Never mind about that right now. You just have to believe me. Leo's gone. I need to prove that to you, before I can tell you *why* he's gone. Why I'm back."

"You're not Adrian, Leo. I don't know if this is some kind of joke, if you're playing me for some reason. Or if you've lost your fucking mind. But your dad is dead. You can't be –"

"Ask me anything, Nick." Leo glanced around the garage. His eye fell on *One Wilde Ride.* He brightened. "You want to go for a boat ride? You want to see me waterski?"

"If you were really Adrian, you'd know it's too cold to waterski."

"But it won't always be too cold. Would that prove it to you, Nick? If chickenshit Leo, who was always afraid of the water, got up on skis on his first try, would that convince you?" Leo frowned again. "Probably not. You don't know how to ski, either. You were never much for the water yourself, any more than Leo was."

"Stop talking about yourself in the third person."

"Maybe we should go talk to Penny and Bellona. Maybe you'll believe them. They recognized me right away."

"What about your grandmother? Surely she'd recognize her own son . . ."

"No. Not yet. She's still mourning . . . I don't have the words to tell her yet. But – would that convince you, Nick? If I told her that I was back, and she said, 'Of course you are'? She's waited for me for almost eighteen years, Nick. Would that convince you?"

Nick leaned closer to Leo and narrowed his eyes. "I don't know what you're trying to pull here, Cuz. But if you start telling that grieving old woman that you're her dead son, back from the grave . . . I will personally punch you in the mouth. She's got enough on her plate, without believing that her grandson has lost his fucking mind."

Leo considered his cousin for a moment. "I'm going to go get my guitar and my amp –"

"Where'd you get an amp, anyway?"

"I picked it up at Guitar Center. And a lead. It's just a little one. What happened to my Marshall?"

Nick smiled. Leo could've guessed that Adrian had had a Marshall amp. It was a common enough type. Whoever had taught him how to fake playing had probably mentioned the brand.

"I don't know how you learned those riffs, Leo. It's got a be some kind of a trick –"

"Remember that cross-eyed girl, Nick? The one you got rid of by telling her I was going with Tracy? Remember Emily? You told her I had a rash."

All expression left Nick's face.

"I'm going to go get my axe, Nick. And while I'm gone, I want you to think up a logical, sane, scientific explanation for how I could know about those girls."

"Adrian could've told your mom. She could've –"

"Except you know that I – that *Adrian* never had too many heart to hearts with Randi about the girls he dated. And even if he did – you know that Randi never had too many heart to hearts with Leo about anything Adrian said. Ever. It's not like they had a lot of what you'd call history together, now did they?"

Leo frowned for a third time – Nick caught a trace of bitterness. *He's bitter because Randi never told him about his dad. Nobody ever told him about his dad but me.* But that wasn't entirely fair, Nick thought. Surely Daina and Ian, and the old ladies, had talked to Leo about his father. But they couldn't know about the cross-eyed girl. Or the rash.

"I'll be right back, Nick. I also want you to think about how I could know the words and music to *One More Time Today.*"

"The music was on my computer. You just printed it out."

"But I don't know how to read music. I don't know how to play the guitar."

"You got somebody else –"

100

"How do I know the lyrics? I'm going to make you believe this. You're my best friend now, Nick. I had to tell you first. Bobby used to be my best friend, but . . . Bobby got old. Bobby's sad. If I can convince you, then maybe together we can convince him . . . And then . . . It'll be just like the old days –"

"Stop it, Leo. It's not funny anymore." Nick thought that if the kid said, *We can get the band back together,* he'd have to slap him. He remembered Bobby's pain, his outrage, when he thought that Adrian's son was mocking his memory. *Wait 'til he hears about this dog and pony show.*

"I want you to pretend, just pretend, that what I'm telling you is possible, Nick. I want you to suspend disbelief." Leo looked at his watch. "Give me an hour. If I can't convince you that I'm Adrian in an hour, I'll never bring it up again. What do you say?"

Nick's mind was a maelstrom. He'd always been a logical person, and what Leo was saying was just nuts . . . Impossible, supernatural . . . But . . . But . . . How had he learned to play the guitar? How did he know the words to a song that Adrian had never written down? It was just nuts, it was insane . . .

But somewhere in all those swirling emotions – *oh my God, what a compounded tragedy it would be if Leo's lost his mind –* somewhere in all those swirling emotions, Nick recognized hope.

Adrian. What Nick wouldn't give to have Adrian back.

"You've got one hour." He went outside and watched Leo trot across the street, then he got his guitar and amp out of the back of his car.

TWENTY-SEVEN

It didn't take an hour to convince Nick.

Leo was pleased to see that Nick had brought his Strat with him. They found a couple of thick orange extension cords and snaked them from their amps to the outlet in the wall. They sat across from each other in the folding chairs, guitars in their laps. It was just like the old days.

"What should we begin with?" Leo asked.

Nick narrowed his eyes. It was the phrase that Adrian had always used to start their shtick. The crowd thought it was all impromptu, just warm-up band banter, but it was all rehearsed. If Leo knew the sequence of tunes . . .

Nick played the intro to *Back in Black,* then stopped. Waited.

Leo grinned. "Too metal."

Nick blanched. Maybe it was just a coincidence . . . He played *Pretty Woman.* When he got to the part where Adrian would start singing, he stopped again.

Leo said, "Too old."

Nick mimicked the bassline from *Money.* When he stopped again, Leo said, "Still too old. You know what my dad always says, Cuz. *Something from this decade."*

When Nick hesitated, Leo played the beginning of *Addicted to Love.* When he hesitated again, Leo said, "That was your cue, Cuz," and busted into the immortal opening riff to *(I Can't Get No) Satisfaction.*

Leo smiled at Nick's open-mouthed astonishment. "What next?" Nick was speechless. "Bobby would play the bassline to *Disco Inferno.* And I'd say –"

"Disco's dead, Cuz," Nick supplied.

Nick imitated the strings in *Viva La Vida,* and looked for recognition in Leo's eyes. It was one of his favorite songs. Leo had the CD in his car and whenever they drove anywhere, Nick would have to listen to him belt out, *I hear Jerusalem bells are ringing, Roman Cavalry choirs are singing . . .*

But Leo blinked in confusion. Nick was convinced his muddle was genuine. Adrian died in 1991; he'd never heard Coldplay.

Leo shook his head. "No, that's not right. I don't know what that is. Next up was *Play That Funky Music."* Leo played it. "Then I'd say, 'Disco's dead, Nick. Before you were born.' And then Bobby would play *Iron Man."*

Leo continued to stare at his cousin. Disbelief warred with hope within Nick. Sure, Leo was a great kid, but he was no Adrian Wilde. If by some incredible, metaphysical miracle . . . It was impossible, but how could Leo know Urban Equinox's entire act? Unless, it was true. Unless he was Adrian. . .

Leo played *One More Time Today* again, sang the lyrics. They were haunting, considering what had happened to Adrian, mere days after he came up with the song, before he ever got a chance to write it down . . .

"If you think you'll miss me
Why don't you just kiss me
One more time today?

If I must be going
And you say you're knowing
There will come a day

Sometimes when I kiss you
Tell me that you want to
Make sure I can stay

Next I'm just a house rat
Lucky like a black cat
Send me on my way

Then you say you're sorry
'Come on with me, baby
There's still time to play'

Promise that I'll miss you
If you let me kiss you
One more time today."

Nick heard the side door to the garage open. As the last chord died away, Leo looked up and smiled. Nick glanced over his shoulder, figuring that one of the kid's stoney girlfriends had returned, and hadn't even been polite enough to knock.

He was mistaken. He took in Daina's sad, worn countenance, and thought again that it would only make her sadder to see her grandson with his dad's guitar. Again Nick was mistaken. A look of astonishment crossed Daina's face. It became joy.

"Oh, my God! *Adrian!*"

She crossed the garage. Leo leaned the Charvel against the spool table, stood up and jubilantly embraced her.

What did I tell ya, Cuz? Nick heard Adrian's voice in his head. *She knows who I am. Do you?*

TWENTY-EIGHT

Nick went outside to lend privacy to the incomprehensible reunion between mother and son.

Again, he wished for a drink.

He remembered a logic class he'd taken in college. Professor Lopez had been so stern and pedantic as to make Adrian's grandfather Jameson seem like a hippie in comparison. *William of Occam stated, Entities should not be multiplied unnecessarily,* the professor had intoned to his class. When everyone looked mystified, he tried again. *If you have two theories that each explain the observed facts, then you should use the simplest theory until more evidence comes along.* Still nothing. *The explanation requiring the fewest assumptions is most likely to be correct.* Professor Lopez had then grinned at his baffled class and added, *God's existence cannot be deduced by reason alone.*

Maybe someone could've taught Leo all those riffs since Thanksgiving. Maybe he was a prodigy, although Nick recalled that Leo always sang *Viva la Vida* off key. Maybe he'd learned to read music, and that's how he knew the chords to *One More Time Today*.

If that wasn't fantastic enough, maybe Leo had also miraculously learned to sing in a month, because he wasn't off key anymore.

Perhaps Adrian had told Ian about the cross-eyed girl and the rash. Maybe the stories had somehow filtered down to Randi, and maybe she'd told Leo. Maybe Randi had carefully memorized the song order of the banter-shtick the band used to do, and had also related that to Leo, the kid who cared nothing for music. Yet, despite that, maybe he'd also carefully memorized it.

But that was all highly improbable. *The explanation requiring the fewest assumptions is most likely to be correct.* Even if it's insane . . .

Maybe Leo was gone and Adrian was returned. That was the simplest explanation, even the most likely one, considering the facts, no matter how crazy it was. Adrian returned would explain how he knew the stories about the girls, and how to play the guitar, and Urban Equinox's pre-set set list. It would explain how he could suddenly carry a tune, and how he knew the lyrics and the chords to *One More Time Today*. It would explain how his mother recognized him.

It was the only explanation for how Nick could hear Adrian's voice in his head. *God's existence cannot be deduced by reason alone.*

Nick called his brother.

"Did you take that video down yet?" Bobby snarled in greeting.

"What I need you to do concerns that. I need you to pack up your wife and come out to Daina and Ian's house. Bring your bass. And bring that bottle of Chivas that I know Dad gave you for Christmas."

Bobby was silent for a moment. "My bass is in storage, Nick. And why should I come all the way out there –"

"You've never been a part of Leo's life, Bobby," Nick said with all the accusation he could muster. "Because you miss Adrian, you've never been able to bring yourself to give his son the time of day. Now . . . Now Leo wants to explain to you why he made that clip. He explained it to me, and . . . Trust me when I tell you that you're not going to believe it at first.

"But if you give him a chance, if you listen to the things he's gonna tell you . . . I think you'll believe him, just like I do, Bobby. And once you believe him . . . I think today might wind up being one of the happiest days of your life."

Bobby remained silent. Nick thought he could feel his brother's suspicion through the phone.

"Oh, for Christ's sake, Bobby! What else have you got to do today? You were Adrian's best friend." *But you got old. That's why he came to me first.*

"His kid wants to talk to you! It's the least you can do! You owe it to him."

"I told you before – don't tell me what I owe, Nick."

"I swear to Christ, Bobby – if you don't do this one thing – for me, for Leo . . . *for Adrian* – I swear to God, I'll never speak to you again."

"Don't threaten me with that shit, Nick. I'm your brother."

"Then be my brother and do what I'm asking you. Call it a birthday present. Come out here and talk to Leo."

"What does he want to talk to me about?"

Nick laughed. "You wouldn't believe me if I told you. You have to talk to *him.*"

Bobby considered. He didn't want to drive all the way out to Parcay Street on the day after Christmas. He hadn't been out there in years. But he didn't want to fight with his brother anymore, either. Maybe it was time to finally face Adrian's son.

"All right. I guess you're right. I guess it's the least I can do, if the kid wants to talk to me."

"Great. Bring Tracy. And bring that Chivas."

TWENTY-NINE

Nick went back into the garage. Leo and Daina were smiling and chatting. Twenty years had fallen off of Daina's face and bearing.

Nick asked quietly, "How did this . . . How did this *happen*, Aunt Daina?"

Her smile was euphoric. "Once upon a time, it was prophesied that Adrian Wilde was going to die, upon reaching his majority. Fate cannot be contravened, Nick. It's immutable. So, Adrian died." Daina sighed, but it was not with grief. It was almost a smug sigh. "But we had prepared for fate's inevitability, and through calling upon the universal forces . . ."

"The Incantations of Thoth," Leo explained.

"My aunts can explain it more thoroughly to you, Nick. They are undoubtedly proud of their success." Daina smiled fondly at Leo. She lightly touched his cheek.

"Suffice it to say that the transmigration of Adrian's soul was channeled, directed. We've simply been waiting for all these years for him to return to us." She looked curiously at Leo, again touched his face. "Why did you make us wait so long, son? Your father . . ." Daina's expression clouded.

"He knew, Mom. He recognized me, a little before . . ." Leo's own happy smile dimmed. "He knew, Mom. Whatever triggered me remembering who I was, who I am . . . It had just happened. Dad recognized me."

In the sad silence that followed, Nick said, "Bobby's on his way."

Leo's smile bloomed again. "Great. I want you to tell him. Do you think he'll believe it?"

Nick shrugged. "I guess we'll find out."

Daina's smile was glorious, self-satisfied. "Welcome back, Adrian. I'll let you boys have your reunion. Bring Nick and Bobby up to your aunts' when you're done."

Bring Nick and Bobby up to your aunts' when you're done, Nick thought. *Just like it was time for a regular ol' visit, just like our cousin's return from the great beyond,* the transmigration of his soul, *was an everyday occurrence.*

Leo nodded and kissed Daina on the cheek.

"I'll see you soon, Nick," she said, and still smiling joyfully, she left the garage.

THIRTY

Leo found another chair folded up against the wall beside *One Wilde Ride*. He set it up in front of the table in anticipation of Bobby and Tracy's arrival. He tossed the empty Budweisers into a trash can in the corner of the garage, then sat down and looked at his cousin.

"You wanna know why, don't you, Nick? Why now? Why not when Leo was two or five or ten, like something out of a gothic novel?"

Nick nodded and shook his head at the same time. He sat down across from his cousin again.

"But you do believe that I'm Adrian? I have to be certain of that, before I tell you anything more. You don't just think I've gone around the bend? You don't think that Mom's just a sad, hopeful, delusional old woman?"

Nick shook his head. *"God's existence cannot be deduced by reason alone."*

"What?"

Nick shook his head again. None of the Wilde clan had ever been religious. Daina hadn't credited God with this miracle – what had she said? *Through calling upon the universal forces . . .*

"The explanation requiring the fewest assumptions is most likely to be correct," Nick said. "I can believe that you're Adrian returned from the grave easier than I can believe that you learned how to play guitar *just like Adrian* in a month's time. And our old set list, and *One More Time Today . . .*"

Leo grinned. "Wait 'til you see me waterski."

Then his smile abruptly evaporated. "I think that Leo didn't like the water because Gil thought it would be fun to duck him in the bathtub one time when he was about five.

"Just a random act of cruelty. Leo was in the tub, playing with his toys. Gil walked in, then suddenly, he said, 'Whoopsie-daisy!' and slammed Leo under the water. He hit the back of his head on the tub. Gil held him under for a moment, let him thrash around for a second, let him get a good *I'm drowning* panic on. Then Gil let him up.

"Leo started to cry. He was hysterical."

It was so bizarre to hear Leo talk about himself in the third person. Nick believed that he was Adrian now – it was the simplest explanation – but it would all take a little getting used to.

"Even Gil threatening to duck him again couldn't make him stop crying. Randi came in and asked what was wrong. Gil said Leo slipped and bumped his head."

Leo picked up the Charvel but didn't turn on its amp. "Gil did shit like that to him all the time, Nick. I remember it all. It didn't happen to me, but I remember it happening to *him*. Like I said, it's like a story someone told me. Or . . . Like I was there, but I wasn't there . . ." He shook his head.

Nick waited.

"Gil would just randomly smack Leo, when he was little. Sometimes in front of Randi, but mostly when they were alone. He was a bastard."

"Does she know that you're . . .?"

"No. I don't think she'd believe it." Leo shrugged. "I dunno. Maybe I'll tell her, if she ever snaps out of her depression."

Nick thought about all the ramifications of *that*. Gil was gone, and her son was gone, but Adrian was back. Randi had loved Adrian once . . . But Adrian looked like Leo now, and he'd look like Leo most especially to his mother . . . Nick shook his head. *Complicated* didn't begin to describe this new reality.

"What did Randi do when Gil would smack Leo?"

Nick had never realized that Gil was arbitrarily abusive. Nick knew that he was strict, but . . . *Well, what should I expect? He was a murderer, after all.*

"Ah, she'd object, but not too much. She'd tell Leo all the time to try and make sure not to piss Gil off. She'd tell him to go into his room, or go outside and play. But it was impossible for him to avoid Gil all the time." Again Leo shook his head.

"As he got older, Gil hit Leo less, but he'd still shove him, and yell at him. Insult him, put him down. *You're as worthless as your ol' man.* That was one of his favorites."

Leo paused, pondering memories that were not his own. After a minute, he shook his head as if to clear it, and looked at his cousin again.

"Leo hated Gil, Nick. But even after you told him that you thought that Gil killed me, Leo didn't believe it. *He's a son of a bitch, but he's not a killer. He's mean, but he's a chickenshit. He wouldn't risk going to the chair* . . . That's what Leo thought. Until . . ."

Leo leaned the Charvel against the table and stood. "Here's what happened, Nick. It was the next day. The day after Leo found those articles on the *Press-Enterprise* site, the day after you told him that Gil killed me. He was sitting on the boat." Leo walked over to *One Wilde Ride.*

"He'd just decided that Gil couldn't have done it. He wasn't a murderer. Leo took out his phone to text the mousy girl. Sheryl . . ." Leo smiled at his cousin. "Ah, Sheryl was sweet, Nick. She was Leo's first . . . His only . . ."

"It happened at my place, didn't it?"

Leo smiled, nodded. "She was sweet, but I was glad when she stopped calling him. She wasn't really my type, and it wouldn't have been right to keep it up with her. It would've been like sleeping with someone else's girlfriend, in a way. I'm not who she thought I was anymore."

He looked back at Ian's boat. "Leo was sitting right there. Gil comes in, tells him to get down.

"Leo doesn't move fast enough. Gil drags him off the boat, then slams his head down on it." Leo assumed the position Gil had placed him in, arms outstretched on the bow.

"Gil's holding Leo down by the back of the neck. He takes this big knife out of his pocket, opens it in his teeth with one hand, still holding Leo down with the other.

"Then Dad – Ian – walks in the garage and asks him what the fuck he's doing.

"Gil looked over his shoulder . . . He put the knife down, right here." Leo scrabbled at the place, near his outstretched left hand.

"Gil said, 'Back off, old man. This isn't any of your . . .'

"I grabbed the knife and pushed back, Nick. I pushed Gil off of me, and I spun around . . ." the young man that was now Adrian Wilde re-enacted the scene. "And I stabbed him as hard as I could in the side of the neck."

Nick blinked in shock. "You . . . Leo –"

"No. It was me, Nick. Leo was gone, the minute Gil took out that knife. Leo wouldn't have fought back. I was suddenly there . . . Like I say, where I'd been before, I dunno . . ." He shrugged. "I saw the knife . . . I knew Gil was going to kill me . . . So . . . I defended myself."

"You killed Gil?"

Leo nodded. "He flailed around on the floor for a second . . . Then he stopped. I looked up and told Dad, 'He was gonna kill me . . . *again.* Just like Nick said. It was self-defense.'

111

"Dad knew immediately that it was me. He said my name. Then AnTeen showed up."

"What?"

"I'd taken off my shirt, washed my hands." Leo crossed the garage to the sink. "I stuffed my shirt and the knife in here." He opened the cabinet beneath it. It was empty.

"We heard a car door slam in the driveway. We went out the door . . . It was AnTeen. Dad took a few steps, then collapsed." Leo sat back down in the folding chair, put his face in his hands. "That's why I couldn't talk to Mom, Nick. The shock . . . I killed Dad!"

Nick stared at Leo, then looked around at the scene of the crime, playing it through his mind again. Gil fell there. Leo washed his hands there, in the sink . . . But it wasn't Leo. It was Adrian.

Adrian saw the knife beside his hand, sensed Gil's threat. Leo was gone . . . *Adrian retaliated. Adrian defended himself.*

Gil's last act of violence against his stepson had drawn Adrian back from the grave.

"You didn't kill Ian. Maybe the shock of seeing that worthless son of a bitch die, but . . . If you say he recognized you . . ."

Leo nodded, his face still in his hands. "He called me *Adrian.*"

"Then I'm sure he was happy." Nick reached out and put his hand on his cousin's shoulder. "If he knew it was you . . . Then you made his last moments happy . . . *Adrian.*"

The seventeen-year-old boy that had been Leo Wilde looked up at Nick then, and Nick saw the tears, the grief. But he saw something else – at last, he *saw* Adrian.

If he'd harbored a single doubt – if for one second Nick had thought that maybe Leo had gone berserk and murdered Gil, and the guilt had made his mind snap, made him believe he was his dad – the look in his cousin's eyes removed it. There was no guilt. Only sorrow at Ian's loss.

Nick had never seen any strong emotions on Leo's face at any time in his life – joy, fear, delight, disappointment – all had been tempered by Leo's constant, cautious watchfulness. The only time Nick had ever seen Leo let his guard down had been his show of tears at Ian's funeral.

He was already Adrian then, Nick realized. And beyond a shadow of a doubt, Nick knew that he was Adrian now.

"What did you do with the . . . Oh, Christ, Adrian!" Nick realized that, his cousin's supernatural resurrection notwithstanding, he was now an accessory to murder. "What did you do with the body?"

The boy shook his head. "When Dad collapsed, I ran up the hill to tell Mom. She ran back down to help Dad, but Penny and Bellona didn't move. They just stared at me.

"'Welcome home, Capo,' Aunt Penny said. They knew it was me. I told them that there was a *mess* in the garage. I didn't tell them what it was . . . But they said they'd handle it.

"They told me to go take care of Dad. I ran back down the hill. The ambulance was already here, and right on the other side of the wall . . .

"When we got back from the hospital, I went to fetch Penny and Bellona to take care of Mom. They didn't say anything. They were grieving, Nick. We all were. But I had to go and check.

"Gil's body was gone. The knife, my shirt, *the blood* . . . All gone. Even Leo's busted phone. Gone."

Nick considered. If the old gals had been instrumental in bringing Adrian back from the other side, he supposed that getting rid of a dead body would've been *mere child's play* for them. Nick grinned at the expression. He had no sympathy for Gil. He'd gotten away with murder for eighteen years, and his comeuppance had been of the most literally karmic kind. The man he'd killed had come back from the dead and killed *him.*

"Hod dayum, Cuz!" They embraced, and Nick felt his own tears spill down his cheeks. Adrian was back. *"What a long, strange trip it's been!"*

THIRTY-ONE

Bobby and Tracy sat in the folding chairs. Tracy looked at her brother-in-law and Adrian's son blankly. Bobby's anger about the disrespectful video still simmered. He was suspicious about whatever it was that Leo wanted from him, and he was ready to let his anger explode again if the need arose, if Leo refused to take that clip off the internet. He had to take it down. It just wasn't right.

Leo stared expressionlessly at them. He was holding Adrian's guitar, and again Bobby was struck by the kid's resemblance to his father. After a moment, Bobby looked away. It hurt too much to look at Leo, sitting there, carelessly cradling that black and yellow Charvel, because he wasn't Adrian. Adrian was dead, murdered, shot down like a dog. Adrian's absence, the utter senselessness of his death – these things had colored all the years of Bobby's life. Not a day had passed when he hadn't mourned his best friend.

And now his best friend's son wanted to talk to him. Nick had said it was about that video . . . Bobby put his anger on low boil.

They all looked at each other in silence for another moment, then Nick said, "Did you bring that Chivas?" Bobby wordlessly handed him the familiar dark blue bag with the gold tassels. Nick grinned. "Will you do the honors, Cuz? Go fetch us some glasses? Some ice?"

Leo set the Charvel down and left the garage.

"What the fuck is going on, Nick?" Bobby asked. Tracy blinked at her husband's anger, at his unaccustomed profanity. "I didn't come out here in the middle of the day to drink twelve-year-old Scotch with you and an underage kid."

"You're gonna need a drink in a minute, my brutha. I know I need one. And as far as the underage kid goes . . . Win, lose, or draw, whether you believe it or not . . . After what he has to tell you . . . Trust me. You're gonna need a drink."

Leo returned with glasses and ice. Nick poured a generous shot in each and handed them around. "A toast!" he proposed. "To absent friends!" He and Leo shared a smile and downed their drinks. After a moment's hesitation, Tracy and Bobby sipped theirs.

"Your young cousin has asked me to explain something to you," Nick began. "Because you don't know him – and, as it turns out, you're not going to *get* to know him – he thought it might be better if you hear it from me.

"I'm gonna ask you to keep your fat mouth shut until I'm done, Bobby." Bobby glared at his brother, and set the flame a little higher on his anger. "No leaping up and storming off until I'm finished. Agreed?"

Bobby nodded silently.

"First, I want you to know that I believe it. As Pink Floyd once said, *The evidence before the court is incontrovertible, there's no need for the jury to retire . . ."*

"That's a little before Leo's time, Nick," Tracy said, with a nervous laugh. "It's practically before your time."

"The classics endure." Nick sighed and poured himself another shot. "There's no easy way to say this, so I'm just going to start. Just like he told me earlier today, Leo is not the man he used to be. Leo is not Leo at all, anymore. Through the supernatural ministrations of the old ladies at the top of the hill –"

"Through *The Incantations of Thoth,"* Leo explained.

"– our beloved cousin Adrian has been returned to us."

Bobby and his wife looked at Nick in silence. Then Tracy supplied another Pink Floyd line: *"Crazy, over the rainbow, I am crazy. Bars in the window . . ."*

"There must have been a door there in the wall when I came in . . ." Bobby added. He didn't smile. "What the fuck are you talking about, Nick?"

"You think that you're looking at Leo. But Leo's gone, my brothers and only friends." Nick drained his glass again. "Adrian has taken his place."

Bobby set his glass down on the table. He rose. "I knew this was gonna be some kind of sick joke. I don't know what's going on with you, Nick. First that video, now this bullshit." The anger he felt couldn't mask the pain in his eyes when he said to Adrian's son, "Look, Leo, I'm sorry. But you're not your dad. I don't care how many guitar lessons you take, how many crazy ideas my brother puts in your head. You're not Adrian. You're never gonna be –"

"Sit down, Bobby. Leo asked me for an hour to explain, to show me, to make me believe. It didn't take nearly that long. You owe it to –"

"I'm just about sick and tired of you telling me what I owe, Nick."

"Sit down, Bobby. You said you'd hear me out."

Bobby shared one of those telepathic glances with Tracy, the ones that come from a lifetime of marriage. *Sit down and listen to him, Bobby. It's obvious that he's lost his mind. It'll be easier for you to explain it to the doctors if you hear him out.*

Bobby sat.

"Never mind the mechanism of this miracle." Nick waved his hand. "I have it on good authority that Penny and Bellona can explain the *how* to us. What I want you to do right now is to just go with the possibility. Accept that it is possible that Adrian is returned."

"What happened to Leo?" Tracy asked.

"Leo's gone," Leo said. "He's been superseded. He was temporary. He was never really . . . He never really existed."

Bobby and Tracy looked at him as if the Chivas bottle had suddenly spoke.

"Never mind about Leo," Nick insisted. "I want you to accept the possibility that Adrian has returned from the great beyond. Can you accept it?"

Tracy shared another glance with her husband. *Humor him,* it said. *He's your brother.*

They looked back at Nick and nodded.

"Good. Now we're going to prove it to you." He smiled at his cousin. "Tell Bobby something that only Adrian could know."

Leo considered for a moment, then smiled. "The first time you guys had sex, Bobby brought you a dozen red roses," he said to Tracy. "There was candlelight. You wore a black lace garter with a pearl and a little silver letter *R* on it. For *Robert*. It was . . ." Leo counted in his head. "1987. You guys were fifteen."

Bobby glowered at his brother. "You could've told him that."

"I didn't know anything about that," Nick replied in surprise.

"You told Tracy that you'd love her forever," Leo continued. "And you said she said the same thing. And you made Adrian promise to never tell anyone, especially not Nick, because he'd make fun of you being so . . . *mushy*. That was the word you used."

Bobby continued to look at his brother. "Well, apparently Adrian did tell you."

Nick shook his head. "I would've made fun of you. I *will* make fun of you, now and in the future. I never would've taken you for a romantic, Bobby."

"How about the time . . . Oh, you're gonna love this one, Nick." Leo winked. "How about the time when you blew a tube in your amp, Bobby . . . I don't know where the hell you, were, Nick. Or you either, Trace."

Tracy blinked. Few people in her life had ever called her *Trace*. Adrian had been one of them.

"It was just one of those days," the kid continued. "Nothing went right. I broke two strings, and couldn't find any new ones. Bobby blew a tube in his amp, so we said, 'Fuck it. *Now is the time to ski, shall we about it?*' We hooked up the boat to Dad's old truck and went."

Nick remembered that expression. It was something that Ian and Rob had always said, and Adrian had picked it up. He downed his drink and poured himself another one.

"When we got to Elsinore, we met two girls hanging around at the marina. They asked us to take them for a ride, so . . . They had funny names. Country names." Leo paused. "Dusty and . . . What was the other one?"

"You tell me," Bobby growled. Nick watched him toss back his Chivas and refill his glass.

"Darlene . . . No. It was *Earlene*. Dusty and Earlene! We rode around the lake with them most of the day. Neither of them could ski, I remember that. Earlene was quite impressed that we had a band. She wanted to come to our next show. She said she'd never met a real bass player before."

Tracy's mouth had dropped opened at Leo's tale. She'd never heard anything about Bobby and Adrian picking up girls together.

Leo noticed her amazement. "All that made Bobby mighty nervous, let me tell you, Trace. Some strange chick showing up at our next show, saying they'd taken a boat ride together . . ." Leo nodded and shook his head at the same time. Again Tracy blinked. It was Adrian's gesture.

"All that would've required too much explanation, so Cousin Bobby suggested that it was time for us all to go back to the marina. It had been nice meeting them and all, but it was time for him to be getting back home to his girlfriend.

"Dusty pouted. We had been rather hitting it off . . . I told her I didn't have a girlfriend."

"You never had a girlfriend," Nick said.

"I had lots of girlfriends, Cuz," Leo said with a wicked grin.

"Indeed you did. I'll drink to that." Nick refilled Leo's glass and his own. "To Adrian's many girlfriends!" They downed their shots, and Tracy noted that for a seventeen-year-old kid, Leo drank like a champ.

"I understood Bobby's nervousness. Here was Earlene, all over him, practically sitting in his lap – she didn't care about his girlfriend. So we pulled the boat out.

"Bobby was in a mad rush to get rid of this friendly chick, so he walked her up to their car. I lingered on the ramp with Dusty for a few minutes. She helped me stow the skis and the ice chest in the truck, and then she said, if I'd like, we could get in the truck and she would . . ."

Leo grinned at Nick and he grinned back. "I said that we couldn't be doing all that on the launch, but maybe in the parking lot, so we got into the truck and drove up there.

"The place was practically deserted for a Saturday afternoon, and I spotted Bobby right away. Earlene had him pushed up against the side of her car." Leo laughed, slapped his knee. "He was shaking his head. *Thanks, I'm sure you're a nice girl and all, but I've got a girlfriend . . .*

"I pulled up next to them. Bobby had never been so glad to see me in his life. He opened the door to the truck and just stared at Dusty. It was an awkward moment. I told her I'd call her later, after I dropped the boat off. She found a pen in her purse, and wrote her number on my hand." Leo grinned. "I thought that was a nice touch. She stuck her tongue out at Bobby, and got out of the truck.

"He jumped in, slammed the door. 'Hurry, Cuz,' he said. 'Or else they'll follow us.' I put the truck in gear and drove outta there. All the while, Bobby was looking out the back window, making sure we hadn't *picked up a tail,* as they say on *Jake and The Fatman."*

Jake and The Fatman? Tracy thought. Jesus! That show hadn't been on for *years!* That hadn't been on since before Adrian died . . .

"I laughed at him," Leo was saying. "I laughed at him until the tears ran down my face. Bobby was always such a good boy, Trace. Loyal to the core. 'I swear, Adrian, if you ever tell anybody about this . . .'

"And I said, 'I swear, Bobby. On my life. I'll never tell anyone that you got attacked by a girl named Earlene at Lake Elsinore.' And I never have. Until now."

Bobby gulped his Chivas.

Leo picked up the Charvel, strummed it. "Remember what Mr. Johnson used to say, Bobby? *'Play clean, Adrian. I'm hearing extra noise on the lower strings.'* I had that problem cleared up by the time Nick started taking lessons, and –"

"Adrian?" Bobby said softly. "Is it really you?"

118

"Ask me anything, Cuz."

"Remember that girl from Guitar Center? I was about sixteen. She asked me –"

"She asked you if you'd like to go home with her and teach her how to play the bass," Leo said.

"And you said –"

"I said, 'He'd love to, honey, but his mom's waiting for us in the car.'"

"Really?" Nick said to his brother. "Somebody else tried to pick you up?"

"All the time," Leo said. "I was always rescuing him."

"Hot damn, Adrian!" Bobby said in amazement. "It really is you!"

Tracy looked at her husband in astonishment. She couldn't believe he was buying it. Sure, there were some coincidences: Leo mentioning that old cop show, his knowing about some embarrassing incident at Lake Elsinore, at Guitar Center. His knowing about their first time. But Adrian could've told those stories to Nick, and Nick could've told Leo. But why were they doing this?

"Too bad you didn't bring your bass, Bobby," Nick said. "He remembers the whole set, all our old banter. Remember? *Disco's dead, Nick. Before you were born.*" Nick set his glass down on the table and picked up his Stratocaster. "Play *One More Time Today*, Adrian. I'll try to keep up."

They played the song. Tracy didn't remember it very well. Adrian had sung the lyrics, played the music only once or twice. That was right before she'd gone to Europe with Bobby and his family, right before . . .

Tracy looked at her husband, saw the tears standing in his eyes. But they were joyful tears. He looked happier than she'd seen him in a long time, since . . . She listened to Nick and Leo play, listened to Leo sing. *Nick could've taught the kid how to play the guitar,* she thought, *or someone else could've taught him.*

Knowing how to play the guitar, knowing a few old family stories, didn't make him Adrian. Bobby smiled at her, took her hand in his and squeezed it. It was clear to Tracy that her husband believed, just like that – this incomprehensible, impossible bullshit. Bobby believed that Adrian, whom he'd loved like a brother – maybe *more* than his brother – his best friend, for whom he'd mourned every day for the past eighteen years – he believed that

119

Adrian was with them again, in the person of the son he'd never known.

Tracy didn't believe – sure, there were some coincidences – but people didn't return from the grave. People didn't *supersede* the personalities of others. It was impossible.

But it was also impossible to ignore her husband's joyful, shining face. Tracy loved Bobby. She had loved him, had been *in love* with him from the moment they'd met at Mr. Johnson's house. She'd missed Adrian, too, but not like Bobby had. Adrian's death had cast a shadow over their lives, and as she listened to his son play his last tune, Tracy saw that shadow lifted from Bobby.

They sat around in the garage for the rest of the afternoon. Nick and Leo played the old favorites. The four of them sang. They got drunk together.

Nick was amazed at how easily his brother had accepted the incredible metaphysical truth of their cousin's return. But on the other hand, he thought, of the three of them, Bobby had been the hardest hit, the most inconsolable over Adrian's murder. Of course he'd buy it, because he *wanted to. Of all the people in the world,* Nick said to himself, *no one is happier to have Adrian back than Bobby.*

Nick watched Tracy watch her husband. He wasn't sure if Tracy believed or not – it was unbelievable, incredible, impossible, after all. She might still maintain some skepticism. But Nick sensed that she'd go along with it for her husband.

"What should we call you?" Bobby said at one point.

"I guess, just call me *Leo*. Otherwise –"

"Crazy, toys in the attic, I am crazy," Bobby sang another verse from that old Pink Floyd tune. *"Truly gone fishing. They must have taken my marbles away . . ."* He giggled and poured himself another shot.

Nick nodded. "If we start calling you *Adrian,* they'll lock us all up. You first."

Leo grinned, and Tracy, who was feeling quite light-headed and fuzzy from the Chivas, thought for a second that she could almost see Adrian in his smile.

"We should get the band back together," Nick jokingly suggested.

"We should!" Bobby said enthusiastically.

"Right," Nick said. "All of us pushing forty, with a seventeen-year-old front."

"He's not just a seventeen-year-old front, Nick," Bobby said. Nick noticed a little slur in his brother's words. "He's Adrian's son! People would be amazed at how much he plays just like his dad!"

"Like there's anybody that remembers us. The band. Adrian, or the rest of us." Nick was a little taken aback that Bobby had taken his drunken, off-the-cuff remark to heart. "We'd look ridiculous, Bobby."

"Hell, Nick. Eddie's son's been playing bass for Van Halen for a couple years now."

"Nick was never a big Van Halen fan," Leo said.

"And we were never Van Halen," Tracy commented. She was also appalled at the idea of getting the band back together.

"Three old people, fronted by a kid." Nick shook his head. He picked up the Chivas bottle, noticed that it was almost empty. "We're gonna need some more Scotch. Hey, Leo. Why don't you run up to the liquor store and pick us up another bottle? Oh, wait. You're only seventeen." Nick grinned at his cousin. "I must say that I see a great deal of irony in the fact that you're the kid, now. After all these years, it's not me anymore. I think that I'm finally getting the last laugh."

"I won't be a kid forever, my brutha. My *majority* is just around the corner. Eighteen, anyway."

Let's see that you live through your majority *this time,* Nick thought. Adrian grinned at him.

"Still," Nick said, "I'm too old to be in a band with a teenager. All the groupies would be jailbait. No reason we can't play together again, though. Take some walks down Memory Lane. But no getting the band back together, Bobby. That would just be insane."

Like the rest of this isn't, Tracy thought.

THIRTY-TWO

In mourning, in *seclusion,* Randi was tormented by bad dreams.

Sometimes, it would start out pleasantly enough. She'd be in bed with Adrian . . . Randi hadn't dreamt of Adrian in all the years since his murder, but lately, since Gil had disappeared, she dreamed of him frequently. Randi figured that it was the sleeping pills that Doctor Samuel had prescribed for her. He'd said that they were known to produce vivid dreams.

She and Adrian were making love and it was sweet and wonderful. Randi could see him smile again. In her sleep, she breathed in his scent, felt his touch, his kiss. It would be just as awesome as it had been . . .

Then the door would burst open and the masked intruder would shoot him, all over again.

But instead of gesturing at her with the shotgun, indicating that she should run, lest she be next, in her dream, the killer would lower his weapon. He'd pull off the ski mask, and it would be Gil, just like Nick had tried to tell her, all those years ago.

"I told you I'd kill you if you ever touched her," Gil would say to Adrian's bleeding body, crumpled against the wall.

Randi would scream then, and sometimes her scream would wake her up. Other times, she'd just keep screaming until the blackness of the sleeping pills again overwhelmed her unconscious mind.

In another dream, she'd be in bed with Gil. They, too, would be making love, and it would be comfortable and familiar. Then once again, the bedroom door would slam open. This time, the intruder would shoot Gil, and when he took off his mask, it was Adrian.

He looked the same as Randi remembered him: gorgeous. He'd smile that killer Adrian smile at her and say, "I've missed you, Randi. Kiss me."

In her dream, Randi would wonder why she'd so easily forgotten Gil as she went to kiss Adrian. She'd practically forgotten about Adrian for all these years, but ever since Gil had disappeared, he'd been in her dreams.

Randi would close her eyes in anticipation of kissing Adrian, but then she'd smell the rot. She'd open her eyes to discover that Adrian had turned into a grinning corpse, like something from a horror movie.

"Kiss me, Randi," he'd croak, and she'd scream and fight her way through the sedatives to wakefulness, or once again, she'd drift back into dreamless oblivion.

Like any other educated witch, Randi knew that there was meaning in these dreams. She dealt out the Tarot, again and again, but could glean nothing from the cards. They seemed to tell her that Adrian was near, but that was just ridiculous. Adrian's ashes were near, in a cabinet beside his father's, at Penny and Bellona's. But Adrian was dead.

She felt that perhaps the statement that *Adrian was near* was a coded admonishment that, in her grief, she'd been neglecting Leo. Randi vowed to herself that she'd shake off this depression. She'd talk to her son, laugh with him once more, tell him how much she loved him . . .

But then Randi would start to think about Gil again. She knew in her heart that Gil was dead. That was what the dreams were telling her. Someone had murdered Gil. Maybe he'd walked up to the store that morning, while Leo was taking her to the airport, and someone had jumped out and mugged him on the way. Maybe they'd been hiding in Allan Coleman's old, abandoned shop.

So real was this idea to Randi – someone had murdered Gil on the way to the market – that she'd called the police and suggested to them that they look around for clues in the vicinity. When the cop asked how she'd come to the conclusion that her missing husband had been murdered, and *right there,* Randi had told him that she'd dreamt it.

"I'll send a forensic team out immediately," the cop had told her. Randi had said thank you and hung up, and it hadn't occurred to her for several minutes that the cop had been having her on.

The investigation of Gil's disappearance had been shipped to the cold case files, and they weren't going to probe further based on a grieving wife's dream. Gil's file was probably right next to Adrian's, in the same cabinet. An unsolved murder and an unsolved disappearance, all on the same block, and their investigations had turned up nothing. Another reason that she despised cops.

But Randi was sure that Gil was dead, nonetheless, and his loss crippled her, more than the accident had crippled her. The pain from that had finally subsided, but the pain from this . . .

Randi missed Gil pitifully, even though the last couple years of their marriage hadn't been the best. She could never understand why he'd hated Leo so passionately, and it pained Randi whenever Gil would yell at him or hit him, when, as he got older, she'd see the answering hatred in Leo's eyes.

But still, she'd loved Gil, despite all the bad things that had happened. Despite what he'd done with Nadine, despite his cruelty to her son, Randi had loved Gil.

She knew he was dead, that someone had murdered him and hidden his body. She knew that it couldn't have been Adrian – Adrian was dead himself, murdered also, by a crazed, bloodthirsty robber that hadn't even bothered to steal anything.

Nick had insisted that Gil had shot Adrian. But that was impossible. Gil couldn't kill anything. She'd never even seen him touch those guns – and hadn't he gotten rid of them, so they wouldn't be a danger to Leo? Gil had loved Leo when he was a baby . . .

Randi decided that the juxtapositions in her dreams – Gil killing Adrian and Adrian killing Gil – were a product of Nick's long ago accusations. In reality, Gil hadn't killed Adrian, and of course, there was no way that Adrian could've killed Gil.

But they were both dead, regardless. Someone had murdered Gil, just as surely as someone had burst in and murdered Adrian. Randi was sure of it.

And she'd cry then. Both of the men she'd loved were gone, senselessly murdered. Randi would tell herself that she'd talk to Leo again, just as soon as she could stop crying. Perhaps tomorrow. And then she'd take another pill and get back in bed, and hope that she wouldn't dream this time.

THIRTY-THREE

The party to see out the Year of Our Lord 2009 was held at Daina and her late husband's house. Bobby and his brother and cousin had gone to his storage place in the week after Christmas. They brought along a new battery and a big can of gas, and with a little work, they got the old band truck to turn over. The registration was long expired, and it wasn't insured, but normally conservative Bobby threw caution to the wind. He was more than sure he could talk himself out of ticket if they should get pulled over. They loaded up all of Urban Equinox's instruments, amps and stands, cables and pedals, brought them to the house, and stuffed them into the garage. It was a little cramped in there, beside *One Wilde Ride,* but they managed to set everything up. Had there been fans, they would've had to stand in the driveway.

Bobby kept saying that it was just like the old days, and it was, almost, except that, just as Nick had said, the brothers Wilde (and Tracy) were all pushing forty; their Number One fan was still immobilized with grief over her missing husband; and Adrian was returned from the dead as a not quite eighteen-year-old boy.

There were no guests at the party, only family: Daina, Penny and Bellona, Bobby and Tracy, Nick and Leo. Bobby said it was easier that way. No one had to pretend that Leo was still Leo, and he said that the band was rusty, anyway. Daina and Penny and Bellona would do for an audience, he said, until they recovered their skills.

Bobby was overjoyed, and Tracy had no trouble pretending that Leo was Adrian, especially since the music was good, and the memories were great, and the liquor flowed. She concentrated on the coincidences, the things that had so easily convinced her husband. Leo knew their old set list; he played guitar as well as Adrian had; he remembered incidents that had happened to the four of them. She ignored the fact that she didn't believe in the transmigration of the soul, that the kid couldn't possibly be Adrian reborn.

But Tracy hadn't known Leo, and as the evening wore on, she began to tell herself to think of it this way: Adrian had been on a journey for the last eighteen years, and while he'd been away – in Shangri-La, perhaps – he'd hadn't aged a day. People told themselves fanciful stories every day, Tracy reasoned. That didn't make them crazy. She was willing to accept a little bit of insanity to see her husband happy again, regardless.

Penny and Bellona retired early, as they had prayers to say and auguries to scry before the clock struck midnight and ushered in 2010. Daina and Tracy went into the house to make coffee, in an attempt to sober Bobby up a tad. He'd overindulged in New Year's Eve cheer and refused to budge from the couch until the room stopped spinning.

Nick and Leo stood in the driveway, waiting for the year to end. The moon was full, the night clear and starry, and it again struck Nick that a miracle had occurred. Adrian was returned to them. Tonight while they played, it was almost as though he'd never been gone.

Because Leo was young, if Nick concentrated only at him, it seemed as if it was December 31st, 1990, all over again, the last New Year's Eve they'd played together. It was only when Nick looked at Bobby, grown a trifle paunchy at thirty-seven, or when he noted the hint of crows' feet around Tracy's eyes, that he was recalled to the present. Nick and his brother and his sister-in-law were grown old, while Adrian was still twenty-one, with the face and physique of his seventeen-year-old son.

"You couldn't talk Randi into coming?" he asked.

Leo shook his head. "I almost thought she was gonna make it. She got up, got dressed. But then she mentioned something that Gil had said or done on some other New Year's Eve. She started to cry and went back to bed."

"Maybe you should let her know who you are, Cuz," Nick said with just the whisper of a drunken leer. "Maybe it would cheer her up. Maybe you could –"

"Maybe *you* should go over there and cheer her up," Leo returned. "I remember another New Year's Eve, about a million years ago, when you couldn't have been happier because she kissed you."

"She didn't kiss me. She let *me* kiss *her*. I was just a kid."

"You're not a kid anymore. Maybe you should look into it."

"Maybe I should." Nick made a step as if he would walk down the driveway, cross the street and go see the woman that he'd once loved. Cheer her up. Then he stopped, shook his head. "But I don't think so. The last guy that tried to cheer her up wound up dead."

Leo's eyebrows went up. "That's not likely to happen to you."

"You never know, my brutha. Strange things transpire around here. I don't think I could . . . *concentrate* for thinking about it."

Nick shook his head again, and his expression sobered a bit. "That ship has sailed, Adrian. I could never . . . The thought never really crossed my mind again after she went back to that cheating, murdering son of a bitch.

"I tried to tell her once that he did it, you know that? She refused to listen. She told me if I ever mentioned it again, she'd stop speaking to me. After that . . . I didn't think I was in love with her anymore. I didn't bring it up, because I didn't want her to cut me out of Leo's life."

"You were the only friend he had, Nick. I appreciate that you were always there for him."

"It couldn't have been any other way, Cuz. He was your boy."

Adrian looked across the street at the house where he lived. It had been AnTeen's house when he was a kid, then Allan's for a minute. Then it'd been his house, the first time he was Adrian, for an even shorter period of time. Then it was the house in which Leo had grown up, dodging Gil's punches and invective for seventeen years . . .

Penny and Bellona still held title to it. When he again reached his majority, it would again be his house, held in the name of Leo Wilde. Places remained the same. Only the people that occupied them changed.

"Do you think she knows that Gil did it?" Adrian asked his cousin. "I mean, do you think that she knows, deep down, but just won't admit it to herself?"

"People believe what they wanna believe, now don't they, Cuz? Despite all evidence to the contrary. The powers that be would lock me up – me and you and my brother and his wife, your mom and her aunts – if they knew what we believe." Nick shrugged. "I don't know how she couldn't know, Adrian. Gil was a jealous asshole, and nobody knew it better than Randi did. I'm telling you. It couldn't have been anybody but him."

"I know it was him."

Nick looked at his cousin in surprise. "You know for sure? How do you know? Randi said he wore a mask. I've always believed it. It couldn't have been anyone but him. *I know for sure.* But how do you know? Do you know because you were – are all mysteries revealed on the other side?"

Adrian shook his head. "I don't remember the other side, my brutha. I remember being with Randi . . . Then Gil had my head pinned down on the bow of the boat, with a knife in his hand. Where

I was in between . . ." He shook his head again. "Maybe I was with Leo all his life, only he didn't know it and I didn't know it.

"I know Gil did it because he told me, Nick. He said to Leo, 'I'm done, kid, done with putting up with you *and* your shit. Just like I was done with putting up with your daddy's shit, once upon a time.'

"Just the day before, you'd told Leo that Gil had murdered me, Nick. Now Gil was telling Leo that he'd done it, because he was . . . He was gonna do it again."

"I was gonna ask you about all that, Adrian, but I didn't really know how to say it. You said you killed Gil in self-defense . . . But you also said Ian came in. Gil wouldn't have stabbed you in front of him. But you . . . You finished it anyway. So I was thinking . . . Maybe it wasn't entirely in self-defense . . ."

"Maybe not." Adrian offered Leo's innocent, boyish grin. "What goes around comes around."

Nick's own grin returned. He looked across the street, returned to their earlier discussion: Randi's need to be cheered up.

"I dunno, maybe I *should* visit the grieving widow, turn on the ol' Wilde charm." But then Nick shook his head again. "Nah. She was never interested in me. She only had eyes for you. That's why I think you should tell her. I think she'd be thrilled. She'd forget all about Gil. You guys could reminisce. Maybe the two of you could –"

Leo's eyebrows went up again in surprise. "You're drunk, Nick."

"Nobody liked you better than she did, Cuz. If you let her know that you're back . . . I'm just saying . . ." Nick considered what he was proposing, how much Randi had loved Adrian, and here he was, young again. Here was Adrian, even if he looked like . . . Nick realized that the suggestion was a little too over the top, even for him. "I'm sure that it would really cheer her up, that's all," he concluded quickly.

THIRTY-FOUR

Leo gave his mother a box of chocolates and a dozen roses for Valentine's Day, trying to coax her back to the land of the living. Randi was touched. She told him thanks, gave him a hug. But then she went back to reading the Tarot and again ignored him. *At least she's staying up and awake more during the day,* he thought. *Maybe she's coming out of it.*

Adrian wondered what it was for which Randi searched, what questions she was asking of the universal forces. He figured that she was attempting to learn what had become of her husband. Adrian half expected a séance next. But like waterskiing and playing the guitar, witchcraft was another one of his father's pastimes that Leo had never expressed any curiosity about, so neither his aunts nor his mother nor his grandmother had instructed him. For all Leo had ever been taught, Randi might be simply playing solitaire with the wands and cups, the swords and pentacles. It occurred to Adrian that it would seem odd to Randi if her son suddenly showed an interest in the Tarot at this late date, so he left her to her fortunetelling without comment.

Randi at last roused herself from her extended fugue on Easter Sunday. It was a time of pagan festivity, too, the season to celebrate rebirth and renewal, and Randi decided that maybe it was time to see how springtime was treating her little corner of the world. Jesus, after all, was not the only deity to have died and been resurrected. The same was true of Osiris and Dionysus. Persephone had spent the three months of winter in Hades and now Demeter rejoiced in her return – it was the explanation for the vernal flowering of nature. Randi decided that it would be refreshing to go up the hill and visit Penny and Bellona, to light a yellow, a green, and a purple candle with them.

The Christian observance fell on April 4th, four days before Leo's eighteenth birthday. Randi felt a pang of guilt for having neglected him since Gil's disappearance. It'd been nearly a year: Ian had passed and Gil had gone missing on Saturday, May 9th, 2009, barely a month after her son's last birthday. Randi realized that she'd hardly had any interaction with her boy in all that time. She'd hardly even had a conversation with him.

All that had to change. It was the season of renewal, and Randi again vowed to herself that she'd stop ignoring Leo. The time had arrived to stop feeling sorry for herself, to get back to living. Gil was gone, but Leo was here. Leo was the future.

Though she'd scarcely have admitted it to a living soul, one of the reasons that Randi felt a surge of life again had to do with the new dimension to the frequent dreams she'd been having. She thought they were brought on by the sedative she'd been prescribed, so she presented Doctor Samuel with a happy, smiling face and told him that she was feeling so much better, but she still had trouble falling asleep. The good doctor was happy to oblige with a refill of her Ambien prescription. Several times.

Randi's dreams were all sweet now. No more nightmares of Gil assassinating Adrian, and of Adrian in turn murdering Gil. Gil was in fact absent from Randi's dreams entirely. Adrian's own shocking ending was not revisited, nor did he turn into a grinning, rotting corpse anymore.

Yet Randi's dreams were still filled with him. Since Gil was gone from her life, it was suddenly as if Adrian had returned to it. It was almost as if there'd never been a Gil, as if the only man Randi had ever loved had been Adrian.

She'd be at a party, watching him and Urban Equinox perform. The old tunes seemed to drift lazily on the air, and he'd sing only to her. Or she'd be walking upon the forested path to Penny and Bellona's with him, hand in hand. He'd smile at her, kiss her on the cheek. Sometimes, they'd be bouncing along over the chop in Ian's boat, the wind in their hair.

None of these events had ever taken place in real life. Adrian might've sung to her alone once or twice during rehearsals, or maybe Randi had just convinced herself that he had. But when he performed in front of a crowd, Adrian had belonged to the whole audience. Unless he'd been interested in one particular girl, and then he might sing to her . . . *But it was never me,* Randi remembered.

Randi had never held hands with Adrian, he'd never fondly kissed her on the cheek. Randi had never been aboard a boat in her life, least of all *One Wilde Ride.* But in her dreams, Randi did all these things with Adrian. In her dreams, they had more than just one night together. They had that for which Randi had secretly longed, from the moment that she'd met Adrian at Mohini's: they had a relationship.

The best part of her dream-relationship with Adrian, the best part of the dreams themselves, was that they always concluded the same way. Her dreams always ended up with Randi and Adrian in bed together, and no one murdered him. On the best nights, her dreams started off there. Randi was convinced that it had to be the Ambien that made him so intensely alive to her then, so real. When she dreamed, it was like her one and only night with him. Randi could feel Adrian's skin against her own, she could taste his mouth . . .

THIRTY-FIVE

Randi knocked on Leo's bedroom door on Easter morning, to see if he'd like to accompany her up the hill. There was no answer, so she opened the door and peeked around it, thinking that perhaps he had slept in. But her son wasn't there, and she had no idea where he might be. Randi reflected that she had no idea where he'd been, nor what he'd been doing, for almost a year now, and again she promised herself that she'd spend more time with him.

Randi called Leo as she walked up the path to the old witches' house.

"What can I get for you, Mom?" he said, instead of *hello*.

Randi was taken aback. Was that how she'd treated him for the past year? As a servant? As someone to step and fetch for her?

"I thought you might like to visit your Aunt Penny and Aunt Bellona with me."

Leo laughed pleasantly. "That sounds like a great idea, Mom. I'll meet you there."

So he's nearby, Randy thought. *Maybe just up at the market.* She told her son okay, and hung up.

The Ambien ads mentioned the possibility of hallucinations, and when Randi stepped onto the deck, she thought she was having one. Five people were sitting around the little table. There was Penny and Bellona, and Daina, looking as fresh as a flower herself. There was a teenage girl that Randi didn't know.

And there was Adrian. Although the weather was mild, he was wearing a dark blue tank top. He was saying something to the girl, while peeling an electric-orange-colored hard-boiled egg. He was wearing furry, pink and white bunny ears atop his long, feathered black hair.

Randi stopped, and the group turned and looked at her. Silence reigned. A heartbeat passed. Then Leo said, "Mom!"

He set down his Easter egg, half peeled. He arose, crossed the deck, and hugged her.

Randi was amazed at the change in Leo's appearance. Only yesterday, it seemed, he was just a little boy, but now he'd become tall and strong. He'd let his hair grow out. He was wearing it shoulder-length, parted in the middle, just like Adrian. Only yesterday, Leo had been just a child, but today, her boy's resemblance to his late father was uncanny.

For another moment, no one spoke, and Randi felt that they were all staring at her. *It's because I've been depressed for so long, in seclusion,* she thought. *They're all surprised to see me.* Then Daina smiled in welcome, as did Penny and Bellona. Even the girl smiled.

Leo put his arm around Randi's shoulders and walked with her across the deck. "Mom, this is my friend Angie," he said. "Angie, this is my mom."

Angie stood and offered her hand. "Nice to meet you, Mrs. Wilde."

A short, surprised laugh escaped from Randi before she could stop it. "This is Mrs. Wilde," she said, indicating Daina. "I'm Mrs. Hogan."

Angie looked at Leo in confusion, and Randi decided that she didn't want to go into it at the moment, how she'd never been Mrs. Wilde, how she'd been Mrs. Hogan, because Mr. Wilde was dead, and now Mr. Hogan was dead, too . . .

"Please," she said to the girl, with more pleading than she'd intended. "Just call me *Randi.*"

"Nice to meet you, Randi." They shook hands, and Angie sat back down.

Leo pulled out a chair for his mother, the one in which he'd been sitting, then sat beside Angie.

Conversation started again. Randi didn't join in right away, because she was noticing that Leo and Angie were sitting very close together. *Any closer, and she'd be sitting in his lap,* Randi thought in amazement.

She studied the girl. Angie was pretty, but she was dressed a little . . . *scantily,* for the season, in Randi's estimation. She was wearing a bright pink, somewhat low-cut halter top, displaying her flat tummy to its best advantage, and brilliant white shorts, which showed off her shapely legs. Like Leo, she was clothed as if it were the height of summer instead of not-yet-balmy April. Penny and Bellona and Daina and Randi herself were still wearing long sleeves. It couldn't have been more than sixty-five degrees, and once the sun went down, it would get downright chilly.

Yet the young people were dressed for summer, already showing a lot of skin. Randi realized with a start that they were showing it for each other: as she watched, Leo put his arm around Angie and gave her a little squeeze.

Is this my son's girlfriend?

133

Randi forgot all about Leo's resemblance to Adrian for the moment as she studied the two of them. They still sat with their thighs pressed together. Leo leaned back against the railing and casually draped his arm around the small of her back.

Randi decided that Angie was a little too *mature* for Leo, even though they were obviously the same age. Randi thought she was a mite trampy, with her immodest, rushing-the-season get-up, and she didn't fail to notice the way Angie ogled Leo a shade too appreciatively out of the corner of her eye.

The mother in Randi was appalled. She wouldn't have thought that her shy, quiet boy would've gone for such a slutty-looking young woman. On the other hand, she'd never known her shy boy to sport bunny ears on Easter, either. Angie giggled loudly at something Leo said, and Randi thought she would've expected Leo to pick a girl as shy as himself, a *quiet girl.* Angie didn't seem like Leo's type.

But then Randi realized that she didn't know *Leo's type,* now did she? She'd never seen her son with a girl before. He'd been just a baby, but on this spring day, Randy recognized that Leo was now a young man. He was almost eighteen. He was an adult, fine and tall and good-looking, just as his father had been . . .

Leo noticed his mother staring at him. "Do you want to have an Easter egg hunt, Mom? Like when I was a kid?"

Randi couldn't remember more than a handful of Easter egg hunts with Leo. When he was a toddler, maybe, but after he'd started kindergarten, the whole idea had just been annoying to Gil. Leo must be speaking of Easter egg hunts he'd had with his aunts and his grandmother.

"The winner gets the bunny ears." Leo took them off and put them on Randi's head. He smiled happily at her, his blue eyes guileless. Innocent.

He might look like his dad . . . Ah, Adrian! He might have a trampy girlfriend who obviously knows more about life than he does . . . But he still wants to hunt Easter eggs. He's still my little boy . . .

134

THIRTY-SIX

Penny and Bellona had been fond of Leo. They'd been kind to him. But they'd never taken an overly active part in his life. They'd babysat when he was little, bought him the requisite toys and presents, but they'd never believed that he actually existed. They'd spent his life waiting for their beloved Capo, the Boss, to emerge.

Nadine no longer visited, and Lily was busy with the shop. Randi hadn't come out of her house in nearly a year. So Penny and Bellona were pleased to have Adrian back, if for no other reason than that he was far more serious about witchcraft than he'd been in his first life. He frequently burnt a candle with his aunts now. He said his prayers, and engaged in the required rituals on the Sabbats. He'd become devout, almost, a true believer, as had Daina.

The two of them had always believed: they'd been raised in the traditions. But while before they'd been laissez-faire in their observances, now they were more heartfelt in their rites, more thoughtful in their ceremonies. Now they couldn't help but believe utterly.

Daina reveled in her son's return. She never ceased to be amazed at how completely he *was Adrian.* Not only the memories, and the turn of phrase . . . Once again, Daina could observe Adrian's clever, deft hands: when he'd play guitar for her, when he'd absently walk a quarter across his knuckles; when he'd deal a Tarot lay. When she would call his name, he'd fix her with that same old confident, expectant Adrian stare. Leo would look her in the eye only if he was making a point, underlining a lie. Daina, too, had been fond of Leo, but she, too, had spent his life watching for her son's return.

Although he'd never told Daina anything about what had happened to Gil, Adrian had described the circumstances of Gil's demise to his aunts. They had a stake in it, so to speak. Adrian told them how Gil had admitted to killing Adrian because he'd aimed to kill Leo at that moment. Penny had remarked that karma was a bitch. Fate would not allow a second murder.

"Mr. Hogan's bragging was the trigger for you to return and avenge yourself. Order has been restored. It had been fated that you had to die young. You accepted it, did not foolishly try to hide from it or fight against it. Your initial fate was accomplished, and now you have returned . . ."

The old seer glanced at her sister. They wondered what Adrian would do with his life, now that fate had gifted it back to him.

THIRTY-SEVEN

Four days after Easter, Penny and Bellona threw Leo a party for his eighteenth birthday, small but of a fine variety.

The birthday boy again sat with his grandmother and his aunts at the little table on their deck. Bellona remarked that while eighteen was a seminal milestone in a young man's life, it was really just the signal of responsibilities yet to come. He was no longer a child, but was not yet an adult.

"In what way am I not an adult?" Leo protested. "I can get married, sign a contract, go to war –"

"Go to jail," Bellona said.

"I'm experiencing a rush of déjà vu," Daina said with a wink. "It occurs to me that the four of us have had this conversation before."

"Indeed," Penny recalled. "I said, 'But you can't yet buy a drink,' next."

Adrian looked at the beer in his hand, supplied by his cousin. "Sometimes I forget that I'm not supposed to drink yet. Leo never did."

Penny nodded. "And in that way, you're not an adult yet, at least not chronologically." She smiled at Daina. "I remember this conversation that we've already had. It was when we were discussing Adrian's majority."

"His impending doom," Bellona added.

"Have you scryed my new future?" Adrian asked. "Will I outlive twenty-one this time?"

"A long and happy life have we seen for you," Bellona said with a twinkle in her eye. *"You may rely on it."*

"As long as there are no more unfortunate missteps, like that one involving the stolen car," Penny said primly.

"We didn't know it was stolen, Aunt Penny," Adrian replied with an innocent smile.

"Ah, how boyish you can be, Capo, my little, evil, lost and returned soul. You can bring shy Leo back in a heartbeat, to those who don't know you." Penny glanced at Randi and Angie, chatting with Nick, Bobby, and Tracy across the deck, out of earshot. "I'm sure that young Angie would be surprised to hear anyone call Leo Wilde shy – because she never knew him, did she?"

Adrian shook his head. "Leo didn't drink, and he didn't trust girls. He didn't trust anyone, least of all . . ." Adrian looked over his shoulder at Randi.

"You know that she was aware of *The Incantations of Thoth,* Capo," Penny said slowly.

Adrian tried to hide his astonishment when he looked back at his aunt. "No. I was not aware of it. Do tell."

"After the murder . . . Randi was distraught. So we told her that you weren't really gone." Penny smiled at her sister. "Remember, Bell? She thought that we were referring to a séance."

"She was still working for Lily, then. The Spiritualists had been in Mohini's, filling her mind with their misguided ideas."

"We told her what would come to pass," Penny continued. "We told her that she was pregnant, that the child she carried possessed your soul. That he would *be you.* We told her that all we had to do was wait for you to come back."

Adrian looked over his shoulder at Randi again. He wondered how she'd taken *all that.* He knew that she'd been a confident believer in the universal forces, a knowledgeable practitioner of the old arts. She'd patiently performed her banishing rituals, lit her candles, said her prayers, read her Tarot.

But Adrian also knew that Randi was a simple creature. Her mind was straightforward, her wants and desires plain and easily discernable. Randi was not given to deep, philosophical meditations, and the ramifications of *The Incantations of Thoth* were complicated, far-reaching.

He turned back to his aunts and his mother. "Did she believe it?"

Daina shook her head. "I don't think so. She said she did, but I think it was just in an attempt to comfort me." Now Daina looked over her shoulder. "She's such a sweet thing."

Adrian was not so sure about how sweet Randi was. As he'd discussed with Nick, it seemed that there was no way that Randi couldn't have known who it was that had murdered him. Yet she'd gone back to Gil, married him, made a life with him. And she'd stood by and done nothing while Gil proceeded to mistreat her son for his entire existence.

"So perhaps you should tell her," Penny said, studying the young man carefully. "Bring her back into our circle. It was quite a sacrifice she made, becoming the vessel of your rebirth. Perhaps it would be only fair to let her know that her expense has produced

137

dividends." Penny paused, then said, "After all, she could just as easily have gotten rid of you –"

"Killed me twice," Adrian said. *Her expense has produced dividends,* he thought with a touch of resentment. *Her* expense. *She came to me, and because she wanted me so much,* my expense *got me killed. And had it not been for all the supernatural machinations . . . She didn't believe all that anyway. Her* expense *produced a little boy, whom she allowed Gil to berate and smack around for seventeen years.*

Penny shrugged. "It was her prerogative. Yet she chose not to exercise it, and here you are. Perhaps you should consider telling her –"

"I'll consider it," Adrian said evenly. "But not just yet. She's just gotten over her husband's . . . disappearance. I think I should wait a little while longer. The fact that I'm back, that *her expense has produced dividends* . . . I think that would all come as quite a shock to her. She doesn't need another shock right now. I think I'll wait a little while."

Penny nodded. "As you will."

THIRTY-EIGHT

Randi had been surprised to see Nick give Leo a six-pack for his birthday, and she'd been even more surprised to see him commence to drink it.

"He's eighteen, Randi, for Christ's sake," Nick had said in response to her disapproving frown. "He's not a kid anymore. Stop being so hypocritically maternal. We all drank when we were eighteen."

Randi had also been surprised that Bobby and Tracy had shown up for her son's birthday party. Again, Nick said, "He's eighteen, Randi. They thought it was time that they got to know Adrian's son."

He's eighteen, he's eighteen, he's not a kid anymore, Nick kept telling her. Leo had been her baby just the other day . . . Now he was drinking beer. And now there was this girl.

Randi thought her son's girlfriend was a little too flirty with Nick, as they stood there talking. Angie leaned in too close to him, she touched him on the arm too often. Randi reflected that maybe she was just imagining it: maybe Angie wasn't too flirty with Nick. Maybe she was just flirty, period. She was dressed in short-shorts and another low-cut top – a V-neck t-shirt this time – no tummy on display. The fact that Randi had dressed the same way at Angie's age was not lost on the disapproving mom. The look had worked for Randi, and she'd discovered that it was working for Angie, too.

If Randi had any doubts that her son wasn't a little kid anymore . . .

Earlier, Bobby and Tracy had just arrived for the party. Nick was inside, admiring the cake with Daina and her aunts, so Randi went outside to look for Leo. She walked around the corner of the house, and found him with his girlfriend.

Angie had Leo pushed up against the siding. Her arms around his neck, she kissed him eagerly, pressed her half-dressed body against his. Leo kissed her back – Randi knew that she shouldn't be watching them, but it was such a shock to see her little boy with a girl – Leo kissed Angie back, and there was nothing shy or boyish about it.

Leo stopped, whispered something into his girlfriend's ear. Angie giggled, and Randi stepped quickly back around the house, mortified at the thought that they might look over and see her standing there. Randi suddenly wondered if they'd already . . . *No, he's just a kid . . . But he's not a kid anymore. He's eighteen, he's reached his* majority.

By the time Randi was eighteen, she was certainly no kid. She'd already been living with Gil for two years.

Randi realized that she'd been just about Angie's age when she'd first met Adrian. She remembered how much she'd been in love with him at his own eighteenth birthday party, right at this very house, how she would've given anything to demonstrate her love to him.

Leo was more careful about life than Adrian had been at eighteen, and this girl . . . If Leo and this girl were . . . She had to be his first. Adrian had been far more outgoing than his son. He'd been a musician, and Randi didn't like to think about how many girls Adrian had undoubtedly been with by the time he was eighteen.

Yeah, Leo's more reserved than his father at the same age. Angie's his first girlfriend. Adrian didn't have time for a girlfriend when he was eighteen, but he had plenty of time for girls . . .

No, Leo isn't a kid anymore. Jesus, he looks so much like Adrian! And because he does . . . Randi doubted if Angie would be his only girlfriend.

THIRTY-NINE

Adrian was at odds and ends. He was twenty-one, he was eighteen, he was returned from the dead. He had been acclimatized to the times: he'd learned how to use a cellphone, how to use the internet, from three old women and his cousin. He didn't want to go to college – he'd returned from the other side, for God's sake – he surely didn't want to waste his new life going to college.

Now that he was eighteen, Adrian had plenty of his own money. There was Ian's life insurance: Leo had been the beneficiary, and the funds had been held in trust until he was eighteen. When he'd been Adrian the first time, he'd thought it only prudent to obtain his own life insurance – what with the prognostications of his impending doom and all – Daina had been the beneficiary for her son's policy. She'd also put the proceeds in trust for Leo, and once he turned eighteen, she signed the account over to him.

Leo was set. He couldn't afford to be jetting off to Europe, he wasn't going to be buying a mansion or a new car or a new boat. But he already had a house, as well as a car and a boat, all paid for. Adrian wasn't wealthy, but still, he'd never have to work a day in his life. And so far, the desire to do so hadn't struck him.

Adrian thought that he could concentrate on music again, but then he remembered Nick's expression: *that ship has sailed.* His band had moved on in life, and Adrian's taste in music had always been behind the times, anyway. *Something from this decade, son,* Ian used to tell him. Now, Adrian reflected, Ian would say, *Something from this century.*

Adrian still believed that the classics endured, but no one wanted to hear *Johnny B. Goode* or *Iron Man* or even *(I Can't Get No) Satisfaction* played by an eighteen-year-old kid. Even the songs he'd written for Urban Equinox seemed dated.

Adrian could take or leave contemporary music, yet he thought that if he really wanted to have another band, he could play the new stuff. He could just scare up some kids his own age . . .

But Adrian had started to be annoyed with kids his own age, Leo's age. Kids from *this century*. Angie and her friends were all eighteen, like Leo. But Adrian was not Leo, and he wasn't even remotely eighteen. He counted Leo's recent birthday as his first, reborn – he considered himself to be twenty-two. And it was certainly an older, been-around-the-block, back from the grave twenty-two. Angie and her friends and their tempests in texted teacups had begun to wear on his nerves.

Adrian didn't love Angie. She was just the same as every other eighteen-year-old girl he'd known, in two lifetimes. She was transparent; she wanted him only because he was attractive, because he knew his way around the ol' four-poster far better than the other young men she'd known. She loved *that*. Adrian knew that she confused loving that with loving him.

In his first incarnation, Adrian hadn't wasted too much of his time on girls that loved him. He didn't want to hurt anyone, so he'd been circumspect in his choices. He'd avoided the girls that had been obviously infatuated with him. *Except for that one,* he thought, *and look how disastrously that had turned out.*

As Adrian again, he also possessed Leo's watchfulness. Leo had always mistrusted girls. Once he'd realized what they wanted from him, he'd always wondered at the *why* of it; he'd always been disappointed that they didn't want to know him *as a person.* They didn't want to explore the sad little boy that he actually was. Leo had also avoided women because he was somewhat of a prude: girls' immediate willingness had appalled him a little bit.

Adrian had never been so maudlin. He'd owned the confidence that had come from a lifetime of love from his parents and aunts, his cousins. Adrian had never wanted anyone to feel sorry for him, as perhaps Leo secretly had.

Adrian had never minded girls' willingness. They had a right to go after what they wanted, after all. He'd just never wanted to lead any of them on, had never wanted to stand accused of breaking anyone's heart.

But now Adrian was less cautious. While he'd always known that girls wanted him for their own agendas, now he thought that they had a right to those agendas, too. If Angie wanted to risk falling in love with him, why should he not allow her to take whatever risk she chose?

If Angie thought she was in love with him, why should he discourage her? He didn't encourage her – he never said *I love you, too* – so why should he deprive her of her fantasy? It made her happy for the moment, and if it made her sad eventually . . . Well, that wasn't his problem right now.

Adrian harbored a little resentment at the forces of the universe. He'd lived twice, and neither time had he been granted true love. He would've been embarrassed to speak the thought out loud: it sounded sentimental, girlish, *mushy*. His cousin Nick dated lots of women, and would laugh at Adrian's desire for that one and only. In that way, Nick was like his Uncle Rob. But Rob was an old man now, alone. Adrian had lived twice. He didn't want to end up alone.

It seemed to Adrian that love was all around him. Except for Nick and Rob, everyone had found it effortlessly. Randi had loved him once, and after he was murdered, she'd gone on to live happily ever after with his murderer. Adrian thought that he should perhaps feel a little guilty about putting an end to Randi's marriage, but he didn't. What goes around comes around.

Gil had mistreated Leo for his entire life, and he'd escaped punishment for his capital crime for seventeen years. He'd basked in Randi's love all that time. Gil got what he deserved, and if it made Randi sad, well . . . Adrian was still not convinced that maybe she didn't deserve her sadness. Leo's mother had to have realized who'd killed Leo's father, even if she refused to admit it to herself. If her only punishment was a little sadness, Adrian thought that she was getting off easily.

Bobby and Tracy had found love – *when they were fourteen years old, for Christ's sake!* And in the intervening years it'd never faltered, never even wavered. Adrian could tell by the way they looked at each other: his cousin and his wife were still as devoted to each other as they'd ever been.

Adrian's parents had also shared a loving devotion, right to the very end. Adrian knew that Daina was cheered by his reappearance, but he also knew that, once the initial agonized pangs of grief had subsided, once Daina had gotten used to the absence of Ian's person in her life – his smile, his voice, his scent – Daina was devastated no longer. She knew in her heart that she'd see the love of her life again. They were halves to one whole. Adrian knew that his mother believed that she and Ian had shared previous lives, as they'd shared this one. They'd share future lives.

Adrian had already lived one life, and now had embarked upon another one. He'd not known true love in the first, nor had he any prospects for it now. With whom would he share a future life? Adrian was resentful; he didn't want to wait for another life to find love. He wanted to experience it *now*.

FORTY

Bobby and Nick and Tracy occasionally came over on the weekends and played music with their young cousin. Nick told Randi that the brothers Wilde had decided to teach Adrian's son how to sing and play the guitar, but Randi couldn't help but notice that they seemed to only play old stuff. She thought that if they were going to take the effort to teach Leo, they should teach him something new. Something current.

Randi was pleased that Bobby had come to terms with Adrian's death at last. His acceptance manifested itself in the immense joy Bobby suddenly seemed to take out of buddying around with his cousin's son. Leo had replaced Adrian for Bobby; he had a new Adrian.

Randi almost had a new Adrian, too: he still visited her in dreamland every now and then.

Seeing Leo in front of the mike, playing Adrian's guitar, made Randi uncomfortable, however, so after the first couple of times, she didn't watch them perform anymore. Seeing Leo with Adrian's guitar didn't make Randi sad, didn't make her miss Adrian more, didn't make her again mourn his senseless loss.

Randi had neither missed nor mourned Adrian for too long. She hadn't really known him; she'd only desired him. And that desire had produced Leo, and she could remember Adrian anytime she looked at him. But Randi had never had more than the random pleasant recollection of Adrian, because she'd shared her life with Gil.

Watching Leo front the reformed, now geriatric Urban Equinox made Randi uncomfortable for a different reason. Leo was a quick study, Nick had told her – he'd picked up playing the guitar effortlessly, learned the old songs easily. Randi didn't like to watch them because at times, it seemed to her that Leo *actually was Adrian.* When he sang, when he played – the resemblance was inescapable.

Randi hadn't forgotten the old witches' tale. She hadn't forgotten the promises of *The Incantations of Thoth.* Still, she'd never believed any of it. Randi had never believed that Leo was anyone other than Leo, her shy, quiet, watchful boy. All his life, she'd looked for signs that he could be Adrian. Randi had never seen a single one.

Even now that he'd become so grown up, with his long hair and his girlfriend and his father's guitar, Leo resembled Adrian, but he was not Adrian. He still gazed upon Randi with his own reserved, watchful expression. Adrian had never been reserved. He'd always been open, fun-loving. Leo was not Adrian, no matter how much he looked like him. If Leo was Adrian returned, he'd tell her.

It had been a ridiculous, impossible proposition nineteen years ago, and it was just as ridiculous now. Leo was not Adrian, and it made Randi uncomfortable to watch him sing and play Adrian's guitar, because when she did so, the possibilities of *The Incantations of Thoth* always sprang to her mind.

Gil was gone. Randi thought that she'd welcome Adrian back . . . But that would mean that her son would be gone . . .

Randi shook her head. It was ridiculous. The boy simply resembled his dad, and he seemed even more like Adrian when he was with Adrian's cousins, his old bandmates. But Randi knew from the way Leo looked at her . . . He was still her little boy. She was his mom. Leo was not Adrian.

FORTY-ONE

Randi had shaken off her depression, had reached the final stage of grief, had accepted the loss of her husband.

But that didn't mean that she didn't still take the occasional Vicodin to help her through the day. And of course, there was dreamland to visit, where Adrian dwelt. Randi never missed her nightly dose of Doctor Samuel's Ambien.

Some mornings, Randi woke up groggy from the medication. Her eyes would flutter open, and it would take her a few moments to remember where she was in the world, to recall where she was *in time*. If she'd been with Adrian in her dreams, it would take a minute to remember that Adrian was dead. He wasn't here in bed with her as it had seemed, just seconds before.

On a morning about a month after Leo's birthday party, Randi thought she was awake. She thought she'd opened her eyes. But there was Adrian, lying beside her, his head propped up on his hand. He looked down at her expressionlessly.

She recalled that long ago 4th of July, when she'd made up her mind to seduce him. Randi grinned at him now, in this staggeringly realistic dream, and said, "Remember that night? The first time we . . ." It had been only that one time, but there had been many more since, in other dreams. Though none of them had been as lifelike as this one . . .

"You were crying," he replied, still without expression.

"I said, 'Kiss me, Adrian!'" Randi put her arms around his neck, as she had on that night. But she didn't kiss him; instead, she buried her face in his shoulder. Because he visited her so gloriously in her dreams, Randi admitted, "Oh, Adrian! I miss you so much."

Leo let her snuggle into his neck for a moment, but when she started to move the rest of herself closer to him, he said, "Wake up, Mom. You're dreaming."

Randi slowly disengaged herself from her son's neck. She looked up at him, horrified. "Oh, my God, *Leo!* I thought you were . . ."

Ever since his birthday party . . . Leo had let his hair grow long, and Randi had seen him kissing that girl. He played the guitar now . . . Any more, he looked so much like Adrian. That's why she'd thought *he was Adrian* . . .

But why is he in bed with me?

Randi sat up quickly, pulled the sheet around her. She'd been asleep, and Leo had just crawled into bed with her, like he used to do when he was a little boy, whenever Gil took the boat out, whenever he knew his stepfather would be gone . . .

She'd been half asleep. She'd thought that she was dreaming of Adrian again. *Oh my God, I almost kissed him, I almost . . .*

Randi looked over her shoulder at her son. Leo was still lying in the same position, on his side, his head propped on his hand, looking up blankly at her. With his hair longer, he looked *so much* like Adrian . . .

"I need a pill."

"I bet you do."

FORTY-TWO

Randi didn't make any comment to Leo about the odd way he'd chosen to wake her up. He hopped out of bed, fetched her pills and a glass of water, told her good morning and left the room. She got dressed and went out to the kitchen, but he was gone. *Probably off to see Angie.*

She figured that she'd been shocked by the whole thing far more than Leo had been – she'd thought she was dreaming, thought he was Adrian – but he couldn't know any of that. He'd just laid down beside her, waiting for her to wake up, like he used to do when he was little. Randi decided there was no reason to discuss it with him.

But a few weeks later, Randi thought she was about to dream of Adrian again. She thought she could smell the scent he used to wear, but she could also hear birds chirping outside. She knew she was awake.

Randi opened her eyes. Leo had his head propped up on his hand again. He smiled at her.

Christ, he even smells like Adrian!

"You have to stop doing this, Leo," Randi said, embarrassed, annoyed. "You're too old to be getting into bed with your mother."

Leo didn't move.

"Get out of my bed, Leo. It's not . . . proper. You're making me . . ."

"Nervous?" Leo grinned at her now.

Jesus! Randi thought. *He looks so much like Adrian! He was just my shy little baby a few months ago, but now! Christ!*

Leo rolled gracefully out of his mother's bed. "How'd you like to walk up to the store with me? We never talk anymore. Unless you don't want to. Maybe you want to go back to sleep."

"I'd love to take a walk with you, Leo. I'll be out in a minute."

When she came out into the living room, her son was sitting on the couch, again holding Adrian's old guitar. Leo was concentrating as he strummed the strings. Mercifully, little sound came out, because the amp wasn't on. Randi wasn't in the mood for *(I Can't Get No) Satisfaction* so early in the morning.

"Nick and I are going to go buy a new Marshall today. Dad's wasn't in Bobby's storage. Do you have any idea where it is?"

"His what?"

"His Marshall, Mom. It's an amplifier." Leo gestured at the small one attached to the Charvel.

"I never knew what happened to your dad's things, Leo. His aunts . . . His parents . . . The house was empty when we moved in."

"You never thought about what happened to all his stuff . . ." Leo let the statement die. "Tell me again about Dad's accident, Mom. What kind of car did he have? I tried to find something about it on the internet, but . . ." Leo shrugged, but he watched her carefully.

He knows, Randi realized suddenly. *Somebody told him. Probably Nick. Goddamned Nick. He knows and now he's testing me, to see if I'll lie to him again. Well, he's old enough to know – he already knows.*

Randi was annoyed that Leo was testing her, and she was also a little disconcerted with waking up and finding him lying next to her again. He was too old for that. *He looks so much like Adrian . . . What if I'm more than half asleep some time . . .* Randi shuddered. *I'm gonna have to start locking my door.*

She sat down in a chair across from him. Leo still watched her expectantly. *God, when he's holding that guitar . . . If I squint my eyes just a little bit, I almost expect him to start singing one of Adrian's favorites . . . My, my, my, I'm once bitten twice shy, baby . . .*

Randi cleared her throat. "I haven't been honest with you about your father's death, Leo. It happened before you were born . . ."

The night you were conceived. But Randi wasn't going to tell him that.

"Soon you were a little boy. Your grandmother and your aunts and I decided to tell you that –"

"He was in heaven."

"And that was good enough for a little boy," Randi replied, letting her annoyance show a little bit. *He knows,* she thought again.

"Then, when you were about twelve, and you asked *how,* we told you about the car accident."

"And now I'm asking again."

Randi blinked at his tone. The thought crossed her mind that ol' slutty Angie had kissed the shy right on out of her son. Before he'd starting hanging out with her . . . The old Leo would never have been so . . . direct.

Randi decided that she could be direct, too, since she was sure he already knew, that he was just challenging her honesty.

"And now you're an adult, a big, grown-up, tough guy. So I'll tell you the truth, now. Since you think you're old enough to hear it."

Randi softened a little bit. "Your father was murdered, Leo. Shot." Randi kenned immediately that she'd been too harsh. She saw a flash of pain, of disbelief, in his innocent blue eyes.

"Was it an argument? Did somebody jump him? How . . . Why?"

"The police said the motive was robbery. Someone broke in . . ."

"And they never caught anyone? Did they ever even have any suspects?"

Randi shook her head, looked down at the floor, thinking once again how much she hated cops. They'd been worthless. Their so-called *investigation* had gone nowhere.

"Nick said . . ."

Randi glanced up sharply at him. Leo stared at her steadily again, suspicion in his eyes. The innocent expression was gone.

"What did Nick say? If Nick already told you, why are you asking me?"

"I wanted to hear it from you."

"What did Nick say?"

"Nick said Gil did it. He said Gil was jealous –"

"That's ridiculous, Leo. Gil was in Bakersfield, with . . ."

Oh, Christ, he doesn't need to hear about that. How his father died, yeah, but what went on between Gil and that old bitch . . . That filthiness isn't any of his business.

"The cops interviewed Gil, Leo. He was out of town. There were witnesses that saw him in Bakersfield. No one ever suspected him –"

"Except for Nick."

"Goddamn Nick," Randi said softly. "If anybody was jealous, it was him. He hated Gil. He wanted me to be with him . . . Someone broke in and shot Adrian . . . Nobody thought it was Gil, except for Nick. It was ridiculous. Gil wouldn't hurt anybody."

"Except for me. All my life." Leo looked at her reproachfully for a split-second, then the expression was gone, replaced by the watchfulness that Randi had always seen in his eyes. "Who do you think did it?"

Randi shook her head. "I don't know, Leo. Your dad didn't have an enemy in the world. The police said it was *a robbery gone awry.*"

"So you don't think Nick's right? You don't think that Gil killed my dad?"

What does he want from me? Randi thought. *Goddamn Nick! He's poisoned Leo's mind . . .*

But then Randi remembered how Gil had treated Leo, how he'd yelled at him, berated him, how he'd hit him . . . Gil had loved Leo when he was a baby, but then his attitude had changed. Nick didn't have to poison Leo's mind against Gil. Gil had done that on his own.

Gil hadn't cared for Leo, *but he loved me.*

Randi's first inclination was to slap Leo, to lash out at him for accusing the man that had loved her of such a horrible, senseless act. Gil had loved her, despite his faults, and he wasn't here to defend himself. He was dead, murdered, just like Adrian.

Randi took a deep breath, got a hold of her emotions. "No, Leo," she said calmly. "Gil didn't kill your dad. He was a good, honest, loving man. You guys didn't get along, but he couldn't hurt anyone."

You guys didn't get along, and I'm sorry about that. That's what she should've said, Adrian thought. But Randi didn't apologize. She never had. *She stood by all of Leo's life and never said a word to Gil about the monstrous way he treated him, and she still can't apologize for it, not even now . . .*

"I don't want to ever hear you say that Gil had something to do with your father's death again, Leo," Randi was saying. "I won't listen to you speak ill of the dead."

A look of frank surprise crossed Leo's face. "How do you know he's dead?"

"I dreamed it."

"You *dreamed . . .?*"

Randi remembered her nightmares. Gil killed Adrian and Adrian returned from the grave and killed Gil. All of that was the product of Nick's influence.

"I dreamed that someone mugged him," she told her son. "On the way to the market. They took his body away somewhere, buried it. That's what I dreamed."

It was a useful lie, just like the one they'd told Leo about Adrian's mythical, fatal car accident. The main thing was that she'd dreamed that Gil was dead. Murdered. It was none of Leo's business what she'd actually dreamed. Randi didn't want him to know that Nick's lies had also crept into her subconscious. Randi knew that Gil was dead. That was all that mattered.

There would be no big reveal about Gil's death, like she'd just delivered to her son about the true manner of his father's passing. No one would ever discover that Randi had guessed the truth, unless the stereotypical man-out-walking-his-dog stumbled across Gil's body someday.

Randi lied to Leo, told him that she'd dreamt about the mugging. It was close enough. She hadn't dreamt it exactly that way, but she believed it, nonetheless. Gil was dead. Randi knew that someone had murdered him, as surely as she knew someone had murdered Adrian. Hell, maybe it was the same guy. That's all Leo needed to know.

FORTY-THREE

A few days later, Adrian and Nick were out in Daina's garage, waiting for Bobby and Tracy. The four of them had decided to round out *One More Time Today:* they were going to help Tracy come up with a drum part for it, write a bridge, a guitar solo or two.

"I almost told Randi who I am," Adrian said conversationally to his cousin.

Nick looked up from adjusting his strings. He blinked in surprise.

Adrian grinned. "I crawled in next to her while she was sleeping. She woke up, but she thought she was dreaming. She said, 'Oh, Adrian, I miss you so much!' Then she put her arms around my neck, nuzzled me a little bit . . ."

Nick blanched. He wasn't sure he wanted to hear this. "What did you do?"

"I said, 'Wake up, Mom. You're dreaming.'"

"So . . . You didn't tell her?"

Adrian shook his head. "The next time –"

"The next time?"

Adrian's grin widened. "The next time, she was pissed. 'Get out of my bed, Leo,' she told me. "You're too old to be –"

"So you still didn't tell her?"

Again Adrian shook his head. "I still don't think she'll believe it."

Nick was relieved. He wasn't sure what Randi would do when she found out that her son was gone, that his father was returned. It would be . . . *complicated.* It would be quite *the family secret.*

Nick grinned wickedly. "Hell, Cuz, you never used to be a tease. I think you've gotten a little mean since you were dead."

"There is a distinct possibility, my brutha."

FORTY-FOUR

Nadine Germaine was bored. She lived comfortably off the savings that she'd amassed over a lifetime, plus, since she'd turned sixty-two the month before, she'd opted to start receiving her small Social Security benefits, instead of waiting until she was sixty-five. Hell, she might not live that long.

Retirement was less than thrilling, however. She worked at Mohini's with Lily a few hours a week, but the new crop of devotees was more annoying to her than the last. Nothing had changed since she was a teenager: those that embraced the arts later in life, those who hadn't been raised in the traditions as she'd been − witchcraft seemed to be about nothing but sex to them.

There was a local coven in Riverside now. Its leader was some middle-aged tart who went by the pseudonym of *Penelope*. Nadine was sure it wasn't her actual name. It was too mythical of a moniker to be real. Lily catered to her, sold her the requisite ritual items, and told Nadine of the celebrations the coven undertook in the wooded areas around Reche Canyon: "Boys with boys, girls with girls. All in the name of the universal forces." Lily snorted in disgust. "That's not what magic is about."

No, Nadine thought. *Magic isn't about anonymous sex.* It never had been. She was not sure what magic was about anymore, because it hadn't served her well. Not well at all. But she knew it wasn't about *that.*

Magic seemed to be about eternal youth for Lily. She seemed a well-preserved fifty these days, far younger than Nadine. If Nadine hadn't been aware of the old gal's powers, she might've believed that Lily had had a few nips and tucks performed, a lift here and there.

When she'd been a teenager, and even a young adult, Nadine had believed that it had been through earthly means that Lily maintained the illusion of youth. But now, in her own old age, Nadine knew better. It wasn't cosmetics or even plastic surgery that allowed Lily to look so young. She'd made some pact with the unseen.

Nadine thought about asking Lily to reveal her secret, but she didn't really want to be young again. Now that the famous line was finally true − *the heyday in the blood is tame, it's humble, and waits upon the judgment* − Nadine saw that youth was foolish. It chased shadows.

Nadine's life was empty as a result of the foolishness of her youth. Ian was gone, Gil was gone, and her memories of both of them were insufficient. She was past the age for travel, but still she longed for some spice in her life. A new adventure. Some intrigue perhaps. No boyfriends, or anything like that. Nadine was past the age of physical longings – the men she'd loved, one with her heart and soul, the other with her body – they were gone. But still she craved something interesting to amuse her, nonetheless.

She hadn't visited the denizens of Parcay Street since she'd paid her last respects with them at Ian's funeral; that'd been more than eighteen months ago. Penny had told her not to darken their doorway again, but what of it? What was Penny going to do, curse her? Life, fate, had cursed Nadine more than one ancient beldame ever could.

Nadine reckoned that the weird sisters hadn't told Daina that once upon a time, Nadine had herself cursed Daina's son. It would've only added to their niece's pain, at a time when she was already grieving for her lost husband. No, Penny and Bellona wouldn't have told Daina that the seeming prayer that Nadine had recited at Adrian's funeral – cumbersome though it was – had actually been an oath against his soul. There was no need for her aunts to tell Daina of Nadine's bitter wish. The universal forces had not heard her curse, after all. Adrian had returned. His soul was alive and well again.

So technically, Nadine reasoned, *Daina and I are still friends . . .*

It had been eighteen months. Nadine imagined that all who could be induced to believe, everyone who'd rejoice at the black-haired monkey's return, was now aware of it. His aunts, his mother, perhaps his cousins . . . Nadine wondered how Randi was dealing with the fact of her lover's return in the person of her son.

What a unique living arrangement they must have adopted! Nadine thought. *I have to see that for myself!*

155

FORTY-FIVE

A plethora of conflicting emotions played through Randi's mind when she answered the bell a day after Christmas and beheld Nadine standing on her doorstep. There was surprise, there was confusion. There was a little touch of satisfaction: Nadine was old. Gil wouldn't have looked twice at her now. There was a sharp, painful flare of hope – did the old witch have some news of Gil?

But that hope died as quickly as it had flamed. Randi's husband was dead. Nadine couldn't have any news of him.

"What do you want?" she asked simply.

"Where's Adrian?"

"What?" Had the old whore lost her mind?

Nadine studied the younger woman. There was no guile, no craft to her expression. Randi had never been very crafty, anyway. There was nothing in her eyes but shocked surprise at Nadine's query. Incredulously, Nadine thought, *Is it possible that she doesn't know?*

"Pardon me," she said quickly. "I misspoke. Where's Leo?"

"He's off somewhere with his girlfriend," Randi replied immediately.

His girlfriend? It is possible! She doesn't know! Of all the people in the world – why hasn't Adrian told Randi that he's back?

"What do you want with my son?" Randi asked warily.

"Nothing, particularly," Nadine replied. "I was just in the neighborhood. It's the holiday season, so I thought I'd stop in and say hello. I thought that we could catch up –"

"You've got to be kidding," Randi stated flatly. "I have absolutely nothing to say to you."

"Perhaps I have a few things to say to you. Enlightening things. *Yes, definitely. You may rely on it.* May I come in?"

Randi hesitated, uncertain. She surely didn't want to take any walks down Memory Lane with this old bitch. Gil had apologized, over and over . . . *It was a mistake, baby! Just one of those things. I've never loved anybody but you . . .* And as much as she was capable, Randi had forgiven him.

She knew that men sometimes did these things, but Randi had forgiven Gil because he had loved her. He'd married her, had helped her to raise the boy that wasn't even his. Gil had cut off all ties with Nadine, had never seen her again – hadn't she been surprised when Randi told her that he'd disappeared?

Maybe she does have some news. The hope flared again. The flame was small – Randi knew that Gil was dead – but maybe somehow, against all the odds, this old cow knew something about it. And it was Christmastime . . .

Randi opened the door and let her nemesis into the house.

"What a lovely tree!" Nadine said.

"Thanks. Leo put it up."

Like a good hostess, Randi offered Nadine a cup of coffee. Nadine assented, and Randi went out to the kitchen and poured them each a cup. She had a fancy sugar bowl tucked away in a cabinet; it had been a wedding present from Gil's mom. *Jesus, how the years have slipped away!*

Randi found the sugar bowl, with its silver spoon. She wiped the dust off of them, poured the sugar in. As an afterthought, she dumped the remainder of a bag of Milano cookies onto a plate. They were Leo's favorites and he'd be upset that they were gone, but this was just the oddest thing, Nadine showing up on her porch, the day after Christmas. *What does she want?*

Randi scared up a tray from another cabinet, and set the coffees and the snacks upon it. *Why am I acting like this?* she asked herself.

Unwillingly, Randi recalled that she'd once looked up to Nadine. She'd always seemed so sophisticated, educated, a world traveler. Randi recalled that she'd come to hate these qualities about the older woman, because she thought that they'd also been what must've appealed to Gil.

Randi answered her own question: *There's no need to be rude. She came all the way out here to tell me something . . . Gil broke it off with her, years ago. It's the holidays. There's no call for me to be a bitch to her.*

"Cookies?" Nadine's eyes widened in delight when Randi set the tray down on the coffee table. "How nice of you, Randi!"

Damned right it's nice of me. But then, I'm a nice person. You, on the other hand . . . What do you want?

Nadine selected a Milano, nibbled it daintily. She dumped a spoonful of sugar into her coffee, stirred, sipped. Randi thought about apologizing for not having any creamer: she always took her coffee black. But then she thought better of it. She'd displayed enough holiday hospitality to her dead husband's whore.

Randi watched her guest. Waited.

At last Nadine sighed. "First of all, I want to apologize for my . . . deception, all those years ago, with Gil. I'm afraid that I appealed to a certain wayward nature in him –"

"I don't really want to talk about that."

Nadine ignored her protest. "I knew it was wrong . . . But it was just one of those things."

Jesus, they even used the same expression for it!

"If it means anything, Randi . . . I was never trying to take him away from you. He was just an attractive young man . . . A diversion. I knew he'd never leave you, and I didn't want him to. I knew how much he loved you."

Randi picked up her coffee cup. She didn't have a response.

"Still," Nadine continued, "I knew it was wrong. So I want you to know that I'm sorry."

"Do you want me to say I forgive you?" *Maybe that's why she's here. It's the season for forgiveness, is it not?*

Nadine shook her head. "No. Forgiveness isn't necessary, although I'd accept it." She offered Randi a small smile. "What I'd seek would be . . . understanding, perhaps. You're about the same age that I was when I first met Gil. You're alone, like I was. I'd like to imagine that perhaps now you can understand. An attractive, attentive young man . . ."

Randi thought of her dream-Adrian. He was certainly young, attractive and attentive. But he wasn't real. He didn't have a girlfriend already.

". . . and sometimes one allows one's morality to be compromised." Nadine offered Randi that small smile again, and allowed herself another cookie.

Her apology had been delivered. Nadine didn't give a tinker's damn if Randi accepted it, if she *understood.* That wasn't why Nadine was here. Randi was sweet and gullible and good-hearted, things Nadine had never been; things Gil had certainly never been. Such betrayals happened to people like Randi. Nice guys finish last.

Nadine changed the subject. Now it was time to get to the meat of the matter. She wanted to uncover why the dark miracle of Adrian's return had been hidden from Randi.

She asked curiously, "Do you still practice the old arts? I remember, once upon a time . . . Penny and Bellona said that you were quite enthusiastic. Quite adept. A leader of rituals. A celebrant."

"I had fallen off," Randi said. "But I've resumed, since Easter. I practice *solitaire,* and sometimes with Penny and Bellona. And Daina."

Of course Daina has returned to the old ways, Nadine thought. *I imagine she is downright pious now, since her worthless brat has been returned to her. I was always devout, but that didn't matter . . . Daina was blood to them, whether she adhered to the old ways or not, so they stole Ian from me and gave him to her . . .*

"Your son doesn't practice with you?"

"Leo?" Randy laughed. "Not hardly."

"Well, I know that his father practiced . . . a little."

He's undoubtedly become devout now, too, Nadine reckoned. *Just what they always wanted – a fervent warlock in the family . . . A devoted witch that wasn't blood to them wasn't good enough.*

Randi sighed. "Leo never knew his father." *But you know that,* she thought. "He looks a lot like Adrian these days . . ."

I'll bet he does. Nadine smiled to herself.

". . . but he's never been much like his dad. He's always been quiet and shy, although lately, he's come out of his shell a little bit, since he's been going with Angie."

Nadine remembered how mature Adrian had been when he was Leo's age. She doubted that being dead had made him any less adventuresome with the ladies.

Randi didn't elaborate on her son's relationship with his girlfriend. "Like I say, he's quiet, not outgoing like Adrian was. They're not alike very much at all . . . Leo's got a steady girlfriend, where Adrian never had time . . ." *for just one girl . . .*

Randi continued quickly, "Leo doesn't like the water, either, like Adrian did. They're not at all alike. Although, he did learn to play the guitar this past summer."

"Really?" *Musician sheer,* Nadine thought. *I curse his name . . .*

Randi nodded. "You remember Bobby and Nick? Adrian's cousins? They taught Leo how to play. They practice in Daina's garage."

"Just like the old days."

Nadine thought Randi appeared a bit flustered by this statement. Maybe she was a little more . . . *disconcerted* with Leo's resemblance to Adrian than she was letting on. Now was the time to zero in.

"Are you familiar with the concept of the transmigration of the soul, Randi?"

Randi's eyes widened in surprise. "You mean *The Incantations of Thoth?*"

"The incantations of . . . what?"

Shut up, Randi told herself. *She's just talking about the old arts.* It was only a coincidence that Nadine would bring up *the transmigration of the soul,* the thing that Randi thought about every time she saw Leo with Adrian's guitar . . .

Randi shook her head. "Nothing. What did you say? The translation . . ."

"The *transmigration* of the soul. It means reincarnation."

Randi shook her head firmly, pursed her lips to demonstrate that she was not familiar with the idea. "I've heard of it, but I don't know anything about how it works." *Nope. Nothing at all,* her expression said.

"How it works is of course one of the great mysteries," Nadine said loftily. "But I believe that it is possible. That it does indeed happen. Allow me to tell you a little story."

Nadine related to Randi how, at the moment of Ian's collapse, her son had cried, "Help him, AnTeen!" The anecdote mean nothing to Randi – Nadine had to explain that no one on the planet had ever called her *AnTeen,* except for Adrian.

She went on to tell Randi that Leo had said, "What's wrong, Dad?"

"Not, *Grandpa,* Randi," Nadine stressed. "He said, 'What's wrong, *Dad?*' Ian already knew. He wasn't at all surprised that Leo called him *Dad.*"

"He knew what? What did he know?" *It can't be true,* Randi thought.

"Ian knew that Leo was gone. I think that Adrian's emergence must've just occurred. I think that the shock of it induced Ian's heart attack.

"Regardless, your son's gone, Randi. He's *been gone,* honey. For over a year now. Adrian is back. It's his mind . . . His thoughts, his memories, his personality that now inhabit Leo's body."

"But it can't be. He would've told me . . . How do you know? You've never heard of *The Incantations of Thoth?*"

Nadine shook her head. "What is that?

No, Randi thought. *I won't tell her. She says she doesn't know, so maybe this is some kind of a trick. She's making it all up . . . She wants something from me, and it's just a coincidence that she's*

160

taking this route to get it, telling me stories about Adrian being reincarnated . . .

"It was just a fable that Penny told me once. About the translation —"

"The transmigration of the soul," Nadine corrected her again. "And then there was Leo's grief at Ian's funeral. He was devastated. He was never that close to Ian —"

"How do you know?"

"I visited, Randi. Penny and Bellona . . . Daina, Ian . . . They were family to me." *Ian was, anyway. Ian was my soulmate . . .*

"I went out of my way to make sure I never ran into you. Or Gil. But I visited Penny and Bellona, and Daina and Ian. I saw Leo a lot."

He never mentioned it to me, Randi thought. *But then Leo's never been a big talker. He'll speak if spoken to, but he never has been one to volunteer too much information.*

"I watched Leo grow up, Randi. That thing you said about his being afraid of the water? I already knew about that, because *Ian* told me about it. I always thought he took it personally, to tell you the truth. Waterskiing was life to him, up until Adrian died." Nadine paused. "Leo was a modern kid, Randi. Ian was an old scholar. They weren't close. Were they?"

Randi shook her head. "But Ian was still his grandpa. Leo loved him."

"Of course," Nadine allowed. "But he was grief-stricken at the funeral, Randi. You said that Leo was always shy. I always thought so, too. I always thought he kept his feelings to himself. But he *wept* at Ian's funeral. He was *bereft.* He was as Adrian would've been at his father's funeral."

"I don't believe it," Randi stated. "It's impossible."

"There's something else, Randi," Nadine said slowly.

"Lots of young men learn to play guitar," Randi objected. "Adrian played. Nick and Bobby . . . It's only natural that Leo would want to learn, with them as relatives. Of course he'd want to learn. That doesn't make him Adrian reincarnated."

"I'm not talking about that, Randi. What I'm talking about . . . It has to do with Gil."

FORTY-SIX

Eileen Coleman's mother was ill, so Eileen returned to Riverside in September of 2010. She transferred from her management position at Orange Coast Title in Whittier; the higher ups were glad to send her back to the Inland Empire. They were looking for a paralegal to answer to the head Underwriting Attorney, and they were confident that a go-getter like Eileen would bring competence and experience to the position.

Carmen had been attending Whittier College, but she was more than happy to transfer her accumulated credits to the University of California, Riverside. She was the first one in her family to attend college as a full-time student. Her father had been a high school dropout, and her mother had spent many grueling years going to night school.

All the way into her mid-teens, Carmen had watched her mother sitting at the dining room table, studying the ins and outs of buying and selling real estate, title abstracts, property surveys, insurance policies, loan documents; the whys and wherefores of property taxes; real estate law. Eileen's hard work had paid off. She had a high level position with Orange Coast these days. Carmen was very proud of her mother's accomplishments.

Eileen had worked with a steady ferocity to better herself after she'd been forced to move back in with Mrs. Artus, after Allan had lost his business and their home. Eileen's mother had been unyielding: of course she'd welcome Eileen and her granddaughter, but that *fat deadbeat* had to come up with his own accommodations. A man who couldn't support his wife and child was no man to Eileen's mother.

Her mother's welcome was tempered with criticism. Eileen came to see herself as the poster child for *marry in haste, repent it leisure*. At first, Eileen chafed under her mother's scorn. She always leapt to defend Allan – he was a kind and loving husband and father.

"Kind and loving doesn't pay the bills, Eileen," her mother would reply. "He needs to be hardworking and reliable. He needs to provide for you and Carmen. Why, when you were a baby, your father took on a second job, so we could put the down payment on this house. Your husband won't even get *one* job."

"He runs his own business, Mom!"

"He ran his own business into the ground, Eileen. He's obviously no businessman. He's lazy. He doesn't make any money.

If he really cared about you and his child, he'd go to work for someone else."

Mrs. Artus continued to point out her husband's lack of ambition, and by May 1991, Eileen reluctantly agreed with her. Eileen filed for divorce from Allan.

And that's when she discovered that he wasn't really just the charming, slightly shady ne'er do well that she'd always believed him to be: a graduate of the School of Hard Knocks, but still basically a kind and good man. When he discovered that his wife was serious about leaving him, Allan threatened the life of the process server that delivered the bad news. And then he really got mean.

He started calling Mrs. Artus's house at all hours of the night, calling Eileen all manner of vile names, telling her that she wouldn't get away with taking his baby from him. Eileen filed a restraining order against him, but still, he was permitted visitation with Carmen under California law. Eileen was troubled. What could Allan possibly be doing to entertain a toddler during visitation? He didn't even have a home to which to take her, just the shop in Moreno Valley.

Carmen made an appointment to talk to the court mediator, and expressed her worries over her baby's safety.

The mediator said, "Well, if your daughter comes back with bruises, then you can have the order amended. You can ask for supervised visitation."

Eileen was appalled. "If my daughter comes back with bruises, then it'll be too late."

The mediator shrugged. "Mr. Coleman has parental rights, too."

Mrs. Artus had little sympathy for her daughter's plight. "You married him," she would say.

Eileen's mother studied the divorce documents. "It's says you can't leave the state. But it doesn't say you can leave town. I say you ask for a transfer."

There was a position available at the Whittier office. It was a lateral transfer, and Eileen had to take a small cut in pay, but it was worth it to get away from Allan. He still visited his child on her birthday and holidays, but the every other Saturday nightmare ceased. It was too far to drive just to harangue his ex-wife, and he didn't really know what to do with a little kid, anyway.

Eileen found a tiny apartment, and Mrs. Artus subsidized the rent for a time, while Eileen went to night school, until she received a few promotions and started making better money. Birthdays and holidays were still dreadful: Allan took great relish in expressing his hatred for his ex-wife. But sometimes he missed Thanksgiving, because he had no relatives with which to dine with his daughter. Or he couldn't make it down to Whittier for Christmas.

And as she got to be eight and nine and ten years old, Carmen could go down to the curb and meet her father alone. Eileen didn't have to speak to him anymore.

Eileen persevered in night school. She'd married Allan because he was a little bit dangerous; he was a been-around-the-big-ol'-block bad-ass, while she'd still been just a fairly innocent teenager, and his worldliness had appealed to her. But once Carmen was here . . . Allan's unwillingness to find a decent job, his not quite on the up and up business dealings – there'd been that incident with the stolen Corvette, and God only knew what was going on at the new shop – it all made Eileen realize that a tough guy didn't really make for what she needed now.

The first years were difficult – Allan frequently called and threatened, even though he didn't visit very often – and night school and work and childcare wore on Eileen. But eventually things got better. She got promoted, started making more money. Carmen grew up and didn't need as much constant, expensive supervision.

Then Allan got arrested and imprisoned when Carmen was fourteen. Eileen considered it to be the best news ever: she wouldn't be hearing his vitriol on her answering machine anymore, wouldn't wonder if he was going to turn up to threaten her at any moment. Eileen didn't care what he'd been arrested for. She didn't want to know.

Allan wrote letters only to Carmen, and sometimes, the phone would ring and there'd be a recorded voice that said, "This is a call from a California State Prison . . ." He'd speak to his daughter for a few minutes. He didn't ask to speak to Eileen and she wouldn't have talked to him if he did.

With Allan safely tucked away where Eileen had no doubt that he belonged, she felt free to date again. She met George Wade through her job, when Carmen was about fifteen. He was a successful realtor, charming and educated; nothing at all like her ex-husband.

Eileen allowed herself to be charmed. Life had not been a bed of roses for her since she'd married in haste as a foolish teenager. Like Allan, George was a few years older than Eileen. Unlike Allan, he made plenty of money, had a nice home. When he invited Eileen to share it with him, when he asked her to marry him, Eileen consented immediately.

Fate did not allow Eileen to be lucky in love, however. George wasn't a fat deadbeat like Allan. He was quite the opposite: driven, almost shark-like in his real estate dealings. Before their marriage had fallen apart, Allan had always told Eileen how sweet and wonderful she was. But George, on the other hand, looked down on his wife because she'd chosen to have a child early in life, and therefore didn't have as much education as he did. He intimated that he thought that her disastrous decisions when she was young must mean that Eileen was a little stupid. He began to mention how much he had given her, how much better off she was since he'd deigned to marry her.

Eileen had put up with enough bullshit from the men in her life. After three years of unhappy marriage, Eileen took her daughter and moved out of George's big house. She returned to the same modest apartment complex where they'd lived before. Eileen filed for divorce.

Unlike Allan, George wasn't upset about it. No connection between them remained. There was no reason for him to even call her anymore. In the two years since the end of their marriage, Eileen hadn't even received so much as an email from her second ex-husband. And that was fine with her.

FORTY-SEVEN

After a month or so in Riverside again, Eileen found that she was enjoying life back in her hometown. The stern woman that had railed at her in her youth was gone. Mrs. Artus was proud of her daughter's success in life, after such a rocky start, and she was grateful for Eileen's help. She was thrilled that Carmen was living with them, too.

Her illness improved: the crippling arthritis with which she was afflicted seemed to loosen its grip upon her somewhat. She still needed assistance with a few everyday tasks – that's why Eileen had come back home – but overall, life was looking up for Eileen's mother, as well as for Eileen and Carmen.

They had a wonderful Christmas season together, with a tree and lights, and a Honey-Baked Ham for Christmas dinner. Carmen bought her mother a laptop computer. "Now you can sit in the living room and watch TV with us while you work," she told Eileen. "You don't have to be chained to that old desktop in your room."

Eileen was fairly well versed with computers, but Carmen was a whiz, so Eileen asked her to personalize the laptop for her. Carmen did so. The day after Christmas, she was perusing a few pictures on Google when her mother came up behind her at the dining room table and looked over her shoulder.

"Are you done yet?" Eileen said with a smile. "I'm kinda anxious to mess around with it a little."

Carmen smiled. "It's all yours, Mom."

Eileen looked at the screen. Carmen had left up a picture of a young man. He had long, dark brown hair. He was wearing a flannel shirt with the sleeves cut off, was holding a black guitar. He had big green eyes, and grinned a sly, killer smile at the camera. Eileen felt a vibration pass through her. She was suddenly, inexplicably reminded of . . .

"Who is this?"

"Oh, that's Joshua Martin, Mom. He's a singer. I don't really care for him with long hair, but if you click back . . ." She hit the back arrow key, and the screen was filled with little pictures of Joshua Martin. Carmen clicked one of them, showing the musician with shorter hair, in concert, jamming with his bassist on stage.

"He just came out with a new CD," Carmen said. *"Reflections on a Peach."* She smiled. "I was going to go pick up a copy of it. I love the way he sings."

Eileen clicked back to the Google page filled with pictures. She chose another one of Joshua Martin with long hair. He didn't really look like . . . But he was the same *type*. Young, attractive, a musician. The memory had been summoned for Eileen and it remained. It danced around in her brain like a Mexican Jumping Bean.

"He's cute," she told her daughter. "He reminds me of someone I used to know. A long time ago. When you were just a baby."

Carmen kissed Eileen on the cheek. "Merry Christmas, Mom. I'm gonna go help Grandma. She wants to make some deviled eggs."

"Always my favorite," Eileen said, still looking at the picture of the young rock star.

"Enjoy your computer. But don't be going to any porn sites, now," Carmen warned with a grin. "You'll pick up a virus."

Just like in real life.

Eileen fixed her daughter with an expression that communicated how unlikely it was that she'd be visiting any porn sites. Eileen hadn't even been on a date since she'd divorced George. Carmen believed that romance, emotional or physical, just wasn't something her mother cared about.

"Go boil eggs."

FORTY-EIGHT

Randi glanced over at the Christmas tree for a moment, slurped her coffee to disguise her surprise. *This is more than just a Yuletide visit,* she thought, *more than just a request for forgiveness. Nadine does have some information about Gil . . .*

Nadine sighed. "There's no statute of limitations on murder, Randi. Since Gil's gone, I doubt that I could be prosecuted as an accessory, but you never know. So I'll trust you to keep what I'm going to tell you in confidence. With the perpetrator gone, it really doesn't matter anymore, but still . . ."

"What are you talking about, Nadine?" Randi set her coffee cup down. It rattled on the table, because her hands were shaking. "If you know who killed Gil . . . If you had something to do with it . . ."

Nadine looked at her curiously. "How do you know Gil's dead?"

"I . . . I dreamed it." Randi supplied the same lie that she'd told Leo. "I dreamed that someone jumped him on the way to the market . . ." Randi narrowed her eyes. A touch of hysteria tinged her voice. "Are you telling me now that you . . . That you had something to do with it?"

Nadine shook her head firmly. "No, Randi. You misunderstand me. Like I said when you came to my house – I haven't seen him in years." *Best to maintain that lie.*

"I might be able to offer a guess as to what happened to him, but I'll get to that in a minute. When I spoke of murder, I wasn't talking about Gil's disappearance. I was talking about Adrian."

Nadine paused significantly. She took the time to have another cookie. Randi waited.

At last Nadine said, "Do you have any idea who killed Adrian, Randi? Any idea at all? Just an *inkling,* perhaps?" She watched the younger woman carefully. Randi was artless, and Nadine was convinced that she'd be able to tell if she spoke anything other than what she believed.

Randi shook her head. "The cops said it was a burglary. The guy was surprised that we were . . . That there was anybody inside a dark house on the 4th of July. They said that he must've panicked, shot Adrian so he wouldn't get caught breaking and entering."

Randi seemed to be telling the truth. Nadine said, "But he let you go. Why do you think that is?"

"What was I gonna do?" *I was naked, deafened, splattered with Adrian's blood.* "He had a gun." The memory of the twin barrels of the shotgun returned to Randi: huge like caves, pointed at her . . .

"But you were still a witness. A witness to murder."

"He wore a mask. I couldn't see who he was. There was no reason that he'd have to kill me, too."

"Especially not if he loved you."

Randi wanted to say, *What?* but found that the word stuck in her throat. Speechless, she waited for Nadine to continue.

"You called my cousin's house to tell Gil that you'd found out about our . . ." *No, not relationship,* Nadine thought. "To tell him that you'd found out about our *indiscretion." Yes, that's better.* "You told him that you were leaving him.

"Gil was upset, Randi. Distressed. Like I said, I always knew how much he loved you. And now, here you were, saying that you were leaving him . . . I asked him where it was that you would go.

"He said, 'To her Mom's, I guess.'"

A maleficent gleam flashed in Nadine's eyes. It was gone in a split-second. "That's why I spoke of being an accessory. I'm afraid that I inadvertently put Gil onto it."

"What are you talking about, Nadine?" Randi repeated.

"Remember the first time we met, Randi? At Adrian's eighteenth birthday party? I hadn't seen him for years. He was just a gangly boy, the last time I'd seen him. But the way you said his name . . . I asked you if he was your boyfriend, remember?"

Randi didn't particularly remember, but . . .

"Once I saw Adrian again, I understood why a pretty young thing such as yourself would have a crush on him. He had grown up. He was attractive. *Sexy.* He reminded me of his father . . . I had a little bit of a crush on Ian myself, back in the old days." Nadine shook her head. *No need to go into that right now.*

"I always knew how much you liked Adrian, Randi. How much you *wanted* him. So, when Gil said that you were leaving him, that you'd go back to your mom's . . . I knew better. I knew that you'd go to Adrian. So I said as much to Gil."

Randi's eyes widened. A horror began to form in her, like a tiny bubble in her brain.

"My cousin and her husband were going to a baseball game. I told Gil how long it would last – there was a fireworks show scheduled for afterwards – I told him that there was plenty of time for him to drive back to Riverside, to *handle* the situation, and then come back to Bakersfield. He could say that he couldn't find me in the crowd . . ."

"No," Randi whispered. The bubble burst in her mind. It was like a physical manifestation: she felt a flash of pain. Nadine was repeating everything that Nick had always said . . .

"I'm afraid so, Randi."

Nadine considered the Milanos, thought about just one more, then decided against it. Too much sugar upset her stomach.

She looked at the younger woman again. "Gil wanted to prevent you from running to Adrian, so he came back here. But he was just a little bit too late, wasn't he?"

"No," Randi repeated, utterly horrified. "Gil couldn't hurt anyone. The cops would've figured it out."

"Gil had an alibi. I provided it for him."

Nadine decided on another cookie anyway. They were so tasty. If they disagreed with her later, she could always take some Pepto.

"When he came back to Bakersfield, he met me at the stadium gate. We never spoke of it . . ." Nadine nibbled her Milano. "And then, he broke it off with me. He married you, and you lived happily ever after. Until . . ."

"No. It's not true! Gil couldn't hurt anybody!"

Randi thought of how much Gil had hated Leo, the living reminder of the one night that she'd spent with Adrian. Gil *had* been too late. He hadn't returned until the following morning, and by then, Adrian was dead and she was pregnant. Gil hadn't stopped her from going to Adrian, and Leo must've always reminded him of Adrian, of what they'd done together.

But that didn't mean Gil had been the one that'd murdered him.

"Believe it or not, Randi. But I think you'll believe it a little bit more after you consider the circumstances surrounding Gil's disappearance for a moment. You say you dreamed he was mugged?"

No! Randi's mind screamed. *I dreamed just what you said! Gil killed Adrian, and then Adrian killed Gil! Then he'd turn into a rotting corpse because he was dead . . .* Randi marveled at the logic of her dreams. There was no way that Adrian could've murdered Gil like she'd dreamed, because he was dead. It was impossible. Unless . . .

Randi nodded speechlessly at Nadine. The mugging story was good enough. She wasn't going to admit to what she'd actually dreamt, that Gil had killed Adrian, and then Adrian . . .

Adrian had returned.

"On the day that Ian died, I had come over here to visit Daina."

Nadine reminded herself to keep the story straight. She and Gil had broken it off years earlier. She'd never seen him again afterward, once he'd married Randi. She hadn't been here to see him. He hadn't called and told her that Randi was out of town. They hadn't planned on taking a boat ride together. Nadine had been present on Parcay Street on that fateful day because she was here to visit *Daina.*

"Adrian returned from the other side that day, Randi. Like I said before, I think it must've just happened. The shock sent Ian into cardiac arrest. But he *knew* who it was who called him *Dad.* It wasn't Leo."

Another thought struck Nadine, and she blinked in astonishment that it had never occurred to her before. She'd always believed that Adrian Wilde, returned from the great beyond, had caused Gil's disappearance, but maybe she'd always had the timing of it wrong.

She'd supposed that Ian had *just* become aware of his son's return, and the knowledge had given him a fatal shock. Then Adrian had come back home from the hospital after his father was gone, bereft, guilty that the surprise of his return had killed Ian. He had come upon Gil, returned from wherever he'd been earlier that morning, and in his grief and anger, Adrian had exercised his vengeance.

But maybe that's not how it happened at all, Nadine thought now.

She recalled that Leo and Ian had seemed nervous when they came out of the garage to meet her. Ian had been pale, and he'd closed the garage door firmly behind him. He'd seemed in a hurry to get into the house.

Ian was aware that his son was returned from the grave, but perhaps it *hadn't* just happened! Perhaps it had happened days or weeks earlier. Perhaps father and son had already reminisced, sat around and laughed and joked like it was Old Home Week . . .

Perhaps it hadn't been Adrian's return that had shocked his father onto death.

Perhaps Ian had walked into the garage . . . Gil would've been over there, getting the boat ready. Perhaps Adrian had been lying in wait for him, ready to exact his revenge . . .

Maybe Ian walked in, right after Adrian killed Gil. The shock of seeing *that* was what had brought on his heart attack!

Nadine realized that Randi was staring at her. Her eyes fairly bulged from their sockets.

"Adrian killed Gil. I'm sure of it. He came back from the grave and avenged himself. Your son has blood on his hands, Randi, except that he's not your son anymore."

"NO!" Randi sprang to her feet. "Gil didn't kill Adrian! Leo is not Adrian, and he didn't murder Gil! Somebody mugged Gil, hid his body . . . I dreamed it . . ." Randi crumpled back into the chair, put her face in her hands, sobbed.

"I bet it happened in Daina's garage," Nadine was saying. "Did the police . . .?"

Randi felt a surge of hope, and she was stunned that it came to her at the thought of the police.

"If Adrian . . ." *No!* Randi's mind insisted. *Adrian is dead!* "If Leo . . ."

Randi stopped. Now there was a thought. Leo was seventeen when Gil disappeared. Maybe he had snapped, after a lifetime of Gil's torment. Maybe Nadine was right, partially. Adrian hadn't returned in the person of his son to assassinate Gil. He hadn't had to. Maybe Leo had just gone berserk . . .

But it was all insane. Leo surely couldn't hurt anyone. Not her shy, quiet, fearful boy . . .

But he wasn't so shy anymore, was he?

"If *someone* shot Gil in Daina's garage, the police would've found evidence. Blood, DNA . . . forensics, like on TV."

"Why do you think he was shot? Are there any guns around?"

Because I dreamed it that way, Randi thought. She shook her head again. No one on Parcay Street possessed any guns. *See? It was all ridiculous.*

"Adrian didn't have to shoot him, Randi. That would've made too much noise. If you say there were no guns around, Adrian could've stabbed him, hit him over the head with something. Strangled him."

And Ian . . . Ian saw it! Nadine was convinced of it now. Ian saw Adrian murder Gil and the shock of it was too much for him. He could accept that his son was returned from the grave, but he couldn't accept him as a murderer . . .

Randi still clung desperately to her picture of the competence of the police. She'd been taught as a child that a policeman was always her friend, that they punished wrongdoers, that they always got their man. It had only been after Gil had made her carry a fake ID that she'd come to fear the police, to hate them . . .

"If Gil died in the garage, the police would've found evidence there."

"Did they even investigate? They had no reason to think it was a crime scene."

"No." Randi shook her head. "There were only two guys. They came out and spoke to me, and Penny and Bellona. They didn't talk to Daina, because she was sedated. They talked to Leo . . ."

Oh, my God! Could my son have murdered Gil?

"So they didn't look at the garage as a crime scene. They might not have even gone into the garage."

It was impossible. Leo, her sweet little boy! He couldn't have slaughtered Gil in cold blood, he couldn't have . . .

"What did he do with body?"

Nadine nodded in the direction of the house in the woods. *"They* would know what to do. They'd do anything to protect Adrian. He was returned from the dead, Randi! They couldn't have him going to the chair!" That malefic sparkle ignited in Nadine's eyes again. "They're old witches, steeped in magic. I'm sure that they could make a body disappear. Effortlessly."

Randi realized that she had a headache. It was positively fierce, like a migraine. There were lightning bolts in front of her eyes.

Insanely, she thought of Mrs. Kravitz, from the ancient reruns of *Bewitched* she'd seen after school when she was a kid. *I've got a sick headache, just like Mrs. Kravitz,* Randi thought. *She'd get one whenever she saw some bit of Samantha's witchcraft. Whenever she saw some little thing that she knew couldn't be possible . . .*

Nadine noticed that Randi had gone pale, that she squeezed her forehead as if in pain. "I'm sorry to be the one to bring you all this awful news, honey. Especially at Christmastime. I don't know why Adrian hasn't let you know –"

"I'm going to have to ask you to leave, Nadine," Randi said. "I don't feel very good. I think I need to lie down." *Just like Mrs. Kravitz.*

"Of course, dear. I'm so sorry." Nadine found a pen and an old receipt in her purse. "Here's my number. If you need anything . . . If you'd just like to talk . . ."

Because apparently you can't talk to any of them *about it.* Nadine still couldn't imagine why Adrian hadn't told her. He didn't have to tell her about Gil . . .

Against her will, Randi said, "Thanks. I probably will call you."

Then a flare of defiance sparked in her mind: *No, I won't call you, you crazy, evil old bitch! This is all bullshit! Gil didn't kill Adrian, and Leo isn't Adrian! But Leo could've done it, without any supernatural help at all, because Leo hated Gil. He could've done it . . .*

"I just need to lie down right now." *I need to take a pill. Maybe two . . .*

"Of course, Randi," Nadine repeated. "Thanks for the cookies. They were delicious. I'll just see myself out."

FORTY-NINE

The idea had been planted in Eileen's mind by her daughter's picture of Joshua Martin, the rock star. She hadn't thought of Adrian Wilde in years . . .

This guy didn't really look like him, but he was the same type. His photograph had reminded Eileen of Adrian, and now . . .

She was single, footloose and fancy free. In another week, it would be a new year. Maybe it was time to get back out into the world again. Time to live a little.

A refreshing hope bloomed in Eileen. *Oh, my God! Sexy, flawless Adrian!*

She took a deep breath. *Here goes nothing.*

Eileen typed *Adrian Wilde* into the Google search box. She was delighted to see the first link: *Adrian Wilde Profiles | Facebook. View the profiles of people named Adrian Wilde on Facebook. Join Facebook to connect with Adrian Wilde and others you may know.*

That was a great start! Eileen called Carmen back from the kitchen and asked her to help her join Facebook.

Carmen blinked. "Really? Why?"

"I'm looking for a guy I used to know. Adrian Wilde. Remember, I used to have his picture? Holding you, when you were a baby?"

Carmen remembered. She'd seen the picture enough times, whenever her mom would be looking for something in the big cardboard box she now kept in her grandmother's attic. It was full of old pictures, papers, tax returns – Eileen had never been much for organizing things. She just threw all the stuff she deemed important into that big old box. And whenever she went to look for something, every couple of years usually, she always found that picture. Carmen reckoned it must be right on top.

And then Carmen heard the story again, about this guy that her mother had known when Carmen was just a baby, when her mom and dad had still been married. Mom had had an enormous crush on this guy. *He was so cute, Carmen! I thought I was in love with him!*

Carmen's dad had lost the shop when she was just a baby; he and Eileen had lost the house at the same time. They'd divorced not long after, and Eileen had taken her daughter and moved to Whittier. Carmen knew the story. It was the history of her family.

The old cardboard box had moved with them, and every couple of years, Carmen had heard the story of Adrian Wilde and the hellacious crush her mother had once had on him. Her long lost love. The one that got away.

"Did you ever . . . While you were still married to Dad?"

Eileen shook her head. "It was never anything like that."

But it was going to be, it would've been, if your worthless father hadn't come back home at exactly the wrong moment . . .

"Then how can you say that you were in love with him, Mom? It sounds like you barely even knew him."

"It was just one of those things, Carmen. I thought about him all the time. I couldn't get him out of my head. He was the best looking man I'd ever seen. Oh, my God, Carmen! He was so fine, so sexy! I just wanted to . . ."

Eileen noticed that her daughter was staring at her. It was really not the kind of subject matter that Carmen was used to hearing her mother discuss. Eileen had never talked a lot about romance with her daughter. Eileen had not experienced much of it, except for her long-ago dreams of Adrian . . .

"That's a kind of love," she finished quickly.

Carmen's expression communicated that she wasn't sure that being unable to stop thinking about a virtual stranger was the definition of love. Wanting to sleep with someone you barely even knew . . . That wasn't a kind of love. It was a kind of obsession.

She said, "Why have you waited all these years? If he was so *special* to you, why didn't you look him up right after you and Dad got divorced?"

Eileen shook her head again. "I don't know. Things were tough for a long time after I left your father. Life took over. I didn't have time to go chasing after some dream. But I thought about him a lot over the years . . ."

"Every time you found his picture again."

Carmen had always thought that the guy was all right looking. The long hair seemed a little dated. She'd never cared for men that wore their hair long, not even Joshua Martin. Mostly Carmen looked at herself in the picture – it was hard to realize that the little fat baby that the cute-enough guy was holding was her. He didn't look like anything special to Carmen, and it was difficult to imagine her mother having a crush on anyone. Her mom had never gone on dates when she was little, had never had much to say about the opposite sex at all.

Carmen thought her mother had been a little somber and withdrawn since her second marriage had ended, two years ago.

Eileen hadn't gone out on a single date since. But now she seemed to be coming back to life, looking up old boyfriends . . .

"You should join one of those dating sites, Mom," Carmen suggested.

"Maybe I will," Eileen said with a little smile. "Adrian's probably married. But it would be great to talk to him again. God, Carmen! He was incredible! Help me with this Facebook thing."

Carmen made a quick profile for her mom on Facebook, showed her how to search for people. The first Adrian Wilde she found was black, age twenty. That wasn't her old flame. The next three weren't him, either.

"Maybe he doesn't use the Facebook," Eileen said. "After all, I didn't have it 'til just now. We old people . . . He's probably married. He wouldn't need something like this."

"You're not old, Mom."

"I'm not married, either," Eileen said with a little grin. "I can see how this might be useful if you're single, but Adrian's probably married. He was so cute, Carmen. He probably wouldn't have –"

"What was his middle name?"

Eileen tried to recall if she'd ever heard Adrian's middle name. *Ah, Adrian!* She didn't remember a whole lot of details like that about him, because she'd never known a whole lot of details like that about him. What she *had* known, that he was absolutely the sexiest man she'd ever seen, that he'd actually kissed her once . . . All that didn't translate to a Facebook search.

What was his middle name? Eileen tried to remember conversations she'd had with the girl that'd cleaned house for her. Randi . . . Randi Green . . . Randi had known Adrian better than Eileen had, but not much. Eileen recalled with some satisfaction that Adrian hadn't been interested in Randi, either.

But Randi had been friends with his aunts. She'd followed his band, hung out with them, so she would've probably known his middle name. Eileen thought back across the years, and after a moment, a conversation came back to her.

"Tell me about Adrian."

Eileen recalled that the uncommunicative girl had become nervous, said that her boyfriend didn't like Adrian.

"But you do," Eileen had pressed.

Randi had grinned, shook her head in the affirmative. "Yes," she'd said. "I like him very much. Adrian Robert Wilde . . ."

"His middle name is Robert," Eileen told her daughter.

177

"Okay. Put that in the search box."

The search came up empty. Adrian Robert Wilde didn't have a Facebook page.

Carmen's phone beeped. "It's Clint," she told her mother, and started to leave the room. Eileen frowned. She didn't care for Carmen's current boyfriend. She thought he was shifty.

"Just Google his full name," Carmen said over her shoulder. "I'm sure something will come up." Carmen closed the hall door behind her.

All right, Eileen said to herself. She called up Google again, typed in *Adrian Robert Wilde.* She hit *Enter,* and was surprised that a page full of results appeared. *Now we're getting somewhere!* The first one said:

Adrian Wilde - Ancestry.com - Search
search.ancestry.com/sse.dll? . . . Adrian . . .Wilde
Ancestry.com Inc.
California Birth Index, 1905-1995. Birth, Baptism &
Christening. Name: Adrian R. Wilde . . .

Adrian R. Wilde, Born 7/4/1970 in California . . .
www.californiabirthindex.org/fullname/wilde/adrian
View Adrian R. Wilde's birth record on
CaliforniaBirthIndex.org, the best place to find free birth
records for people like Adrian R. Wilde . . .

Adrian Wilde Birth Records
birth-records.findthebest-gen.com/d/b/Adrian-Wilde
Find birth records for Adrian Wilde. Over 50 million
births from around the world. Research . . .

Well, yes, I know he was born, Eileen thought. *But what's he doing now? Is he still in California? Is he single?* She hadn't seen an entry that said *Adrian Wilde Marriage Records.* That gave her hope.

But then she scrolled down, and the next entry made Eileen gasp.

Adrian R. Wilde Obituary - Tributes.com
www.tributes.com/show/Adrian-R.-Wilde
July 4, 1991 - Death record and obituary for
Adrian R. Wilde from Riverside, California.

It couldn't be true. Adrian couldn't be dead. It had to be someone else. Eileen ignored the link from Tributes.com and scrolled further. The next entry gave Eileen a mother's maiden name. She didn't even have to click on it.

Person Details for Adrian R. Wilde,
California, Birth Index . . .
http://familysearch.org
Name: Adrian R. Wilde. Event Type: Birth.
Event Date: 4 Jul 1970. Event Place: Riverside,
California, United States. Gender: Male.
Mother's Name: Cooper . . .

But a mother's maiden name was no help to Eileen, as she'd never known Adrian's mother's maiden name. The next one mentioned death again.

Wilde Social Security Death Index (SSDI) Records
www.genealogybank.com/gbnk/ssdi/?lname=Wilde
Wilde Death Records in the Social Security Death
Index (SSDI). Wilde matches 9 death records in the
Social Security Death Index (SSDI). View any of these . . .

Eileen clicked warily. There had to be some mistake. Adrian couldn't be dead . . .

None of the nine records for deceased Wildes bore Adrian's first name. Eileen figured that one link couldn't list all the dead Wildes that there probably were, but still she sighed in relief. *See? He's not dead. The entry on that tribute site? That has to be for some other Adrian Wilde . . .*

Eileen scrolled down to the end of the page. There were links for other people named Wilde: an *Ian* and a *Marta;* a *Jameson* with a Ph.D. after his name. Eileen went to the next page and found more of the same. There was an AMA entry for a *Doctor William Wilde,* a Facebook page for a *Doctor Robert Wilde,* a Smith's Medical Systems employee profile for a *Robert William Wilde*, a Community Hospital Pediatric Nursing commendation link for a *Tracy Wilde,* a Facebook page for a *Nick Wilde . . .*

But no more entries for *Adrian R. Wilde.*

179

Eileen clicked back to the first page. The link to Tributes.com was the fourth one down. *July 4, 1991 - Death record and obituary for Adrian R. Wilde from Riverside, California.*

But it couldn't be him.

After seeing Carmen's pictures of Joshua Martin, Eileen had been filled with elation. The rock star had reminded her of Adrian. Fine, sexy Adrian. It'd all come back in a flash, the longing, the fantasies, the obsession. She remembered the one incredible kiss they'd shared, as if it'd been yesterday instead of twenty years before.

It was again as it was every time she'd run across his picture over the years. *Ah, Adrian!* She'd always think of him for a few hours or a few days, then reality would again capture her attention. The grind of reality: her baby was sick, her ex-husband was a nightmare, her paycheck was scanty, school was a bitch. Adrian had been a part of her past then, a memory from better days. An idyllic moment out of time, from before she'd become sadder but wiser. But now . . . Eileen was happy, settled, comfortable. Maybe now incredible Adrian could be a part of her future.

The idea of it, the impossible, incredible, just-maybe *hope,* burned in her. There were no impediments in her life now: she had no husband, her child was grown. He was probably married, but even if he was . . .

Ah, Christ, wouldn't it be something else to see Adrian Wilde again?

It was almost 2011. Everyone was on the internet. Eileen thought, dreamed, that it would be easy to find him, to connect with him, to resume where they'd left off, to consummate that one, promise-filled kiss . . .

Ah, Jesus, what I wouldn't give, what I wouldn't do to see him again!

Eileen sighed and clicked the Tributes.com link. If Adrian was dead, she might as well find out for sure.

There was a box on the left hand side with a picture of blue skies. The caption said, *Add a Photo.* Eileen was relieved that whoever this Adrian had been, no one had posted his photo. Although that would've clinched it, wouldn't it? Her hopes would've been crushed irrevocably had she seen his picture.

Beneath the photo box it said, *Adrian R. Wilde, July 4, 1970 – July 4, 1991, Riverside, California.* And to the right of that, the same information was repeated: *Adrian was born on July 4th, 1970 and passed away on July 4th, 1991.*

The birth year was right: Eileen knew that Adrian was the same age as she was.

But she'd never known his birthday, so this could still be just a coincidence. There were a number of Adrian Wildes on Facebook, and none of them had been him. There could be another one that was also from Riverside, that had been born the same year. It didn't have to be the one that Eileen knew, the one that she'd loved . . .

Eileen counted back over the years. The last time she'd seen Adrian, the one time that he'd kissed her . . . It had been on Hallowe'en. She recalled that she'd bought a little bunny costume for Carmen, really just footy-pajamas with ears attached. She was too young to actually go trick or treating. She was barely even walking. Carmen had turned a year old the previous August, so it had to have been . . . 1990. Eileen had been twenty. Adrian had also been twenty, unless his birthday was after Hallowe'en.

Eileen looked at the dates on the obituary again. This Adrian had lived barely another eight months. He'd died on his birthday. He'd only been twenty-one.

It just couldn't be the Adrian that she knew. It just. Could. Not. Be.

Eileen clicked on the links on the Tributes.com page for this Adrian Wilde that could not be the one that she'd known. She could light a candle, send condolences, sign the memory book. She could post a memory . . .

The only memory Eileen had of Adrian was the single kiss they'd shared. Her only memory was of how much she'd wanted him, how much she'd loved him . . .

None of the links had any entries. Whoever had set up the page had thought enough of this Adrian to make a tribute for him, but maybe they hadn't been computer savvy enough to put up his picture. They apparently hadn't told any of his friends and relatives about the post.

This Adrian had died a long time ago. Almost twenty years. Eileen didn't think there was an internet back then. Perhaps this post was a recent thing, something an old friend or relative had decided to do, since the nineteenth anniversary of his death had just passed last summer. Maybe that's why the links were empty of memories and condolences.

181

Eileen closed the site, closed the internet, closed her brand new laptop. She tried to resign herself to the idea that Adrian Wilde was dead. She'd waited too long to look for him.

But the spark of hope that had flared to life when she'd seen the photo of Joshua Martin refused to be extinguished. This dead Adrian, of the empty tribute page . . . It couldn't be the same one.

Beautiful, sexy Adrian Wilde, whom she'd just decided to find again . . . He couldn't be dead. He just couldn't be. Life could not possibly be that unfair.

Eileen thought about Adrian, and the little remembrances were like kindling to the fire of her hope. She remembered his smile, his voice . . . She'd not said more than a hundred words to her sexy, black-haired neighbor, but she remembered his smooth, dark voice. She'd sometimes stood in the shadows of her garage and listened to him sing, as his band rehearsed across the street. Adrian had been so talented, *so gorgeous* . . . He just couldn't be dead.

There was only one way to find out. The internet was good for research, for what it was worth, but this time it had delivered more questions than answers. It was no substitute for real-world sleuthing. If Eileen truly wanted to find Adrian again, she wasn't going to be able to do it from the comfort of her mother's dining room table. She was going to have to go out into the world. She'd have to go back to Parcay Street, knock on his door.

He might not live there anymore, but maybe his mom and dad still did, or his aunts that had lived up the hill. It was the first place to start. As soon as the holidays had passed, she'd go out and look for Adrian.

Life was finally good for Eileen. If she could find Adrian . . . It could be great.

FIFTY

Randi took to her bed again during the week between Christmas and New Year's Eve, after Nadine had appeared out of nowhere and brought with her all these horrible, impossible theories.

Leo was dismayed.

"You've been doing so well, Mom! Ever since Easter. What are you sad about now?"

Christ! He looks so much like Adrian! But he's not Adrian! He can't be! If he was, he'd tell me . . .

"I'm not sad, Leo. All that's in the past." *All the bodies, long buried. In the past.* "I've just been feeling a little tired. Maybe I've got the flu. If it keeps up, I'll make an appointment with Doctor Samuel next week."

"Bobby and Tracy and Nick are coming over tonight. Just like last year. We're gonna jam. I hope you're feeling up to joining us this time."

"Maybe." *But probably not.*

It never seemed more likely that Leo was his father reincarnated than when he was standing in front of a microphone, singing, *jamming,* playing Adrian's old black and yellow Charvel.

"Even if I don't make it over there, I'll be with you in spirit." Randi smiled faintly. "I'll still be able to hear you. Play a couple for me. Tell Bobby to play *I Ran.*"

Leo hesitated. Artificially, it seemed to Randi. "I don't know if I've heard that one, Mom."

"It was from a band called *Flock of Seagulls,* from a long, long time ago. Their music was called *new wave.* In the 80s. I think they only had the one hit . . . *I Ran.* It wasn't really the kind of music your dad's band played, but that song was one of Bobby's favorites. From when he was a kid."

Jesus, how the years have slipped away! Randi thought again.

"I'll ask him about it," Leo said. He gave her a hug, then left the house.

FIFTY-ONE

Bobby and Nick and their cousin were tuning up in the garage. It was about nine o'clock on New Year's Eve. Goodbye, 2010!

"Who's all coming to this shindig?" Nick asked. "Your little girlfriend? Maybe some of her friends?" He leered in jest. All of Angie's friends were far too young for him; in years, in temperament.

Adrian shook his head. "She is my girlfriend no longer, Cuz. She dumped me. Right before Christmas."

"Don't be so broke up about it," Bobby said with a grin.

"*She* dumped *you?* That's a first. You must be slipping, Cuz."

Adrian shrugged. "Times have changed, my brutha, but apparently I haven't. She took up with some college boy. Justin Somebody. She told me that I just didn't have enough ambition for her."

"Well, you don't do a whole lot, do you?" Nick said.

Adrian smiled craftily. "I've got my whole life ahead of me this time, Cuz." *I want to live a little this time.* Nick grinned at him.

"So, no audience?" Bobby said with a touch of disappointment. "Your mom and your aunts are fine, but I get the impression that our music doesn't . . . *reach* them." He grinned at the silliness of that. "What about Randi?"

Adrian shook his head. "Maybe. But she's been in bed all week again, so I doubt it. Says she got the flu. But she did make a request, though." He grinned at Bobby. "She wants you to play *I Ran.*"

"Christ!" Nick said. "Not that old dog."

"It was actually called *I Ran (So Far Away),*" Bobby said defensively. "It's a classic."

Nick snorted. "Right. From when you were ten years old. You just liked the haircut."

"You remember that?" Adrian said. "You couldn't've been more than seven or eight."

"I remember he'd stand in front of the mirror for days, trying to get those side flips just right."

"I thought that's what a musician should look like." Bobby grinned at Adrian. "You wanted to be Eddie Van Halen."

Again Nick snorted. "He was overrated, too. But at least they had some great guitars. Not like Flock of Seagulls –"

"*A* Flock of Seagulls," Bobby corrected.

"I dunno, Nick. The solo in *I Ran* is pretty good." Adrian turned on his amp and played it. When the last chord died away, he said, "Sure, it's not *Black Dog,* but it's okay –"

"I thought you didn't know how to play that song."

The cousins hadn't noticed Randi walk up the driveway, over the sound of the new Marshall.

There was a moment of silence, then Nick said, "When did he tell you that?"

Randi looked at him expressionlessly. "A couple hours ago. When he asked if I was coming to the party."

Nick grinned. "Well, there ya go. A couple of hours ago, he didn't know it." Nick glanced at his cousin. "A couple of hours is all it takes. Less than that, actually. I told you before, Randi, the kid's a natural. A prodigy. Just like his dad."

Randi looked at her son. "Apparently."

"You want us to play the whole thing, Mom?"

"No. I can't stay. I'm still feeling a little tired. I brought you a jacket. It's supposed to get cold tonight." Randi took the hooded sweatshirt that she'd draped over her arm and held it out to him. Leo set the Charvel on its stand and obediently put it on.

"Sure we couldn't interest you in just one song, Randi?" Nick asked.

"No, thanks. But I found a bottle of Johnnie Walker under the sink, if you'd like to have it."

"Black or red?"

"Black."

Nick grinned. "It's not Chivas, but I'm never one to turn down free whiskey."

"Come back home with me and get it, Leo."

"All right."

They started down the driveway, and Nick called, "Happy New Year, Randi. I hope you feel better soon."

Randi waved over her shoulder, but didn't turn around.

FIFTY-TWO

Randi set the dusty bottle of Scotch on the kitchen table.

"It must've been Gil's," she said simply. "I always preferred gin." There was no alcohol in the house nowadays, because Randi didn't dare take a drink anymore. Not with all the pills the doctor had prescribed for her.

When Leo reached for the bottle, Randi said, "Sit down, Leo. I need to talk to you."

Leo sat and she sat down across from him.

"Your AnTeen stopped by to see me, the day after Christmas."

"Who?"

Randi looked keenly at him. Had he given that little artificial hesitation again?

"Nadine."

"Who?" Leo repeated.

"Nadine Germaine. She's a friend of your grandmother's. She says she used to visit your grandma and your aunts all the time. She says she watched you grow up. I never saw her over there, but . . ."

Now Leo nodded. "Okay. Grandma's friend. The older lady. I haven't seen her in a long time. Not since –"

"Since Gil disappeared."

"I was gonna say, not since Grandpa died."

This news of AnTeen's visit was a revelation, and apparently Randi had something to say about it. Leo waited.

"Nadine had some interesting thoughts about your grandpa's heart attack, and about Gil's disappearance." Randi leaned forward and stared at her son. She spoke softly, rapidly. "Did you murder Gil, Leo?"

"What? That's nuts, Mom! Did that old lady tell you that?"

Randi leaned back in her chair again. "Maybe I should say, *Did you murder Gil . . . Adrian?*"

The change that passed across his features mesmerized Randi. She watched the expression she'd seen for his entire life – Leo's cautious, watchful gaze – Randi watched it fall away, disappear. He blinked, and Leo was gone. Adrian – confident, in control – looked steadily at her now.

He grinned. "What gave me away? The guitar?"

Randi was speechless for a moment. *It's all true. The promise of The Incantations of Thoth is fulfilled. Adrian's back.* A tear ran down her face for Leo, her lost little boy.

Adrian stared at her emotionlessly now, his grin vanished. Randi wiped the tear away.

"No. Nothing gave you away. I looked for a sign of your return for your . . . for *Leo's* whole life. I never saw it. Even now, I told myself that you just wanted to play music because your cousins did." She paused. "Nadine told me."

"Really?" Adrian replied glibly. "And who told her?"

"She figured it out all on her own. When Ian collapsed . . . She told me that you said, 'Help him, AnTeen.' She said that you called Ian *Dad,* and that he wasn't surprised by it, even in the middle of a heart attack."

Adrian waited for her to continue. When it seemed that she would not, he said, "What else did she tell you? You said something about Gil?"

It was impossible, but it was true, beyond a shadow of a doubt. Adrian was sitting across from her. Her little boy was gone. Another tear threatened, but Randi sniffed it back. She reckoned that Leo had been gone for some time now, going on two years, and it had taken that filthy old witch to make her see it.

The signs had been there, but Randi had ignored them. The sudden interest in music, the sudden interest in that trampy girl. Leo's resemblance to Adrian had become undeniable, *because he was Adrian.* But Randi had denied it, despite the fact that he'd inexplicably crawled in bed with her twice, despite the fact that she'd almost mistaken him for his father on both occasions . . .

But there was no denying it now.

"Nadine was full of confessions."

"Do tell." He grinned again. It was Adrian's expression. There was absolutely no doubt in Randi's mind now.

"She told me that she sicced Gil on you. That he came back here, to stop us from . . . Then he went back to Bakersfield. She told me that she alibied him." Randi watched Adrian carefully. She noted no surprise in his eyes, so she said as much. "None of this seems to come as a shock to you."

He shrugged, noncommittal. "That's just what Nick always said."

"Nadine said that you killed Gil."

"I say I did not." A moment of silence passed. They stared at each other. Finally Adrian said, "What proof did she offer?"

Randi shrugged. "Nothing that would stand up in court."

Adrian paused for another moment. He studied her face.

187

At last he said, "If Gil murdered me, don't you think he had it coming? I'm not saying I did it . . . But supposing I did, what of it, Randi? *And thine eye shall not pity; but life shall go for life, eye for eye, tooth for tooth . . .*

"Something Dad said once. You know how he was always quoting things. I suppose that's from the Bible."

When Randi was about ten years old, Mrs. Green's beat-up old dryer had called it quits. They didn't have any money for a new one right away, so Randi's Mom had strung a clothesline in the dusty, grassless backyard.

Randi remembered a time when she'd been helping her mother hang out bed sheets on this clothesline. The washer that they'd had wasn't the best either: it didn't spin very well, and the sheets were heavy with water. Randi stood on a little step stool and attempted to sling one of the soppy sheets over the line. But she heaved too much over, and the sheet slithered to the ground with an audible, wet, flapping noise.

Now Randi heard the same noise in her mind again. She thought she felt the pain of another sick headache coming on, but then it subsided.

She'd lain in bed for a week, contemplating all the revelations that Nadine had told her. Gil shot Adrian, out of jealousy, to keep Randi from sleeping with him. That was shock enough to her mental health. Randi had never once suspected Gil of the murder.

Then Nadine had said that Adrian was returned from the other side, reincarnated in the person of her son, just as Penny and Bellona and Daina had always believed he would be. Then Nadine had delivered her final bombshell. Not only was Adrian returned, he had murdered Gil in revenge. Penny and Bellona had disappeared Gil's remains.

Randi had turned all these ideas over and over in her mind. Some evil, some miraculous. She arrived at a decision: there was no way to know if any of it was true, unless she came right out and asked the young man that shared the house with her. She considered how to bring it up. If it wasn't true, then Leo would think she was insane, asking him if he was somehow the father he'd never known, back from the dead.

But when Randi heard Leo effortlessly, flawlessly play the guitar solo to that old song . . . Leo had told her that he'd never heard of it, yet he'd played it, and Randi had known he was Adrian right then. It was true – not only was Adrian returned, but he was lying to her about it.

Why wouldn't he tell her? Unless the rest of Nadine's awful story was also true.

"Why didn't you tell me that you were back?" she asked him now.

Adrian grinned wickedly. "I tried to." Randi saw not a scintilla of Leo. Only confident, knowing, *sexy* Adrian remained. He said, "I didn't think you'd believe it."

In the week since Nadine's visit, Randi had made herself believe it. She'd had discussions with herself: *if I accept that it's all true, then how will I proceed?*

Randi had convinced herself that she'd be able to go on, to continue. If her baby boy was no more, she'd just look at Adrian as a nice young man that she had once known, when she was younger. She was old now, but he was just as he'd once been, friendly, a talented musician . . .

"You loved me once," Adrian said. It wasn't a question. He'd always known it.

Randi nodded. She'd been infatuated with his beauty, his charm, his talent. All of her affection for him had been heightened by the fact that he wouldn't give her the time of day.

"But as soon as I was gone, you forgot about me. You went back to Gil."

"I never forgot about you!" Randi protested immediately.

Randi's love for Adrian had been unreturned, therefore, she'd more than loved him. She'd worshipped him. And when her never requited fantasy had at last come to pass . . .

One night with Adrian had been sufficient. It had been everything that Randi had ever hoped it would be. In the intervening years, she'd kept the memory like a secret treasure. She'd taken it out and looked at it every so often. She'd relished it.

Randi had lived her life with Gil, and she'd never spoken of Adrian. She'd never dwelt on what might have been. But still, Randi had never forgotten him.

"How could I forget you?" *I had that one glorious night . . .* "I had Leo to remember you by."

Adrian grinned humorlessly. "Yet you allowed Gil to make his life miserable."

"I'm sorry about that."

Randi couldn't apologize to Leo himself, Adrian reflected, *but she can apologize to his father.* He didn't know if that was better or worse.

"I begged him to be nicer to Leo. But what was I supposed to do? He was my husband. It's not like he beat Leo. He never actually *hurt* him. And besides —"

"Besides, what difference does it make now? They're both gone." Adrian studied her with a slightly self-satisfied smile. He stood. "Nick's gonna wonder where I am with this Scotch."

Adrian put his hand on the bottle, but didn't pick it up. "I know you've been lonely, Randi. I could come back later if you want, after the party . . ."

Randi just looked up at him, wide-eyed, speechless with horrified disbelief.

Adrian shrugged. "Suit yourself." He picked up the Johnnie Walker. "Happy New Year. *Mom.*"

He left the kitchen, left the house. Randi jumped at the sound of the front door closing.

She'd told herself that she'd be able to handle it, if it was all true. Gil was gone, Leo was gone . . . Adrian was back.

He was undeniably Adrian, and he'd just made a rather blatant pass at her, as if he wanted to take up right where they'd left off, twenty years ago. And some tiny voice in Randi's head had responded. It had whispered, *Why not?*

Randi felt her sanity slipping away. Its departure was what made that wet, flapping sound in her head, just like the heavy sheet had done as it slithered from the clothes line. Rational parts of her mind grabbed for it – *It'll all be okay! Adrian's back, but that doesn't mean we have to . . .*

But it was too late. Randi couldn't cope. *Adrian murdered Gil, and now he wants me to . . .*

Randi arose and went to her bedroom. She locked the door. She shook an Ambien out of its bottle, and then a Vicodin out of its bottle. She washed them down with the glass of water from the bedside table.

I can't think about this anymore. I won't *think about it.*

Randy slid in beneath the covers and closed her eyes.

FIFTY-THREE

"Happy New Year, my bruthas," Adrian said. He handed the dusty bottle of Black Label to Nick. "I don't know if it's going to be entirely happy for all of us, however."

Bobby and Nick waited for an explanation.

Adrian sighed. "Randi knows."

"You finally told her?" Nick said in wonder. "How did she take it?"

Adrian shook his head. "I didn't tell her. Apparently, AnTeen stopped by the day after Christmas. She told her."

"What?" Nick exclaimed. "How does *she* know?"

"She knows a lot of things. What she doesn't know, she guessed."

Nick heard his cousin's voice in his head: *She told Randi that she sicced Gil on me.* Nick's mouth dropped open. He closed it quickly.

"She told Randi that she knew I was back, because I said *AnTeen* when Dad collapsed."

Nick knew the whole story: how Gil had been about to murder Leo, how the act had somehow precipitated Adrian's emergence. Adrian had then taken his vengeance. Ian had realized that Leo was Adrian returned at that moment, right before his heart had failed him.

But Bobby didn't know about any of that. Bobby hadn't ever asked about the *whens* and *whys* and *wherefores* of his cousin's return. He believed that Adrian was back and he rejoiced in it, but he'd never asked for any clarification about the timing of it.

So Adrian explained it to him now. Sort of. "I'd realized who I was, and Dad recognized me. We were standing in the garage. Dad was amazed, Bobby, just like you were. But he believed it, just like you do. We heard a car door slam in the driveway, so we went out to see who was there. It was AnTeen.

"Dad took a few steps . . . He fell . . . I said, 'Help him, AnTeen!'" Adrian shrugged again. "Nobody ever called her that but me. She knew. She's a witch, just like my aunts."

Bobby rolled his eyes. All his life, he'd heard that the other side of his cousin's family tree dabbled in the supernatural. *I guess I have to believe it now,* Bobby thought with a start.

"So she had no trouble believing it."

"Does Randi believe it?" Bobby asked.

Adrian nodded and shook his head at the same time. "She believes it. But I don't think she's taking it too well. I think she's having a little trouble with all of the ramifications."

Again, Nick heard Adrian's voice in his mind: *AnTeen told Randi that I killed Gil.*

Nick mouth dropped open a second time. *How does she know?*

She guessed. I think all of it might be a little too much for Randi . . .

Adrian twirled his finger beside his temple.

"I'm sure she'll be okay," Bobby said. It had been difficult enough for him to accept the miracle of Adrian's return. He didn't want to think too closely about what its *ramifications* might mean to Randi.

Adrian shrugged, picked up his guitar. "What should we begin with?"

FIFTY-FOUR

On Sunday, January 2nd, 2011, Eileen paused outside the fence to Adrian's old house. She'd never stepped foot in the yard, had never been on the porch, had certainly never been inside her neighbor's home. She'd watched him glide languidly up the street from it to meet Allan enough times; watching Adrian's approach had often been the highlight of Eileen's day.

Allen would always go outside to greet him, then they'd walk on up to the shop. Eileen had concocted elaborate fantasies in her mind, but they really weren't elaborate at all: Allan would go on up to the shop alone, and Adrian would come up on the porch, knock on the door . . .

And then it actually happened. Adrian showed up on that Hallowe'en evening, when Allan wasn't home. He'd told her that he liked her. He'd kissed her, gathered her up in his arms. All her fantasies were going to come true . . . And then Allan came home.

Eileen had never spoken to Adrian again.

After their divorce, he was one of Allan's favorite accusations: "You just want to get rid of me so you can go after Adrian. I saw how you looked at him, you slutty bitch. You never loved me."

And Eileen would hang up on him. She'd loved Allan once, but he'd killed that love. No thought of Adrian had ever entered into her decision to divorce Allan, and afterwards, life was just too difficult.

And then she'd find that picture, when she'd needed a tax return or Carmen's shot record or some other vital statistic, and she'd remember how she'd schemed to get it. The little plastic camera, how she'd told Adrian to hold the baby so she could get *her* picture. She'd actually gotten a couple of shots of him that day, but they'd disappeared over the years, perhaps slid to the bottom of the box. But that one – the best one – was always there on top.

Eileen hesitated outside the gate. She'd stood at this fence and exchanged a few words with Adrian's mother no more than thrice. It was on this tenuous connection that Eileen depended: she hoped the old woman still lived there, that she'd remember her brief neighbor. If a stranger answered the door, Eileen would walk up the footpath and check to see if his aunts were still there. They might remember her. They'd made her a casserole right after Carmen was born.

Eileen had to know for sure. The internet was too vague. It simply couldn't be true. It had to be some other Adrian Wilde. He couldn't be dead, couldn't have been dead for almost twenty years.

Eileen took a deep breath and opened the gate. Now was the *momento de la verdad* – the moment of truth – when she'd find out for sure. Either Adrian was dead – she'd let a lifetime pass her by without ever thinking to go back and find him – or, he was still alive, maybe even here, and now she'd perhaps get a chance with him.

All of Eileen's body, her soul, her spirit, rebelled against the idea that he could be dead. After all these years, if she couldn't finally, at last, make something with Adrian – he was probably married – maybe they could at least resume a friendship. Something. She was old now, but so was he. Maybe he wasn't married, maybe he was divorced, just as she was . . .

But her mind knew the truth, even if the rest of her being defied the information she'd seen online. Adrian was dead.

But it could all be just a coincidence. This was the only way to find out for sure.

Eileen knocked on the door, and after a moment, Adrian himself opened it. He looked blankly, politely at her.

A wave of relief washed over Eileen. It was an actual physical sensation: she rocked back on her heels. *Oh, my God, he looks exactly the same!*

It was as if Adrian hadn't aged a day: he still had the same long, black hair that she'd always ached to run through her fingers, the same flawless, almost boyish mouth that she'd kissed just once, and had ever after longed to kiss again . . .

He was even wearing the same kind of tank top he used to wear in the old days, the kind that displayed the perfection of his arms and shoulders. *Oh my God, he's beautiful!*

Eileen whispered his name and she saw a spark of recognition in his depthless blue eyes. He hadn't known her at first – she certainly had changed over the years, even if he had not – but Eileen was so sure that he recognized her now that she threw propriety to the wind and hugged him tightly to her. They'd kissed once, after all. She'd loved him . . .

Adrian allowed himself to be hugged, but he didn't hug Eileen in return. After a moment, she felt self-conscious and stepped back. The recognition that she was sure she'd seen in his eyes was gone. Just an open watchfulness remained.

"Adrian?" Eileen said in dismay. "Don't you remember me?"

He looked down sheepishly, boyishly, for a moment, then met her eyes again. His eyes were so blue, it caused Eileen to flinch. They were just like she remembered them.

"I'm sorry. I'm Leo. Adrian was my dad."

Of course. This couldn't be Adrian. Eileen should've seen it right away: the soft mouth, the jet-black hair – no gray. Not a single line or wrinkle. This was a boy; this was *his boy*.

"Pardon me," Eileen apologized. "You look so much like him."

Through the prism of time, Leo looked so much like him that Eileen could not remember that Adrian had looked any different from his son. She hadn't seen Adrian in twenty years: this is what Adrian looked like. There had to be some difference – she reminded herself to find that picture again – but until she did so, Leo *was* Adrian to Eileen, just as beautiful and irresistible as he'd been when they were both twenty.

But this young man wasn't Adrian. Time had to have taken youth from Adrian, just as it had from her, just as it takes it from everybody. Adrian had to be gray by now, or at least on his way. Or maybe bald, or even fat. He was obviously married: here was his son.

"Is your father here?"

Again the sheepish glance down, then a look of sadness. "I'm sorry," Leo repeated. "My father's dead."

Though she'd suspected that it would be so all along, the finality of it hit Eileen like a punch in the gut. She felt as though the wind had been knocked out of her. She gasped for breath for a moment. The hope that had grown and thrived inside her for the past week shriveled, blackened. It was as if a torch had been put to an orchid. Adrian was dead. The truth of it scalded. *It hurt.*

Adrian was dead, for nineteen and a half years. She caught her breath, put a rein on her emotions. She quickly wiped away the tear that ran down one cheek.

Eileen looked at his boy. He was watching her. Eileen reckoned that he couldn't have been very old when it happened, because he wasn't very old now. Not to mention that it had happened barely eight or nine months after Eileen had seen Adrian last. He'd had no woman, no child, then. Eileen realized that Adrian had to have died before his son was even born.

"Is your mother . . ." *No, not his mother. I don't even know who his mother is!* "Does your *grandmother* still live here?"

The sheepish smile. "Yes. She's up the hill right now. With my aunts. Would you like me to go get her?"

195

FIFTY-FIVE

Adrian was back. The memories he'd of Leo's life had faded: they weren't even like a story someone had told him about anymore. They were more like something he might've read in passing on the internet once, a news article about people he didn't know.

He and Nick were telepathic, just like the old days. That useful phenomenon had returned immediately. And Adrian could read fragments of thoughts from adoring women, just like he'd always been able to do. Right now, Eileen was thinking about how much Leo looked like Adrian, how beautiful he was . . .

Adrian was even getting flashes of precognition again. He saw that Eileen was going to say, "I wouldn't want you to go to any trouble."

So he preempted her. "Why don't you just come up there with me? My grandma will be glad to see you. She always likes to talk to anyone that knew Dad."

Eileen nodded.

"Hold on just a second." He ducked into the house and shrugged into a flannel shirt. It was chilly. It was January.

Only the second day of the bright new year and all my hopes are destroyed, Eileen thought.

Another tear threatened. Eileen was still shocked into speechlessness by the truth. There was now an empty place in her mind, in her soul, where the hope of seeing Adrian again had lived for a short while. Now that hope had died. Adrian was gone. She'd waited too long. She would never, ever see him again.

Eileen knew that she'd have a good, long cry over Adrian's death when she got home. But she couldn't just leave. She thought it would only be polite to say a few words to his mother, since she'd just showed up on her doorstep unannounced. That would be the respectful thing to do, and besides, Eileen found that she liked looking at Adrian's son.

Leo closed the front door and the two of them started up the hill.

As they walked up the path, he looked at her curiously. "You went out with my dad?"

Eileen blushed. Of course he'd think that. She'd hugged him after all, when she thought he was Adrian.

"No, nothing like that. We were just friends."

I hardly even knew him. But he was incredible, and you look just like him . . .

"He worked for my ex-husband for a little while. It was a long time ago. We used to live in the house across the street."

"Really?" Leo smiled, and Eileen thought her heart skipped a beat, just like it used to do when Adrian smiled. "That's where I live. With my mom."

Eileen wondered about Leo's mother. It must've been a whirlwind courtship. Adrian had died eight or nine months after Eileen had seen him last. A very short time for him to have met a girl and fallen in love . . . Eileen thought again that Leo's mother had to have still been pregnant with him when his father died.

Eileen considered that in a different world, she'd like to have a little girl talk with Leo's mother. If Adrian wasn't dead, of course. With his being gone, it would just be unfitting, ghoulish . . . But if Adrian was still alive, Eileen thought she'd like to ask Leo's mother what he'd been like, what it was like to kiss him, more than just once, what it was like to . . .

She realized that Leo was looking at her; it was her turn to speak. Again Eileen blushed. "It's a small world," she stammered.

You have no idea, Adrian thought.

He was pleased to see Eileen again. He liked the idea that there was someone else in the world who remembered him, besides his immediate family. On the other hand, Eileen wasn't just some random person who remembered him. Of all the people in the world, if someone had asked Adrian who he thought might never forget him, he would've had to say Eileen. No one had even wanted him like Eileen had. Adrian recalled the sparking, helpless, unconcealable desire in her mind, on her face. Randi's yen for him had been but a passing glance in comparison.

The years had been kind to her. She'd kept her great figure; her face was unlined; her hair was still a rich, chestnut brown. Adrian supposed that she might dye it. Randi left the few streaks of gray that fate had given her, but Adrian knew that Tracy dyed her hair, because it was a different color than it had been twenty years ago.

Adrian reflected that he, too, would be getting old. Gray, perhaps; maybe fat, or bald. Bobby's once dark auburn hair had lightened, thinned. He'd grown a trifle stout. Even Nick had put on a few pounds.

And I'm still nineteen, Adrian thought, *in looks, anyway. I found the fountain of youth. All I had to do was die to achieve it.*

He was glad to hear Eileen mention that Allan was now her ex-husband. He wondered if her divorce from the fat old car thief had prompted her to look up Adrian again. He smiled to himself. It was just as obvious as it had ever been that she still harbored the same desire. Now that he'd given her the bad news, she seemed to have transferred the old yen onto his son.

Damn, he's cute, she kept thinking. *He looks just like Adrian . . .*

They'd reached the house. Leo indicated the stairs that went up to the deck. "Have you ever been here before?" he asked politely.

Eileen shook her head. "I only met Adrian's aunts once," she told him. "They brought me lasagna, right after my daughter was born."

Adrian wondered what . . . Candace? No, that wasn't it. He'd never been very good with names. He concentrated. Karen? No, that wasn't it either. Carmen! That was her name. She'd just been a little baby the last time he'd seen her, just barely walking. She'd had big tan eyes similar to her mom's, and little blonde ringlets. She'd looked just like Allan. Adrian wondered what she looked like now.

They stepped onto the deck. Daina and his aunts and Randi were sitting at the little table in the corner, as they always were. He'd seen them there, throughout his life as Adrian, the first time. He'd seen them there while he was Leo. They were still there. *Some things never change,* he mused.

"Ladies, this is —"

"Eileen? Is it you?"

Eileen blinked blankly at the woman that had spoken her name. She'd recognized the old ladies right away, because they didn't seem to have changed at all. They were just whitehaired now, instead of gray. The other woman was Daina, Adrian's mother. Eileen had always thought she was beautiful. Adrian had inherited his shiny black hair from her. The black was gone now, but the two decades since Eileen had seen her last had been kind to Daina. She was still beautiful.

The woman that had said her name was about Eileen's age. She had black hair, too, streaked with gray. She looked familiar . . . After a second, Eileen realized that it was Randi.

"Yes, Randi. It's me."

Randi leapt up and unexpectedly hugged Eileen. "Oh, my God! It's been so long! The things I have to tell you!" Randi glanced over her shoulder at the rest of the group. *Fearfully,* it seemed to Eileen.

"It's great to see you, Randi!" Eileen returned her hug. She noticed that Randi still stared apprehensively at the others. She seemed to have forgotten that Eileen was standing right next to her. "I'm looking forward to catching up."

Randi turned her attention to Eileen again, and her worried expression vanished. She smiled. "I can't wait."

Penny and Bellona and Daina looked politely, blankly, at Eileen. She saw no recognition in their eyes.

"You remember Eileen, don't you?" Randi said. "Eileen Coleman. She used to live in my house. With her husband and little girl?"

Now they recognized her. "Of course!" Daina said. "How have you been, Eileen?"

"How's your little girl?" Bellona asked. "She's all grown up now!"

"She turned twenty-one last August," Eileen replied.

"My, how the years fly by," Penny said. Eileen failed to notice that she said it to Leo, or that he grinned at his aunt in silent, amused reply.

An awkward moment skipped by, and Eileen realized that they were all probably wondering what she was doing there.

"I'm so sorry to hear that Adrian passed," she said at last.

Eileen decided that she wouldn't mention her internet search for Adrian. That might seem a trifle odd to his family. Carmen had looked at her like she was *obsessed* with the man she'd known for just a brief time, so long ago. After seeing Joshua Martin's picture, after being reminded of Adrian, after feeling that hope, maybe she had been obsessed for a moment. Maybe she had been obsessed twenty years ago. *Adrian was incredible.* But now he was gone.

"I just moved back to Riverside a few months ago, and I was in the neighborhood . . ."

Does anybody ever believe that? I was just in the neighborhood, after twenty years. Thought I'd just drop right on in and look up gorgeous Adrian Wilde again, see if he might be single . . .

"I knocked on your door, Daina. Leo told me. I'm so sorry."

"It was a car accident," Randi blurted out.

Eileen looked at her in surprise. Somehow, it seemed inappropriate that Randi would just come right out and say how Adrian had died. Eileen had always found Randi to be shy in the old days; she hadn't ever been able to get much conversation out of her. Eileen couldn't remember anything they'd ever talked about, except for a few brief words about Randi's crush on Adrian.

But she'd gotten directly to the point, now. Eileen noticed that Randi looked fearful again. But that wasn't exactly right. Not fearful. Randi looked haunted, perhaps a little . . . crazy.

"Please sit down, Eileen," Daina said with a sigh. "We've got a lot of catching up to do."

"Oh!" Randi said, with an odd, not apropos enthusiasm. "Let me tell it."

FIFTY-SIX

The people that dwelt on Parcay Street still kept a few secrets from each other.

Nick and Bobby had heard mention of *The Incantations of Thoth,* and they believed that Adrian, miraculously, was back from the other side. They didn't know that it had been Adrian himself that had recited the potent words, however. They didn't know that their cousin had initialized his own future return. Nick and Bobby knew nothing of Adrian's practice of witchcraft, neither now, nor in his first life.

The first time, it had been just an odd family tradition, and Adrian had been a little embarrassed by it, hadn't mentioned it to his mainstream cousins. Now Adrian knew the old ways to be a source of unspeakable power: they'd brought him back from the dead.

Nick, and even Bobby and his wife, could no longer deny that some kinds of magic existed. Adrian had laid the blame and the miracle of his return at his eccentric aunts' witchy feet. If his cousins were curious about specifics, they could query Penny and Bellona. Adrian thought that was unlikely.

The old witches and Nick knew the trigger for Adrian's return. They knew that Gil had murdered Adrian in a jealous rage; they knew he'd intended to kill Leo. They knew that Adrian, fresh from wherever he had been for seventeen years, had exacted his revenge.

Daina knew none of these details. She believed that Adrian had just returned one day, as it had been promised that he would.

Nadine had figured it all out on her own, and for reasons Adrian couldn't understand, she'd felt compelled to tell the tale to Randi. The day before, Adrian had gone up the hill to fill his aunts in on the new development.

"I got up this morning, and she was staring at the wall again," he'd told them. "She's not taking it well. What I want to know is, why would AnTeen want me dead? Why would she incite Gil to kill me? Why would she tell Randi about it all?"

Penny sighed. "It seems that no stone ever remains unturned in this family. No secret is ever forgotten."

Adrian waited.

"Nadine was once in love with your father, Capo."

"I knew it!" he exclaimed. "I used to get a vibe from her. Something about Dad." He looked at his aunts in surprise. "Did Dad

. . . Did he throw her over? Dump her for Mom?" *Did my parents lie to me about it?*

Bellona shook her head. "Fate offered Ian a crossroads. A choice. He chose your mother."

"But did he and AnTeen ever . . . He at least knew that she liked him, right?"

Penny shrugged, noncommittal. "Maybe he knew she liked him, but she never spoke up. There was never anything between them. Nadine missed her chance. Once Ian met Daina, he never thought about another woman.

"Nadine was a silly witch when she was younger, Capo. She insisted on interpreting her own Tarot. She saw foretold there just what she wanted to see. Ian was her *soulmate*. They were destined to be together." Penny flapped her hands in dismissal. "It was simply not the case."

"And when it didn't happen, just like we told her that it wouldn't . . ."

"She seethed. She hated," Penny hissed. "She cursed. Daina had stolen Ian from her. 'Deen convinced herself that we'd helped to bring this betrayal about. We were all against her. So she left."

"But she kept coming back," Adrian said. He remembered AnTeen's infrequent visits, how she'd always seemed cold, malevolent. Now he knew why.

"We had told her that Ian would always be in her life," Bellona said. "Just not in the way she wanted him to be. So she remained on friendly terms with Daina so she could come back and visit. So she could see Ian."

"This is all water under the bridge," Penny said dismissively. "You asked why she hated you? She hated your parents' happiness, and you were a living symbol of that. She knew about the prediction of your early demise –"

"Why did she know about that?" Adrian demanded. "If you knew that she hated me, why would you tell her –"

"Fate is immutable, Adrian," Penny said sternly. "No one knows that better than you. You were only three years old when she learned of the prophecy. Nadine's knowledge that your life was to be brief didn't matter, as she could neither prolong it nor shorten it. It would happen when it happened."

"But she made it happen! She sicced Gil on me!"

"Perhaps he would've come on his own," Bellona said. "Or perhaps it would've happened some other way. *If it be not now, yet it will come: the readiness is all.* You were ready. All is as it should be."

Adrian considered for a moment. "And Mom doesn't know about any of this?"

"Bell and I took an oath," Penny revealed. "We swore that we'd never tell Daina that Nadine had once –"

"Coveted her man," Bellona said. "That's how she put it."

"'Deen was never around that often, anyway," Penny said. "Why make your mother feel bad about things that were beyond her control? The silly, jealous witch never posed any kind of threat. It would've happened regardless. It was fated."

"So Mom doesn't know that AnTeen hated her? That she hated me?"

Penny shook her head. "There's enough ugliness in the world. We didn't think it was necessary to soil your mother with this bit of it."

"I always knew there was something evil about her," Adrian said.

Penny smiled humorlessly. "Not evil, Capo. Just bitter."

"Maybe she told Randi that I killed her beloved husband because she thought Randi would go berserk and off me all over again," he suggested.

"Maybe," Bellona opined. "But that's not going to happen."

"No. Randi's not going to kill anybody, but the news might've made her go a little berserk, regardless. Like I say, she's staring at the wall again. She's having trouble accepting everything."

"She'll come to terms with it eventually," Bellona said. "And if she doesn't, we'll just . . . care for her."

"A little madness in this family can be excused," Penny said.

FIFTY-SEVEN

So when Randi volunteered to tell Eileen of all the Byzantine intrigues and otherworldly events that had occurred over the last twenty years, Adrian and his aunts waited.

Daina knew enough: she knew that her son was back from the other side; she knew that there was no Leo. Daina knew that Randi had been acting a little odd for the last two days, since Adrian had revealed all to her. She also waited.

The truth was incomprehensible. If Randi spilled it, the family would just deny it. They'd twirl their fingers beside their temples, roll their eyes.

What's that you say, Mrs. Robinson? Daina thought. *Laugh about it, shout about it, when you've got to choose. Every way you look at it you lose . . .*

None of them believed that Randi would attempt to tell Eileen the truth. There'd be no benefit in it to her. Eileen would think she'd lost her mind. But if Randi *had* lost her mind . . .

They waited.

"Let's see," Randi began. "It wasn't long after you moved away. I'd broken up with my boyfriend. You remember Gil, Eileen?"

Eileen nodded. *The blondie, with the dark green eyes.*

"I was finally single, and Adrian finally saw the light." Randi glanced mildly at Leo, and continued to hold his gaze as she spoke. "He realized that I loved him, that I would always love him." She looked at Eileen and grinned conspiratorially. "One night . . . Leo was conceived."

Eileen was astonished. Her mouth fell open. *Randi* was Leo's mother! The shy, quiet girl that Eileen could never coax into a conversation, had achieved her fondest wish. To be with Adrian.

That was my fondest wish, too. And now it's too late.

Eileen recalled her earlier idea, that if Adrian was still alive, she'd like to talk to the woman that had brought his child into the world. Eileen reckoned that she'd been friends with Randi once . . .

But such a discussion would still be inappropriate. Adrian was dead, and talking about the love of her past might be painful to Randi. She'd never been a big talker, and it seemed to Eileen that Randi might not be all there anymore. A vacant light seemed to dance behind her eyes. Eileen wondered how long she'd been that way.

"Adrian was thrilled!" Randi continued. "He told me that the prospect of having a baby was the best thing that could ever happen to him, even if he lived two lifetimes."

Leo exchanged a glance with his Aunt Penny.

"Alas, Adrian was not fated to meet his son." Randi's words were sad, but her expression was not. It was as if she was recounting a melancholy fairy tale, not a tragedy that had actually occurred in her life.

It has *been almost twenty years,* Eileen thought. *Maybe her grief has passed.*

"A tractor-trailer rig ran the light, right down the street, at the corner of Jurupa and Van Buren. Adrian was coming home, turning left . . ." Randi clapped her hands together, and Eileen jumped. *"Wham!* He died instantly."

Daina was surprised at the ferocity of Randi's account. The details of Adrian's mythical car accident had never been manufactured, had never been fleshed out. But Randi had come up with a fairly gruesome story on the spot. She'd dispatched Adrian in one fell swoop. No ambulance ride, no life-saving techniques, no deathbed with grieving family gathered around. A tractor-trailer rig ran the light. He died instantly. Daina shivered.

"After Leo was born, Gil came back. He took pity on me, a single mother, all alone in the world. We got married, and he raised Leo as his own. He was a good man and I loved him very much. He passed away suddenly, in 2009."

Daina raised her eyebrows at this chapter in the fiction. The possibility that Gil could be dead had never crossed her mind. She had always figured that he'd just taken off for greener pastures. Daina looked at her aunts. Penny shrugged. *It's as good an explanation as any,* her expression said.

"I'm so sorry to hear that, Randi," Eileen said softly. She patted Randi's hand.

"Thank you." Randi shrugged. "I imagine that you came here to see Adrian, anyway. It's not like you knew any of the rest of them very well." Randi spoke as if the rest of them weren't sitting right there.

Eileen didn't know how to respond. It was true, but she hadn't expected Randi to lay it out so blatantly. She felt blindsided.

"I . . . I didn't really know Adrian all that well, either. I was just in the neighborhood . . ."

"I heard him mention you to his cousin Nick once, Eileen," Randi continued with a sly smile. "Adrian said he thought you had a little crush on him."

"Well . . ." Eileen was flustered. Now she looked like a nutcase, just dropping in unannounced, looking for some guy she'd had a thing for twenty years earlier.

"It's okay, dear," Bellona soothed. "Lots of young ladies liked Adrian."

Eileen smiled gratefully at her.

Then, inexplicably, Randi softly warbled an old Led Zeppelin tune: *"And if you say to me tomorrow, 'Oh, what fun it all would be!' Then what's to stop us, pretty baby, but what is and what should never be?"*

In the uncomfortable silence that followed – what does one say to someone who attempts to embarrass one, then busts out with ancient, non-sequitur rock and roll? – Leo smiled at Eileen. She had to remind herself: *he's not Adrian. He's about Adrian's age, the last time I saw him, but he's not Adrian.*

But then another line from the same Zeppelin tune played, unbidden, through Eileen's mind: *So if you wake up with the sunrise, and all your dreams are still as new, and happiness is what you need so bad . . . Girl, the answer lies with you . . .*

He's so gorgeous . . . Just like Adrian. Eileen broke eye contact with Leo, and looked down at the table. She didn't want to be admiring a kid – *Christ, he's younger than Carmen!*

But his eyes are so blue . . . Adrian's gone. There's no crime in just looking at him . . .

Leo again smiled when Eileen glanced back at him.

Daina cleared her throat. "Well, it doesn't matter why you came to see us, Eileen. We're glad you're here. We were just about to have brunch. Would you like to join us?"

"Yes," Eileen said immediately. "Thank you."

If Eileen stayed for brunch, she'd get to look at Leo for a while longer. Sure, he was just a kid, and she should be ashamed of herself – she *was* ashamed of herself – but what could it hurt?

206

FIFTY-EIGHT

Eileen enjoyed brunch with Adrian's family. Penny and Bellona served a delicious casserole: hash browns stuffed with bacon and onions and green peppers, smothered in cheddar cheese.

Conversation turned away from the sad past. The little group discussed things from recent history. They talked about the clean-up efforts from the BP oil spill, hoped nothing so awful would ever happen near California's coast.

Bellona said that it'd gotten tough to have brown skin in Arizona – there'd been talk of discriminatory new laws and racial profiling in their neighbor state to the east.

Daina mused that America was perhaps not the land of opportunity that it had once been. She mentioned some people's growing fear and hatred of Muslims, as evidenced by the protests that had occurred when there'd been talk of a mosque near the 9/11 site.

Penny commented that every faith had some extremists, some *crazies* – Eileen couldn't help but notice that she glanced at Randi when she said the word – but no faith should be judged on the fringe groups alone.

As they talked and dined, Eileen noticed that Leo helped his aunts and his grandmother at every turn. He brought out plates and silverware, hopped up and fetched anything that was found lacking at the table. He was obviously a good boy.

And good-looking, Eileen couldn't help but think, as she watched him carry the last of the dishes back into the house. When Eileen turned her attention back to the ladies, she found that Randi was staring at her with that same sly smile on her face. The expression unnerved Eileen a little bit – had she been looking at Leo a little too appreciatively? She'd just glanced after him as he crossed the deck. There was nothing wrong with that.

Eileen told herself that Randi was just a little off. She perceived that Leo's mother smiled slyly or frowned ponderously, seemingly for no reason, many times during brunch.

Leo helped his aunts bring out tea. While she was enjoying a cup, Eileen's phone beeped.

"That'll be Carmen," she said. "She's probably wondering where I've been."

"You'll have to bring her with you, the next time you visit, dear," Bellona said. "We'd love to see her."

"Definitely," Randi said. "I'm sure she and Leo would hit it off. They're about the same age. Leo will be nineteen in April, and you said that Carmen's just twenty-one."

Again that knowing smile. It seemed to Eileen that Randi put an unusual emphasis on the fact that her son was only nineteen. Then Eileen thought that perhaps it was her own guilty conscience – she had been rather staring at him, and he *was* only nineteen. *He looks so much like Adrian . . .*

Randi picked up her phone from the table. "What's your number, Eileen? We should have dinner sometime this week. I don't get to cook as much as I used to. Leo's always off somewhere with Angie."

"Angie and I broke up, Mom," Leo informed her. "Before Christmas."

"Well." Randi seemed a little confused that she didn't know this fact. "I never liked her, anyway." She smiled. "All the more reason for you to meet Eileen's daughter. We can all have dinner together."

"Carmen has a boyfriend," Eileen said quickly. She regretted her haste: Randi's smile widened.

"Bring him along, too."

Eileen gave Randi her cell number, and after a few more pleasantries with the other ladies, it was time for Eileen to take her leave. They invited her to come back and visit anytime.

Leo walked with her back down the hill to her car.

"It was so nice meeting you, Eileen," he said, after she'd gotten into it and put the key in the ignition.

"You, too, Leo." *You look so much like your dad. Poor Adrian . . . Poor me.*

"It would be great if you'd come back and visit them," he said, and nodded up the hill. "None of them ever get out much. They never go any farther than the market. Especially my mom. It would be nice for her to have a friend."

Eileen was touched. "Tell your mom to call me. I'd love to chat with her. I don't know anybody here anymore, either." *And if I buddy up to your mom, then I'll get to look at you . . .* Eileen pushed that thought away.

"I'll do that. Drive careful, now. Hope to see you soon."

Eileen turned her car around at the end of the cul-de-sac. Leo smiled and waved as she passed him.

FIFTY-NINE

Leo didn't have to make the suggestion that Randi call Eileen. Eileen had barely walked in the door to her mother's house when her phone rang.

"It was wonderful to see you again!" Randi chirped.

"You, too, Randi."

Eileen reflected that she was telling a little fib. It had actually been a little weird seeing Randi again, what with her odd smiles and uncomfortable outbursts. *But maybe they were only uncomfortable to me,* Eileen thought, *because I was leering at her son . . .*

Randi had hit the nail precisely on the head: Eileen had shown up out of the blue because she was looking for Adrian. She'd had a crush on him once. It was only uncomfortable because Randi had laid it all out so plainly in front of Adrian's mother and aunts. And his son. Eileen thought perhaps she was being unkind.

"Would you still like to come out for dinner? How about Friday?" The hope in her former housekeeper's voice decided Eileen. She *was* being unkind. There was no reason not to be friendly with Randi. Eileen had told Leo the truth: she didn't know anyone in Riverside anymore. Why not have dinner with Randi?

"Friday sounds great. What time?"

"Whenever you'd like. I'm here all day."

Eileen remembered Leo's words: *None of them ever get out much, especially my mom. It would be nice for her to have a friend.* She could be friends with Randi. Why not?

"How about six o'clock?" Eileen said. She figured she'd just leave straight from work.

"That sounds great. And be sure to bring Carmen."

"Carmen's going to be out of town next weekend. With her boyfriend. They're going to Las Vegas." Eileen frowned. She didn't care for Clint.

"Not to get married, I hope?" Randi said with a giggle.

"No. They're going to see The Blue Man Group."

"Carmen's smarter than we were, huh? She's too young to get married!"

Eileen found herself warming up to Randi. They had a lot in common. They'd both had their children young. *And we're both all alone. Allan's in jail – thank God! – and Randi's husband died. And Adrian died, too . . .*

"I'd like to think that Carmen isn't even considering marriage yet," she told Randi. "And I hope she doesn't ever consider marrying the one she's going with now."

"I know what you mean. Leo's girlfriend – Angie – she was a tramp. I didn't like her at all. I would've thought that he would've picked a nicer girl the first time. Someone quiet and shy, like he is." Randi paused. "But then . . . Well, Leo's changed a lot lately. He's not really . . . who he used to be."

"Clint hasn't changed Carmen, not yet," Eileen commiserated. "She's only been seeing him since we moved back to town. I guess he was the student assigned to show her around at UCR, and they just hit it off . . ."

Had Randi really said that the absent, un-met, allegedly trampy Angie was Leo's *first* girlfriend? Eileen found it hard to believe that a young man as attractive as Leo, someone that looked so much like Adrian, wouldn't have had lots of girlfriends. But his mother would know. Randi said that he was quiet, shy.

Eileen again felt guilty for so thoroughly noticing his attractiveness. *He's just a boy, for God's sake. Quiet, shy. I should be ashamed of myself. If he didn't look so much like Adrian, why . . . Why, I wouldn't even have noticed him . . .*

"I know a few spells," Randi was saying. "If you have anything that belongs to her boyfriend . . . An article of clothing, something like that. We can say a few words, and then maybe he won't be interested in Carmen anymore. Those kinds of charms never worked for me, but –"

"What?" Eileen hadn't been paying attention to Randi because she was too busy deriding herself for noticing Leo.

"Never mind. It's not important. I'll see you at six on Friday! I can't wait!"

"Me, too, Randi. See you then."

210

SIXTY

Eileen's dinner with Randi was delightful. The food was good: Randi made pork chops and mashed potatoes, cornbread, a green salad and ice tea. The conversation was light, blithe. Leo and Daina joined them for dinner, but then both left afterwards to pursue other activities. Daina invited Eileen to have lunch with her the next day, and Eileen said she'd be there.

After Randi's son and his grandmother departed, the two single mothers' conversation again turned to their children. Since they were at Randi's house, she had baby pictures on hand. She dragged out the past for Eileen to see, starting with a thin scrapbook of Urban Equinox photos.

Eileen's enjoyment of the old pictures of Adrian and his band was tempered by the memory that Adrian was no more. She scanned the pictures for the differences in appearance between him and his son that had to exist, but still found the resemblance uncanny. Adrian's face was a little thinner than Leo's, his eyes perhaps a darker shade of blue. But that might've been just the lighting in the photos.

The most striking difference between father and son was in the expression. Adrian was always smiling, in every picture, sometimes laughing. He was young, confident; he was good-looking, sexy, and he knew it. Adrian had the world by the ass, as Eileen's grandpa used to say: a vibrant, *aliveness* came from the old photos. Again, Eileen railed in her mind against the cruel, indifferent universe that had taken him away from Randi, from his son, from her.

Leo had his father's beautiful smile, but in the short time she'd known him, Eileen had noticed that he didn't show it as often as Adrian had. Leo had smiled at her a few times, and it'd been glorious, just like the few times Adrian had smiled at her, but Leo also had a watchful quality that Adrian had never possessed.

He's shy, just like his mother said. Again, Eileen felt guilty that she'd noticed Leo at all, that she continued to think about him.

"Leo looks so much like his father," Eileen commented to his mother, as Randi closed the band scrapbook and opened Leo's baby book.

"Yes, I thought that *you'd* notice that," Randi replied. She flashed that same sly, naughty smile at Eileen for a moment. Then it was gone.

"He always has reminded me of Adrian." Randi showed Eileen a picture of a blue-eyed, black-haired, newborn baby boy. "But in the last year or so . . ." Randi shook her head. "He really looks like Adrian these days."

In the next picture, Gil was holding his stepson. He smiled happily out across the years, and Eileen recalled that he'd been quite the looker himself, in a crafty, wolfish kind of way.

Like the gentlemen of legend, Eileen had once preferred blondes, but two things had broken her of that singular preference. She'd married a blonde that had turned out to be a shiftless, cruel, criminal monster. And she'd met black-haired Adrian Wilde, the best looking man she'd ever seen.

Eileen looked at a few more pictures of Gil holding baby Leo. He had been a cute blondie. He was no Adrian, but he hadn't been unattractive. She recalled that he'd had the most striking, dark green eyes. Eileen wondered how he'd died. She figured that Randi would get around to telling her eventually.

Eileen had hundreds of baby pictures of Carmen, thousands of pictures of her childhood, her school years, her adolescence. Randi's collection was similar: here was Leo taking a bath, here was Leo riding a pony, here was Leo hunting Easter eggs.

But oddly, after his kindergarten portrait, Randi seemed to have lost interest in recording the events of her son's life. There were one or two birthday parties, but that seemed to be all. After kindergarten, the only pictures Randi had kept of Leo were his school portraits, and those were still in the envelopes in which they'd come. The cellophane made an old-fashioned crinkly sound as Randi pulled a few of them out.

The walk through Leo's life was thereby truncated; there just weren't very many pictures. The last one was of him in his cap and gown from high school graduation, standing beside his grandmother. Daina looked pale, drawn, elderly. She offered a weak smile. Leo didn't smile at all. He looked very sad.

"His grandfather had passed the month before," Randi explained. "And Gil . . . Gil left us the same month."

"I'm so sorry," Eileen said again.

"The only thing that got me through it was Leo," Randi replied. She took the album from Eileen and put it back on the shelf with the one from the band. "And even then, I was depressed. I stayed in my room, in seclusion, for almost a year. And by then . . . My little boy had grown up.

"One day, he was just a child, and the next, he was . . . a different person. All of a sudden, he looked like just like Adrian, from the last time I'd seen him." Randi smiled faintly, and Eileen saw that vacant light flare in her eyes again, light blue, like the flame from a gas torch. "He'd let his hair grow long, started playing the guitar. He practices with Bobby and Nick, in Daina's garage. Just like the old days. Sometimes, when he sings, it seems like *he is Adrian.*"

Randi held Eileen's gaze for another moment. That strange, mad light in Randi's eyes made her guest uncomfortable. Eileen reckoned that Randi had had more than her share of tragedy: losing Adrian before his child was even born, then, later, losing her father-in-law and her second husband in the same month. Eileen's own life, which she'd always considered to be so rough, was mild in comparison. No one had ever died on her, except for her father, and she'd been just a kid then. The years had marched on, and Eileen's childhood grief had passed. She didn't remember Don Artus at all.

Eileen reflected that she might be a little crazy too, if she'd suffered the same losses as Randi.

Randi blinked and the haunted look was gone. Only a cheerful, pretty, forty-year-old woman remained. "Would you like some dessert?" she asked. "I just remembered. I made an apple pie."

SIXTY-ONE

The next day, Eileen's lunch with Daina started off on a somber note. The younger woman mentioned that Randi had told her that Daina's husband had passed, and Eileen offered her condolences.

A shadow crossed Daina's features. She thanked Eileen for her sympathies, then said, "Living without Ian . . . It's the greatest tragedy of my life." Daina blinked, as if surprised at her own words, and quickly added, "After losing my son, of course."

"I'm so sorry about that, too," Eileen said genuinely. She'd hardly known Adrian, but she'd loved him. Losing Adrian, without ever getting the chance to find him again – Eileen reflected that Adrian's now irrevocable absence was the greatest tragedy in *her* life.

Daina sighed. "I have my memories, and I have Leo to remind me of him." She sighed again. "But Ian . . . I miss Ian every day. He was the love of my life."

"Tell me about him, Daina." Eileen smiled kindly. "Tell me all about him – how you met, how you fell in love. I never had a love of my life." *Except for Adrian.* "Just two awful husbands." Eileen smiled to communicate that she was over both of them.

Daina also smiled. "It's really kind of a funny story. I'd been dating Ian's cousin Will, and my best friend, Nadine, she was dating Will's twin brother, Rob."

Daina frowned. *My best friend . . .* She hadn't seen her one-time best friend since Ian's funeral. Nadine hadn't visited, hadn't even called. *But then again, we were really only close as children . . . Once I met Ian, Nadine drifted away . . .*

Daina looked at Eileen, realized that she was waiting for her to continue. "I'd heard Rob and Will talk about *Cousin Ian*, heard them say that he was a ladies' man." Daina grinned and Eileen could see the beautiful young girl that she'd once been.

"I heard that he'd taught Nadine to waterski, and she and Rob went skiing with him and his girlfriend all the time. But I'd never met him. Here's the funny part. I broke up with Will – actually, he broke up with me – and he started going with Ian's girlfriend. Marta. They'd broken up, too.

"Eventually, Will and Marta would get married . . . But I'm getting ahead of myself. All the years run together after a while, when you're as old as I am." Daina smiled again. She didn't seem old at all at the moment.

"Nadine threw a Hallowe'en party, right here in this house. That was the night I met Ian. He was wearing this gladiator costume . . . It was love at first sight. For both of us."

Daina told Eileen the history of her life with her husband. Eileen found the story to be charming – it was enjoyable to hear all the cute details about what a happy marriage was like.

Eileen had never been much of a romantic. She'd married in haste and repented in leisure. Twice. Reality for Eileen was that men were nothing to write home about. The two that she'd known . . . Neither had been the love of Eileen's life. Not by a long stretch.

The love of Eileen's life had only been a fantasy, someone she'd barely even known. The love of Eileen's life had been Daina's son. And all the hopes of that were now gone. The love of Eileen's life would now never be. Adrian was gone, as permanently as was his father.

But unlike Eileen, Daina had been allowed to live her life with the man she'd loved from the first moment she met him. Eileen enjoyed listening to Daina tell their story.

SIXTY-TWO

Eileen began to visit the ladies of Parcay Street on a regular basis. Despite the loss of her lifetime love and partner, Daina was always chipper and upbeat. Eileen learned that Daina believed that she'd see Ian again, on the other side, in another life. Eileen admired her belief, her faith. She wished that she could believe in one thing in this world that could bring her as much comfort as Daina's belief did. She wished that she could believe that she'd see Adrian again, in another life.

Eileen didn't believe that, but she did get to see Leo when she visited with his grandmother, and that was sufficient for *this* life. He'd always smile at her, pause and ask her how she was. Surely, Eileen enjoyed her visits with Daina, and with the old ladies, too. They always had tea or a little snack for Eileen, and they never failed to make her laugh with funny stories. Sometimes the stories were even a little risqué – tales of loves and lovers from their long-ago, wild youths.

But when Eileen was honest with herself, she had to admit that the main reason she visited was to see Leo. He was just a boy, but Eileen had discovered that she *needed* to see his shy smile, at least a couple of times a week.

Inexplicably, Daina and her aunts seemed to accept this. To Eileen's amazement, they even seemed to encourage it. If Leo was not present when she arrived, one of them would always call him, and he'd come on up the hill. They'd insist that he have a seat, stay and visit. Eileen flattered herself that Leo didn't take much coaxing – it seemed that he enjoyed chatting with her almost as much as she enjoyed seeing him.

"I think Leo has a little bit of a crush on you, dear," Bellona even said once, after the young man had departed.

"That's just silly . . ." Eileen blushed. *What would people say? I'm old enough to be his mother. He's younger than my daughter!*

"Stranger things have happened," Penny observed with a rare smile.

Eileen sought to divert the conversation away from any preposterous innuendoes concerning herself and Leo. "It's such a shame that he never got to meet his father. He looks so much like him."

"He was such a shy little boy –" Daina began.

"That's what Randi said."

"But in the last couple of years, we've seen Adrian *come out in him,* so to speak." Daina smiled at her aunts and they smiled back at her.

"Since his stepfather . . . died," Bellona said. "He was rather a bully, and –"

"Really?" Eileen said in surprise. "I only met him once. Randi said –"

"Randi loved him, poor child. I'm sure that she still misses him terribly." Bellona paused significantly, mentioning without words that perhaps it was Randi's lingering grief at the loss of her husband that made her seem not quite all there, at times. "But to tell you the truth, none of the rest of us miss him. He was rather a beast to Leo, and since he's been gone, Leo has become a more outgoing, happy young man."

"He plays music with his cousins." Daina said. "Remember I told you about Will and Marta, Eileen?" Eileen nodded. "Their sons. Bobby and Nick. They taught Leo how to play the guitar, and now Leo sings for their band instead of Adrian."

"Sometimes it's just like having Adrian back." Randi stepped onto the deck. "Hi, Eileen. Leo told me that you were here."

"I was going to come down and see you in a little bit," Eileen explained.

"I've saved you the trip," Randi replied with a smile.

It was another tiny fib on Eileen's part. She enjoyed the older women's company, even when Leo wasn't around, but she probably wouldn't have gone to see Randi, if she could help it.

It wasn't that Eileen didn't like Randi. She would have dinner with her whenever she'd ask. It was just that Randi was odd, moody. She said outrageous things sometimes, things that made Eileen uncomfortable, because they were true.

"I've noticed you looking at Leo," Randi said one evening, as she cleared away the dinner dishes.

Eileen didn't know how to respond to the comment. Should she deny it? Admit it? Share a little joke with the kid's mother about how cute he was? How desirable, even to a forty-year-old woman?

Eileen didn't think so. She opened her mouth to say something, *anything,* because Randi's remark demanded an answer. But Eileen had nothing. She closed her mouth again and remained silent.

"It's okay," Randi allowed, as if Eileen had accidently dropped a few crumbs on the carpet. "I know it's because he looks so much like Adrian."

Eileen nodded, but still didn't speak. If she agreed that Leo looked like Adrian, then that would mean she was admitting to *looking* at him, Randi's initial supposition. Eileen wasn't going to admit that, not to his slightly off-center mother. It was just something that she didn't want to discuss with Leo's *mother.*

"I know how it is, Eileen." Again, that conspiratorial smile, totally inappropriate. "Well, actually, I don't know personally. I'm through with all that . . ."

All what? Eileen thought apprehensively.

"I knew a woman once. She had an affair with a younger man. She said that he was attractive and attentive, and she was lonely, just like you."

"I'm not lonely, Randi. I have Carmen, and my mother . . . And you."

"But it's not the same thing, is it? I used to dream of Adrian . . ."

Randi dreamed of Adrian no longer. She still had trouble falling asleep, because sometimes the reality of Adrian's return, the idea that he'd murdered Gil . . . Sometimes these thoughts tumbled over and over in her mind until she thought she'd scream. But she dreamed of Adrian no more. She'd gone through five or six different sleeping pills with Doctor Samuel, until they found one that knocked her out soundly. If Randi dreamed at all – of Adrian or otherwise – she no longer remembered her dreams in the morning.

"This woman told me that the attentions of a friendly young man, sometimes they *allow one's morality to be compromised.* That's how she put it."

Denial leapt immediately to Eileen's lips. "Randi, I'm not interested in Leo. I would never –"

"I'm just letting you know that he's not as shy as he used to be. These days, it's all an act."

"I'm not –"

"I just wouldn't want you to start anything that you're not sure about, Eileen. And then be surprised when Leo finishes it for you." Randi's smile was practically a leer.

Then she blinked and the expression was gone. "I see your glass is almost empty. Would you like some more iced tea?"

"Yes . . . Please. Thank you."

It was just this kind of embarrassing exchange that made Eileen not want to visit Randi. She didn't always say inappropriate things – whole evenings had passed without Eileen ever feeling uncomfortable. But when Randi said something unsuitable, it was always in relation to her son, and Eileen's attraction to him.

SIXTY-THREE

"Where are you going, Mom?" Carmen asked.

Eileen was humming to herself. Carmen had noticed a lot of that lately. Humming, smiling. If she didn't know better, Carmen would've thought that her mother had a secret boyfriend.

"I'm just going out to have dinner with Daina and her aunts."

Carmen knew that Daina was that guy's mom, the one that Eileen had had the crush on, all those years ago. Carmen had come home the day after New Year's to find her mother sitting in the living room, in the dark, crying.

Carmen had held Eileen while she cried it out. She was shocked at her mother's complete, abject grief. She couldn't understand how Eileen could be so upset about someone that she hadn't seen in twenty years. Eileen said he'd been dead for all that time, so how could she be so broken up about it?

"I loved him, Carmen!" Eileen had sobbed. "And now I'll never see him again!"

But you haven't seen him . . .

Carmen didn't understand how her mother could so deeply feel the loss of someone she'd never really known. But her mom said she'd loved the guy, and Carmen felt pity for her sadness.

Carmen had never been anything but ambivalent about the idea of love. She was sure that her father had loved her mother, but when things didn't work out, that love had turned into the most virulent hatred. Carmen wasn't sure she wanted to feel anything like that. She'd liked a lot of guys; she liked Clint just fine. But if he didn't call her tomorrow, she wouldn't be too broken up about it. Carmen didn't love Clint. She'd never been in love.

After the initial blow of that guy's death, Carmen's mom had started visiting with *his* mom and her aunts. In the wake of tragedy, she'd found new friends. She went back to being cheerful again.

"Well, you have fun," Carmen said.

"You'll have to come with me sometime," Eileen said. "They're very nice ladies."

"I'll be sure to do that."

The idea of hanging out with a bunch of old women appealed to Carmen not at all. She loved her grandma and her mother, and would listen patiently to their stories of the past. She figured she owed them that. But old strangers' stories . . .

Carmen intended to avoid dinner as long as possible.

SIXTY-FOUR

As she drove out to Parcay Street, Eileen stopped humming and asked herself why she'd still failed to mention Adrian's son (or Randi, for that matter) to her daughter. *It just slipped my mind* was a bald-faced lie. In the four months since she'd met him, Leo had been foremost in her mind, just like his father had been, once upon a time.

I don't think about him in exactly the same way, Eileen told herself. *I don't think about . . .*

But maybe she did, a little. It was a guilty, secret fantasy. She'd never act on it, not in a million years. He was just a boy, a shy, innocent boy. Nineteen, today.

That was why Eileen was humming. Penny and Bellona were throwing a surprise birthday party for Leo, and Randi had invited her to it. Eileen had just stopped home for a moment after work to freshen up before heading out for the festivities.

Why haven't I mentioned him to Carmen? she asked herself again. They were close in age, just like Randi had said. *She's far closer to his age than I am. But Carmen already has a boyfriend. She wouldn't be interested in Leo, no matter how cute he is.*

Eileen pushed the whole train of thought from her mind, because she didn't want to admit to herself that maybe Carmen might be interested in Leo. He was certainly better looking than Clint, and maybe the thought of Carmen dating Leo didn't sit too well in Eileen's mind. But that was all ridiculous. Carmen, and Leo, too, could date whomever they chose. It surely wasn't any of Eileen's business.

She told herself that there was nothing untoward about her *feelings* for Leo. *That's just crazy. I don't have any feelings for him. I just like to look at him.*

Sometimes, Eileen would glance at Leo and find that he was already looking at her. He'd smile at her then, his blue eyes friendly, guileless. Innocent. He was beautiful. Eileen would smile back at him.

Then she'd feel guilty for smiling at a nineteen-year-old *boy,* and she would look away. She'd join in the conversation around the dinner table again, then after a while, her gaze would once again be drawn back to Adrian's son. *It's not like he's a child,* she'd think. *He's nineteen, an adult . . .*

Eileen would reflect that she was certainly an adult when she was nineteen. She was married, had a baby. Eileen had never noticed men her own age when she was nineteen. She'd considered herself grown, superior to them in experience, older than them in worldliness. Eileen remembered thinking that Randi was just a kid, even though they were the same age, because Randi didn't have the same responsibilities that Eileen had. *Randi got them all soon enough, however . . .*

Eileen had always preferred older men. She'd always thought that they knew what they were doing more than her peers, that they were more in control of their lives. Through two marriages to men older than herself, Eileen had learned that that was all an illusion. If you wanted stability in your life, *you* had to have control, not some man. You had to do things for yourself, not abdicate the helm to someone else.

Eileen told herself that she liked to look at Leo because she'd never looked twice at a young man when she was young. *Except for Adrian.* Eileen was in awe of Leo's beauty, his vibrant, healthy youth. He was sexy, like his father had been, just because he was young.

Then guilt would strike her again. Despite what Randi had said about him – *he's not as shy as he used to be; these days, it's all an act* – Eileen didn't believe it. Adrian had been young and beautiful when she'd known him, like Leo was now, but Adrian hadn't been shy. He'd kissed her. They'd been about to commit adultery, whereas Leo had only had one girlfriend, and for some reason unfathomable to Eileen, she'd dumped him. Maybe it was because he *was* shy. These young girls today . . . They surely weren't shy.

Leo had no idea of the things she thought about him, not a clue, and Eileen felt like a dirty old woman for thinking them. But she couldn't help herself. He looked so much like Adrian, and Adrian hadn't been shy . . .

222

SIXTY-FIVE

The cover story for the surprise party: Eileen was meeting Randi and Leo at their house, then the three of them were scheduled to go up the hill and have dinner with Penny and Bellona. It was 7:30, April – the sun had already set as they walked up the path. The houselights were on when they climbed the steps, but the deck was dark. When Leo stepped onto it, someone inside turned on the floods, and a small group of people yelled, "Surprise!"

Leo was entirely, utterly surprised. Eileen thought he looked positively dumbfounded.

"Happy birthday, son!" Randi said, and gave him a little pat on the shoulder. Eileen thought it was odd that she didn't hug him.

"That's right. I guess it is my birthday," Leo said.

You're nineteen, Nick's voice said in his head. *Still not old enough to buy a drink.*

There was a short whine a feedback, and then the electric guitar version of *Happy Birthday* began. Eileen looked across the deck. There was Penny and Bellona and Daina and another dark-haired woman that Eileen didn't know. They'd stepped aside to reveal a band.

The small crowd sang *Happy Birthday,* then Randi and Daina and her aunts went into the house to get the cake. Leo introduced Eileen to those that remained.

"This is my Aunt Lily, Eileen," he said of the dark-haired woman. She was about fifty, Eileen reckoned. Her black hair was streaked elegantly with white, and she had luminous green eyes. She was striking in a witchy, Lily Munster kind of way.

"So nice to meet you," Lily said to Eileen, then promptly ignored her. She smiled craftily at the birthday boy. "It's been *so long* since I've seen you . . . *Leo.* You look *exceptional,* as always. How has fate been treating you?"

"Not as well as it's been treating you," he said and gave her a luxuriant hug. "You look lovely."

"It's all the clean living," she said, and kissed Leo's cheek. "Many happy returns." Now she looked at Eileen. "Nice meeting you," she said again. "I'll just go help the other ladies." Aunt Lily glided across the deck. She turned once and winked at Leo, then continued on into the house.

"This is my cousin Bobby, and his wife, Tracy. This is my friend, Eileen."

The redheaded bass player put his guitar pick in his mouth and shook hands with Eileen. The drummer nodded at her from behind the kit. Bobby turned to say something to his wife, and Leo introduced Eileen to the other guitar player.

"Did you ever meet Eileen, Nick? She used to live across the street. She was Allan Coleman's wife."

Nick looked at his cousin in astonishment. No, he'd never met Eileen, and Adrian knew it. But he'd heard enough about her.

"Hod dayum, Nick!" Adrian had told him. "The heat comes off of her like a brushfire." He'd held his hands out to imaginary flames, as if to warm them. "She doesn't even try to hide it. Her ol' man – *I haven't failed to notice that Eileen has taken a shine to you – what do you intend to do about that?"*

"What did you say?"

"I told him the same thing I told Gil. I'm not interested in someone else's woman. But, sheesh, Nick!" Adrian had offered his trademark killer smile. "I'm never going over there again, if I can help it. She might jump me. I don't think she'd take no for an answer."

And they'd laughed about it then, fifteen-year-old Nick, who'd barely even kissed a girl, and his twenty-year-old cousin, who had *a way with the ladies.*

Then the house across the street had been sold, empty. Adrian had moved in, then Adrian had died. Nick had never again thought about the married woman that had once had such a hot yen for his cousin.

He peered at her appraisingly now. She was beautiful, with darkish brown hair and enormous, sparkling hazel eyes. She was a few years older than Nick, just the way he liked his women. Older, calmer. Eileen was Randi's age. Adrian's age, had he lived.

"No, we never met," Eileen said, and smiled at him.

"I'm Nick Wilde," he told her. He gestured at the bass player, still talking to his wife. "Bobby's my brother. Leo's my cousin."

Nick thought that Eileen had a lovely smile. She offered her hand and he shook it. It was soft and warm, and he thought that she let it linger in his for a moment.

She was *Allan Coleman's wife* . . . Nick surreptitiously glanced at her left hand. *No wedding ring.* He flipped the switch on the ol' Wilde charm. "What brings you back to the old neighborhood?"

"She was looking for Adrian." Randi had returned from inside. She stared unwaveringly at Nick, and one corner of her mouth

224

crooked up in half a smile. "Eileen and I used to be friends, in the old days. Now we're friends again."

Randi gave Eileen a little hug. *She didn't hug her son, but she hugs me,* Eileen thought. *She's so strange . . .*

"Eileen comes out to visit us all the time," Randi continued. "We're like one big, happy family. Me and Eileen and Leo . . ."

At this odd statement, Nick glanced at his cousin in surprise. Leo smiled blankly at him. Nick noticed that Randi's own smile had grown into a smug grin. Finally, Nick looked again at Eileen. She was smiling at Leo. *Fondly.*

Well, I be a son of a bitch! Nick thought. *But, no, she couldn't be thinking . . . Just because he looks like Adrian . . . She's old enough to be his mother.* Nick pushed the ridiculous thought aside.

"Well, I'm part of the family, too." Eileen smiled at Nick when he said so, and he felt a spurt of warmth flood through him. "Welcome."

"Thank you, Nick. You're all so nice."

"Shall we light this candle?" Leo said. He reached for a black and yellow guitar, sitting on a stand next to the microphone.

"No music yet," Randi said. "That's why I came back out here. Cake and ice cream first."

The cake was on the little table, ablaze with nineteen candles. Leo took a deep breath and blew them all out. His guests applauded.

What did you wish for, Cuz?

Adrian watched Nick glance at Eileen, then back again.

A long and happy life, my brutha. I have no idea what you're talking about.

"Happy birthday, Leo!" Eileen gave him a quick hug. She was just being friendly, congratulatory. It was his birthday, after all.

No idea at all. Adrian winked at his cousin.

To Eileen's secret delight, Leo hugged her back. *His aunts say he's got a little crush on me . . . I wonder what he wished for?*

Eileen knew what she would've wished for. *But that's just crazy. He's shy, he's just a boy . . .*

Eileen at last admitted to herself that she might have a little bit of a crush on Leo. *Adrian's son . .*

SIXTY-SIX

They all had cake and ice cream, chatted, congratulated Leo on his nineteen years of life.

Adrian was bored. He wasn't Leo and he wasn't a shy and inexperienced nineteen, no matter how necessary it was to pretend to be so. He could read Eileen's mind. She was older now, so she was in control of herself enough to mostly hide it in her expression, but she couldn't hide it in her thoughts. She was thinking wild, wholly inappropriate thoughts about Leo, whom she believed to be innocent and uncorrupted. Adrian discovered that he liked that.

"Come on," he said to Nick. "I'm gonna be fat by the time I'm twenty, if I eat any more cake. Let's play."

Leo leapt up gracefully. Eileen thought he'd never be fat. He was too energetic, too alive . . .

Lily rolled her eyes. "Your music . . . It's a little young for me." Again she winked at Leo.

Randi snorted. "All they play are oldies."

"Still . . . Ladies? Shall we retire inside? Allow the young people their fun?"

The only one here who's young is Leo, Eileen thought. *The rest of us . . . We'll never see young again.* Although Nick was a little bit younger than her. He had dark red hair and beautiful, light green eyes. He smiled at her and Eileen smiled back. *He's cute.*

"Come on, Nick," Leo said again, and the little moment that Nick and Eileen had shared was gone.

Nick arose and followed his cousin, and Bobby and Tracy. Penny and Bellona, Randi, Daina and Lily beat a quick retreat into house.

"What's the name of this band?" Eileen smiled at Leo, at Nick, as they picked up their guitars. They smiled back.

"Oh, my God! A fan!" Bobby said. "We haven't had any fans in a long time."

"More like just a spectator," Nick said and grinned at Eileen. "She hasn't heard us yet."

"We're called Urban Equinox," Leo breathed into the mike. "And thanks for the audition."

"Clever," Eileen commented.

She was happy. Here was Nick, smiling at her. She found Nick attractive. She liked him, she really did . . . But Leo was smiling at her, too, and she found Leo *exceedingly* attractive, even though she knew that she shouldn't.

"But it's gonna be a minute," Leo said.

Nick rolled his eyes. *Goddamn it, Cuz! You rush me over here . . .* "Now what?"

"One, two, three, four," Leo counted the strings on his guitar. "Shit. Did you guys drop this bringing it up here? Two broken strings!"

"I'd like to drop it," Nick said, sotto voce, to Eileen. "Isn't that the ugliest guitar you've ever seen? He's, uh, his *dad* was a big Eddie Van Halen fan. But I think that's a poor excuse to have a hideous guitar."

"Let's go look in the garage," Bobby suggested. "If you've got another set, that's where they're gonna be."

"We'll be right back, Eileen," Leo said. He and Bobby set down their instruments, crossed the deck, and hurried down the steps.

Nick looked pointedly at his sister-in-law, still perched behind her drum kit. Tracy was used to interpreting unspoken messages from men named Wilde, and she understood Nick's immediately, clearly. He wanted to be alone with Eileen.

"I'll just go see what Randi's doing," she said, standing and laying her sticks down on the seat. "Maybe have another piece of cake."

Nick smiled gratefully at her. Once she went into the house, he said to Eileen, "So were you and Adrian close?"

Eileen looked at him curiously. What had Randi said, with her ribald smile? *I heard Adrian mention you to his cousin Nick once. He said he thought you had a little crush on him.*

So Adrian's cousin already knew how close Eileen had not been with Adrian. Was he testing her? Eileen realized that maybe she was being a little paranoid. It was a result of Randi's statements about her *looking* at Leo; it was an outgrowth of her own guilty conscience.

Eileen and Nick had never met. He probably didn't remember a comment Adrian had made about some woman that'd liked him, twenty years ago.

"No," she told Nick. "We weren't close at all. I barely even knew him."

Right, Nick thought. *That's why you just showed up out of the blue.* This kind of deceit was why he didn't trust women. *But on the other hand, what do I expect her to say? 'I barely even knew him, but I sincerely wanted to do him, twenty years ago?'*

227

For some reason, Eileen felt that she could be honest with Nick. Up to a point, of course. "My daughter showed me a picture of some singer on the internet. Joshua Martin? Have you heard of him?"

Nick nodded. "He's pretty good, actually. He plays a Stratocaster, not unlike mine." Nick gestured at his guitar.

"I haven't heard him," Eileen admitted. "My daughter just showed me his picture. And he reminded me of Adrian. I just moved back to town a few months ago, so I decided to look Adrian up, see if he still lived here." Eileen didn't feel it necessary to tell Nick about the internet search either. "I knocked on Daina's door. When Leo answered, I thought he was Adrian."

I bet you did, Nick thought. *How impossibly amazed would you be if I told you that Leo is Adrian? That he knows you're here because he reminds you of his dad, because he remembers how much you liked his dad? Because he is his dad?*

"I was sorry to hear that Adrian was gone. Did they ever charge the guy?"

Nick's mouth fell open. *"What?"*

"Randi said that a tractor trailer ran the light down the street and hit Adrian's car. I was just wondering if he was charged in any way. Vehicular homicide, or something like that."

Nick stared incredulously at Eileen. It took him a moment to put two and two together, but it finally gelled for him. The mythical car accident. The story that the family had told Leo, when he'd asked about what had happened to his father.

But there'd never been any details. Randi must've just made something up. Nick realized that Eileen was waiting for his reply. He shook his head. "I don't know. I never heard."

Nick seemed rattled for a moment, and Eileen decided that perhaps she'd been too direct in her question about Adrian's accident. "It's just so sad –"

"What else did Randi tell you?" Nick interrupted.

It could be absolutely anything these days, he thought. It was just as Adrian had said: Randi didn't seem to be taking the new reality well. She blurted out things better left unsaid. She had a wild, crazy look to her sometimes. *But at least she's not depressed any more . . .*

"Randi's had a rough life, hasn't she?"

Has she? Nick nodded slowly, uncertainly.

228

"She lost Adrian. Then, she told me that she also lost her second husband. I always thought that I'd had a rough life, but hers has been so sad."

Nick waited for Eileen to commiserate with him about the tragic, awful, horrible manner of Gil's death – whatever it was that Randi had told her – but when she didn't comment further, Nick realized that perhaps Randi hadn't gotten around to manufacturing that detail yet.

Nick changed the subject. "I don't believe you've had a rough life," he said with a smile and a look of faux suspicion. "You're too pretty."

Eileen liked the compliment. It wasn't the best line she'd ever heard, but she'd not failed to notice that Nick wasn't wearing a wedding ring, and she figured that Nick was probably used to picking up younger women that might actually believe they were pretty, just because the attractive, green-eyed redhead told them that he thought so.

It's not the compliment itself that I like so much, Eileen thought. *I just like it because* he *said it.*

She sighed, didn't acknowledge Nick's praise except with a little smile. "My life wasn't rough like Randi's. I've just been through two bad marriages. The second one ended two years ago." Eileen smiled ruefully. "I've always been what you call *unlucky in love,* I guess."

Maybe your luck's about to change, Nick thought. He opened his mouth to say just that – Nicholas Franklin Wilde surely wasn't shy – when Leo vaulted over the closed gate at the top of the steps. Bobby, who was not nineteen, just today, opened it behind him, a little out of breath.

Nick heard Adrian's voice in his head: *What'cha doin', Cuz?*

Leo said, "Where's my drummer?"

"She's in the house. Eating cake." *Your timing sucks, my brutha.*

Timing's a function of fate, Cuz. You can't blame me for a bad entrance. I am but a pawn . . .

"Go get her, will ya, Bobby?" Leo said. "I'm sure Eileen can't wait to hear us play."

He picked up his guitar – Nick was right, it was ugly – and carried it across the deck. He sat on the bench and quickly replaced the broken strings. Eileen was surprised that he didn't ask for guidance from his cousin – Randi had indicated that Leo hadn't been playing the guitar for very long. But on the other hand, Eileen didn't know anything about guitars. Maybe changing the strings was one of the first things one learned.

Leo came back across the deck, plugged the Charvel into its amp and turned it on. He strummed a few notes, made one or two adjustments, strummed again. He smiled at Nick.

"Perfect." Nick smiled back at him.

I've been doing this for a minute, Cuz.

You had a rather long interruption. Seventeen years.

It's like riding a bicycle. You never forget.

Unless you're someone else in the meantime . . .

Nick said to Eileen, "The kid's a prodigy."

The kid's something, that's for sure, Eileen thought. She smiled at Leo.

Bobby returned from the house, holding hands with his wife. Eileen thought that was cute. "Let's do this. Can't keep our new fan waiting any longer."

Tracy sat behind her drums, and Bobby and Nick picked up their instruments. They looked at Leo, and he smiled back at them.

"What should we begin with?"

Nick played the intro to *Back in Black.*

Leo grinned. "Too metal." But before the rest of the band could start *Pretty Woman,* the next part-of-a-song in their shtick, Leo said, "I'm thinking we oughta change things up a little bit." He turned around and looked at his drummer. "Remember your moment of rebellion, Trace? *I wanna sing, too,* you said. *I wanna be bad.* And you had the perfect song. Made Bobby blush. Remember *Never Say Never?"*

Tracy might've blushed herself, but it was dim back there behind the drums, so Eileen wasn't sure. "Christ, Leo," Tracy said.

"You remember it though? Bobby? Nick?"

The bassist and his brother nodded.

"Trace?"

"Yeah, I remember it. But I'm not gonna sing it."

"That's okay." Leo turned around and looked innocuously at Eileen. "I'll sing it."

"If you insist," Tracy said.

They began the old new wave tune, with all its exuberant drums and chugging guitars. Leo mumbled through the first verse. Apparently he didn't remember it as well as he thought he did.

Remember it? Eileen said to herself. *Hell, I barely remember it. It must've been from . . . I couldn't've been more than eleven or twelve . . . 1982, maybe? I remember it because I didn't want my mom to hear it. I thought that the lyrics were so dirty . . . cool, though. Tracy must've thought so, too, to want to sing such a nasty old song . . . But Leo . . . 1982 was ten years before he was even born. No wonder he doesn't know all the words.*

Leo came in on the line that went *Sunsuit girls must be discreet.* He mumbled through the next verse, too, then busted out with the chorus, grinning at Eileen:

> *"I might like you better if we slept together*
> *I might like you better if we slept together*
> *I might like you better if we slept together*
> *There's somethin' in your eyes that says maybe*
> *That's never, never say never . . ."*

They played the bridge and Nick looked up to see that Eileen had a little surprised smile on her face. But she wasn't smiling at him. She was smiling at Leo. Nick's own smile evaporated.

Leo flubbed the next verse. *Never Say Never* had indeed been Tracy's protest song, and Urban Equinox had played it only a few times. Bobby had not appreciated the way the guys in the audience had grinned at his beloved when she stridently sang, *I might like you better if we slept together.*

The song had been old already when Tracy had dug it up from God-only-knew where, during her brief, almost-punk, *I wanna sing, too,* girl-power phase. She'd also unearthed and insisted that the band learn Joan Jett's *Bad Reputation.*

Nick had always thought the lines, *And everyone can say what they wanna to say, it never gets better, anyway; so why should I care about a bad reputation, anyway?* applied more to his smart-ass self, or Adrian-the-ladies-man, than they did to Tracy.

She'd looked wild and reckless in the old days – a girl drummer! *How Mom freaked out when Bobby brought her home, holding her hand!*

But Tracy had never been wild, and certainly never reckless. She'd only ever had eyes for Bobby. But just like Bobby thought a musician should have an outrageous hairdo, and Adrian wanted to be Eddie Van Halen, Tracy had wanted to project a bad-girl, rock star image. She'd wanted people to think she was a tough chick. She was

231

a drummer, after all. So she'd made them play a couple of bad-girl songs.

Even though it was clear that Adrian didn't remember the verses to the obscure old tune, Nick didn't fail to notice that he was right on time with the chorus again. Nick also noticed that Eileen smiled inquisitively at him when he sang, *I might like you better if we slept together; there's somethin' in your eyes that says maybe, that's never, never say never.*

Eileen had said she'd had a rough life. She'd had a baby early, like Randi. She'd been married to that fat thief once, and then she'd told Nick that she was divorced again now, after a second bad marriage. Apparently, she didn't have any prospects, if she was telling him all this. *Unlucky in love.*

So Nick was not surprised to see the appreciation in Eileen's eyes for the song's next sentiment: *Old couple walks by, as ugly as sin, but he's got her, she's got him . . .*

Leo sang the chorus again, and then abruptly stopped playing. The band jangled to a stop. Everyone laughed but Nick.

Adrian had never been much for playing entire songs anyway, *and Leo didn't have to,* Nick thought furiously. *Not this time. He communicated what he wanted to Eileen. He's toying with her. The son of a bitch.*

He's gonna do it to me again.

SIXTY-SEVEN

Eileen thoroughly enjoyed Leo Wilde's surprise nineteenth birthday party.

She was thrilled when he sang that impish old song to her; it was like he could read her mind. *I'd* definitely *like you better if we slept together, you flawless, gorgeous young thing!*

Eileen's mind swung madly between elation and guilt: Leo was flirting with her; Leo was younger than her daughter. She felt relieved, therefore, when after their set, Leo once again offered her only that shy, blank, friendly smile. He wasn't flirting with her anymore. Perhaps she'd only imagined it, in the first place. Perhaps it'd been only depraved wishful thinking. Leo had only seemed to be worldly, *knowing* – just like Adrian – while he was holding his father's guitar. Now, he was just shy, artless Leo again.

Eileen suddenly understood the universal appeal of musicians. It was the beat that the young girls liked so much, the wicked lyrics. They just transferred all those warm feelings onto the singer . . . Leo wasn't necessarily flirting with her. He'd just sang an inescapably flirty song. But it was sure fun to think about.

Eileen also enjoyed being around Nick. He was funny and clever and attentive, just self-deprecating enough for her to know that he was actually confident. He was cute. He was a few years younger than her, but not so young that anyone would bat an eyelash if they were to become involved. Not like Leo. *Christ, the scandal!*

They sat around on the deck in the flood-lit dark and talked, then Urban Equinox played another set. Eileen watched Leo sing, watched Nick play the guitar.

Just like Randi had said, they played mostly oldies. Eileen knew the lyrics to a million old songs. She'd listened to the radio a lot in her life, because she'd never gotten out much after high school. She recognized everything that they played, except for their own compositions. Eileen supposed that the band was good, but she didn't know much about the nuts and bolts of playing music, or about musicians.

Eileen turned to Randi to ask her if it'd been Adrian that had written the band's songs, the ones she didn't recognize. She was going to say that Leo seemed to know all of the unfamiliar ones that Nick suggested that they play.

Randi was staring at the table in front of her, her eyes big and round. She looked over at Eileen when she said her name, and Eileen saw that the vacant blue light was back. Randi was panting a little bit. Alarmed, Eileen thought she might be having some kind of a panic attack.

"What's wrong, Randi?"

"You seem to like watching Leo sing," Randi stated.

Eileen was again flustered – she *did* enjoy watching Leo sing, probably entirely too much. She said, "They're very good." *Leo, especially.*

"I love their music," Bellona confessed. She glanced mildly at Randi, repeated Eileen's sentiment. "Are you okay, dear?"

"I was just thinking about the old days. Eileen and . . . Adrian . . ." Randi stared at Eileen for a moment.

She looks like a crazy person, Eileen thought. *What about me and Adrian? There was no me and Adrian.*

"I don't feel very good." Randi laughed nervously. "Too much cake, maybe. I think maybe I should go lie down." She stood up suddenly, knocking over a glass with her elbow. It shattered on the deck. The band stopped.

Randi locked eyes with Leo. "Happy birthday, *son,*" she called to him. "Sorry to abandon you, but you're a big boy. I feel a little dizzy. I'm going to go back home."

"Okay," Leo said neutrally.

Eileen noticed that he made no move to cross the deck to see to his mother. *Maybe he's used to it. Maybe this happens all the time.*

Randi took a few steps toward the gate to the staircase, then she paused, leaned against the railing, put a hand to her brow.

"I'll go with you, Randi." Eileen volunteered, because no one else had offered. Randi had obviously taken ill; she might faint or fall on the dark path back to her house.

"Thanks, Eileen. Goodnight, everybody."

There were murmured goodnights. Eileen picked up her purse – she didn't know how long she'd be gone – and assisted Randi down the steps. By the time they reached the turn in the path that led down the hill, the band had started up again.

SIXTY-EIGHT

Randi had watched Adrian flirt with Eileen, sing to her. *He never sang to me.*

The mad thoughts had flowed freely through her unhinged mind for four months now, ever since she'd learned the truth: *he's not Leo anymore. He looks so much like Adrian because he* is *Adrian. He made a pass at me, crawled in bed with me twice, trying to get me to see . . .*

And then Randi would be appalled at that train of thought, at the possibility that she could just *let it happen . . .* She'd then quickly remind herself that Adrian had murdered Gil . . .

And now he was flirting with Eileen.

It didn't matter that he was only nineteen and Eileen was old enough to be his mother, because he *wasn't Leo.* Adrian remembered Eileen from when all three of them were nineteen.

It must seem like only yesterday to him.

Randi remembered overhearing Adrian, back in the day, when he was telling Nick about the painter's wife and the crush she had on him. Now Adrian was Leo, and Leo looked so much like Adrian that Eileen didn't seem to care that he was just a nineteen-year-old kid. Randi had seen how Eileen stared at him, watched him . . .

But he wasn't really a nineteen-year-old boy, was he? He was Adrian Wilde, ladies' man. And he'd been smiling at Eileen all night, *singing to her . . .*

Randi wanted to tell Eileen the truth, but she knew that it was impossible. Eileen would think that she was crazy. All the thoughts tumbling through her mind were *making her crazy,* and none of the people she lived with seemed to care. Not Leo – Leo was gone. Adrian didn't care. He'd been nothing but cold to her since his dark secret had been revealed. There'd been no more repeat performances of him sliding into bed beside her, because Randi kept her door locked. She wasn't sure she could trust herself . . .

Daina and Penny and Bellona didn't care that Randi was unable to cope with the situation, that it was making her lose her mind. They just smiled kindly at her, patted her hand, didn't speak about it. Adrian was returned: that was all that mattered to them. They didn't care that he was making her crazy because she kept thinking of how much she'd once loved him. They didn't care that he'd murdered Gil . . .

Eileen walked slowly down the path with Randi. When they arrived at the house, she fetched Randi's pills for her and a glass of water.

But even after taking two of the anti-anxiety meds that Dr. Samuel had prescribed, Randi's heart still beat furiously. She still panted. All the ideas in her mind . . . Eileen . . . Adrian . . . Adrian was going to make a pass at Eileen next, and Eileen would go along with it . . .

Eileen was concerned. Randi was alternately pale or flushed. She panted. "Maybe I should take you to the hospital."

"It's just nerves," Randi wheezed. "I just get a little scared sometimes."

"What are you scared of?"

Randi laughed shakily. "I'm not really sure. It'll pass soon."

But the seconds ticked by and Randi's episode didn't pass. She seemed to become more agitated, even though she didn't speak. Eileen got the impression that Randi wanted to say something, but Eileen didn't encourage her to unburden herself. Eileen didn't particularly want to hear the craziness that was playing behind Randi's eyes come out of her mouth.

"Is there anyone I can call for you? Someone that you can talk to?" *Because you clearly need to talk to somebody, and you just as clearly don't want to talk to me. And I don't particularly want to listen to you.*

"Should I call Leo?" Randi's eyes became rounder. She shook her head. *Why is she afraid of Leo?* "Daina?"

Again Randi shook her head. "Look in my purse," she gasped. "There's a scrap of paper. A number."

Eileen scrabbled through Randi's large purse, past empty pill bottles, lipstick tubes, a pair of sunglasses, nail clippers, Randi's phone. She pulled out a small wad of old receipts and pawed through them until she found the number. *Nadine.* Eileen dialed the number on her own phone.

"Hi. You don't know me – my name's Eileen. I'm here with Randi . . ." *No, not* Wilde. *She and Adrian hadn't been married. What's Randi's last name?* Eileen realized that she didn't know all that much about Randi, just that she'd loved Adrian once, had borne his son . . . *Leo . . .*

"Put her on," the voice on the phone commanded. Eileen handed the phone to her distraught companion.

"Nadine? I just can't take it anymore, Nadine!" Randi sobbed. "I feel like I'm losing my grip! Could you . . ." Randi listened to the voice on the phone. She sniffled. "Okay. I will. I'll see you soon." Randi handed the phone back to Eileen. "She wants to talk to you."

Eileen said, "Hello?"

"I'll be right there," the voice said. "I'm just downtown. Can you stay with her until I get there?"

"Of course."

"Thanks. Don't let her take any more of those damned pills."

"Okay." Eileen hung up and slipped her phone back into her purse.

She looked nervously at Randi. The woman on the phone had mentioned pills. There were empty bottles in Randi's purse, and Eileen had fetched her a full bottle from beside her bed, but she hadn't watched Randi take them.

"How many pills did you take, Randi?" Eileen blurted out.

Randi had caught her breath. She was calmer, now that her friend was coming. "I'm not suicidal, Eileen." The wild light flared in her eyes again for a second. "I'm just a little distracted. I only took two."

Eileen nodded. *You're distracted, all right.* She wondered what it was that was bothering Randi, but then she decided it was none of her business, and that she didn't really want to know. She didn't really care for Randi too much, with her embarrassing outbursts. Always some pointed remark about Leo. *You seem to like watching Leo sing.*

So? What was wrong with that?

Randi and Eileen sat in silence as the time inched past. Finally, after about twenty minutes, the doorbell rang. Eileen leapt up and admitted a handsome older woman.

She introduced herself quickly, thanked Eileen for staying until she arrived. Then she turned to Randi. "What's a'matter, honey?"

Randi burst into tears, sobbed incoherently.

Again Nadine cursed the witches that she'd cursed for a lifetime. She hadn't always done right by Randi in the past, but the poor thing was a quivering mess now because of *them. Why did they pick her?* Nadine wondered. *She's so simple and kind-hearted. Adrian's return has undone her.*

Nadine sat on the couch beside Randi. She cradled her in her arms, soothed her, cooed to her as though she was the baby that she'd never had.

"Thanks for looking after her," Nadine said to Eileen in dismissal. "I'll take care of her now."

"Okay." Eileen didn't mind being dismissed. She was relieved to be getting out of there. "I hope you feel better soon, Randi." Eileen quickly, quietly, let herself out of the house.

She didn't hesitate, didn't debate whether she should just go on home, or if she should go back up and tell Randi's son how his mother was doing. Eileen was sure he'd want to know. Besides, it was his birthday. She wanted to wish him a happy one again. She wanted to tell him goodbye.

The witchy-looking woman, Leo's Aunt Lily, had departed, but the rest of them were sitting around the little table, laughing and talking, unconcerned with Randi's sudden illness. Again Eileen thought that perhaps she had these attacks frequently. Perhaps the family was used to them.

They stopped talking and looked at Eileen expectantly when she approached. "She's doing better now. Her friend came to sit with her."

Adrian saw what had occurred. It was the first time he'd ever seen a *past event,* and it made him blink. He saw Eileen open the door to his house, saw AnTeen stalk in, her face the picture of concern.

He was appalled. "Her friend Nadine?" Leo asked, just to make sure.

"Yes. Randi asked me to call her." Eileen watched the family's expressions: Leo made eye contact with his aunts; Penny pursed her lips and scowled. Bellona looked surprised, as did Bobby and Tracy.

Daina seemed downright shocked. "Nadine? *Really?"*

"I forgot to tell you," Leo said expressionlessly. "Nadine came to see Mom the day after Christmas."

"She came to see Randi?" Daina asked in disbelief.

Nick grinned. "Maybe she wants to bury the hatchet. Maybe she wants to apologize for what she did with –"

"Thanks for looking after her, Eileen," Penny said quickly. *No need to hang out the dirty laundry in front of our new friend.*

"It's nothing," Eileen replied just as quickly. She sensed that there was some family undercurrent afoot here, but it wasn't any of her business, so she didn't want to seem too interested in it.

There was a heartbeat of silence, then she said, "It's getting late. I just wanted to tell you that your mom's all right, and wish you happy birthday, Leo." He smiled at her. "Goodnight, everybody."

They told her goodnight. As she turned to go, Nick jumped up and offered to see her to her car. Eileen wished that it had been Leo that was going to be walking with her on the dark path, but quickly pushed the thought away. Nick was pleasant and cute, and just a tiny bit younger than her. Nick would do just fine.

SIXTY-NINE

The following morning, Nadine walked up the hill to the old witches' house. She'd slept on the couch at Randi's. If Leo had come home, Nadine hadn't see him.

Nadine stopped in the open entrance to the French doors. Penny and Bellona were bustling around in the kitchen, making breakfast. Nadine reflected that it was a quaint domestic scene that she'd witnessed hundreds of times when she was a child. It had given her a feeling of safety and belonging, then. When Nadine was a schoolgirl, she'd always happily skip inside and offer to help her beloved aunts.

But they were beloved no longer. Nadine leaned against the door frame and waited until one of them noticed her.

Penny paused at the sink. She looked up, out the window. Then she turned and said, "Bell. Look what the cat dragged in."

Bellona glanced at her sister and then at the doorway. She smiled.

Nadine looked over her shoulder at the railing to the deck. Three unfamiliar cats dined from dishes set up there for them. She said to Penny, "I don't know any of these cats."

"You've been gone a long time," Bellona said. "Welcome home."

Penny glanced irritably at her sister. "What is it that you want, Nadine?"

"May I come in?"

"Of course!" Bellona pulled out a chair at the kitchen table. "Would you like some breakfast?"

"Yes. Thank you. I've missed your cooking." Nadine took the pro-offered chair.

Penny looked expectantly at her. She'd ceased her meal preparation, so Bellona took up the slack, turning off the flame under the skillet and scooping bacon and eggs onto a platter. Penny waited.

Nadine sighed. "I've decided to take your advice. No more curses, no more hatred. This life is almost gone, and like you said, I've wasted it. *Out, out, brief candle!* It's time to make amends. Randi needs me."

Penny snorted. "Is that a fact?"

Nadine nodded. "I'm sure you've noticed. She had that woman call me last night. She was hysterical, couldn't stop crying She kept mumbling about *The Incantations of Thoth.*" Nadine studied Penny carefully. "What is that?"

"It was the method by which Adrian was returned," Bellona supplied. "An ancient, obscure spell. Unspeakably powerful —"

"But you already know of Adrian's return," Penny said. She shot a warning glance at her sister: *Shut up!*

"Yes." Bellona set a plate in front of her and Nadine smiled in thanks, then looked back at Penny. "But I've never heard of —"

"The *Incantations* are not what troubles Randi, are they, 'Deen? Adrian told us that it was you who revealed his return to her. He told us that you fed her some claptrap, told her that he'd done away with her husband. You told her that Mr. Hogan had murdered Adrian, and Adrian had in turn wrought his revenge." Penny stared steadily at Nadine, then abruptly looked away. She seated herself at the table and continued. "What's past is past, 'Deen. *What's done cannot be undone.*

"Randi is a new soul. She's callow, untempered by the often unfair, sometimes cruel fires of fate. Why did you feel it necessary to ply her with your evil theories? Surely you knew these lies would put her around the bend?"

"What lies did I tell? Gil killed Adrian. I know, because I set him to it. Are you saying that Adrian didn't murder Gil, as was his right?"

"If Mr. Hogan murdered Adrian, he was an instrument of fate," Bellona said. "Perhaps fate has dealt with him."

"The inexorable hand of providence," Penny intoned, studying Nadine. "No one escapes its justice. Is that why you're here, 'Deen? Is that why you want to *help* Randi? Do you fear judgment for your part in Adrian's demise?"

"I fear nothing," Nadine retorted haughtily. "Adrian would've died, regardless of any action on my part. He was doomed. It was prophesied." Nadine paused. She glanced at Bellona, then addressed Penny again. "You say that Randi is a new soul. I agree. She is naïve, good-hearted, unaware of the myriad unfairnesses of this world. Why did you choose her? Surely *you* knew that Adrian returning in the person of her son would undo her? The man she loved, *desired . . ."*

"Adrian chose her, not us," Bellona said. "The time had come, and he . . ." She ceased at another glare from her sister.

"All things cannot be as we would wish them, 'Deen," Penny said. "Perhaps Randi was a poor choice, an imperfect vessel."

"But necessity dictated that it could be no other," Bellona said. She sighed. "I agree that the young woman Adrian chose for such a

241

singular ordeal should've been stronger, or at least less likely to bow to societal pressures."

When Penny and Nadine looked at her in surprise, Bellona continued arrogantly, "We are initiated in the old ways. *We cannot be confined within the weak list of a country's fashion: we are the makers of manners; and the liberty that follows our places stops the mouth of all find-faults.*

"Randi needs to accept *that there is no Leo.* He's Adrian, the man she once loved. No one would care if she would –"

"The state would care!" Nadine protested.

Bellona shrugged. "The state can just mind its own business."

Penny ignored her sister. "Perhaps you *can* help Randi, 'Deen. Show her that a miracle has occurred, help her to cope with it. Help her get the inescapable reality of it straight in her mind. Adrian is returned. He is a young man again. She doesn't have to –"

"The first step is to get her off of those pills," Nadine opined. "The quackery of modern medicine never ceases to amaze me. All they want to do is make money for themselves." She took a piece of paper out of her purse. "Lily should have all of these on hand."

Penny read the list. "Some of these are powerful, 'Deen. Soporific. Dream-inducing. Hallucinogenic. Are you sure you know the proper mixtures, the proper spells?"

"Rome wasn't built in a day," Nadine sniffed. "I plan to wean Randi off of those awful pharmaceuticals slowly. I studied potion lore extensively while I was overseas. Some of the African shamans . . . Besides, Randi deserves some sweet dreams for a change."

Bellona took the list from her sister, and her eyebrows went up at some of the ingredients. "I'll text this list to Lily," she volunteered.

"Have that woman pick it up," Nadine suggested. "Randi says she's here all the time, anyway. What's her name?"

"Eileen," Penny supplied.

"Right. Put her to some use. Lily can tell her it's herbal tea." Nadine smirked darkly. "Randi tells me that she had a thing for Adrian, that she looks at Adrian-reborn like he's on the menu. She's a little long in the tooth for *Leo*, though, don't you think?"

Now Penny's eyebrows rose. "You've got to be kidding, 'Deen. A few decades difference in age never bothered you."

Nadine shrugged. "It was only seventeen years. And Gil was a grown man. Leo's just a boy."

"There is no Leo," Bellona reminded her.

SEVENTY

After Randi's *episode* – in her mind, Eileen termed it *a nervous breakdown* – Eileen let a few weeks pass before she returned to visit her friends on Parcay Street. She still spoke to Randi on the phone, told her that she hoped she was feeling better. Randi said she was right as rain.

Eileen also talked to Daina, and tried to gauge from the older woman's words if things had calmed down, if Randi had indeed returned to normal. Daina was noncommittal. Eileen got the impression that she pitied Randi and her *illness,* and didn't like to talk about it.

Daina even put her grandson on the phone, so he could say hi. Leo said hi, told Eileen cheerfully that he missed her. That clinched it. Eileen could stay away from Parcay Street no longer. She missed him, too.

When Daina came back on the line, she invited Eileen to lunch at her aunts', and Eileen immediately accepted.

It was a bright, sunny, late April Saturday, and Eileen was again humming to herself. She missed Leo's friendly smile. He was charming, without even realizing that he was – Eileen was sure of that. He was just a good-looking, naïve boy. Eileen again felt ashamed of herself for thinking the things that she did about him. *Why, he probably wouldn't even know what I was talking about. He'd be shocked at a woman the same age as his mother, making such a suggestion, asking him if he'd like to . . .*

As she started up the deck steps, Eileen heard Nick's voice. She paused.

"You look a trifle tore back this morning, Cuz."

"Yeah," Bobby said. "Where were you last night? I thought we were gonna work on the new song."

"Sorry I didn't call," Leo said. "I dropped off an order of candles to Aunt Lily last night, right before she closed. She'd asked about them, when she was here for my birthday. I was gonna hurry right back, so we could figure out that bridge, but . . ." Leo laughed. "I was walking by that bar down the street from Mohini's. What's it called?"

"Mickey's," Nick supplied. "We should see if we can get a gig there some time. When you're old enough to get in." He grinned. "Rolling Blackout's the house band, but maybe they wouldn't mind sharing the stage with us some Saturday night. It's a nice little place."

Eileen had met Carmen and Clint once or twice at Mickey's for a quick beer. It *was* a nice little place. She'd never heard of Rolling Blackout.

"So, I'm just walking down the public sidewalk, minding my own business," Leo continued. "This chick is standing in the doorway to the bar, and as I walk by, she says, 'Hey, Raven. Let me buy you a drink.'"

"Raven?" Bobby asked.

"I kid you not, my brutha."

It's all that beautiful black hair, Eileen thought. *Maybe I shouldn't be listening to this,* she told herself, but she didn't move.

"I said, 'The ID in my pocket says I'm nineteen, honey,' and I pointed at the sign on the door."

You Must Be 21, Eileen thought.

"I said, 'I can't go in there.' Just then, her friend comes out of the door –"

"What did these chicks look like?" Bobby asked.

"The first one was a blonde. Little. Cute. Maybe twenty-five. Her friend was a little taller, skinnier. She had pinkish hair. She was even cuter, probably twenty-two or three." Leo paused. "So the blonde says to her friend, 'Raven here says he's not twenty-one.'

"Pinky looks me up and down, and says, 'Is he eighteen?'

"'Nineteen,' I told her. 'Just a couple of weeks ago.'

"She looks at me for another minute then says, 'Would you like a drink, anyway, Raven? We've got a bottle back at our place. It's just around the corner.'"

"Christ!" Nick said. "Just like the old days."

Old days? Eileen thought. Surely Nick was talking about his own old days. *Leo's too young to've had any old days yet . . .*

"So I said, 'Sure, I'll have a drink with you guys.' I introduced myself as we walked to their place. The blonde said she didn't care for my name. She said she liked *Raven* better."

"Don't tell me," Nick said. "Let me guess. You told her that she could call you anything she wanted."

"Oh, Raven!" Bobby said in a high, girlish voice.

Leo laughed. "The blonde was Betty –"

"And the other one was Veronica," Bobby opined.

"How did you know?" Leo asked.

There's that innocence, Eileen thought, at his tone of voice.

245

"Were these working girls?" Nick asked.

"Why do you always think that, Cuz?" Leo said in annoyance. "I don't know any *working girls*. Sheesh."

"Sheesh, Nick," Bobby said derisively. "Who are you talking to? When did our cousin ever have to pay –"

"They were just nice young ladies. Lonely. Bored." Leo paused. "So, we went back to their place, had a couple of drinks, smoked a little weed."

Really? Eileen thought. She couldn't imagine Leo smoking pot. He seemed so conservative, responsible. Eileen remembered how much he always helped his aunts and his grandmother. She could see Adrian smoking weed, definitely. He'd been friends with Allan, and Allan was the original pothead. But Eileen could not picture shy Leo toking up. Maybe his mother was right. Maybe his shyness was all an act.

"Don't leave us hanging, Cuz," Bobby said. "One thing led to another, and . . ."

Again Leo laughed. "Yeah. One thing led to another. I liked Veronica more than Betty, and she certainly liked me. Apparently, I was showing her a little more attention, and –"

"Someone always gets their feelings hurt with those things," Bobby said.

"How would you know?" Nick asked curiously.

"Like you know," his brother replied.

"Anyway," Leo said, "Betty says to Veronica –"

"'Hey! It's my turn!'" Nick supplied. Bobby giggled.

Leo laughed once more. "Something like that. And I said, 'Ladies, ladies! There's no need to fight. You guys are friends –'"

"'There's enough of me to go around,'" Nick supplied. Again his brother giggled.

"So . . . yeah. That's why you didn't hear from me last night. I didn't get home 'till like four. AnTeen was sleeping on the goddamn couch again. I'm getting about sick of that."

Nick ignored Leo's mention of his mother's friend. "Christ, *Leo,* you're worse than you used to be. Weren't you always the one looking for true love?"

"Ah, maybe not so much anymore. Maybe all that's just for the lucky guys, like Bobby." Leo chortled. "Maybe I'm down for a little more fun this time."

"You had enough fun the last time," Nick observed.

246

"Betty and Veronica loved me. Truly. For the evening, anyway."

"Hot damn, Cuz," Bobby said. "If it was anybody but you, I'd think you made it up."

Anybody but . . . He's just a kid!

Eileen heard shuffling footsteps on the deck above her, then Bellona's chirpy voice. "Would you start the barbeque, Robert? Penny's onion burgers are all ready to go."

"Yes, ma'am," Bobby said.

Eileen heard his feet hit the deck; he must've had them up on the table. She waited for another heartbeat, then climbed the rest of the way up the steps.

Leo smiled when she opened the gate, the same friendly, boyish smile he always gave her. Had someone related the conversation that she'd just overheard to her, Eileen would not have believed it. *He looks so innocent . . .*

But she *had* overheard it. *Ladies, ladies! There's no need to fight . . .*

Suddenly, something dawned on Eileen, and it was like the most spectacular sunrise ever: breathtaking Leo Wilde was no innocent. Not in the least. There was no possible way he could look as good as he did and not have women hitting on him. Eileen didn't know how she'd never realized it before.

It didn't matter that he was only nineteen. He was still a red-blooded American boy, and had no doubt been responding to girls' advances for a few years now. Sometimes two at a time, as evidenced by his story. The naïve, good-boy act was just that, an act.

All the guilt Eileen had been wading through – had she actually be daydreaming about a nineteen-year-old *boy?* And so boyish had he seemed – guileless, blinking those big blue eyes at her, so like his father's . . .

But now Eileen saw that it was all a sham, just as Randi had told her. *Warned her.* Leo was no innocent. He was young, true. He was *incredible,* just as Adrian had been. And he was by no means the baby that he pretended to be. Eileen smiled to herself.

SEVENTY-ONE

Bobby grilled Penny's onion burgers to perfection. They were delicious, as was all the old ladies' cuisine. Eileen chatted with Leo and Diana and her aunts and Bobby. Nick smiled at her. Tracy was absent from the meal, because she was covering someone's shift at the hospital. Randi was also absent, which didn't bother Eileen in the slightest. She was off somewhere shopping with her friend. Leo mentioned irritably that Nadine seemed to be there all the time anymore.

"'Deen wouldn't have been my first choice," Penny said, "but it's good that Randi has some companionship."

They shared the same man after all, Nick thought to his cousin. Adrian grinned at him.

"I'm a little miffed," Daina said. "She hasn't even stopped by and said hi to me."

"You'll get over it," Penny stated flatly.

Daina sighed. "Indeed."

Eileen wondered what the skeletons in the closet looked like: why were they so down on Nadine? She seemed nice enough.

But Eileen couldn't really worry about any of that now. In fact, she was having a little difficulty holding up her end of the conversation. Try as she might, Eileen couldn't get the picture out of her mind: Adrian's son, entertaining two women . . .

She reflected that maybe he'd made the whole thing up. The idea that two girls would just step out of a bar, pick up a stranger – *a nineteen-year-old kid!* – and take him right on home was hard to believe. And the idea that it was Leo . . . But Leo was fine. Hadn't she been secretly, guiltily thinking about the same kind of thing?

In her mind, Eileen had never worked out any concrete details to her imagined liaison with Leo. She didn't have a nearby, empty apartment, like those lucky young women. Leo lived with his crazy mother, and Eileen lived with her mother, too, as if she was also a kid. And Carmen also lived there. They couldn't go to his house; they couldn't go to her house. Eileen had just imagined a non-specific room, dim – she wasn't nineteen, after all – candlelit, maybe. A soft bed, Leo there with her . . .

Maybe he was making it all up. But his older, wiser cousins had believed him. There'd not been a single syllable of doubt offered against his outrageous story. If it was all true . . . *My, what a bad boy he must really be . . .*

After lunch, Leo and his cousins left to go work on their new song. It was okay with Eileen, because she found she could better concentrate on her conversation with Daina and her aunts once Leo was gone. He still lingered, *cavorted,* in the back of her mind, but once he was out of her presence, she could again think.

Eileen stayed at Penny and Bellona's for the entire afternoon. She truly enjoyed the older ladies' company, even when Leo wasn't there. His being there just made her enjoy herself more. As the sun set, Carmen called and asked if her mother would like to go to the movies.

"Clint has some family thing," she said. "And I never see you anymore."

It was an unusual request. Her daughter was an independent young woman. Eileen had always been busy with school while she was growing up, and had had little time to entertain her, so Carmen had learned to entertain herself.

Eileen wondered vaguely if there was trouble in paradise. Carmen spent damn near every Saturday night out with Clint. She hoped that *some family thing* was a euphemism for *I don't want to see him right now.*

Out of courtesy, Eileen asked the ladies of Parcay Street if they'd like to go to the movies, too. She knew they'd decline. Just like Leo had told her, they never went much further than the market.

Mother and daughter went to see *Water for Elephants,* and that night Eileen dreamt of romance with Leo under the big top, on the trapeze . . .

SEVENTY-TWO

Eileen slept in the next day, and woke up refreshed. She only felt marginally guilty about her dream of Leo and the circus. One had no control over one's dreams, after all, and it had seemed so real. She felt as though she could still feel the texture of his hair on her fingertips, the taste of him on her lips . . .

Whatever tiff Carmen and Clint had sustained was apparently forgotten. She breezed out the door to meet him while Eileen was having her coffee. Even Mrs. Artus had something to do that Sunday: one of her old friends was in town visiting her grandchildren, and stopped by to take her to the mall.

Eileen sat on the front porch and sipped her coffee, and her mind once again returned to Leo and the story he'd told his cousins the day before. *His aunts said he's got a crush on me . . . He's always so friendly, so attentive. Maybe all I'd have to do is ask him . . .*

Eileen smiled to herself. The whole idea was insane. What would her mother think? Her daughter? *But on the other hand, they wouldn't have to know, now would they? It could be our little secret. Me and Leo . . .*

Impulsively, Eileen took out her phone and sent him a text. *What'cha doin'?* she said, just like she was his age.

Not a damn thing, he answered instantly. *Mom's gone again. Nick's coming over later, but right now, I'm here all by myself.*

Eileen shivered. Leo. Home alone. *All by himself.*

I'm bored, he texted. *Come see me.*

Eileen arose and went into the house to retrieve her purse and car keys before she quite realized that she had done so. Leo was bored. He wanted her to come out and see him. *He wants me to entertain him. Like Betty and Veronica . . .*

Eileen stopped and took a deep breath. This was insane. Then she picked up her purse, locked the door, and left the house.

SEVENTY-THREE

This is nuts. Crazy. Insane. All the synonyms for absurdity played over and over in Eileen's mind. It was *lunacy,* that she should be so excited to be going out to meet a nineteen-year-old *boy.* It was *madness* that she was going at all.

But Leo Wilde said he was bored, and even though she was almost as old as Betty and Veronica combined, Eileen couldn't stop thinking about similar ways to amuse him . . .

Eileen parked her car in Randi's driveway, and checked her look in the rearview mirror. Satisfied – she was not unaware that she looked great for forty – Eileen got out of the car, smoothed her clothes, took a deep breath.

And then she just gave in to it: Leo was fine, as sexy as his father ever was, and she was just as helplessly attracted to him as she had been to Adrian. The age difference be damned. He was young, but he was no boy . . .

Eileen rang the bell. Leo opened the door immediately and welcomed her inside. *He was waiting for me . . .*

Eileen thought she caught the faint aroma of marijuana smoke. *But he wouldn't smoke pot in his mother's house . . .* Then she remembered that his mother wasn't home.

Leo closed the door, turned the deadbolt. Eileen wondered if it was the same one that had been on the door when she'd lived there, twenty years ago. She wondered if you still had to jiggle the key in it to get it to open.

Eileen realized that it had been in this very room, long before Leo had even been a twinkle in his incredible father's eye . . . Carmen had been in her playpen, not far from where Leo was standing right now. *This can't be happening. I must be dreaming.*

Oh, my God, Leo, I want you so bad!

Adrian turned at her thought and smiled at her. He could feel Eileen's desire, hot like a wildfire, exactly as it had been all those years ago. He wondered if he was up to it, after the adventure he'd had the night before last. But then he remembered that he was nineteen, that he'd been up for any and all such undertakings when he was nineteen the last time.

"You wanna watch a movie, or . . . something? There's a TV in my room."

"Sure," she said softly. "Whatever you want."

Eileen's big hazel eyes glowed with anticipation. She didn't want to watch a movie. The look on her face made that clear.

Oh, what the hell, Adrian thought. *Randi's gonna be gone for hours . . .* He put his hand on her cheek, ran his thumb lightly across her lips. Eileen shuddered. Adrian made her wait for a heartbeat, then kissed her, ever so slowly.

Without hesitation, Eileen kissed him back passionately. She tangled her hands in his hair, molded her body against his.

Oh, yeah, Adrian thought, *this is going to be fun.*

Oh, my God! It's really gonna happen this time! It's the momento la verdad *all over again, and Allan's not going to show up this time . . .*

The doorbell rang.

You've gotta be kidding me! Adrian said to himself. "Hold that thought," he told Eileen, and turned to answer the door.

"Wait!" Eileen reached out and wiped the lipstick from his mouth. It was a darker shade than she'd worn all those years ago . . .

Am I good? Adrian thought. But that would just freak her out.

"Okay. It's gone."

Adrian arranged his face to resemble Leo's characteristic boyishness, and opened the door.

Allan was standing on the porch. Eileen thought she might faint.

He looked at her over Leo's shoulder, and he was clearly not surprised to see her there. There was a split-second of silence, then he said to Leo, "You've gotta be Adrian's boy. You look just like him."

Allan narrowed his eyes, studied Leo. "I don't guess you remember him very much. You must've been just a baby . . . I was sorry to hear that he was killed." The fat painter offered his hand. "I'm Allan Coleman. Your dad used to work for me."

Leo blinked in astonishment and shook his hand.

When did you get out? and *What are you doing here?* fled from Eileen's mind. Instead she blurted out, "How do *you* know Adrian's dead?"

"I've known about it since the day after it happened, honey. It was right after you left me." Allan grinned humorlessly. "The cops told me. They thought I did it." He looked at Leo again. "You sure look a lot like your dad, kid. That must be why my wife's here."

"I'm not your wife, Allan."

He stepped past Leo into the house. "What, no big welcoming hug, Eileen? I spend seven years locked up and no one's glad to see me, except my daughter."

"You saw –"

"Earlier today. I've been out for about a week. I thought it was time to see her. She wouldn't tell me where she lived. That must be your influence. So I had her meet me at the Del Taco downtown. She was glad to see me, I think. She's really grown up.

"I asked her how you were doing. I told her that I wanted to apologize to you for the shitty way I treated you before I went in."

Adrian saw that Allan wasn't here to apologize to his ex-wife. Not at all. He planned to start it all over again, right where he'd left off – the threatening phone calls, the sudden appearances . . .

"Carmen said you weren't home at the moment. We got to talking, and she said that you'd been spending a lot of time with our old neighbors out on Parcay Street." He glanced at Leo. "He's a little young for you, isn't he? What are you, kid? Eighteen?"

"I can see you'd like to have a moment with your ex-wife, Mr. Coleman," Leo said politely. "If you'll excuse me . . ." He darted out the still open door and closed it behind him.

"What do you want, Allan?" Eileen asked. She felt a twinge of fear. He was a bastard before; now he was an ex-convict, too. She was sure that seven years in prison hadn't sweetened his disposition.

"You're one sick puppy, you know that? I know he looks like Adrian, but Christ, Eileen! He's just a kid! You're old enough to be his mother –"

"I'm friends with his mother. You remember Randi? Randi's his mother."

Allan grinned. "So Adrian finally gave in to her, huh? She had it bad for him. Just like you did." Allan shook his head. "Jesus, Eileen! How desperate are you? He's just a kid –"

"What do you want?"

"Don't worry. I'm not gonna hurt you. You're not worth going back to prison over. I'm not gonna hurt your teenage boyfriend, either. But I might scare him a little bit." Allan grinned maliciously. "Don't get me wrong – it's not that I want you. You're just a dirty bitch.

"But nobody else is gonna have you, either. I aim to scare them all off. You're gonna be all alone, just like me, Eileen. You ruined my life, so now I'm gonna ruin yours. I had seven years to think about it." Allan's grin grew. "Hell, since you've decided to start cruising the high schools, it'll be easy. It doesn't take much to scare boys –"

Leo came back through the door. He grinned mischievously.

"Hey, Mr. Coleman, guess what? My mom told me all about you and Dad's little adventure with the Corvette. So I got to thinking, just now . . . In honor of your showing up uninvited, I thought I'd give it a try myself. I remembered that there was an old slide hammer in the garage. You must've left it here. This used to be your house, right?

"Look outside. See that Honda Accord? I just stole it from the market. It wasn't locked, so it was easy. It's still running. Was I quick, or what?" Leo winked at Eileen.

He took his phone out of his pocket. "Now I'm gonna call the cops. Tell them I saw some shady-looking old fat guy . . . He abandoned that car, right in front of my house. I thought I saw a gun in his hand, maybe . . . I dunno.

"I'm sure they'll come right out. Hell, the owner's probably called his car in stolen already. It's brand new, isn't it? A 2011?"

Leo looked out the window. The Accord was parked haphazardly in the street, illegally, blocking Eileen's car into the driveway.

"Now, if you're still here, I'll say that you forced your way in, that you were threatening me and your wife."

Allan's mouth dropped open.

Leo paused, his finger above the *Send* button on his phone. "You need to leave now, Mr. Coleman . . . sir. And don't ever come back."

Allan growled, "I'm not done with you, Eileen."

"I think you are, Mr. Coleman . . . sir. Your daughter's of age. If you want to see her, if she wants to see you, you can just talk to *her*. Her mother doesn't have to have anything to do with it."

"You got me this time, kid. But next time . . ."

"There's not gonna be a next time, Fat Boy," Leo growled. "If you ever show up here again, I'll put a bullet between your eyes."

Allan was amazed. He thought he saw fearless, smart-assed Adrian Wilde for a split-second in his kid's face. Then it was gone, and Allan instantly forgot about it, because some snot-nosed kid wasn't going to threaten him, wasn't going to get away with calling him *Fat Boy* . . .

Allan swung on Leo, but the kid dodged it. "Look what you made me do, Mr. Coleman! I've pushed the button. Even if I don't say anything, the cops'll *triangulate* a 9-1-1 cellphone call."

Allan didn't know if that was true or not, but he knew he couldn't be picked up anywhere near a stolen car. And this kid would rat him out. He glared balefully at Eileen and her young boyfriend, then fled the house as fast as his fat legs could carry him.

Eileen was speechless, dumbfounded. *He's no boy,* she thought again. *He's not afraid of Allan at all . . .*

Leo grinned. "It's all bullshit, Eileen. I don't know how to steal a car, and I don't own a gun. That's Nick's Accord. I've got a key to it. It was parked in my mom – my *grandma's* – driveway. Nick's in the house, I guess, making himself a little snack or something. We're gonna rehearse."

Eileen threw herself into Leo's arms and kissed him again. He quickly broke the kiss, and looked innocently at her. But Eileen could see that he was faking it, and Adrian knew she could see it, so he again thought, *oh, what the hell,* and kissed her like he knew she wanted it, hungrily, passionately.

Eileen just had time to think, *Oh, my God, he's incredible,* before Leo broke their kiss again, because, since he'd returned from the great beyond, Adrian Wilde *had* become a tease.

"Hold that thought," Adrian said again, and again ran his thumb lightly over Eileen's kiss-swollen mouth, a mouth that positively *ached* for him. "Goddamned Nick showed up early. If I don't go over there, he'll come over here looking for me. He'll wonder what your car's doing in the driveway."

"You can come over and hang out with us, but all this . . ." Leo grinned wickedly. "We're gonna have to put this off 'til another time. When we don't have so many unexpected *visitors.*" He kissed Eileen quickly. "Come on. Let's go."

Adrian wiped his mouth on the back of his hand, just in case there was any more lipstick there. He smiled at Eileen, wordlessly asking if the evidence was gone. She nodded and smiled back at him.

As they hopped into Nick's Honda and turned it around in the cul-de-sac, Adrian wondered how long it would be before Eileen started calling him or texting him. *Maybe I'll ask her to send a couple of pictures,* he thought. *Hot damn, but it's a wonderful time to be alive!*

He grinned to himself and parked Nick's car back in Daina's driveway.

Nick was sitting in a folding chair in the open garage, adjusting the strings on his guitar. When he heard the car door slam in the driveway, he started to say, "What the hell, A —" but then he heard the other door close and looked up. Eileen was standing beside his cousin. Nick finished his thought. "Why did you move my car, Leo? I come outside and my brand new car's suddenly in the middle of the street. Then some fat guy runs by."

"It's a long story." *You gotta stop calling me Adrian, Cuz.*

Eileen's phone beeped. *I just saw Dad a little while ago,* Carmen's text said.

Me too, she replied.

Where are u? R u ok?

I'm fine.

Can u come home? I'm a little freaked out.

I'll b right there. 20 minutes or so.

Ok.

"I guess I can't stay after all," Eileen said. "I have to go see my daughter." Nick thought she looked at Leo silently for too long, although he didn't look back at her. At last she said, "I'll see you soon."

"Okay." Leo walked into the garage and picked up his guitar.

"'Bye, Nick."

Nick said goodbye. When she had walked down the driveway, out of earshot, he turned to Adrian. "What's going on, *Leo?*"

Adrian looked up at Nick's accusatory tone. He hadn't told his cousin about the heat he'd read coming off of Eileen this time around. He hadn't talked to Nick about Eileen at all. He was supposedly nineteen, and she was forty, with quite the hard-on for him. It was a little untoward, was it not?

He offered Leo's innocent smile. "Whatever are you talking about, Cuz?"

Nick nodded over his shoulder. "You seem awfully chummy with Eileen."

Adrian shrugged, noncommittal. "She comes out to visit Randi and Mom. We talk sometimes. You know, she had a crush on me in a previous life . . ."

I knew it! He's playing her!

"But you're just a kid now. She wouldn't . . . Shit, she's old enough to be your mother . . ."

Adrian grinned and switched on his amp. "Here's an oldie for you Nick. A little Jackson Browne." Adrian sang:

"Now can you see those dark clouds gathering up ahead?
They're going to wash this planet clean, like the Bible said
Now you can hold on steady, and try to be ready
But everybody's gonna get wet
Don't think it won't happen
Just because it hasn't happened yet."

Adrian grinned at him as the last chord died away.

Nick hadn't said it in a lifetime. He hadn't said it since his cousin had returned from the grave, but he said it now. "Fuck you, Adrian."

Nick watched Eileen back out of Randi's driveway. He set his guitar on its stand and hastened down to the street. Eileen stopped her car, rolled down her window.

While she was talking to Nick, Eileen briefly glanced up at the garage. Adrian could feel her eyes on him, but because he knew that she wanted him to, he didn't look back at her. Instead, he just smiled to himself and studied the guitar pedals on the floor.

After a few minutes, Nick came back, the picture of smug self-satisfaction. "Go buy me a beer, will ya, Leo? I feel like celebrating." He slapped his knee. "Damn! I keep forgetting. You're just an underage boy."

"What are you celebrating?"

Nick turned and watched Eileen's car pull out onto Jurupa Road. "I've got a date tonight. Might even stay out past your bedtime."

Leo's black eyebrows went up in surprise. "Is that a fact? Well, you kids have fun."

"You can count on it."

SEVENTY-FOUR

Eileen didn't realize that she'd accepted Nick's invitation to dinner until she pulled out onto the main road. There was traffic, and she had to pay attention to driving now, so the mist cleared from her head. But moments before, her mind had been awhirl. She'd been *distracted.* She felt the way Randi looked sometimes.

She should've been worried about Allan's reappearance, about its effect on Carmen, but none of that concerned her. One call to her mother's lawyer, and Eileen would have another restraining order against Allan quicker than he could say, *You're a dirty bitch.* He didn't have her cellphone number, didn't know where she lived or where she worked. And if he found any of these things out, if Allan so much as *called* her, she'd tell him that the next time he called, *her* next call would be to the cops. Just like Leo had said, Carmen was grown. Eileen didn't have to deal with her father anymore.

Eileen could not possibly care less about her ex-husband. He was nothing more to her than *the wind blowing,* as he'd once been so fond of saying.

Yet still her mind had been a spinning maelstrom while she spoke to Nick. *Leo.* Leo, Leo, Leo! Eileen had agreed to Nick's invitation so he'd stop talking to her, so she could tell him goodbye and go home and think about Leo . . .

But as she drove, the insanity of what had happened returned to Eileen. Leo was no boy. She knew that now, just from kissing him, from the fearless stunt he'd pulled to rid them of Allan. But he *was* only nineteen. What would her mother say? What would Carmen say? It was crazy. Even if they tried to keep it a secret, they'd inevitably get caught. There was no place for them to go . . .

The thoughts flip-flopped over and over in her mind.

By the time she got home, Eileen discovered that she was glad that she'd accepted Nick's request for a date. Going out to dinner with Nick would get her mind off of his young cousin.

SEVENTY-FIVE

Nick didn't linger at Daina's house. Working on the new song was forgotten – Urban Equinox was never going to play in front of a crowd again, anyway, so who cared if they had any new songs? Nick wanted to go home and prepare for his date with Eileen.

Adrian was unconcerned. It was true that he'd been a little surprised that Eileen had so readily accepted his cousin's invitation to dinner, scant moments after he'd just kissed her, *but she's probably a little flustered by the whole thing,* he thought with a grin. *Nick's a nice guy and all,* but Adrian knew the depth and breadth of Eileen's desire.

People had to eat. She had to have dinner with someone. Why not Nick? Adrian knew Eileen undoubtedly had to think about what had happened, had to take stock of the situation.

The situation was that Eileen had as big of a thing for Adrian's boy as she'd ever had for his dad. It was maybe even a little bit worse, a little bit better, because of the age difference. Adrian smiled to himself. He knew she'd be back.

He went home and sat in the living room and messed around on the internet on his laptop for a while. Randi and AnTeen returned, laden with shopping bags from the mall.

Adrian frowned when they came in. He was not at all happy with their new friendship. He didn't appreciate the fact that the woman that had sicced his murderer on him was at his house all the time. *Daily.* AnTeen was *always there.* She frequently stayed overnight, sleeping on the couch.

Nadine smiled sweetly at Adrian's frown. His opinion of her presence – his opinion of *anything* – mattered to her not at all. Returned from the grave or not, Nadine would always despise Daina's son.

Randi chirped happily to him about her purchases from the mall. She was either unaware of, or ignored, the tension between him and Nadine.

Probably ignoring it, Adrian thought acidly. *Just like she ignored the inescapable fact that it couldn't have been anybody else but her beloved Gil that shot me. Just like she ignored Gil's abuse of Leo for his whole life.*

"That's great, Randi," he told her, as she held a bright yellow sundress up in front of herself, almost as if she was seeking his approval. "I'm glad to see you're getting out more."

"I owe it all to Nadine," she said, and gave the older woman an impulsive little hug.

"Right." Adrian closed his laptop and set it on the coffee table. He arose. "I'll see you ladies later." He stalked out the door.

Amused at his obvious pique, Nadine called after him, "'Bye, Adrian!"

"Don't call him that, 'Deen," Randi whispered in alarm. "Call him Leo!"

"Sorry, dear," Nadine soothed. "Sometimes I forget the whole charade."

SEVENTY-SIX

Adrian was pissed about AnTeen's blithe, insouciant attitude toward him. It was clear that she felt that she could just come and go as she pleased, stay at his house anytime she wanted, just because she'd befriended Randi.

Well, that's just bullshit. We'll just see about all that.

He sprinted up the path to his aunts' house, stomped up the steps to the deck. He found them sitting at the little table, as he always had, through going on three lifetimes. The two little old whitehaired witches whose ancient wisdom had saved him from oblivion . . .

Adrian pushed the fond thought away. He was angry.

"Where's Mom?" he asked harshly.

Penny's eyebrows rose at his tone. "At home, I would imagine."

"Good." Daina didn't know of Adrian's dislike for Nadine, or of her murderous dislike for him. "What's up with AnTeen being at my house all the time? She practically lives there, anymore."

Penny's surprise continued. "Why would you possibly care? She's keeping Randi company. Lord knows she needs it."

"But it's my house! I don't want someone who wants me dead always at my house!"

"Don't be a spoiled brat, Adrian," Bellona said flatly. "Randi made a tremendous sacrifice on your behalf. She's become a trifle . . ."

"Nuts," Penny supplied.

"And it's probably entirely because of you." Bellona looked at him imperiously for a moment. "Randi's so much happier now. She and 'Deen perform the old rituals together, practically every day. You know how much Randi enjoys the craft. It soothes her. Besides, with 'Deen around, the rest of us won't have to look after her."

"I don't like seeing the accomplice to my murder every day," Adrian reiterated.

"Nor do I," Penny said. "But you have to occasionally think of someone other than yourself, Capo." The old witch couldn't chide him too much: she loved him. "Here's a thought. Why don't you move back to Daina's house?"

"The other bedroom – Dad's study – it's just the way he left it," Adrian said softly. "I wouldn't want to disturb anything. Mom goes in there and sits sometimes. She looks at his old books and papers, she leafs through our family pictures. It's where she goes to think about him. To commune with his memory. I couldn't just move back in there and disturb all that."

"You don't have to disturb anything, dear," Bellona said tenderly. "We've discussed this with Daina. She's at odds and ends in that old house by herself. She'll come back up here with us, back to her old room. You can leave Ian's study the way he left it. Take the other room. Daina can meditate there any time she wants."

"You're grown now, *again.*" Penny flashed a rare smile. "Once more, you need your own space. Daina will come back home to us, and you can have the house to yourself. It's the perfect solution. Daina knows as well as we do how much you want to get away from Randi."

"And how much she wants to get away from you," Bellona added.

Adrian smiled. It *was* the perfect solution. As always, his aunts never failed to come through for him. "I love you guys," he said and hugged them. "I really don't deserve you."

"Oh, you're all right, Capo," Penny demurred. "After our long lifetimes in service to the universal forces, I'd say that we definitely deserve you."

SEVENTY-SEVEN

Nick and Bobby helped their cousin move his belongings back across Parcay Street, and they also assisted with carrying Daina's clothes and a few items of furniture up the hill to her aunts' house. The four of them, movers and moved, were quiet, thoughtful. Each considered the lives they'd lived together, the happinesses, the sadnesses. The tragedies, those predestined and those unanticipated. The strange miracles.

Nick and Bobby and Adrian recalled the day that they'd moved his stuff the first time. The little two bedroom house that he was now leaving had been his then, a Christmas gift from his generous aunts. Adrian had been just starting out in life. They'd all been young. Nick remembered the thrill he'd experienced when Randi allowed him to kiss her on that New Year's Eve at his cousin's house . . .

Daina's memory stretched back farther than her son's and his cousin's. She again saw the day that Penny and Bellona had presented the house to her, the house that she was now leaving.

She and Nadine had been such good friends then! Will and Rob had helped moved Nadine's things from across the street, out of the very same room that Adrian was vacating now. Daina and Nadine had been best friends, dating wealthy, good-looking twin brothers. They'd been footloose and fancy free, just two young, liberated hippie girls on their own for the first time.

Daina remembered the moment that she'd seen Ian, on Hallowe'en. She remembered how gorgeous he'd been in his gladiator costume. Ian had never ceased to be gorgeous to her . . .

She remembered the first time that they'd made love. She thought with a grin that Adrian might've been conceived that very day. She'd plucked Ian from the bedroom to which she was now returning, had brought him home to the bedroom from which she was now leaving. They'd never slept apart a single night after that, except when she was in the hospital giving birth to his son. Now the room in which they'd shared so much joy would be Adrian's.

Daina was once again returning to the room she'd occupied as a child, after her parents had passed. She thought soberly that she'd live there until she died. She wouldn't be moving back and forth between the houses on Parcay Street again. There was no fear in the thought. Once this life was concluded, Daina knew that she'd see Ian again. There was immeasurable solace in that.

The house that Daina had shared with him – ah, what a wonderful life they'd lived there! That house would be Adrian's now. He'd been taken from her for seventeen years, but fate had been kind and returned him. It was a miracle. Everything was as it should be. Things had come full circle.

Daina hoped that Adrian would experience the same kind of happiness that she'd shared with his father in that house, where she'd lived as a child with her long-ago lost parents, where she'd lived with Nadine, then Ian. Where she'd raised her son, then lost him; where she'd found comfort with her husband after Adrian's death; where she'd finally lived alone. She hoped that Adrian would find a girl to love, that they'd get married, have kids . . .

Daina looked forward to watching all the mundane, delightful, future phases of his life.

SEVENTY-EIGHT

The dust had barely settled from Adrian's departure before Nadine moved into his old room, *her* old room. She did not ask the Wilde men for assistance, because she despised the Wilde men. She hired a professional mover, and she and Randi sat on the front porch, sipped ice tea, and made appreciative comments to each other about the healthy young fellows that brought Nadine's bed and nightstand and dresser into the house from the big truck.

The furniture that she no longer needed from her downtown apartment – a couch and a dinette set, various chairs and lamps and end tables – Nadine sold them to the local used furniture dealer. She would not need them again. Her thought had been similar to Daina's: *this is the last place I'll ever live.*

And like Daina, the finality of the idea held no fear for Nadine. She also believed that she'd see Ian in her next incarnation.

The future was bright. Nadine had come to like Randi, as much as she could like anyone. They'd become friends, confidants.

Randi revealed to her the precise methodology of *The Incantations of Thoth,* as Penny and Bellona had explained them to her. Nadine was nonplussed. It was the simplest, yet most bizarre spell of which she'd ever heard.

Since becoming aware of Adrian's return from the other side, Nadine had researched the methods by which the transmigration of a soul could be purposefully redirected. She found that there were myriad spells, many other *incantations* purported to achieve it. Nadine discovered to her delight that the old ways were alive and well on the internet.

There were also all the tales of *natural* reincarnation, souls that had returned without the guidance of any influence from this world. There was the little boy who'd before been a fighter pilot during World War II, who'd gone down in flames at Iwo Jima. Similar to Adrian, another little boy had been his own grandfather: at the tender age of five he was able to verbalize family secrets that there was no other way he could have known. There was the little girl that could name all thirteen members of the family to which she'd belonged in a previous life.

Nadine wasn't particularly interested in the tales of those born again through the random machinations of the universe. That such events occurred was second nature to her. She believed that everyone lived many lives – the fact that some could remember who they'd been before was the anomaly, not the idea of rebirth itself.

She was far more interested in the concept of *guided* transmigration, as had been afforded to Adrian. The sites that offered instructions were manifold – one even claimed that famous people could be called back from the other side and reincarnated, if the enterprising supplicant would only send $39.95 for the spell book – *Your child could be Einstein reborn!*

The powerful Egyptian divinity Thoth was frequently mentioned online. His magical tomes were available for purchase; invocations to summon him were provided. He was said to be the original author of the Tarot deck, after all. But nowhere could Nadine find anything about his *incantations,* as they related to rebirth. Neither in connection with the god, nor anywhere else, did she ever find discussion of how a man could direct the transmigration of *his own soul.* Yet Daina's black-haired, monkey son had accomplished it. *It must be a truly ancient, obscure spell,* Nadine thought.

Randi enjoyed looking at the reincarnation websites also. The subject couldn't help but interest her. She knew firsthand that guided transmigration could be induced to occur: she'd been the vessel of one such miracle.

Randi's favorite website asked for no money, not even a donation. It promised that if all of its requisite rituals and purities were followed to the letter during the first trimester of a woman's pregnancy, then the new baby would possess the soul of whomsoever the petitioner wished.

"It says, 'You will know that the charm has succeeded if the infant bears some physical resemblance to the deceased person, however slight,'" Randi said to Nadine. "Wouldn't that be wonderful if it was true? If it was really possible?"

Nadine smirked. "Unfortunately, it's a little late for either of us to attempt such a grand experiment. We're both a bit past our childbearing years. Besides, who would we bring back?"

SEVENTY-NINE

Nadine slowly weaned Randi off of all the pills she'd been prescribed. She showed the younger woman how to prepare, mix and distill various compounds. If she wished a dreamless sleep, Randi should add a little of this powder to her dinner. If she wished sweet, happy ramblings through the Elysian Fields with the man of her choice, she should tinct her nightcap – Randi was again allowed a little alcohol – with a few drops of the green liquid contained within a certain vial.

Nadine knew that Randi chose Gil to dream about these days – she sought no more visions of Adrian. He lived across the street, stuffed to overflowing with ingratitude for the woman that had made his return possible. He avoided Randi (and Nadine, also) as much as possible.

When she chose to utilize the dream-potion herself, Nadine walked and talked and smiled and laughed and made love with Ian, as she never had in waking life. The contents of the small flask, renewed over and over as the years swept past, had often helped Nadine to cope with her own sterile reality.

Sometimes Nadine would cobble together a concoction of roots and berries, leaves and fungus, and she and Randi would partake of it together. Then they'd sit in the dark and stare at a single candle, and Nadine would regale her with the mechanics of the craft, as she'd studied them overseas. Or she'd tell stories of the old ways, of the loves and betrayals and revenges wrought by witches and warlocks of legend.

On one such evening, Nadine at last told Randi the unhappy saga of her love for Ian, of Daina and her aunts' betrayal. With low-spoken, trembling words, she told Randi how they'd stolen her soulmate from her. Nadine had never related the story of this abomination to one other human being, and the unburdening of it made her feel twenty years younger. Randi listened raptly, wide-eyed and overflowing with pity and commiseration.

"This life hasn't been fair to either of us," she said.

Nadine smiled ruefully in agreement. With minimal effort, under the influence of the witchy blend, Nadine succeeded in convincing Randi that the vast majority of the unfairness that they'd both suffered came as a direct result of the witches across the street. They'd stolen Nadine's soulmate. They'd given him to an undeserving whore, and through her was produced the black-haired monkey that had returned from the grave and murdered the man that Randi and Nadine had both loved.

With very little persuasion, Randi began to see Daina and Penny and Bellona in a new light: as her enemies. And Adrian, too. If Leo had never been born, and thereby Adrian never returned – then Randi would still be living happily ever after with Gil.

It was their fault that she was all alone in the world today, with only Nadine for company. Had Randi not run afoul of these particular witches, had she not been duped, *used* by them, had they not made her the unwitting receptacle of Adrian's rebirth, then Gil would still be alive, and she would've borne *his* child. Not some ungrateful, unnatural monstrosity that would no longer even give her the time of day.

Randi and Nadine practiced the old rites together. And now Nadine had a compatriot in her desire for revenge against the other aging witches that dwelt beside them on Parcay Street.

EIGHTY

The Year of Our Lord 2011 progressed, and Eileen started seeing Nick on a regular basis.

The passionate, forbidden kisses that she'd shared with Leo had frightened her a little bit, and the power of the desire that she felt for him had not abated. It nagged at her, gave her many a sleepless night. Eileen still wanted Leo, but the insanity, the indecency of it, also plagued her. His kiss was like a drug, like a contagion. Eileen was addicted. She was infected. It was insane.

Maybe Nick was the cure.

Eileen still visited with Daina and her aunts, dropped in every now and then to say hi to Randi and Nadine. She made sure that she also ran into Leo, because she could not bear to go for too long without seeing him.

Leo smiled at her as he always had. The only indication that he ever gave of what had passed between them was an occasional pause when he was speaking to her, a little curious tilting of his head, as if he wanted to ask her something. But he never did.

Eileen thought that Leo *was* boyish in that respect: he would not act. He was waiting for her to make another move. To save herself from the temptation, Eileen made sure that she never found herself alone with him.

Eileen visited her friends frequently over the spring and summer, chatted cheerfully with them, enjoyed their good cooking. She smiled blankly at Leo, then went home and furiously fantasized about him. Sometimes she dreamed about him.

But Eileen went out with Nick.

Nick was always a perfect gentleman. He might impulsively take her hand as they walked down the street, but it was always just for a moment. He'd give her a hug when he dropped her at her door, but it was always just a friendly, brotherly one. He'd kissed her quickly on the cheek a few times, in appreciation for something clever she'd said. But he made no further moves past these displays of friendly affection.

Nick was an old soul. He'd been able to glean the motivations of those around him while he was still just a child. In addition to this useful skill, from a very early age, Nick had also had the opportunity to watch his cousin interact with the opposite sex. He'd learned that there were certain signals women displayed when they wanted further attentions from a man. With the ones that had pursued Adrian, these signals had been unmistakable and writ large.

After watching the kaleidoscope of girls that had thrown themselves at his cousin, Nick knew how to tell when a woman wanted him to make a move. He might not be as attractive as Adrian, either in his first incarnation or in his new one, but Nick knew he was just as clever, just as charming. And he also played guitar, maybe even better than Adrian.

Nick had never once made a misstep. He'd never once misread a woman's signals. Nick hadn't gone through as many women as Adrian had, but he'd experienced more than his share, and he'd never been turned down. Not because he was irresistible, but because he could accurately read what they were trying to tell him. If Nick knew he'd be turned down, he didn't waste his time asking.

And so it was with Eileen. Nick liked her immensely. She was beautiful and intelligent, but she was also sober-minded, calm and responsible, traits he valued highly. He thought that he could love her someday, but for the moment, he just enjoyed her company. Nick thought that Eileen liked him, too, even though she had not transmitted any indicators that she wanted to take their relationship to a more physical level. So Nick waited.

He knew that her ex-husband had recently been released from prison. Nick thought that perhaps Eileen was reluctant to rush into anything with him until she found out if Allan was going to start harassing her again. Maybe she wanted to avoid any ugly scenes that might ensue, if her ex thought she had a new boyfriend.

But if he was honest with himself, Nick knew that this excuse for Eileen's unresponsiveness was all bullshit. Eileen's daughter – whom he'd never met – would be twenty-two soon. Nick knew that Eileen no longer had to be present if Allan visited. There was no need for her to see him at all, no need for him to come to her house and perhaps run into her new boyfriend. Allan was in no way an impediment to any relationship that Eileen might decide to start with Nick.

The truth was that Eileen hesitated because she had a thing for Leo. Nick could tell from the way she stared at him, when she thought no one knew that she was looking. Adrian had told him about her incendiary desire, all those years ago. And Leo looked just like Adrian, *because he was Adrian.* How could she not feel the same stirring for the son as she had for his father? Perhaps even more so, because Leo was still a *young* Adrian . . .

But the years were wrong now, especially for Eileen, although Nick knew that Adrian would go for it. Eileen obviously wanted him, and his cousin was down to oblige any girl that so much as smiled in his direction these days. He'd come back from the great beyond as somewhat of a reprobate: gone were the days when he worried about unnecessarily breaking hearts. Gone, too, was that search for his one and only.

Like he'd said, Adrian was out to have fun this time. If some young thing showed an interest, he would show an interest right back. It didn't matter to Adrian anymore if they liked him too much, while he knew that he was just killing time with them. If they were sad when he took off the next day, that was their problem.

Nick thought that Adrian was toying with Eileen. He knew she wanted him. He couldn't help but know it. *Hell, everyone knows it, especially Randi.* Nick thought that this conundrum contributed to Randi's distracted craziness. Randi couldn't have Adrian: that proposition was just too unthinkable to her, though Nick had a fair idea that it wouldn't bother anyone else on Parcay Street, least of all Adrian . . . Randi couldn't bring herself to bend this most ancient of taboos, but neither did she want Eileen, a woman the same age as she was, to have Leo, either.

Leo appeared to be only a nineteen-year-old kid, but he still possessed all of Adrian's charm. Nick's cousin pretended to be shy, boyish Leo around Eileen, yet still she wanted him, against all respectability. Nick reckoned that her perception of this sham innocence was probably the only reason that she hadn't already made a play for him. If he let Adrian out, if he showed Eileen that in-control, grown-up confidence, just once, Nick thought that Eileen would no longer care that Leo was just a kid.

In a flash, Nick understood what Gil must've felt.

Randi had not been able to hide her desire for Adrian, and all Gil could do was stand by and watch it. Nick suddenly understood how furious Gil must've been at the unfairness of it. Adrian did nothing to encourage Randi's affection, but there it was, obvious to all.

Seeing the woman you loved with another man was a bitter pill to swallow, Nick knew. Had he not watched Gil and Randi together? Had he not hated Gil – that cheating, low-life son of a bitch – *because Randi loved him instead of me?*

271

Had Nick not hated Adrian just as thoroughly, even more, really, when he realized that his cousin had disregarded his feelings and taken Randi to bed?

He's gonna do it to me again.

Nick realized with a start that history had a way of repeating itself. Especially when the player at the center of the drama had not aged, was still a vital, eye-catching young man . . .

Nick liked Eileen. Maybe he even loved her. He didn't feel the same burning, all-encompassing yearning that he'd once harbored for Randi, not yet. But then he wasn't a fifteen-year-old boy anymore, either.

This woman that Nick coveted had a thing for his cousin, just as Randi had had a crush on Adrian once. Eileen hid it better than Randi had done, yet it was still there. Eileen had wanted Adrian in the old days, and perhaps that fire had never been completely extinguished. Hadn't she come looking for him, after twenty years? Nick saw that her desire must've flamed to life again when she'd beheld his son. For who was Leo but Adrian, still youthful and exciting, precisely the way Eileen remembered him?

And the threat was there again, too, Nick realized. Randi had had a jealous, dangerous boyfriend, and Eileen had a jealous, dangerous, ex-convict of an ex-husband.

It's gonna happen again . . .

Nick feared for his cousin's safety for a moment. If Leo made a play for Eileen, her ex ol' man was just liable to come along and shoot him all over again.

But that was Adrian's bed, if he chose to jump right back into it. He'd been friends with Allan, once upon a time. Surely, Adrian could judge the amount of threat posed by the painter, far better than Nick could. *If he's willing to take that risk, why should I worry about him?*

Nick felt that rage again. Anytime he truly felt something for a woman, there was his cousin to come along and steal her from him. Nick perceived the dangerousness of jealousy, the inchoate desire to lash out. The emotion had driven Gil to murder, and from what Adrian had told him of Allan, he didn't sound like much more of a sophisticate.

Nick felt jealousy steep and bubble within himself, like some kind of viscous, poisonous tar. The dark thought played through his mind: if only young Leo were out of the picture, Eileen would respond to him . . .

The unfairness of her attraction to the kid gnawed at Nick, flayed him. It made him feel helpless again, just like he'd felt when he'd watched Gil and Randi together. It was the same furious helplessness he'd felt when Ian had told them where Adrian was when he died, and with whom. The same hatred flared in Nick now, as it had when he'd realized that his beloved cousin hadn't paused even a second to contemplate Nick's feelings for Randi. Nope. He'd just gone right on ahead and *fucked* her, and it had gotten him killed.

He's gonna do it to me again.

Nick allowed the bitterness of his jealousy to slosh acidly around in his mind. He understood how the helplessness of the emotion had driven Gil to murder. He saw how Allan could do the same thing. But Gil had been an animal, and he was long gone. Adrian had told Nick that he didn't think Allan would be back.

The only one feeling jealous at the moment was Nick himself.

Shame choked Nick. He quickly tamped down the sudden hatred he felt for his cousin. Adrian was his best friend, blood to him, like his own brother.

He knows I like Eileen. He won't do it to me again.

I hope.

EIGHTY-ONE

Eileen enjoyed going out with Nick. He was funny and smart. Sexy. Sometimes she thought she should just go for it, put down this ridiculous torch she carried for a nineteen-year-old *boy*. She told herself that she'd never again act upon it, so why couldn't she just let it go?

Sometimes she'd catch a little sparkle in Nick's light green eyes, or he would smile at her a certain way, and Eileen would imagine what he'd be like. She would think that she might just suggest that they go back to his place after dinner . . .

But then she'd remember Leo's blue eyes, the promise of things glorious that she'd felt when he'd kissed her, and Eileen's warm feelings for Nick would evaporate. He was a nice guy, and she liked him very much. But it wouldn't be fair to him. She had to get Leo out of her mind first.

Eileen accompanied Nick to the 4th of July family barbeque on Parcay Street. Out of nowhere, Eileen suddenly remembered Adrian's memorial page on Tributes.com. The 4th of July had been his birthday. It had been the day he'd died. He'd only been twenty-one.

But the family didn't observe a somber moment of silence for Adrian's loss. They laughed and joked, ate and drank, as if there'd never been an Adrian Wilde. *Perhaps it's because Leo looks so much like him,* Eileen thought. *No need to mourn Adrian with his son here, because they can see Adrian in Leo. It's probably just like having Adrian back again to his family, just like it is to me . . .*

Leo was looking exceptionally fine this evening. He was wearing a dark blue tank top that showed off the perfection of his tanned arms and shoulders; his long black hair was wild and free. He smiled at Eileen from across the deck and he reminded her so much of his father that she had to look away . . .

Eileen considered Nick, sitting right there beside her. He looked good, too. He smelled good. She liked how the light from the fireworks pooled in his eyes. *I'm going to go home with him tonight,* Eileen told herself. *I'm going to forget all about this impossible thing with Leo. I'm going to go home with Nick tonight.*

Eileen indulged in an uncharacteristic third beer to bolster her resolve, then she slammed a fourth. She patted Nick on the knee, smiled at him, squeezed his hand.

Nick saw the signals at last, the ones that he'd been looking for every time they'd caught dinner and a movie together. When the last rocket from the finale died away, he stood up, stretched theatrically.

"That was spectacular, as always," he said to the assemblage: Daina and her aunts, his brother and sister-in-law, Leo. Randi and Nadine had not attended the festivities. "But Eileen and I . . ." he smiled at her. "We have to go to work tomorrow. So we'll bid you all a happy 4th of July, and say good night."

Adrian smirked at Nick, arched an eyebrow. *Don't do anything I wouldn't do, Cuz.*

Nick returned his smirk smugly. *I don't think there's anything you wouldn't do anymore, my brutha.*

You have no idea, Adrian thought. But he kept the thought to himself.

The family said good night to Nick and Eileen, and the two of them fled quickly down the steps. At the bottom, he grabbed her hand and they ran happily up the path together, like high school kids. At the bend where the path turned to go down the hill, Nick stopped and pulled Eileen against his chest, kissed her. She responded ardently.

Oh, yeah, it's on now, Nick thought gleefully.

They sprinted down the hill, breathlessly made out in the car for a moment. The blood thrummed in Eileen's ears. She positively tingled with excitement. It had been *so many years* since she'd felt this way, since she'd passionately kissed a man. *Except for Leo . . .* Eileen pushed that thought away. She just wouldn't think about Leo anymore, especially not now.

"Have you guys written any more new songs?" she asked Nick.

"What?" he said in surprise. All he could think about was getting her home, so he hadn't heard what she'd said.

"I was just thinking. Maybe you could play something for me. When we get to your place."

"Sure, baby," Nick said and squeezed her knee. "Anything you want." Her kisses had communicated to him what it was that she wanted, and it wasn't to hear him strum his Stratocaster.

They drove in anticipatory silence. Eileen didn't attempt to make any more cutesy conversation. When they reached Nick's building, he again took her hand. Again they sprinted up the steps.

Nick unlocked the door, and once inside, Eileen threw herself into his arms. Nick pushed her back against the door, kissed her mouth, her neck.

This is great, Eileen thought. *This is just what I need . . .*

She closed her eyes, and immediately Leo sprang to her mind.

Nick's kisses, his caresses, had turned her on, but Eileen didn't want Nick. *She wanted Leo.*

It wouldn't be fair to Nick. She wouldn't be thinking of him. She couldn't get Leo out of her mind, and Nick's attentions were just making it worse.

She gently pushed him away. "I'm sorry, Nick. I . . . I just can't right now. I'm . . . I'm drunk. I shouldn't be . . ."

Nick looked at her, nonplussed. He was speechless with disbelief. Such a thing had never, ever happened to him. Nick had gone out with plenty of girls that hadn't been interested: he could tell right away. It didn't matter to Nick. He'd just turn on the ol' Wilde charm and talk up the next one. Women were like new cars: if one wasn't down for a test drive, there was a whole lot full of others.

But when they'd shown an interest, like Eileen had, putting her hand on his knee, kissing him like her life depended on it . . . In his entire life, Nick had never had a girl change her mind on him like this. He didn't know what to say.

"I like you, Nick. I really do. I just shouldn't be drinking and losing control of myself . . ."

You're forty years old, for Christ's sake! How much control do you need? How can you be changing your mind now?

"I'm sorry, Nick. Will you . . . will you call me tomorrow? Can we have dinner?"

"Sure, baby," Nick said softly, gently disappointed. "Anything you want." *Jesus, how Adrian's gonna laugh at me about this.*

"Thanks for being so understanding."

That's me. Understanding Nick Wilde.

"I just . . . I haven't . . . in such a long time . . ." Now Eileen was just rambling. She kissed him quickly, chastely, then turned around and opened the door. "I'll call myself a cab. I'll see you tomorrow." She closed the door and fled down the stairs, taking her phone out of her purse as she went.

Nick sighed, put his forehead against the closed door. *Well, I'll be a son of a bitch . . .*

EIGHTY-TWO

The cab showed up quickly: Nick lived in a nice part of town. By the time she arrived home, Eileen was again sober. She hadn't really been very drunk in the first place. She hopped in her car and drove back to Parcay Street.

EIGHTY-THREE

Adrian sat on the couch in his new-old living room, drinking a beer. He flipped idly through the channels on the TV. It wasn't late, only going on 10:30. Reckoning from Leo's birthday in April, Adrian considered himself twenty-two, and 10:30 certainly wasn't late for a twenty-two-year-old ladies' man that had returned from the other side. Today was his actual birthday, and he cursed the driver's license in his wallet that said he was only nineteen. He couldn't even go to a bar and have himself a celebratory drink with some friendly company.

Adrian had not lived to be old enough to spend any time in bars. Besides, he'd been a musician, had fronted a talented local band with a fair following. He wouldn't have had to frequent bars to pick up girls. They came in droves to the parties that Urban Equinox played. They came *to him*.

But Nick had told him how the bar scene worked. You walk in, look around. The girls were looking, too, that's why they were there. When one of them smiled at you, you smiled back, sent a drink over, strolled up and introduced yourself.

Nick had always been a loner. His brother and his cousin had been his only companions. Bobby was useless as a wingman: he wouldn't even go out with Nick. It wasn't something that happily married men did. And for seventeen years, his cousin had been dead. Now Adrian was returned, but he was still too young to go to the bar. They'd seem an odd pair anyway: his cousin was fifteen years older than Leo.

Nick had laughed and suggested that, when Leo was of age, maybe they could seek out those mother-daughter teams that one sometimes found on the prowl together . . .

Nick told Adrian that it was difficult flying solo, because girls usually went out together, in twos and threes. But he'd been lucky enough. Adrian knew that he wouldn't have any trouble all by himself, but he was still two years away from making the attempt.

It's my birthday. The 4th of July, for God's sake. What am I doing sitting here all alone?

Adrian reflected that he could cruise by the local Starbucks, if they were still open, or find some other place where kids Leo's age hung out. But he didn't want any eighteen or nineteen-year-old girls. Angie had showed him that. She'd been cute and willing, eager and enthusiastic, but she'd also been tiresome and superficial. The latest celebrity faux pas, the most recent viral video to storm across the internet – these were the only things that concerned her.

Adrian couldn't pretend that he harbored any deep-seated moral or philosophical concerns, either. He was just out for a good time. He didn't know what he wanted from a girl, what he wanted out of his miraculously returned life, but he knew that it wasn't Angie or any other girls not yet old enough to even buy a drink.

He wondered idly what Emily was doing these days, or AnneMarie. They were both forty or so, probably married with children, perhaps even grandchildren. If they hadn't grown fat or ugly, the age difference didn't bother Adrian. A good-looking woman was a good-looking woman to him. In his new incarnation, he unknowingly echoed Gil in that sentiment.

Adrian didn't dwell on the age difference. He remembered Emily and AnneMarie – and Randi and Eileen, for that matter – from when they'd been young and beautiful, from when they'd been convinced that they were in love with him. It seemed like only yesterday.

Damn, but wouldn't they be surprised to see me? Hi, I'm Leo Wilde, Adrian's son. Yeah, I know, the resemblance is amazing. I heard stories about you and my dad – from whom had he heard stories? That wasn't important. Maybe Nick had told him. *I heard stories about you and my dad, and if you're single these days, and not doing anything . . .*

That was just ridiculous.

Adrian was a little miffed that Eileen had taken off with his cousin. He knew that she still wanted him, but he had also read her reluctance, her internal arguments with herself, her fight against her desire. He was only nineteen, it wasn't right, what would people think?

God hates a coward, Eileen, Adrian thought with a touch of resentment. *Who cares what people would think? It's not like we'd have to tell anybody . . .*

EIGHTY-FOUR

Leo had summoned Eileen once. He'd texted her, said that he was bored. *Come see me.* Without hesitation, she'd driven out to Randi's house, had made up her mind to give in to her desire, all societal mores be damned.

Leo had kissed her, and it had been incredible. But then her worthless ex-husband had interrupted them, just as he had interrupted her and Adrian twenty years before.

In the three months since her thwarted tryst with a nineteen-year-old boy, Eileen had tried to talk sense to herself. To become involved with Leo would be crazy. Such things were just not done. There could be no future to it. They had nothing in common. He was younger than her daughter. What would people think? She was just too old for him.

What if she got attached to him? How heartbroken would she be when he inevitably found someone his old age? How ridiculously pitiful would she look then?

Eileen didn't think that she'd get attached to Leo. What commonality did they share, other than opposite anatomies and a desire to explore that prosaic, universal phenomenon? Eileen just had this unshakable yen for him, identical to that which she'd had for Adrian. Once her – for lack of a better word – *curiosity* was satisfied, Eileen was certain that she could forget about Leo, and his father as well. She could get on with her life. It was a rather cold way to think about another human being, but Eileen was trying to be realistic with herself.

But then she remembered that she'd also loved Allan once. He was nothing to look at, but she'd been wowed by his confidence, his grown-up-ness, the fact that he was a bad-ass. Eileen had become attached to Allan, had loved him, married him, borne his child. If she could love someone based solely on his personality . . .

She'd loved Adrian based strictly on his looks. And it was the same with Leo.

So, if they became involved, Eileen might get attached to Leo, after all. And that could only end badly. One more reason to maintain control of herself, to stop thinking about him, to give up the insane idea of *being with him* . . .

But tonight, Eileen had come to the conclusion that this thing she had for Leo was making her nuts. It just wasn't going to go away. She'd behaved like some immature, schoolgirl tease with

Nick. He was a nice guy and she liked him very much. He didn't deserve such treatment.

Eileen wasn't going to fight this impossible desire anymore. She was going to go to Leo, and let the chips fall where they may.

She was devious in her resolve. If this was going to happen, it had to remain a secret. She left her car at Allan's old shop, so no one would notice it parked in front of Leo's house so late at night, possibly *overnight*. She had to go to work in the morning, so she'd be gone before Randi or Daina or any of them might have cause to walk up to the market and see her car, not in front of Leo's house, but still in the neighborhood.

She scanned the two driveways as she skulked quickly up Parcay Street: there was Leo's car – *so he's home!* – and there were Nadine's and Randi's, in the driveway across the street. Their house was dark, quiet. There was a glow from a television coming from Leo's living room. Not only was he home, he was awake.

Eileen took a deep breath and rang the bell.

EIGHTY-FIVE

Adrian was surprised to see her. Her thoughts were clouded, jumbled, but that desire still rang in her head like a klaxon, and he sensed a resolution in her. Eileen had come to a decision.

He let a little of his resentment show. "Done with Nick already, are ya?"

I guess I deserve that.

"I didn't . . . I just went home." Eileen glanced across the street nervously. Leo's porch light was on, and if Randi or Nadine just happened to look out the window, they'd see her standing there talking to him, would wonder why she was at his house so late at night . . .

"And now you're here." Adrian sensed her discomfiture. He enjoyed it.

You're just gonna have to let all of it go, baby, if you want to start seducing nineteen-year-old boys . . .

"Yes. Now I'm here."

Eileen hesitated, but the need glowed plainly in her pretty hazel eyes. Adrian stood aside so she could come into the house.

He closed the door behind her, twisted the deadbolt. There was a finality to that gesture that caused Eileen to shiver. There weren't going to be any interruptions this time. *This is crazy, this is crazy, but oh, my God, the way he kissed me . . .*

"You wanna smoke some weed?" Leo said and grinned slyly at her.

Eileen shook her head. She hadn't smoked marijuana since before Carmen was born.

"How about a beer?" Leo gestured at the three remaining in the six-pack carton on the coffee table. "Or maybe a drink?" *Nick left a bottle of . . .* No, it wouldn't do to mention Nick again. "I think there's some Scotch around here somewhere."

Yeah, he's no boy . . .

"Scotch would be great."

Leo went out to the kitchen and made them both a Scotch and soda. Eileen was standing in the middle of the living room when he returned. He sensed that she didn't dare to sit down on the couch. *That would be just too forward, too obvious . . .*

He handed a drink to her and sipped his own. He looked at her mildly, curiously, watchfully. He relished her desire, her hesitance. *You're just gonna have to go for it, honey. A journey of a thousand miles starts with that first step. If you want to journey to the back room with me, you're just gonna have to make your move . . .*

Eileen slurped her Scotch; she stared at him over the rim of the glass. The silence lengthened. At last Leo said, "You wanna watch TV?"

"No." Eileen gulped the remainder of her drink, set the empty glass down on the coffee table. She took a step closer to him.

"I didn't think so." Adrian smiled at her, and took his time setting his own glass down.

Still he waited. Eileen reached out and touched his face. With her other hand, she grasped his shoulder and pulled him against her.

Adrian hesitated another moment, just long enough to feel the doubt blaze through her: *Oh, my God, maybe he doesn't want to . . .*

Then he kissed her, slowly, tenderly, *teasingly.* Eileen responded fervently. The sluice gate on twenty years of desire was opened, and she squeezed him to her. *At last, after a lifetime . . .*

Leo wasn't Adrian, but he looked just like him.

EIGHTY-SIX

Once they got behind closed doors, things progressed just like Eileen had dreamed they would. Leo was confident, in command, impossibly skillful. It was just as Eileen had come to suspect: he was in no manner a shy, innocent, inexperienced boy.

Eileen had never been so excited in her life. She'd never wanted any man as much as she'd wanted Adrian Wilde. Leo wasn't Adrian, but he might as well have been. It was as if Eileen had been granted some kind of mind-blowing do over. She'd missed her chance the first time; the years had passed, Adrian had died. But now everything was reset, the same as it had been twenty years ago: Leo was young, incredibly sexy. Eileen had aged, but Leo was just as Adrian had been the last time she'd seen him. It was everything she'd ever dreamt: incredible, spectacular. Mere words were not enough to describe being in Leo's arms, at long last. It was *so good.*

When they paused to catch their breath, Eileen noticed that the room was lightening. She glanced at the clock on the bedside table: it was ten minutes to six. She was supposed to be at work in forty-five minutes.

Eileen kissed him quickly, then arose and gathered up her clothes from the floor.

"Where are you going?"

"I'm supposed to be at work at 6:30." *I'm not even going to have time for a shower,* she thought. But that was all right. Eileen knew she'd enjoy the memory of him, *the smell of him* on her skin all day . . .

"I don't know, Eileen. You look a little flushed to me. Feverish, maybe. I think you might be coming down with something. I think you should call in sick. Stay here and let Doctor Leo take care of you."

Doctor Leo is certainly good for what ails me . . .

Eileen hesitated. She glanced through the blinds at the brightening July morning. She was rapidly losing the cover of darkness. What if Randi or Daina should drop by later? What would she say she was doing here with him, in the middle of a work day?

"No one should be looking for me today," Leo said, as if answering her thoughts. "If they are, they'll call first." He picked up his phone from the night stand, waved it at her. "Unfortunately, my phone's off. If anyone knocks on the door, I just won't answer. I'm kinda known for that." He smiled at her. Eileen thought his smile was glorious. "Go ahead, call your office. Then come back to bed."

Leo Wilde, her nineteen-year-old lover, was requesting that she stay, that she come back to bed. There was nothing important happening at work today. Orange Coast Title was coming off of a holiday weekend, so the office would be dead. No one would miss her if she called off.

The thought occurred to Eileen that it didn't matter — even if they were closing a deal on the White House, on the Taj Mahal today — they'd just have to muddle through without her.

Eileen couldn't refuse Leo.

EIGHTY-SEVEN

It didn't take long for Eileen to start feeling as though she was living a double life, like a Mafioso or some kind of international spy. To the world at large she was a hard-working, middle-aged title company manager, living at home with her elderly mother and her grown daughter. She visited Daina and her aunts, laughed and dined with them. She occasionally exchanged a few pleasantries with Randi and Nadine. She went on fun-filled, no-intimacy-included dates and outings with a man barely five years her junior.

But after she'd bid adieu to Carmen for the evening, when dinner was concluded with the ladies of Parcay Street, when she returned from the movies with Nick – when night fell – Eileen went to Leo.

The angel and the devil of well-worn cliché frequently perched upon Eileen's shoulders.

It's wrong, it's wrong! the angel cried. *He's only nineteen, you're old enough to be his mother! You're gonna get found out, and then what will your mother say? What will Carmen say? What will Nick – good-hearted, sexy-in-his-own-way Nick – what will he think of you?*

But then the devil would whisper silkily in her ear. *Leo's no boy. He's awesome, positively incredible, better than any man you've ever known. It's just a thing, a once-in-a-lifetime thing. No one's gonna find out . . .*

Like a vampire, Eileen would wait until the sun set, and park at her ex-husband's old, boarded-up shop or at Hilltop Market, and then slink back down the hill to Leo's house.

It was not a mid-life crisis. Eileen didn't feel old, and she had no desire to relive her youth. Her youth had been boring. Hell, most of her life had been boring. Tiresome, sterile, frigid. She'd never taken an interest in a young man before, and if Leo didn't look so much like Adrian, Eileen wouldn't have thought twice about him.

Being with Leo wasn't about reliving a lost, wistfully remembered youth. Because he looked so much like his father, it was about having a little taste of a better, more exciting youth, all the glorious parts that unkind circumstance had made Eileen miss. She was finally getting to experience everything she'd dreamt about when she was twenty. Sometimes, just thinking about it made her tremble.

Incredible, sexy Adrian Wilde . . . Could it really be true that after a lifetime of fantasizing about it, she at last got to touch him, to kiss him, to slide into bed beside him . . .

Well, it was only partially true. She was not twenty, even though Leo was. He was not Adrian, but that was okay, too, because he was an almost identical Adrian surrogate. The situation had its imperfections, but it was a million times closer to living the fantasy than Eileen could've imagined in her wildest dreams.

EIGHTY-EIGHT

Sex had never been the end all and be all of Adrian's life. It was fun, but there were other fun things: writing music, playing with his band, waterskiing; having a drink, smoking a little weed . . .

But for the girls that showed an interest, Adrian thought that physical culmination seemed paramount to them: they *had to have him.* He was always amused by how they'd lose themselves entirely, give themselves over, mind, body, and soul, to their desire, to *him.* The girl that he'd just met, who was idly chewing gum and vacantly looking at the back of an album would moan, she'd writhe, she'd scream his name, just because he gave her what she'd been thinking about while they'd been innocuously discussing music ten minutes earlier. And afterwards, she'd think she was in love with him. Adrian never failed to be astonished with their reactions – it had been fun and all, but it wasn't love.

And if they already thought they were in love with him beforehand, then they were already halfway there the moment he so much as smiled at them.

Once upon a time, Adrian had been especially careful when he chose girls. He preferred ones with a little insouciance; too obvious of a yen for him was a little alarming. In his first incarnation, their abject appreciation had made him feel a little guilty: sure, this was a lot of fun, but it was nothing to lose your mind, your *self,* over, not even for just the afternoon. *Sheesh, honey, get a grip.*

Now, he reveled in the desire they displayed, just for him. It was great to have a woman love you with every nerve, every shred of her being, even if it was just for a little while. He enjoyed their sighs, their unrestrained exclamations of pleasure. He liked to see them lose themselves.

If they remained lost, if they thought they were in love with him afterwards, Adrian didn't feel too bad about it, nowadays. He'd given them what they wanted. If they wanted more than he had to give, that was just the risk that they took when they thought, *Damn, he's cute. I wonder what he'd be like?* and then smiled at him and decided to go ahead and find out.

That delighted oblivion that Adrian saw in their eyes – it must be a portion of that thing of which the poets sang, of which his cousin Bobby spoke, the thing which Ian had possessed – the ability to lose yourself to your lover's touch must be an aspect of love. Adrian had never achieved it. He always enjoyed himself, but he never lost himself. One girl was pretty much the same as all the others to him.

Adrian sometimes wondered what would happen if he pushed all the buttons, flipped all the switches, started the countdown, and then just aborted the blast off. He imagined the astonished look on her face . . . *You were already halfway to nirvana, baby, but I never left town. You closed your eyes and anticipated that shot into orbit, but I'm still here on the ground, checking my watch, wondering what time the sun comes up . . .*

Adrian would never do such a thing. It would preclude his own pleasure, and even if he had never loved a single one of them, Adrian had always at least *liked* the girls that loved him. He'd never been the type to use sex as a weapon, as Pat Benatar had lamented in 1985, when he was only fifteen years old.

But since he'd returned from the other side, Adrian Wilde had become quite a bit more of a gunslinger than he'd once been. If she wanted to stand in the dusty street with him at high noon, Adrian would indulge her. He'd wait for her to draw . . . *Bang, bang, my baby shot me down . . .*

EIGHTY-NINE

And then there was Eileen.

Sometimes, Leo would join her and his womenfolk for lunch. She'd chat with Daina, laugh at one of Bellona's old stories. Eileen was in control of her expression now – the smoldering musings no longer glowed in her eyes when she looked at Leo, when she thought no one knew she was looking. It seemed that Eileen almost disregarded his presence. She'd smile politely, blankly, at him, but he was certainly no more than a nice young man to her.

And all the while, *the things she'd be thinking* – graphically, she'd run through her mind just exactly what she was going to do to Leo the very next moment she got him alone. She'd consider precisely what it was that she wanted him to do to her . . .

When Adrian got her behind closed, locked doors, Eileen's passion for Leo consumed her. She became a wildcat. *Once the lights are out, you'd never know she was forty* . . . His slightest touch, his merest breath, would incite her to the most unspeakable heights of arousal. There was no experience in heaven nor on earth more divinely pleasurable to Eileen than rolling around naked in bed with Leo, kissing him, tangling her fingers in his hair, feeling his skin against hers. Conscious thought would disappear. Her need for him was absolute. There was no societal antagonist that could dilute its dominance, once she unleashed that desire.

With Eileen, Adrian reckoned that he had the perfect arrangement. She loved what they did together. *Christ how she loved that!* But Adrian thought that Eileen was mature enough not to confuse loving that with loving him, as so many younger girls had done.

He knew that Eileen would continue to keep their frequent late-night assignations on the down low, because she was embarrassed, even ashamed, by their age difference. Who could she tell that would understand? Randi, the woman with whom she'd once shared a crush on Leo's daddy? No. Was she gonna tell Nick, her hopeful, age-appropriate swain? Not hardly. Eileen wasn't gonna blab it all over town about their little thing. She wasn't going to start making plans for their future. She knew better.

Adrian was making time with a woman that his cousin liked, but on the other hand, what Nick didn't know wouldn't hurt him. Adrian had not a scintilla of jealousy to him. He had no possessiveness. It bothered him not at all that Eileen was dating Nick. In fact, it amused him that she wasn't duplicitous enough to play them both. The thought never crossed his mind that she *was* playing Nick, after a fashion, and that he was playing his cousin just as much.

Adrian wouldn't care if Eileen up and decided to give Nick a tumble some night. The concept, the purpose of monogamy was lost on Adrian. He understood that appearances had to be kept up: they had names for women that slept with a guy and his cousin as well. He knew Nick would be pissed if he found out, but Adrian would've been surprised to discover how deeply betrayed Nick would've felt. Maybe that was another part of that love that Adrian had never felt: not being able to bear the thought of her with anyone else . . .

Adrian was just having a little bit of fun. Eileen had had a thing for him when he was Adrian the first time, a huge, all-encompassing thing: Adrian had never felt so stupendous a desire as Eileen had unknowingly broadcast, every time she so much as glimpsed him. Now he was simply making all of her dreams come true, at least two or three times a week. What Nick didn't know could not possibly hurt him.

Adrian realized with a jangling start that their set up was almost identical to the one that had existed with Gil and AnTeen. The bitter, malefic witch and that murdering son of a bitch had no doubt believed that what Randi didn't know wouldn't hurt her, either.

Adrian shook his head. *It's not really like that. Sure, Nick likes her, and she likes him, but she* wants *me. It's not like the two of them are living together, like Gil and Randi were. They just go out sometimes. She hasn't even slept with him.*

And AnTeen had other reasons for messing around with Gil. Her agenda included revenge. Eileen's only agenda concerns doing someone that reminds her of Adrian Wilde. I'm just accommodating her. If Eileen wakes up one morning and decides that she wants a respectable relationship, one with a future . . . If she decides that she wants Nick, I'm sure she'll break it off with me. He'd never have to know anything about what's been going on between us.

NINETY

The summer waned.

Through Nadine's friendship and guidance, Randi became the kind of witch that she'd always wanted to be – the mysterious, lonely woman at the end of the path, who knew things about herbs and potions, who could effortlessly scry the glass ball, who could see things yet to come in the cards.

Nadine's instruction on interpretation of the Tarot particular intrigued Randi. She showed her eager student other probable analyses of the wands and pentacles, angles of explanation different than the common, prosaic ones that Penny and Bellona had taught her.

They daily performed rituals to banish evil influences, both upon rising and before retiring at night. They burnt candles and incense, and sent prayers and wishes and curses out upon the smoke to the waiting powers of the universal forces.

Because of the dark miracle that had been accomplished in their midst, the idea of reincarnation fascinated Nadine and Randi. They became rather experts on the ways and means of guided transmigration of the soul, at least as far as the various, sometimes conflicting methodologies were presented on the internet. The idea was a wistful, what-if, hypothetical concept to them, because they both had lost people whom they dearly wished to see again in this life. Ian, Gil . . . Loves lost unfairly, too soon. Men they believed deserved to live again.

The whole idea was a strange and alien concept: what would it be like to gaze into the eyes of a newborn baby and know that you'd known him as an adult, as a friend or lover or husband, twenty, thirty, forty years before? They had long and intricate discussions about it, until Nadine became exasperated with Randi. Of all the people on God's green earth, Randi should be able to say what such a thing was like. Had not her lover returned in the person of her son? But Randi couldn't verbalize the conflicting emotions that she felt whenever she looked at the young man she'd brought into this world, who was her one-time lover reincarnated: amazement checkered with fear, hate mingled with love, revulsion mixed with desire. Randi just didn't want to discuss it.

The idea that it might be possible to resurrect her beloved Ian was a particularly thorny one to Nadine. Such a proposition drove to the core of her faith in the immutable fairness of fate. She truly believed that the gap-toothed, squinty-eyed water skier had been meant to be her soulmate in this life. Of that she was as certain as she was of tomorrow's sunrise. The destiny that had been meant to be had been cruelly turned aside by the ancient, evil witches across the street, aided by their whore of a niece.

But was Nadine as certain of the fact that Ian would be hers in their very next incarnation? Was she positive that his soul was waiting in some limbo now, waiting for her to finish off with her current dreary existence, so that they could be born around the same time, so they could grow up and meet and fall in love and spend their lives together the next time?

If there was a way to bring Ian back now, within the circle of people she knew – she could be like a grandmother figure to him – it would preclude Ian from joining Daina in the next life, because the years would be wrong, the overlap in their lives would not match up. But if it were possible to achieve this, to befriend some young woman of childbearing years, to carry out the requisite spells and rituals to bring Ian's soul back to this world – would Nadine be denying herself a new future with him?

If it were possible, would she want to run the risk of cutting off her metaphysical nose to spite her next-life face? It was a test of her belief – did she truly know Ian would be hers the next time? Or would she rather throw this monkey wrench into the works – if she didn't know for sure if Ian would be hers, would she be contented to make goddamned sure that he wouldn't be Daina's, either? It was an intriguing philosophical conundrum for Nadine.

Randi's thoughts on the subject were simpler: if she was still of childbearing age herself, she thought that she'd like to attempt to resurrect Gil.

She ignored the uncomfortable overtones of lovers becoming sons, becoming lovers, because she'd be far too old to ever love a boy born now. Like Nadine, *the heyday in the blood* was tame for Randi now, and she thought of resurrecting Gil as a boyfriend no more than Nadine thought of returning Ian for such a purpose. Randi thought that she'd just like to give her murdered husband another chance at life, like Adrian had received. If she could still have a baby, and that new life could be Gil's soul returned, it would be like having the son she'd never borne him. In Randi's way of thinking, the baby wouldn't necessarily have Gil's memories and personality, like Adrian did. If she knew that he was Gil, it would be enough. It would not be necessary for him to know it himself.

NINETY-ONE

Daina and Penny and Bellona patiently and good-naturedly observed Adrian and Eileen. They were well aware of what was going on, no matter how much Eileen tried to hide it. She was just there too often: the ladies knew that their conversation was just not that entertaining to a busy woman in her forties. There had to be some other draw that kept bringing her back, and they knew precisely what it was.

There had been no new young women showed up on Adrian's arm, either, wandered in from God-only-knew where, like the old witches' stray cats. If Eileen's perennial presence hadn't shown Adrian's mother and aunts that there was some hanky-panky going on, the glaring absence of a girlfriend for Leo would've convinced them. Adrian reborn wouldn't have remained without a woman all this time, if he didn't already secretly have one.

Eileen was sober, stable and responsible. Daina and her aunts didn't worry that the excesses of her clandestine May-December romance with Leo would go to her head. They each envied her a little bit – who'd not enjoy the love of your youth returned to you in your middle age, still but nineteen years old?

Eileen would've been appalled, flabbergasted, acutely embarrassed, to discover that they knew. She would've blamed herself for somehow betraying the furtive affair, for somehow letting it show through some unguarded word or glance. Leo's attentions had put Eileen into a kind of narcotic, euphoric state. All summer, she felt as though she'd drifted through the days, high and heedless. It seemed like she could only focus on two things: Leo himself, when she was near him; and her job. And even when she was at the office, sometimes she'd catch herself daydreaming about his dark blue eyes, his boyish, incredibly talented mouth . . .

Eileen had become a little absent-minded, a little scatterbrained. That was the result of feeling like she was stoned all the time. The thing was simply impossible, just too good to be true . . .

Sometimes Eileen wondered if she should make a more concentrated effort to get back to reality. She'd lapsed into only a passing, *Hi, how ya doing?* relationship with her mother and her daughter. Her life was about the narrow confines of her sometimes intricate job, and the limitless vistas of pleasure provided by her not-yet-old-enough-to-buy-a-drink lover. Everything else was just a gray area of transition from one to the other.

Sometimes Eileen reflected on the circumstances like a suddenly introspective drug addict might: *I'm neglecting all other endeavors in favor of this exceptional high. The rest of my life is just passing me by. I should concentrate on something else for a minute, like Nick . . .* But no physical depredations happened to Eileen as would have plagued her from actual drug use. There were no hangovers, no painful withdrawal if she didn't see Leo for a few days. There was only an anticipatory longing that would be fulfilled completely the next time they were alone together.

But still, Eileen felt a little guilty. Maybe it wasn't right to be drifting through mid-life as high as a Georgia pine . . .

Everything was coming up roses and lollipops for Adrian Wilde. He was nineteen, but he really wasn't. He had a hot older woman at his beck and call, who made no demands on him other than to let her love him whenever the mood struck her.

But as the summer faded into autumn, Adrian began to feel a little of the old restlessness. He didn't know what else he could possible want: he was in the catbird seat. But he felt an anticipation in the air, as if there were invisible storm clouds massing on the horizon. Adrian felt as if a cloudburst of change was imminent in his life. Existence as he knew it was about to washed away.

But it was an irksome, nebulous presence in his mind. It made him edgy, impatient, sleepless. Just what was coming? Was he going to die again?

Adrian knew that he was walking a tightrope. He didn't think that Nick would kill him if he found out about his affair with Eileen, but his cousin might never talk to him again. That would be an unfortunate side effect of the heedless life he'd been living. Adrian didn't want to lose his best friend, especially over something as temporary as a woman. Was it guilt that was making him feel like some comeuppance was nigh?

Adrian told his aunts about this pesky feeling. He couldn't exactly call it *foreboding* – he didn't feel that something bad was going to happen, necessarily, just that *something* was going to happen.

The infamous seers interpreted his Tarot. The Death card did come up, but it wasn't in the proper quadrant to actually mean death. The skeleton with his scythe, mounted upon his pale horse, rarely signified actual expiration, anyway. He was a concrete manifestation for the elusive portents Adrian sensed: some deep transformation, the completion of one cycle, the transition to a new way of thinking.

Adrian sat across from his aunts, his hands flat on the table beside the cards, his face expectant. Bellona tilted her head, considering possible interpretations.

"You're right, Capo," Penny said, and flipped over another card. "Something is coming. Sudden and unavoidable change."

"What?"

Penny shrugged. "The cards are ambiguous. An attempt at some kind of exact prediction from this lay would be foolish and probably incorrect."

"You can count on it," Bellona added.

"Deal it again," Adrian suggested. He shuffled the cards, meditated on them for a moment.

Penny looked at him pointedly. What the cards had to say wasn't going to change with another deal. They were indefinite right now; they'd remain so. Penny shrugged and dealt again anyway.

"The Ace of Cups: a purity of emotion – love, dreams, memories. Pleasure, instinct. Water; oceans, rivers." Penny turned over another card. "The Two of Wands. Again, the beginning of something new, the question: *what brings true and lasting satisfaction?"*

Adrian shook his head. He had not a clue.

"The Fool." Penny smiled. "That's you, Capo, a soul that has taken on a new body, a new life. It reminds us of your potential, your abilities. Your journey toward knowledge of yourself. In your case, it is a card of adventure." Penny turned over more cards. The Hierophant: "Be still and listen." Judgment: "Limitless, eternal truth and reality." The Four of Wands: "Tradition, celebration." The Ace of Pentacles: *"Magic."*

Penny shrugged again. "It doesn't seem to foretell *bad* news. Just . . . news. Not bad, possibly good or even great. Definitely a change."

"Perhaps Eileen is going to start acting her age," Bellona suggested innocently.

Adrian grinned like the Cheshire cat. Of course they knew. "Perhaps. But she's digging Wonderland right now. I don't see her jumping back through the looking glass anytime soon."

Penny turned over the Seven of Swords, which depicted a figure carrying off a set of swords, while glancing behind him, as if to see if he was being followed. "The abandonment of possibilities, not without reservation." Penny smiled at Adrian. "Perhaps someone's going to push Eileen back through," she suggested.

NINETY-TWO

Nick looked in the mirror sometimes and asked himself, *When, exactly, did I become an idiot?*

His affection for Eileen had only grown over the summer, and it seemed as though the situation was the same for her. They had quite a lot in common. Their political views differed just enough that they had in-depth, spirited, thought-provoking discussions. Their philosophies were similar enough that these discussions never devolved into anger or disrespect or rancor.

They had the same taste in motion pictures, liked the same kind of music. Nick was delighted when she agreed to come back to his place again so he could serenade her with a few old ballads. He could tell it wasn't going to be like the first time: the signals were totally absent. There were no more sly smiles or quick hand squeezes, no more knee pats or breathless kisses up against the door. Eileen had enveloped herself in a no-touch sheath: Nick could see it as plainly as if it was a tangible thing, so he didn't even try.

But still he could tell that she felt something for him. He cooked dinner for her – that was another compatibility – Eileen liked eating Mexican food as much as Nick liked cooking it. She'd sit in the kitchen with him and she'd look at her phone and talk about things for them to do together. They should go to LA for a show; they should take a day trip to Hearst Castle, or the Winchester Mystery House. Sometimes she'd talk vaguely about farther travel destinations: she'd loved to see San Francisco or Seattle with him.

They caught a couple of shows in LA. That was always fun, and it wasn't that far away. They might get back to Riverside in the wee hours, but they always got back. There was no need for overnight accommodations, no need for the uncomfortable fact of their brother/sister relationship to be pointed up, when they ordered separate rooms. That's why Nick hesitated to go out of town with her. He didn't have a sister, but he had a sister-in-law, and the idea of traveling to romantic destinations with Tracy didn't appeal to him, either. Nick already had a sibling and a sibling-in-law. He wanted a companion, a girlfriend, a lover. He wanted Eileen to be all of those things.

But his resolve was waning. They were buddies and all that, really good friends. One could say they were even simpatico. But Eileen's friendship alone couldn't completely captivate Nick anymore, not after eight or nine months. His attention wandered.

Zelda was separated from Link. His real name was Barry, and the two of them had gotten married the previous Valentine's Day. Nick had found the consecration of nuptials on that date to be right in line with the cuteness of their couplehood, and he considered telling her that he'd come down with a 24-hour case of the bubonic plague in order to skip the wedding. But he attended, because Zelda had exuberantly demanded his presence, and she was his friend. He went to their pretty wedding, even though Link/Barry always regarded Nick coolly, suspiciously.

Nick figured that his name was always at the top of the list in Zelda's arsenal of tools to score hit points whenever an argument erupted with her gamer husband. There were her icerods and firerods, her bombs, her magic hammers; her Cane of Byrna and her Book of Muddra. And there was Nick Wilde – *I could always go back to Nick.* It wasn't true: there'd never been a single thing between them, not even a kiss. But Link didn't know that.

The princess and her rescuer had separated after only a few months of marriage. Nick could see a lifetime of break-ups and reconciliations ahead for Barry and Zelda. Nick listened to her bitch about him at lunch all the time. Theirs was the picture, the epitome, of the love-hate relationship. They were perfect for each other; they were toxic to each other. Nick believed that they'd be together 'til death did them part, just as they'd promised before God and the great State of California. There'd just be many little breaks in between.

Zelda was flirty with Nick now that she thought she was through with Link. Unlike Eileen, Zelda didn't have any qualms about putting her hand on his knee when no one else was in the break room. She didn't have any problem telling him that she was sorry that she'd never gotten a chance to go back to his place and hear him play, but she was free tonight, so why not?

Nick knew better. Zelda was cute and perky and definitely down. Modern mores allowed a woman separated from her husband to hit a little strange without too many repercussions. But Nick knew that Link was like malaria in Zelda's blood: she was clear of symptoms at the moment, but she would have a relapse sooner or later. She'd return to Link. Zelda's disease was incurable. And when that inevitability came to pass, pity the fool who had believed that she was truly available and ready to start over. Nick knew better than to be that guy.

So he told Zelda thanks but no thanks, told her he was seeing somebody. And he *was* seeing somebody, but he wasn't seeing enough of her, not seeing the parts he wanted to see, and he was getting a little bit tired of it.

On Friday night, Nick just fell right on off the patient, understanding, platonic companion wagon. Utterly. He and Eileen had a more or less standing date for dinner at the start of every weekend, but when she called with some excuse – her mom was sick or something – Nick had simply said, *Oh, fuck this,* and went out to the local watering hole. Lady Luck smiled on him, grinned at him, sat in his lap – he had the good fortune to meet a gorgeous young woman, some ten years his junior.

Lovely Juliana was in town for the birth of her sister's baby, but she was presently at odds and ends. Her sister was not yet even admitted to the hospital. The baby had overshot his due date, and his aunt-to-be was bored as hell and looking for a little fun. And she just happened to have a thing for redheads. She and Nick didn't leave his apartment, his bedroom, all weekend.

Nick had a vague worry that Juliana was going to keep him tied to the bed, figuratively of course, until her nephew arrived, never mind the fact that he had to be to work on Monday morning. What else did she have to do? She was on vacation. But late Sunday night, the blessed event finally occurred.

Juliana slid silently out of Nick's room, not wishing to wake him. She sent him a text, telling him how much fun she'd had, thanking him for entertaining her while she waited for the baby's birth. She told him that she'd be sure to text him again, the very next time she was in town. And then she was gone, *like the wind blowing.*

It was just as well. Nick was slated to have dinner with Eileen Monday evening, anyway. He checked his look in the mirror after work, before he went to pick her up – no hickeys, no scratches. Auntie Juliana had been something else – she most certainly did like *pelirrojas* and since he fit the bill precisely – she said blue-eyed ones were too common, but a green-eyed one like him was rare (*there is my happily married brother, too,* Nick thought) – she'd expressed her appreciation quite thoroughly.

But she hadn't left any marks. So Nick knew he looked at innocent as a redheaded choirboy when he went to pick Eileen up for dinner. As innocent as shy, young Leo. *And if you believe that, I've got some beachfront land in Fontana for you.* Fontana wasn't on the coast.

Falling face-first off the celibacy train had taken the edge off for Nick. He was able to view Eileen's reluctance to take their association to the next level a little more philosophically. She'd been through two disastrous marriages: *my, my, my, I'm once bitten, twice shy, baby.* Twice bitten, perhaps thrice shy. He couldn't really blame her for taking it slow. Now that he'd undergone an attitude adjustment, Nick thought he could get back to good-naturedly chipping away at her reticence with the ol' Wilde charm.

Nick was convinced that Eileen liked him. She was just hesitant to rush into anything because she'd already rushed into two marriages. Nick could see all that now. He'd just been bitter and irritated before, feeling mightily unloved. Juliana had loved him well enough, and now Nick saw that Eileen's hesitance was a product of her rocky experiences with men in the past.

It didn't have anything to do with the way she looked at Leo, as he'd once jealously assumed. Adrian kept himself hidden. For all he showed Eileen, he was just a kid. A shy, underage boy, younger than her daughter.

Eileen hadn't hesitated to commit to Nick because she had some kind of thing for his cousin, no matter how much she thought he resembled Adrian. That was just nuts. Nick was imagining things that just weren't there.

Or was he?

Urban Equinox didn't practice together as frequently as they had in the old days. Bobby and Tracy were settled in their ways, they had full lives, other pursuits. They'd given up music for seventeen years, after all. But Nick still visited his cousin to jam, nearly every weekend, and frequently in the evenings, after work. It wasn't like either of them had much else to do.

Nick arrived at Adrian's house on the Saturday following his lost weekend with Juliana. The garage door was already open to the bright September afternoon. He parked his car on the street and walked up the driveway.

Eileen was standing back from the mouth of the garage a little bit, holding Adrian's ugly Charvel, the strap over her shoulder. Adrian was standing behind her, her hands over hers on the frets and strings. Nick was struck with the intimacy of it: their faces were entirely too close when she turned her head to grin over her shoulder at him. Their smiles were entirely too familiar.

Nick accidently-on-purpose kicked over an empty beer can; it skittered across the floor. Eileen looked up in surprise at the clatter. Nick asked himself if there was there a flash of guilt in her eyes,

300

before she smiled at him and said, "Leo thinks I have a future in rock and roll."

Nick suddenly thought of all the bands that had been famous twenty years ago, when the irrepressible, irresistible Adrian Wilde had fronted a garage band called Urban Equinox. His band had all been young then: their bass-player was lean, their bad-ass girl drummer sported her own natural blonde hair; their other guitarist, barely more than a boy, had worn his auburn locks in liberty spikes when they played parties.

Urban Equinox had never achieved any fame. They'd never really sought it, and then Adrian had been murdered, and Bobby had buried his music, tried to forget the band in his grief. Nick thought of all the bands that *had* achieved fame, but had then been buried by the march of time, forgotten by their fans. He remembered all the fronts that hadn't been able to take the inevitable fall from hot, fast fame, from adulation to oblivion. How many singers and guitar players had decided it was better to neither fade away nor to rust? How many had stared forty of forty-five in the eye, realized that there was never going to be a comeback? How many drug overdoses, suicides had there been?

Adrian had been given more than just another chance. He hadn't just been allowed to recover a lost youth – he hadn't lived long enough to lose it the first time, yet here he was again, as fresh as a daisy. But Nick had seen youth fade. Like all those despondent, washed-up rock stars of yesteryear, Nick keenly felt the regrets of the years gone by. When he looked at Adrian, Nick felt the nostalgia for his own irrecoverable youth, because his cousin was the same. Adrian was still, he was *again,* the young, clever, desirable musician that he'd been twenty years ago.

And the thing that galled Nick the most about it was that Eileen couldn't help but see him precisely the same way.

"I'm sure you're a prodigy," Nick said to her. He felt a bolt of hatred again, of jealousy. *Don't believe it won't happen just because it hasn't happened yet.*

Before he could stop himself, Nick's mind addressed his cousin: *What the fuck, Adrian?*

Eileen took the strap over her head and handed the guitar to Leo. Again the smile they shared seemed way too intimate.

Adrian glanced mildly at his cousin as he set his axe down on its stand. *Maybe you should try teaching her how to play, my brutha. I'd say she's definitely down to learn. Stop shooting me hard looks and step up, Cuz. God hates a coward.*

NINETY-THREE

On the following Friday afternoon, Leo's doorbell rang. He wasn't expecting anyone: Eileen was up the hill hanging out with his mom and his aunts at the moment. He'd be seeing her later, after dinner, when the sun began to go down, when they could be alone. Leo opened the door and was surprised to see a lovely young blonde woman.

"Hi," she said, a little breathlessly. "I'm looking for Eileen Artus? She said she'd be on Parcay Street. My phone died, and – I see her car on the street, but I'm afraid I don't know which house she's visiting. Since there are only two, I thought I'd start here first. Do you know her?"

"Yes," Adrian said. *I know her quite well, as a matter of fact. She took the afternoon off from work, just so she could be with me.* He smiled at the pretty girl.

"I'm her daughter. Carmen." She offered her hand.

"Wow! You look so much like your dad!" Adrian blurted out as he shook her hand.

Carmen was stunned. Who was this kid? He looked familiar to her . . .

"You . . . You know my dad?"

"Oh . . . Yeah, well . . ."

She's so pretty. . .

But Adrian had to get his mind off of that for the moment. He'd just made a major faux pas. Leo was three years younger than Carmen. Her dad was long gone from the neighborhood before he'd even been a twinkle in his own deceased father's eye. There was no way Leo could've ever met Allan Coleman, no way that he should be able to know that his beautiful daughter resembled him.

Sure, he'd been here recently, harassing his ex-wife, but Adrian didn't want to go into all that. Eileen had shown up that day with a mind to seduce Leo. She would've succeeded, had Carmen's father not showed up out of the clear blue sky. The seduction had come later, so maybe Eileen hadn't mentioned to her daughter that Allan had tracked her down here. Adrian was sure that Eileen hadn't mentioned that Carmen's father had interrupted them making out . . .

She's gorgeous . . .

But Adrian couldn't think about that now. He had to fix his mistake. Carmen was waiting for him to explain how he knew she looked like Allan.

"My dad . . ."

My dad talked about him . . . no, that won't work. I never knew my dad, now did I?

"My dad had some pictures of him. My mom . . ."

Yeah, that's the ticket. Randi had known Allan and Eileen. *Oh, shit! Eileen!* She was up visiting with the family, but soon she'd be back, and she'd want to . . .

Adrian couldn't worry about all that right now, either. He had to make this anachronism go away. He had opened his big mouth, not thinking about who he was supposed to be . . .

Randi was the key. Randi had known Eileen and Allan. She could've told Leo about them. It wasn't like she was going to deny the mythical photos he was making up. Since Nadine had moved in over there, he didn't see Randi too much anymore. He didn't miss her.

"My mom showed me dad's old photos. 'There's Allan Coleman and his wife.'"

Family pictures. Why not?

"'And their little girl,' she told me. 'They used to live right here in this house.'"

"I don't remember this place at all," Carmen said. "But I guess I wasn't even two when we moved."

"Actually, it was that house," Leo pointed across the street. "So . . . yeah. I saw pictures of your dad. You look just like him."

"That's what my mom always says. Usually when she's mad at me." Carmen offered a little giggle. Adrian found it to be adorable. Then she sighed. "I don't know my dad very well. He didn't visit a lot when I was little. And now . . . He just got out of jail."

Carmen looked expectantly at the young man, waiting for a shocked reaction. With most new people she met, Carmen thought it best to get the awful truth out of the way immediately. She knew that they'd judge her. Her dad was that kind of bird that doesn't fly – a jailbird – so, what kind of a person did that make her? In high school, the captain of the swim team had stopped going out with her when he found out that her ol' man was in the slammer. So Carmen told new people up front now, before she got to like them. That way, if their judgment was harsh, they could just go on their way without her wasting any time on them.

Adrian knew all about what kind of a person Allan was, but he didn't think it reflected poorly on his daughter at all. She had nothing to do with it. She'd just said that she barely even knew him.

"I never met my father," Leo told Carmen. "He died before I was born." He offered his hand again, just for another opportunity to touch her. "I'm Leo Wilde."

That's why he looks so familiar! Carmen realized. *That guy, the one Mom had such a crush on, the one that was holding me in her favorite picture. That guy was his dad.*

Carmen's hand lingered in his. She thought Leo was better looking than his dad, but there was still quite a resemblance. He wore his hair the same way. Carmen had never been much for guys with long hair, but it looked good on *him* . . .

Carmen realized that she was staring at him, still holding his hand. She shook it firmly, then took her own hand back.

"My mother told me about your dad," she said. *She was in love with him once . . . No, no need to go into all of that right now.* "She told me that he'd passed. I was sorry to hear about that." *Not as sorry as she was . . .*

Leo shrugged. "Like I say, I never met him." *Damn, she's pretty.* "Your mom's at my aunts' house. It's at the top of the hill. There are actually three houses on Parcay Street. She's visiting with my mom . . ."

Adrian was referring to Daina. He shook his head. Daina was Leo's *grandmother.* He had to remember that. Why was he having so much trouble keeping things straight? It was because Carmen was so attractive. She was muddling his mind.

"She's up there visiting with my aunts and my grandma," he said firmly. Randi, Leo's mom, didn't lunch with the other ladies too often anymore. "The whole matriarchy." Leo flashed a smile.

Carmen smiled back. That was a big word, *matriarchy.* He might be a long-hair, but apparently he was no dummy.

Adrian found her to be even more beautiful when she smiled.

"Would you like to meet them?"

Carmen nodded.

But then a crazy, impossible thought occurred to him. Adrian was well aware of his own charm. It made him fearless. The worst thing that could happen would be that she'd say no . . .

"I just remembered, I have to make a phone call really quick. Would you like to come in? I'll only be a minute, and then we can go up and fetch your mom."

Again Carmen nodded. Leo let her into the house.

"Please, make yourself at home," he said expansively. "I'll be right back." He snatched his phone off of the coffee table and ducked down the hall.

Carmen sat on the couch and looked around the tidy living room. She noted a guitar on a stand. *So he's a musician. I should ask him to play something for me.*

Carmen smiled to herself. She'd just met the guy and was already think about asking him to play a song for her. *How forward I'm getting in my old age,* she said to herself.

But she was bored with Clint. All of his little mannerisms seemed to annoy her anymore. He seemed to be bored with her, too. His mood was always snappish and irritable lately. The thought had crossed Carmen's mind that perhaps Clint was cheating on her: he spent more and more time at school these days. He had a full course load, of course, and five new students to show around. Maybe he was showing one of them more than just around – that was how they'd met, after all, and it hadn't taken him long to suggest more to Carmen than just directions to the quad and cafeteria.

She arose and idly stroked the strings on the black and yellow Charvel. Maybe it was time for a change. This Leo Wilde was cute, long hair and all. He played the guitar . . . Carmen felt a shiver of excitement. She was down to see what might develop.

Adrian closed his bedroom door and called his cousin.

"You got a key to the house in Parker?"

"I do not," Nick said. "But Bobby does."

"Do you think your dad would mind if I went up there for the weekend?"

"My dad hasn't gone up there in years, Cuz. Or Rob, either. Not since . . . Not since your dad died. It's really Bobby's place now."

"Yeah, he mentioned something about us going skiing again, but then nothing ever came of it."

"Bobby was just thinking about how you guys used to ski in the old days. When you were *both* twenty. But he's not twenty anymore. I think he's a little chubby to start waterskiing again."

"Ah, it's like riding a bicycle, Nick. You never forget. You're never too old."

"That's easy for you to say. You've got a forty-year-old memory in a twenty-year-old body."

"Dad would've skied forever, him and Rob, if it wasn't for . . ."

"I think his heart went out of it after you were killed, Cuz."

306

Nick quickly changed the subject. Any mention of Ian always brought Adrian down. The only dark spot to his return from the other side was that he hadn't gotten to spend any time with his dad. Adrian missed Ian.

"Why do you want to go to Arizona all of a sudden?"

"I've got a date." *Maybe,* Adrian thought.

Like the tri-headed dog of legend, three ugly emotions barked in Nick's mind: suspicion, panic, jealousy. He remembered coming upon Adrian and Eileen in the garage the week before. Ostensibly, he'd been playfully trying to teach her to play the guitar. Nick had used the ploy a few times himself in his younger days. No music had ever been learned. The whole idea had soon been forgotten, in fact, and other lessons undertaken. Ones with which Nick and his giggling student were already familiar.

"You're not thinking of taking . . ." Nick stopped, didn't say her name. It was ridiculous. There was nothing going on between Eileen and Adrian, no matter what he thought he'd seen.

Adrian knew whose name Nick had left unspoken. Adrian sensed his cousin's suspicion in his pause. *Does he really like her that much?* Adrian felt an unaccustomed twinge of guilt.

"Now why would I wanna do that, Cuz? I said I had a date."

That should be a weight off of his mind. Maybe he and this beautiful blonde would hit it off while they were out of town together, if she even agreed to go. Maybe this glorious nightmare with Eileen could then come to an end.

Nick was relieved. It was a silly thought, anyway. Leo was almost twenty – Eileen was twice his age. He wasn't interested in her, no matter how she looked at him.

"Who is this chick?"

"Someone I just met. I haven't even asked her if she wants to go yet. I wanted to check and see if it's all right first."

"I'm sure it is. Call Bobby. Good luck." Nick paused. "You don't need luck, do you?"

"No. I play guitar. Just like my good lookin', redheaded cousin." Adrian added, "Tell Eileen I said hi."

"I'll do that," Nick replied, with more gratitude than he had intended. "Have fun."

Adrian called Bobby, told him the that he'd just a met a girl, and he thought it might be fun to take her up to the old vacation house for the weekend.

"They have a key at the ski shop in Parker, Cuz. Mom pays them to go out and check on the place every now and then. To make sure there's no squatters. To make sure it hasn't burned down."

"We'll have to go skiing soon, Bobby. I miss it."

"Me, too, Adrian. We'll definitely do that. But in the meantime, you have fun with your girl."

"Thanks. I'll see you soon."

Adrian disconnected and took a deep breath. The place was his if he wanted to use it. Now all he had to do was talk Carmen into going with him.

"I know this is crazy," he said to her when he went back out into the living room. "I've never done anything like this before . . ." He offered Leo's guileless smile. "But . . . Do you have any plans for the weekend?"

Carmen's mouth fell open. Here she was, just thinking that she might like to get to know this guy a little better, and now he was asking her out . . .

"My cousins have a little house on the Colorado River. In Parker, Arizona. I was just wondering if you might like to go up there with me for the weekend." Her eyes widened and Adrian continued quickly. "It's a big house – three bedrooms." He paused. "Like I say, I know it's crazy. You don't even know me. But I promise, I'm not a murderer or anything like that." *Not much.* "I just thought . . . If you'd like to go . . . It'll be fun."

Carmen opened her mouth again, but no sound came out. *I was just thinking that he was cute . . . I need to think about a million dollars falling out of the sky. See if that works, too.*

"Okay," she said at last. "It does sound like fun."

"Great! We can go . . . right now if you want." *Before your mother comes down to see me.* "I'll show you the path to my aunts' house. You can go see your mom while I pack a few things really quick."

Adrian immediately regretted that suggestion. *Oh, yeah, hey, Mom? I've just been invited to go to Arizona with the nineteen-year-old kid you've been nailing on the down low for the last couple of months . . .*

Of course, Adrian was sure that Carmen didn't know anything about all that. But Eileen might not be overjoyed to hear that Leo had just decided to whisk her daughter away to the river for the weekend. It wasn't like they'd made any promises of fidelity to each other. They didn't *talk much* about what they did at all, they just *did it.*

Eileen had shyly asked Leo once if he had any other *girlfriends.* She'd stumbled over the word in embarrassment. She didn't want anyone to know about them, she said, so she really couldn't think of herself as his *girlfriend.* And she went out to dinner with Nick whenever he asked her. She felt compelled to make it clear to Leo that there was nothing going on there, however . . .

"If you want to see someone else, just let me know. I don't have any claim on you." Adrian could tell that it was awkward for her to say these things. Their situation was complicated.

He could read Eileen's indecision: she loved what they did together, and she loved him in a way, because of it. Then Nick would cross her mind, and she'd again think, *There's no future in this . . .*

"Okay," Leo had told her. "But I don't think I'll be looking for —"

"Just let me know," she'd repeated quickly, and kissed him, just to shut him up. Eileen liked what they had. She just didn't like talking about it.

Adrian hadn't been looking; he enjoyed his little secret thing with Eileen. But here was Carmen, and she was beautiful, and he'd decided on the spot that he wanted to get to know her better.

It was insane. *She's Eileen's* daughter, *for Christ's sake! This is just the kind of crazy shit that's liable to get me shot all over again . . .*

Carmen shook her head at Leo's suggestion that she wait with her mom while he packed.

"That's okay," she told him. "I'll call her later. It's not pressing that I talk to her this minute."

Carmen looked to see if he was surprised. She'd driven all the way out here to scare up her mom, now she'd apparently changed her mind. Carmen really didn't have to talk to Eileen. She'd just been planning to ask her out to the movies again, because Clint said he was studying, but now her plans had changed. Carmen giggled inwardly. Her plans had changed, just like that, and she didn't want to see her mom at all right now. She didn't want to have to explain her spontaneous decision to accompany a complete stranger out of town. *You're just taking off with some guy you just met? What about Clint?*

I might just be done with Clint, Carmen thought, *depending on how this goes.*

Leo was right. It was crazy, reckless, just a spur of the moment thing. But he was cute. Carmen would just text Clint and tell him she wasn't feeling well, in case he was done studying early. She'd tell him that she'd see him . . . later.

Oh, what a tangled web we weave . . . But Carmen didn't care. She liked Leo's big blue eyes. A little recklessness was feeling good.

"Do you know where we live?" she asked him. Leo shook his head. "I was just thinking that I'd go on home and pack a few things myself, then you could come and pick me up."

"Okay." Leo took his phone out of his pocket. "What's your . . ." He smiled. "This is so weird. I've never done anything like this, just asking someone to go out of town with me."

Usually I stay in *town,* Adrian thought.

"I know." Carmen giggled conspiratorially. "Me, either. But it'll be fun." She told Leo her number, and he typed it into his phone, then rang hers.

"So you know it's me," he said and smiled at her again.

He's cute. "We live over by Central Middle School. Do you know where that is?"

Again Leo smiled. "My grandpa used to teach there."

"We live on Rice Road, right across the street."

"I'll call you when I get there."

They looked at each other in silence for a heartbeat. *Should I shake her hand, pat her on the shoulder, kiss her on the cheek?* At last, Adrian decided against touching Carmen in any way.

He just opened the door and let her out.

NINETY-FOUR

"That ain't the way to have fun, son," Adrian sang aloud as he threw a couple of changes of clothes into a duffel bag. *"That ain't the way to have fun, no."*

He paused and texted Eileen. *I'm sorry about missing our afternoon together, but something's come up. I have 2 go out of town 4 the weekend. See u on Monday?*

Sitting at the table on Penny and Bellona's deck, Eileen looked at her phone, read Leo's text. A thin wire of jealousy whipped through her: *he's met a girl, someone his own age . . .*

What else could it be? It wasn't like Leo had any friends, besides his cousins. *Maybe Betty and Veronica called him . . .*

Eileen had tried to tell herself that it was bound to happen eventually. They were just having a little fun together; a fling. Leo didn't, *couldn't* love her, Eileen told herself. *There's not going to be a happily ever after.*

Eileen knew that there was no future in their relationship, but still, the thought of him going out of town with some young girl stung a little bit. She'd asked him to tell her, if, *when,* he met someone else, and she'd hoped that he'd be man enough to do it. She'd hoped that he'd just break it to her, tell her the truth, not slink around behind her back, not play her and his new girlfriend both . . .

I have 2 go out of town 4 the weekend. See u on Monday?

Maybe I'm just overreacting. Leo was adorable, sexy, and the idea that he'd met someone his own age just seemed like the most logical thing to be taking him out of town, even if it was the most painful to consider . . .

But Eileen didn't know anything about what Leo did when they weren't together. Maybe he did have some friends. If he was going off with some girl, surely he wouldn't have said, *See u on Monday?*

Regardless, Eileen didn't have any claim on him. Whatever was going on, she'd just have to deal with it. She'd just hang out with the ladies for the rest of the day.

Ok, she replied.

☺

Adrian put his phone back into his pocket. *That was easy. She's all right,* he thought. *Not possessive or anything crazy like that.*

NINETY-FIVE

Adrian considered talking *One Wilde Ride* with them to Arizona. The prospect of teaching Carmen how to waterski pleased him: showing her how to balance Ian's old Maherajahs; touching her elbow, her knee, her hip. Her skin would be wet and slick from the river . . .

But the registration was expired on the boat and the trailer as well, and even if it wasn't, Leo had nothing so outlandish as a trailer hitch on his car. Ian's old truck was long gone, as was Gil's. Besides, Adrian and Carmen would have to scare up at least one other person if they wanted to ski, and Adrian wanted to be alone with her. That was the whole point of taking her out of town.

Two days and two glorious nights all alone with a beautiful, sparkly-eyed blonde. If they hit it off, Adrian figured he could always teach her how to ski some other time. He didn't realize that it was out of character for him to be thinking ahead to another time with the same girl. He didn't consciously recognize that he was hoping that this one would be around for a while.

In his first life, Adrian had been confident, fearless, the product of loving parents and doting aunts. He'd been raised in the tradition of the supernatural, and it had always lent him a touch of shade, a playful, dark sense of superiority. Through those same traditions, he'd been returned from the abyss. In gratitude, he now devoted a fair amount of his time to the old practices. Adrian would shudder at the melodrama of the term *warlock:* it summoned up pictures of black-cowled covens, ominous, monotone chanting in the dark forest, human sacrifice; a hundred years of Hollywood Satanist stereotypes.

Yet a warlock was precisely what Adrian Wilde was, and a more than competent one. His soul been returned to this plane – that fact enough lent him a little fairy glamour. He paid homage to deities and powers and forces beyond the trinity. He believed in the immutability of fate, yet knew beyond a shadow of a doubt that it was entirely possible to bargain with fate. Like his womenfolk, he could attempt to scry what was to come, although the talent was not his long suit. He could interpret the Tarot. At his aunts' knee, he'd learned herb and potion and poison lore, spells and curses.

Adrian knew the old legends and myths. He'd been taught that male and female were halves to the same whole, that neither was greater than the other, nor complete without the other, although these ideas were more just concepts to him than concrete facts. Adrian had felt superior to practically every woman he'd ever known, and not without cause: most of them had worshipped him, to a greater or lesser degree, whilst he could've taken or left all of them.

But his parents had achieved that oneness, that mutual respect and admiration, that blissful state of being that the poets called love. So Adrian knew it existed, even if he'd given up searching for it for himself since he'd returned from the other side.

If Adrian believed in sin, he would've considered himself sinful now. First the mother: hot, desirous of him as no other. And now the daughter: beautiful, captivating, curious . . .

How unspeakably lucky could one guy get?

NINETY-SIX

The ride to Arizona started in silence.

Carmen was unexpectedly self-conscious – what kind of a tramp must Leo think she was, just agreeing to go out of town with an utter stranger? But he wasn't really a stranger, not like some anonymous pick-up from a bar. Carmen would never in a million year just take off to another state with some guy she met in a bar. Leo wasn't even remotely a stranger like that. Her mother knew him, knew his family, so he was undoubtedly a nice guy.

Then Carmen realized with an abrupt shock that her mom had never mentioned Leo Wilde to her. She'd talked about that guy's mom – that would be Leo's grandmother – and her aunts, and how pleasant it was to hang out with them.

But Eileen had never mentioned any young men in the family, yet Leo had said that he knew her. He'd known where she was when Carmen had come looking for her, had offered to take her right on up there. *So he knows Mom, but she's never mentioned him . . .*

Maybe he was a bad boy, a juvenile delinquent. A black sheep. Maybe he was an embarrassment to his family in some way, and that's why Eileen had never mentioned him.

Carmen looked over at Leo. He smiled blankly back at her. He was cute, but he didn't look like any kind of a rebel, didn't seem like he had a chip on his shoulder about the unfairness of life. She didn't think he had anything to prove. Maybe Eileen hadn't mentioned him because she hadn't had any cause to interact with him too much. Carmen didn't imagine that good-looking Leo would relish hanging out with a bunch of old ladies, any more than she did.

But you'd think Mom would've said something. *He looks so much like his dad, that guy she had such a ferocious crush on . . .*

"What was your dad's name, Leo?" Carmen asked.

He glanced inquiringly at her. "Adrian. It's also my middle name." That would be a good fact for her to know, he thought, in case any of his careless relatives accidently called him by it.

"My mother was very fond of him," Carmen commented.

"You don't say?" Adrian said brightly. How much had Eileen told her daughter about the Adrian of the past? How much had she said about the Leo of the present?

Carmen nodded, offered a little sly grin. "She said she thought she was in love with him. He was the best looking man she'd ever met. That's why I can't understand why she never mentioned you. You look so much like him . . ."

Carmen blushed, recognizing that she'd just paid Leo quite the compliment, albeit through her mother's perceptions. His dad had been attractive, he looked like his dad, so by the transverse property of . . . Whatever. He *was* good-looking. Carmen was sure that she was not the first person that had ever mentioned it to him, inadvertently or otherwise.

"How do you know what my dad looked like?" Adrian asked, almost unable to hide his astonishment. But only almost.

Again, that sly grin. "Mom has a picture of him. She keeps in it a big box with all her important papers, in Grandma's attic. Every couple of years, or whenever she had to find a tax return or something, she'd run across that picture again, show it to me, and tell me all about what an enormous crush she had on your dad, way back when she was still married to *my* dad. I've heard the story a million times. I've looked at your dad's picture, periodically, for as long as I can remember." Carmen paused, smiled at him. "I was just a baby when all this was going on. He's holding me in the picture."

Adrian scanned his memory for a scene of Eileen with a camera. Then he had it: it had been one of the many uncomfortable times when she'd just shown up at the shop to stare at him. Carmen had indeed been just a baby at the time, practically a newborn. Eileen had brought her in some kind of carrier with a handle on it, had thrust her daughter into his arms, said something about wanting to take her picture . . .

Adrian grinned to himself. Because he'd been holding her, Eileen had kept the shot for all these years, separate from Carmen's other baby pictures.

Now Carmen was quite exquisitely all grown up, here with him, and Adrian was a nineteen-year-old kid again. *What a long, strange trip it's been . . .*

Conversation lapsed once more.

Carmen decided not to worry about what kind of person Leo was, nor what he thought of her. She hadn't done anything wrong yet. Agreeing to go with him, that had been a little impulsive, but it didn't automatically mean that she was going to sleep with him. If he thought that, he had another think coming . . .

Adrian didn't know what to say to the stunning young woman that had agreed to take off with him for the weekend, at the drop of a hat, but he figured he'd best come up with something quickly. Silent glances and smiles were okay for a few minutes, but it was a long drive to Parker.

To his delight and consternation, Adrian had discovered that he unable to read Carmen's thoughts. He got a vibe that she liked him, but that really didn't take clairvoyance – she had agreed to come along on this adventure, had she not?

But Carmen wasn't broadcasting any kind of overwhelming desire for him. If she felt it – and Adrian was kinda hoping she did, because he was certainly feeling a little warm for her – she was somehow managing to keep it from dominating her thoughts so much that he could read them.

That was new. It was refreshing. It was great, actually. He'd have to exercise his wit, his charm, his personality, if he wanted to get to know this pretty girl better. He'd have to do something more than just offer that killer smile and say, *Hey, Carmen, do you wanna . . .*

Adrian knew that he was more than up to the task. First, he got straight in his head who he was: Leo Wilde, aged nineteen, whose father had tragically died in a car crash before he was born. Nick had told him that Eileen knew all the details of the mythical car wreck, because Randi had manufactured them for her.

What should he talk to her about?

"What kind of music do you like?"

"What kind of music do you play? I saw your guitar."

"I can play anything you'd like." He grinned bashfully at her to take the arrogance out of the statement.

"Do you sing, too?" Carmen liked his arrogance.

"I do. Request something."

The ride to Arizona was then filled with a cappella singing and lively laughter. Carmen was a firecracker: she had no qualms about singing along with Adrian, even though she was outrageously off-key. Adrian found this flaw to be adorable, and he poked gentle fun at her about it.

"Not everybody can be a rock star," she replied with a giggle.

Carmen liked the way Leo smiled at her, with a kind of fond curiosity, as if everything that she said was interesting or amusing. She was having fun already.

NINETY-SEVEN

It was 7:45 when they parked in front of the ski shop in Parker. The sign on the door said the place closed at six. Apparently no one was buying skis after sundown on a September evening, however, because the shop was deserted when they walked in, manned only by a skinny, dark-haired, teenaged boy. He was sitting behind the counter, leafing idly through a copy of *WaterSki Magazine.* The cover promised to instruct him on *How to Cross Wakes Like a Pro.*

Adrian said hi and told the young man that he'd called earlier about the key to the house up the road.

"Grandma?" the kid called toward the back of the shop. "That guy's here."

A tiny old woman came out at her grandson's summons. Her hair was frizzy, dyed a becoming platinum blonde, though her skin was lined and wrinkled from a lifetime in the desert sun. Her friendly blue eyes twinkled at her customers. She said to the boy, "You can go now, Freddie. I'll make sure your dad gives you overtime."

The kid smiled at the thought of a little extra cash. "Thanks, Grandma!" He kissed her on the cheek and trotted quickly out the door.

"Thanks for staying open for us," Leo told the old woman.

"It's no problem at all," she replied and dropped him a little wink. "I was curious to see which Wilde was going to show up. I haven't seen Rob or Will for years, and Will's son –?"

"Bobby."

"Right. I haven't seen him or his wife in a long time, either." She studied Leo carefully for a moment. "You must be Ian's grandson!" she said at last. "You have his eyes. And your grandmother's black hair."

"You're right. I'm Leo." He offered his hand and she shook it.

"And this is your lovely girlfriend –?"

"Carmen," replied the complete stranger that Adrian had, without putting too fine a point on it, *just picked up.* She also shook the old woman's hand.

Adrian was inordinately pleased that Carmen didn't object to the woman's assumption that she was Leo's girlfriend, that she didn't stammer out something like, *Oh, no, we're only friends. We just met, actually . . .*

"It's a great pleasure to meet you, Leo. I'm Sissy. I used to ski with your grandpa and his cousins, way back in the dawn of time."

"He loved to ski," Leo murmured, half to himself.

"That has to be the understatement of all time," Sissy said, with a girlish giggle. "That's all he did. That, and chase the ladies." She winked at Carmen, then sobered. She said simply, "I miss him."

"We all do," Leo agreed.

A heartbeat passed, then Sissy brightened once again. "Do you ski, Leo?"

"Yes. Yes I do. I use Grandpa's old Maherajahs."

"Christ! Wooden skis! I haven't seen a pair of wooden skis in years! He bought those here, you know. I sold them to him. It was my dad's shop then." Sissy sighed. "Good Lord, how the years have passed."

She hit a button on the cash register. The drawer opened and she removed a house key and handed to Leo.

"If you get a minute while you're in town, come back and see me. I could tell you a few stories about your grandpa that'll curl your hair. He used to take a different girl back to Rob and Will's house very night, whenever he was in town. That was all before he met your grandma, of course."

Sissy sighed again. "Quite the looker was Ian Wilde. And God, could he ski." She studied Leo keenly for another moment. "I remember seeing your dad a couple of summers when he was a kid. You look a lot like him."

"That's what everyone says. Thanks again for waiting for us."

Sissy nodded, and Carmen said it was nice meeting her. "You, too, honey. You guys have fun, and if you need anything, just give me a call."

When they got back into the car, Carmen said, "So, are all the Wilde guys ladies' men?"

In response, Adrian offered her Leo's boyish, slightly confused expression.

"Well, let's see," Carmen explained. "Mom's been seeing another guy named Wilde. Nick? He's your uncle?"

"He's my cousin."

So Eileen had mentioned Nick to her daughter, but not Leo. That was an amusing revelation.

"My mom says Nick's cute. A really nice guy."

Christ save me from being a really nice guy, Adrian thought uncharitably.

"I haven't met him yet. I'm not home a lot . . ."

318

Carmen thought that she shouldn't have said that, as soon as it was out of her mouth. She didn't want Leo to politely inquire where she was if she wasn't at home, what she was doing. Carmen wasn't home a lot because she was always at Clint's place. She didn't want Leo to know that she was seeing someone. Once again, what kind of a person did that make her? She had a boyfriend, but she had just taken off on a whim with the first stranger that had asked her . . .

Carmen continued quickly. "So your cousin's cute, and your dad was the sexiest man alive, according to my mom. And that lady said your grandpa had his share of adventures." Carmen smiled coquettishly at Leo and repeated, "So, are all the Wilde guys ladies' men?"

"I dunno," Leo said. "I've just had one girlfriend, and she dumped me for some college boy."

That was a verifiable fact. It wasn't like Nick or Bobby were going to sit down with pretty Carmen and discuss their young cousin's adventures with Betty and Veronica. And Eileen wasn't going to tell her daughter that Leo Wilde was anything but an inexperienced boy . . .

"I'm single myself," Carmen declared, deciding that she was, right there on the spot.

She was feeling flirty. Night had fallen, and here she was, all alone in a strange town, a strange *state,* with a good-looking, strange man. None of that meant she was going to sleep with him right away, however – Carmen knew better than to do that, especially if she wanted him to stick around. And she definitely wanted Leo to stick around. She thought fleetingly that the time had indeed become nigh to dump Clint . . .

Carmen mentally dismissed her long-time boyfriend, and brought her mind back again to the unusual, not un-exciting situation at hand. She didn't plan on jumping into the sack with Leo as soon as they got to the house, but it was okay to flirt with him a little bit.

"Then this doesn't look bad, our just taking off out of town together," Leo suggested.

Adrian thought it was a truthful, innocuous enough statement to make. He could tell that Carmen was just being playful. She wasn't making hints by mentioning her singleness, talking about his relatives' legendary attractiveness. Carmen wasn't making a pass at Leo, and she wasn't signaling that she wanted him to make a pass at her. She was just telling him in a roundabout way that she thought he was cute, that she liked him a little bit, that she was beginning to feel comfortable with him.

Leo suggested that they stop at the store, because the unused vacation house was sure to be devoid of food. They giggled and whispered to each other, making little snide remarks about the sun-bleached, stringy-looking desert townies that peopled the aisles. It wasn't tourist season, after all, and Leo and Carmen were the only non-locals shopping that evening. They enjoyed displaying their California-bred superiority to each other.

They meshed in the grocery store like an old married couple. Each liked the other's suggestions on what to get to eat, and they anticipated who should go and fetch what. Both were delighted at their easy compatibility on this point.

The house was hot and stuffy, a trifle dusty. Carmen found a rag and wiped off the counters and appliances in the kitchen while Leo fired up the central air. They worked effortlessly as a team in preparation of the meal, and were soon enjoying lime-cilantro pork tacos – Adrian had learned the recipe from his cousin – with rice and beans. They sipped goblets of white wine – Adrian had felt ridiculously self-conscious when Carmen had been required to show her ID to purchase it.

Carmen reminded herself not to overdo it. She wasn't much of a drinker, and with the elation she felt being around cute, fun, good-cook Leo, she thought that the Two Buck Chuck equivalent that she'd bought at the grocery store might go straight to her head.

Adrian had to borrow from his own memories to tell Carmen the history of the house, because Leo had never been there before. Thanks to his stepfather's loving ministrations when he was of kindergarten age, Leo had been petrified of the water. He'd only been on a boat once in his life, and he'd been terrified at the thought of the slimy depths, which his child's imagination had filled with gruesome creatures ready to drag him under.

But Adrian had shared his father's love of boating and waterskiing. Bobby had dug it, too. If they hadn't been so wrapped up in their music, maybe they would've spent more time out on the water with Rob and Ian. Adrian felt a small pang of regret about that. He wished he'd spent more time with his dad. He wished that his murder hadn't taken all the fun out of Ian's favorite pastime for him . . .

But now was not the time to dwell on Ian and the regrets of Adrian's once-removed past. Like his mother, like Nadine, Adrian believed he'd see Ian again in some future incarnation.

He was Leo Wilde now, but he figured that it was safe for him to tell Carmen about skiing and boating via Adrian's memories. It wasn't as if someone was going to suddenly pop up and exclaim to her how odd it was that Leo should all of a sudden have knowledge of these activities. No one was going to inform Carmen that right up until his stepfather *had been lost,* Leo had never been on a boat, that he'd always been afraid of the water.

Carmen mentioned that she hadn't been on fresh water before, but she liked the ocean. She told Leo that she'd taken the big, catamaran-style ferry over to Catalina Island many times. She almost said with whom she'd gone, but quickly caught herself. Adrian didn't fail to notice the little hesitation; someone as gorgeous as Carmen had to have lots of boyfriends. But she hadn't mentioned a single one of them. For all she spoke of anyone that she'd dated, one would think that Carmen had had fewer companions of the opposite sex than boring Leo had known.

Adrian knew better – Carmen was just too pretty, too outgoing. But she said she was single now. He thought that maybe that wouldn't be the case by the end of the weekend. Maybe Leo would be her boyfriend by then. She was gorgeous. Adrian wouldn't be averse to keeping her around for a while, at least until she started to get too clingy.

"And I never got seasick. Not once," Carmen added, as coda to her tale of her trips to Catalina. "I'd like to take a cruise someday. To Mexico or Alaska or somewhere."

Leo smiled at her. "Maybe we can do that, the next time we decide to skip town together."

Carmen smiled back, but didn't speak. *I'd like that,* she thought.

Maybe it'll be soon, Adrian thought.

They shared a moment of silence, each lost in thoughts about the other.

If Carmen had been any other girl, Adrian would've made his move then, because a wistful *spoken* wish about a romantic cruise was usually just as good as a wistful *unspoken* wish to cruise right on into bed with him. But he couldn't read Carmen's thoughts – that might indeed be what she was communicating, but he wasn't sure. He didn't want to mess things up by coming on to her too soon. He didn't want to make her uncomfortable, didn't want to dispel the delightful camaraderie that they were developing. No need to rush it. He had the whole weekend to make a pass at her.

Carmen scattered the silent moment by leaping up and clearing the table. Adrian helped her wash the dishes, and they laughed and playfully splashed each other at the sink. Adrian recognized plenty of opportunities to kiss her, but he failed to take advantage of them. It would've been just that, *taking advantage,* and he was unsure – he didn't want her to be offended and push him away. Then the rest of the weekend would just be prickly. His attempt and her denial of it would become the elephant in the room, crowding out the playful friendship that was emerging.

Adrian didn't truly think that Carmen would push him away if he tried to kiss her – it had never happened to him before – but with this beautiful, fascinating young woman, he just didn't know for sure. So he didn't risk it.

Carmen wanted him to kiss her, but was supremely grateful that he didn't. She liked Leo, past a mere physical attraction. That was a new thing for her.

Carmen had always found interactions with young men to be tiresome, because the question of *would she* or *wouldn't she* always seemed to hang right behind their eyes. All conversation between them was overshadowed by it.

Sometimes she did. Carmen liked sex as much as any other girl, but she often imagined that intercourse just for the hell of it couldn't be the entire reason for associating with the opposite sex. There had to be something more: friendship, intellectual rapport, maybe even love.

But Carmen had never experienced any of that. Her exchanges with men had always consisted of roundabout, generic banter, whose only purpose was to kill time, to serve propriety, before they wound up in bed. Or not. The words, the dialogues, that Carmen had shared with the men she'd known had always been meaningless. Even if she concentrated, it was difficult for her to reconstruct any of their conversations.

This state of the world had been acceptable to Carmen. It was just the way things were. Guys' main objective was to *get at you.* How charming they seemed was simply a function of how well they disguised that undeniable fact.

But Carmen really enjoyed just buddying around with Leo. She knew that she'd like to get to the point of male-female interaction with him eventually, because he was adorable, tall and strong and blue-eyed. Leo was masculine, sexy, a musician. But not yet. Carmen was having too much fun with him, of an entirely new and different kind. Just cooking and eating and laughing and talking was surprisingly enjoyable.

After dinner, Adrian again borrowed from his own memories and taught Carmen how to play poker. He reflected again that Leo's life had truly been empty. Adrian didn't remember much of it anymore; the only skill he'd retained from being Leo for seventeen years was the ability to come up with a credible, instant lie to even out any situation. This was evidenced by how quickly he'd manufactured a plausible tale for Carmen, about how he could know that she looked like her father.

Adrian again reckoned that Leo had spent his entire life just trying to get by, trying to comprehend why his mother didn't love him as much as she loved the cruel bully she'd married, trying to understand what he'd ever done to make Gil hate him so much. He'd accepted it all as his lot in life, had never thought to rebel against its unfairness. Leo had attempted to get along with his arbitrary parents, because he'd been just biding his time, waiting until he was old enough to escape and find a normal life. But in the waiting, the life he'd had passed him by.

Leo had gone to parties, because he liked to observe his peers, then try to figure out the motivations for their behaviors. H'd eventually formed an almost normal relationship with shy, mousy Sheryl, but Adrian realized that Leo had never embraced a single hobby. He didn't like the water, had never learned to play cards or sports or music. He'd enjoyed computer games and the internet, because they'd offered him an escape from the dreary existence that he accepted as the way of the world. Gaming and the web: they were also only a fantasy, another kind of falsehood. Leo had never done much with his short life except visit digital realms and lie to keep the peace.

Carmen was intelligent and picked up the rules to poker quickly. Adrian saw a gambler's enjoyment flash and crackle in her unusual tan eyes, as soon as she grasped how the game worked. The risk was exciting, the possibilities great – all those chips that represented cash could be hers at the draw of a card.

Adrian still took all her "money."

Had she been any other girl, after a while, Adrian would have suggested that he and Carmen play strip poker. She was confident enough in her beauty to sit there in her underwear with him, even though they'd just met, mere hours ago. And Adrian had given her enough confidence in her newly-learned poker-playing abilities that she already believed that she'd soon have him sitting in *his* underwear. Maybe she'd even be surprised to find out that he didn't wear any.

But it was a cheap ploy to hustle a young woman out of her clothes with a deck of cards. Adrian was enjoying talking and laughing with her, learning about her, and he was sincerely enjoying his inability to ken exactly what she was thinking. The liking-him vibe was still there, and it was growing, but Adrian realized to his amazement that Carmen liked him for something else besides just his looks. She sought more from him than simply the customary physical culmination.

Adrian gleaned that Carmen wanted to be friends with Leo. She had the curious desire to get to know him *as a person*. It was the complete lack of that kind of desire that whiny Leo had always lamented, when the young ladies would ignore his boyish hurt in favor of his blue eyes and his cute features and his nice body. They'd never cared *who* he was, past momentarily pondering how someone so attractive could be so quiet and reserved. But the *why* of Leo's shyness, the uncovering of the sad or terrible thing that happened to make him that way, quickly, inevitably ceased to matter to the girls that had taken an interest in him. They no longer cared about the possible causes of Leo's shyness once they aimed to cure him of it.

NINETY-EIGHT

Carmen said, "Since she's been hanging out on Parcay Street, Mom's turned over a new leaf. She's happy again. She hums to herself."

Adrian knew precisely why Eileen had been humming to herself lately, why she just couldn't seem to stay away from Parcay Street for more than a few days. He knew that it had little if anything to do with Daina and Penny and Bellona's clever conversation.

Adrian felt a flash of guilt – *What am I doing? Me and Eileen . . . and now I'm here with her daughter, for Christ's sake . . .*

As she spoke, the dynamic, beautiful Carmen also unknowingly provided Adrian with clues that explained Eileen's behavior, insight into why a middle-aged woman had chosen to ignore all sober respectability and seduce a nineteen-year-old kid.

First, Carmen spoke of her own childhood, relating that the most discomforting aspect of it had been how her happy anticipation of Daddy's visits would, almost without fail, turn to fear.

Allan would finally show up, sometimes after Carmen had waited for him for hours, and at first he'd be warm and friendly. But then he'd turn around and say something mean or threatening to Eileen, effectively shutting that friendliness down in a heartbeat. These crude, cruel remarks, his threats, had shown Carmen the bitter and ugly side to her father.

"He was always trying to get me to pick his side," Carmen told Leo.

And when she was little, Carmen *had* sided with her dad. It was all Eileen's fault that their happy family had been broken up. Everything would've worked out okay, if Mom hadn't had to be a bitch. Carmen loved her daddy then, and she felt sorry for the wrongs her mom had done to him.

Then Allan went to prison when she was fourteen, and Carmen realized that Mom had seen the handwriting on the wall when Carmen was still just a baby. Eileen had done the right thing by divorcing Allan. He was not the most upstanding of citizens, and Eileen had felt it imperative to get Carmen away from his influence.

Eileen had married George Wade, *some guy she met at work,* when Carmen was sixteen. Carmen told Leo that her mom had never dated while Carmen was growing up, so this new guy seemed to have come out of the blue. George hadn't been a deadbeat criminal like Carmen's father was, but he was still a son of a bitch. Strict, humorless.

The successful realtor considered himself superior in education and smarts to his community-college tutored spouse, and he berated and talked down to her so much that Eileen had finally become fed up with it and divorced him.

"'We'll do just fine on our own,' Mom told me, and she was right. We always did just fine, because she saw to it. But after she divorced George, it seemed to me that a kind of sadness settled on her. Until she met your grandmother and your aunts, that is – *the whole matriarchy.*"

Carmen smiled and Adrian noted that not only had Eileen not mentioned her long-ago crush's son to her daughter *(you look so much like him)*, she hadn't mentioned Randi, Leo's slightly bat-shit crazy mother, either. Again, he found the omissions amusing.

NINETY-NINE

As Carmen spoke about her mother, Adrian comprehended that, for Eileen, their fling was an escape from the tedium and monotony of the stable, successful, secure life that she'd worked so hard to establish for herself and her daughter.

He pictured it: as a tender girl, Eileen had been enamored with Allan, ensorcelled by his fearless, criminal bad-assery. Adrian himself had once admired the same qualities in the fat painter. Knowing a bad-guy, being a little bit of a bad-guy yourself under his influence, was fun.

But the fun had ended quickly for Eileen. She paid dearly for the recklessness of marrying a deadbeat. Once her child entered the picture, Eileen was forced to see that she no longer had either the time or the resources to wait around on Allan's shady deals and sometimey paychecks. She needed solidity, permanence, not a jailbird husband and a house in foreclosure. *Duty* reared its ugly head before the young mother. The quest for stability now became paramount to Eileen.

She'd already missed the train to the easy life of a day-school college coed. There would be no lounging around in the Botanical Gardens in the sunshine for Eileen, no quick conversations with happy-go-lucky young men in the quad between classes. She had a baby to support, and in order to provide for herself and Carmen, Eileen had to work during the day and attend school at night. She'd had to knuckle down and get to it.

Adrian understood that Eileen had come to responsibility the hard way.

She had loved him when she was young, because Adrian had been wild and free and sexy to her. The embodiment of anti-responsibility. The young mother had longed to ditch all the baggage she'd so newly acquired, even then, at the very sight of him. Eileen would've thrown propriety to the wind in a heartbeat, would've gone to bed with Adrian, simply because he'd asked her. It had almost occurred.

Eileen would've cheated on her jealous husband, compromised her perceived standing as a good, hard-working wife and mother. She would've risked those unkind appellations: *divorcee, adulteress.* She would've risked the shame that the words would've brought upon her child. All because she wanted Adrian Wilde.

Even when marriage and motherhood and home ownership were still fresh and new to Eileen, she would've chucked them all for Adrian. *He's the sexiest man I've ever seen; you only go through this life once;* any such selfish rationalization would have sufficed. In the end, Eileen had gone for it. The man of her dreams had shown up, ready to go, just as she'd always hoped he might. He'd never even come into the house before, and this glorious opportunity might not ever present itself again.

Adrian wondered if Eileen had ever speculated *why* he'd decided, out of absolutely nowhere, to just come on over to her house and give her want she wanted. He doubted it. The fantasy had been about to come true for Eileen, so the totally inconsequential question of *why* had gone unexamined. Had she won the lottery, Eileen would not have asked *why*. Nor had she questioned the motivation behind the appearance of a suddenly ready and willing Adrian Wilde.

But culmination had never occurred, because the unsuspecting, about-to-be-cuckolded husband had arrived to unknowingly save his young wife from herself. And not a moment too soon.

As Eileen had suspected, as she'd feared, the opportunity to have Adrian had indeed been once-in-a-lifetime. Then the responsibilities and the years had piled up quickly, inexorably, one after another, like snowdrifts. Eileen had barely had a moment to catch her breath, nonetheless go back and attempt to embark upon some fantasy life with her black-haired neighbor, even if he was the sexiest man she'd ever seen.

And when the time had finally been right, when Eileen was at last stable and successful and middle-aged, when she'd reckoned that it might be the season to start living again, she'd been too late. Adrian was dead.

Yet fate was not entirely heartless. Here was Adrian again, in the person of his son, just as young and free and beautiful as he'd been when Eileen had been willing to abandon all the accoutrements of societal approval – a husband and the vows of loyalty she'd made to their marriage – just to possess him.

How could she not go for it now?

When Eileen met Leo, she'd been given that once-in-a-lifetime opportunity a second time. She'd be able to have the one thing from her long ago youth that she'd wanted more than anything else, so she'd enthusiastically jumped at the chance.

The only impairment to Eileen's enjoyment of what she shared with Leo was the glaring, staggering age difference. Eileen was a whopping, eyebrow-raising twenty-one years older than her young lover. The number of years that it took to become an adult – the number of years that Carmen had lived – that was the number of years that separated them. Eileen was sometimes appalled at her own actions, and at those times, their age difference was a bar not to be overcome. Her sense of responsibility, of propriety, her perception of what was done and what was not done forbade all rationalization, and she'd wallow in a bout of the most ashamed guilt.

As he sat in the kitchen of his cousins' vacation home with Eileen's beautiful daughter, Adrian reminded himself (with a great sense of relief) that due to this guilt, Eileen would never reveal her liaison with a nineteen-year-old boy. Not to anyone.

She'd given in to the wild, impossible lure – Leo looked so much like Adrian – but Eileen was too sober-minded, too mature, too accountable to the responsibilities that she'd embraced . . . Adrian knew that because of these strictures (that Eileen had put upon herself) she'd never even dream of attempting to make her on the down low, side action with Leo into any kind of open, real-world, what-other-people-think-be-damned relationship.

So she knows it has to end eventually, Adrian told himself. *She has to know that.*

He looked at Carmen, sitting at the table across from him, pretty and lively, chirping happily, totally unaware of the maelstrom of emotions she was creating in him.

Adrian didn't want to hurt Eileen, *but she's gotta know that we can't go on like we have been forever.* He felt a yellow bolt of guilt. If Adrian continued to hit it off with Carmen, if she continued to enthrall his mind and imagination, then the ending of Leo's affair with Eileen was gonna occur as soon as he got back to Riverside. *The end's gonna come as quite a surprise to her. It's gonna happen far sooner than she imagined.*

Adrian wouldn't lie to Eileen. He wouldn't sneak around behind her back, all the while pretending that nothing had changed between them. Carmen was her daughter, for Christ's sake. Leo would not be so despicable as to cheat on his middle-aged girlfriend with her own daughter.

Adrian didn't want to hurt Eileen. He cringed at the fact that some amount of pain would be unavoidable. He'd just rip the bandage off in one brutal motion. He'd tell her in as gentle a way as possible that it was over. She'd be hurt; she might cry. But the hurt she felt when he ended it could be rationalized – they'd never had a future. Eileen was so ashamed of what she was doing that she couldn't even bear to expose it to the light of day.

But there could be no justification if Adrian neglected to tell her, if he just started seeing Carmen, while Eileen continued blindly on, no more the wiser. Such an act suffered no euphemism. Such an act was *betrayal*, and nothing else.

Adrian felt bad, guilty, but he told himself that only a fool attempted to fight the hand of fate. He'd felt all this coming, had perceived in advance that a change was about to overtake his settled, fortunate, smug, catbird-seat life. The way he'd lived that life, through two incarnations, would never be the same again.

Ending this thing with Eileen, possibly hurting her, was an unavoidable, unfortunate part of what was coming. Adrian could see that now. It only followed, then, that Carmen had to be another part of it. She was beautiful, amazing – but whether she'd be his salvation or his ruin when the approaching thunderheads finally burst – that remained to be seen.

ONE HUNDRED

"I came out to your street today . . ." Carmen was saying.

Had it really been only today? It seemed like she'd started out to fetch her mom a million years ago. It seemed so long ago that dinosaurs had still roamed the earth. Carmen's life had become different, better, exciting, and the space of time in which these marvels had occurred couldn't possibly have been only a few hours. Carmen glanced at the clock on the kitchen wall for confirmation: a few short hours was indeed all the longer it had been.

Earlier, just *today,* Carmen had been reviewing how tedious and irritating Clint had become. She'd been contemplating breaking it off with him, and now she'd done so, even if Clint was as yet unaware of it. The pall, like smoke, that had hung over her mood as a result of their dying relationship had been lifted.

Leo's smile and laughter and just plain *friendliness* had made all her problems disappear. Life was shiny and exciting again, full of possibilities. *The future's so bright, I gotta wear shades,* Carmen thought, as they'd said in some old song she'd heard as a child. She hoped that Leo would be a part of that future. A *big* part.

"I came out to your street today," Carmen repeated, "to ask Mom if she wanted to go to the movies with me. She'd texted earlier that she'd just decided to take the rest of the day off. I probably should've just called . . ." *But then I never would've met you.* "But I was in the mood for a little drive, so I just came on out. I was curious to meet the ladies that's she's been spending so much time with. I wanted to thank them for their friendship with her. She's just been so happy since she's been going out there to see them."

That wasn't entirely true, but it was just a little fib, and Carmen didn't feel bad about it. It was a compliment to Leo's family, and she thought he might like that.

Carmen had actually been looking for her mom simply because she'd been bored: bored with Clint, bored with school, bored with life in general. Carmen hadn't been *particularly* looking forward to making the coffee-klatch's acquaintance, but their company *had* lightened her mother's mood, so she'd been a *little* curious about them . . .

Curiosity killed the cat, Carmen said to herself, *but satisfaction brought him back.*

She'd started out the day bored, maybe a little melancholy, so she'd sought to kill a few hours of it with her work-ditching mother, and had resigned herself to the inevitable chat with the little old ladies that Eileen had befriended. What else did she have to do? Carmen had attended the one class she had on Fridays, went home and made lunch for her grandma, and then had headed out to Parcay Street.

And look what I found. Carmen struggled to remember the word. She already had the definition: *when you find something wonderful while you're looking for something else.* Such good fortune was called . . . *serendipity! That's it! I was looking to spend a little time with Mom, and I* serendipitously *discovered charming, funny, good-looking, not-pushy Leo Wilde.*

Carmen wasn't bored now. Life was definitely looking up.

ONE HUNDRED ONE

The evening wore on. Adrian put Eileen from his mind. She was in another town, another state, and just like Nick, for this weekend, what Eileen didn't know wouldn't hurt her.

The storm was gathering. Adrian could feel that a downpour of Biblical proportions would soon fall upon him. But it probably wasn't going to happen this weekend. He didn't know exactly *what* was going to happen this weekend, and because he didn't know, he reckoned that Eileen was also safe in her ignorance back in Riverside.

Hell, maybe this wasn't going to amount to anything. Adrian couldn't even tell for sure if Carmen liked him. He'd just have to go with the flow. *As always, I am but a pawn in fate's plan. . .* He smiled to himself and put Eileen from his mind. *She's there and I'm here.*

Adrian concentrated on the stunning, tan-eyed girl that was with him.

Carmen asked what having a stepfather had been like for Leo. She'd loathed her stepfather, but she'd only had to put up for him for a few years. In a serious, compassionate tone, she probed gently: what had it been like living your whole life with a man who was not blood to you?

It was flattering to Adrian that Carmen wanted to know Leo's life story, but he glossed over his relationship with Gil, revealing only to Carmen that Leo's stepfather had been distant. He didn't feel it necessary to fill her in on Gil's constant abuse, both physical and psychological: *You're as worthless as your old man.* These painful events hadn't actually happened to Adrian, after all. He had no desire to make Carmen feel sorry for the sad life that he hadn't lived. He wasn't Leo, and he had not a trace of Leo's desire for sympathy.

He told her that for as long as he could remember, Gil had made it clear that he was not Leo's father, that he had little interest in Leo's day to day life, and none whatsoever in his dreams and aspirations. Carmen frowned. Adrian had not wished for her to feel sorry for him, but even the barest outline of the bad hand that Leo had been dealt elicited compassion from her. Carmen was a kind person. Her empathy was deep.

Adrian shrugged, attempted to dispel her unwanted sympathy. "It was what it was. I turned out okay."

Carmen brightened immediately. "You certainly did."

Adrian returned her smile. They again shared a moment of appreciative silence, each thinking wistful thoughts about the other.

Then Adrian blinked in sudden, stunned surprise. Carmen looked at him curiously.

"What was the worst party you ever went to?" he asked quickly, apropos of nothing, changing the subject.

Adrian didn't care about the worst party Carmen had ever attended. He just wanted to get her talking again, so he could examine the bombshell that had just exploded in his mind.

Adrian had suddenly recognized, for the first time ever, that it had been Nick who'd orchestrated the situation in Leo's life that he'd just outlined for Carmen. It had been Nick that had made sure that Leo knew that Gil was in no way blood to him.

Having a stepfather, understanding exactly what that meant, was difficult and confusing for a little kid. He'd be forced to grapple with the alien concept that there had once been someone else in Mom's life, some other, unknown man, different than the one that ate and slept and lived with her now. He didn't know who that person was, could only attempt to imagine what he'd been like. It was a daunting set of circumstances for a kid to consider. He didn't yet comprehend how the interactions between men and women operated – why make him think about his mother's life with anyone other than the only man that he'd ever know? Why put the kid through a lifetime of asking himself painful, unanswerable questions: *Why did my real daddy have to die? Do you miss him, Mommy?*

Why make an innocent child carry the burden of a dead, unknowable father?

Gil could've masqueraded as Leo's father. Adrian was sure that Ian and Daina and Penny and Bellona would've gone along with it, so as to spare Leo the heartache and confusion in his mind. They could've still been Leo's grandma and grandpa and aunts, in some kind of adoptive way. The kid could've been told that they were just kindly neighbors, but that they still all loved him very much. The intricacies of consanguinity held no meaning, no importance to a child, especially when his progenitor was deceased.

Hell, it wasn't even like Adrian had had a life with Randi. There existed neither pretty wedding photos nor quaint, dated home videos, because Leo hadn't been the product of anything as socially acceptable as marriage. He'd been the accidental outcome of a quick roll in the hay, a revenge fuck for Randi, a one-night stand.

334

Randi had loved Gil. He'd been everything to her. There was absolutely no reason why Leo couldn't have been led to believe that his mother's beloved husband was his father.

It had all been on Nick. It had all been his doing, his initiative.

Nick had always been there for Leo, and he'd made sure that the kid always remembered and never forgot that Gil was but a poor substitute for Leo's *real dad,* Nick's cousin. His best friend. Gil was a mean, low-life, controlling son of a bitch – Leo knew that beyond a shadow of a doubt. He lived with the bastard. It was unnecessary for Nick to point it out to him. But Adrian Wilde had been an all-around great guy. Gil was an asshole, but Nick missed his cousin every day, and Leo looked just like him.

Leo of course bore no resemblance to Gil, but he had Randi's black hair and blue eyes. She and Adrian could've almost been brother and sister, based upon their similar coloring. So little Leo wouldn't ever have had occasion to wonder why he didn't look like his dad, if the myth of Gil's paternity had been allowed to fly. Leo wouldn't have wondered why he didn't look like his dad, because he looked like his mom.

But Nick wouldn't stand for any of that bullshit. Gil was not Leo's daddy, and through Nick's constant happy remembrances of Adrian, it hadn't taken the kid long to grasp the difference between Adrian and Gil. Adrian had been Leo's father. He would've been proud of him, would've loved him utterly had he been permitted to live. Gil was simply Randi's husband. He'd stepped in to support mother and child after Adrian's demise, because he loved Randi, and that was the extent of his affection. Gil could not possibly care less about her son. Leo was not his. Why should he waste his time showering love and affection on some other man's child?

Nick had made sure that Leo knew who his father was, even though he was gone, even though Leo could never really know him, because he'd felt it was his duty to honor Adrian's memory, to keep it alive.

Sitting with Carmen in Parker, Arizona, listening to her talk about the worst party she'd ever been to – but not really listening – Adrian wondered suddenly if events, both metaphysical and prosaic, miraculous and profane, would've proceeded differently had Nick not prevented Gil from pretending to be Leo's father.

The question struck Adrian now: if Leo had been led to believe that Gil was his father; if he'd never, thanks to Nick, been told that this was not the case; if Leo had never heard stories about his dad, if he'd never been given the opportunity to think about him, to wonder what he'd been like – if Leo had never known that Adrian Wilde had existed – would Adrian have been able to return as he had?

Carmen was describing the bad party: everyone but her (and her boyfriend, Adrian suspected fleetingly) had already been falling down drunk when she'd arrived. Hilarity ensued, and Carmen was enjoying the retelling of the tale. She didn't notice that Leo was not giving his full attention to her at the moment.

Adrian was remembering that the alpha and omega of Leo's argument with Gil that day had been the fact that Gil was not Leo's father. Adrian blinked in shock. Carmen thought it was at the humor of her story, but it was actually from this realization: had his paternity been kept from Leo, if Nick had permitted Gil to raise him as his own, the whole lethal incident would never have occurred.

"I'm just about through with your shit, son."

Leo's hate-filled, agonized cry, common and clichéd, like something from a Lifetime Channel special on the pitfalls of step-parenting: "I'm not your son!"

"No, you're not my son, but I've still had to put up with your shit, nonetheless. But I'm done, kid, done with putting up with you *and* your shit. Just like I was done with putting up with your daddy's shit, once upon a time."

Gil's confession to Adrian's murder; his intention to cease *putting up with Leo's shit*, once and for all, through the utilization of that big Buck knife; Adrian's sudden reemergence from he knew not where, when he realized (he knew not how) that Gil was going to kill Leo – none of these events would've come to pass if Leo had not been painfully aware, all his life, that Gil was not his father. If Nick had not made it his mission to make sure that Leo knew it.

All of them, everyone Adrian knew, every single one of them: Leo, Randi, Gil, Nick himself, Ian and Daina, her aunts, Eileen, Carmen; if Nick had not told Leo of his true parentage, all of them would've continued through life on an utterly different path.

Adrian came to the stunning conclusion that he would not be here now, he never would've returned from the other side, if it hadn't been for Nick.

Adrian had instigated the transmigration of his own soul when he'd recited *The Incantations of Thoth,* moments before Gil's shotgun sang its song. Metaphysically speaking, there'd never been a Leo Wilde. But Leo might've gone on being Leo forever, nonetheless. Maybe Gil would've treated the kid better if Leo had believed that Gil was his dad. Maybe Leo and Randi and Gil would've lived happily ever after. Maybe they would've been a loving family unit, with only one, harmless, meaningless little lie as the basis of their bliss.

But Nick would not allow it. Nick made sure that Leo knew the truth about the cold, insulting bastard that slept with his mother. Gil was no one to Leo, and this fact had been the root of the incendiary friction that had always existed between the two of them. It had been the reason that Gil's anger had reached the sparking point that day.

Adrian vowed to thank his cousin, and profusely, the very next time he saw him.

And here was another reason that he had to end it with Eileen. Nick was very fond of her, while Adrian was just making time, having fun. Adrian had to break up with Eileen, even if this weekend with Carmen went nowhere. It was the least he could do. He owed *so much* to Nick.

ONE HUNDRED TWO

Eileen had taken off work at noon on Friday on a whim. She thought she might have an enjoyable lunch with her friends, and then an even more enjoyable afternoon spent in bed with Leo . . .

She'd lingered after lunch with Penny and Bellona and Daina, had become involved in conversation with them. Before she had time to traipse down the hill and join her young lover, he'd texted her about some mysterious emergency that was taking him out of town, for the whole weekend.

Damn. The best laid plans of mice and men . . . If you want to hear God laugh, tell him your plans. Oh, well. Leo said that he'd see her on Monday, so Eileen would just have to content herself with that.

Nick had been at work when Adrian had called him about a key to the family's old vacation house. He'd sincerely wished him luck with the new girl. Nick thought it was about goddamned time that nineteen-year-old Leo found himself another girlfriend. If there was always some fresh-faced young chickie on Leo's arm, gazing adoringly at him, perhaps Eileen would take stock of reality and stop looking at him in the same manner. Maybe if Leo had a girlfriend again, Eileen would at last consider Nick.

Nick was glad that Leo was out of town, whether he returned enmeshed in a serious teenage young-love situation or not. Out of sight, out of mind. If Leo wasn't there, Eileen might favor Nick with her undivided attention for a change. Who knew what adventures might occur, if Nick could somehow manage to take her mind off of Leo entirely . . .

After he'd told Adrian to call Bobby to find out about the key, Nick had texted Eileen and asked if she'd like to meet him for a drink at Mickey's, say six or so? Nick thought that would give her a minute to catch her breath after the work day, allow her to go home and freshen up before embarking on the sure-to-be exciting weekend he had in mind.

Eileen texted Nick back, said that she'd be there at the appointed time. She neglected to mention that she was already off work for the day, however.

A lifetime ago, Eileen had always been careful not to mention Adrian to Allan, because he knew of her attraction to their neighbor, and there was no reason for her to rub his nose in it by talking about him. She exercised the same lack of chattiness nowadays, as cover to her secret. Eileen never spoke about Leo to his mother or his grandmother or his aunts. If they mentioned him, Eileen would only comment disinterestedly. He was nobody to her, after all.

And there was certainly no reason to mention to Nick that she was currently at his aunts' house, in the middle of the work day, whilst young Leo – who lived the life of Riley, not working, not going to school – was lazing around just down the hill at the house that had been so generously gifted to him.

Nick probably wouldn't suspect any connection, because she was friends with Leo's womenfolk, after all. But sometimes he looked at her with a trace of resentment – just the tiniest little trace – when she was talking to his cousin. Eileen was certain that Nick had not a clue as to what was going on – he wouldn't keep going out with her if he did – but maybe Eileen's expression wasn't always as neutral as she hoped when she looked at Leo. Nick undoubtedly sensed that part of Eileen's attraction to Leo that she was simply unable to hide. So, just like with Allan, why rub Nick's nose in it? It was completely unnecessary to tell Nick where she was at the moment – that was the glory of cellphones – so Eileen didn't.

Nick snuck out from work a few minutes early. He found that he was in an exceptionally good mood. Perhaps Adrian was going to start acting Leo's age, get himself all coupled-up with some sweet young thing. Such a match would preclude him from offering any more guitar lessons to Eileen. Maybe he wouldn't be at home *all the time* anymore. Maybe he and his new girlfriend would have places to go and people to see and things to do, like young people should. If Leo wasn't around for Eileen to stare at, *every single time* she visited Parcay Street, then maybe she wouldn't constantly be reminded of her long ago thing for Adrian. If Leo wasn't there, then Eileen couldn't stare at him like he *was* Adrian, as if the years hadn't intervened, as if it was 1989 again, and they were *both* only nineteen. Except now she was just as single as he was . . .

Nick whistled cheerfully as he walked the short blocks from his office to Mickey's. He had a good feeling about tonight. Adrian was out of town, no doubt getting all the action that Leo's youth and looks, and his own charisma and confidence, afforded him. Nick was no longer as young as Leo, but the ol' Wilde charm had always been his ally, as well as Adrian's. Nick was feeling like luck might smile on him tonight, too.

He ordered himself a dry martini, just to start the possibility-filled evening off right. While he waited for it, Nick glanced down the bar and discovered that Zelda's husband, Link – *no, his name's Barry* – was sitting only a few stools down.

Before Nick could look away and pretend he hadn't seen him, Barry made eye contact, nodded his recognition of his wife's co-worker. Nick thought that he noted a shade of hostility in Barry's expression. Fearlessness was another trait Nick shared with his cousin. If Link decided he wanted to make some issue out of non-existent extra-marital activities that he suspected between his wife and Nick, Nick would've once been more than happy to oblige him. *Fuckin' and fightin', it's all the same,* just like Bradley said.

But lately, Nick had been feeling his age, trying to embrace a little bit of the dignity that he thought should accompany pushing forty. So lately, when Link frowned at him, Nick would've just gone elsewhere in the bar, to avoid finishing any confrontation the blonde kid might want to start.

But tonight Nick was in an expansive, friendly mood. The milk of human kindness flowed from him at the moment. Why should be continue to allow Zelda's husband to be giving him the stink eye? There was absolutely no reason for it, and Nick should take the effort to make him see that. Why, they should be friends! Nick had once been a little bit of a gamer himself, when Leo was in his early teens (when he was still Leo), and Barry reminded Nick a little of a character from a video game.

Nick took his martini and sat on the barstool next to his co-worker's husband. He smiled. "Are you waiting for Zelda to get off work?"

"Yup." Barry sipped his beer impassively.

"I'm glad to see you guys are working it out," Nick said genuinely. Zelda was cute and perky and friendly, and if she were working it out with her husband, then she wouldn't be flirting with Nick in the break room all the time.

Barry narrowed his eyes and considered this guy from Zelda's office for a moment. Then he shrugged. "Maybe we are, maybe we're not. What are you doing here?"

"I've got a date," Nick replied with a big grin.

Barry was a little surprised by the older man's enthusiasm. Apparently it was a big date. Apparently the woman must be a keeper.

"Good for you," Barry said. "Good luck."

In retrospect, Nick wouldn't be able to say why he said what he said next. But he was in a bouncy mood, and he had a little bit of time to kill.

"Can I ask you for a little advice, L – uh, Barry? Since you're married and all, I thought maybe you might have a little bit of insight."

It was silly, really; ridiculous. Barry and Zelda had been dating since high school. They'd been exclusive since they were teenagers, except of course for those frequent epochs when they'd break up. Then both would be convinced that it was officially over forever. Then both of them would hightail it out onto the boulevard for a little strange . . .

Then they'd reconcile. Zelda had told the whole story to Nick at lunch, during breaks. She and Barry had both been around the block without ever having technically cheated on each other.

Even so, Nick was just kidding. He didn't want any advice from Barry. He was just killing time.

"Okay," Barry said, his expression still neutral. Nick still got the impression that Barry didn't really want to talk to him – Zelda's husband wouldn't be so rude as to just tell Nick to get lost, but Nick also didn't think the big blonde would be sorry to see him go, either.

Nick stopped the bartender and ordered himself another drink, and another beer for Barry. Then he began his tale.

"I've been seeing this girl, almost all year. We go out to dinner, the movies. We went to the beach a couple times –"

"How old is she?" Barry asked.

Nick wondered if Zelda's husband suspected that Nick was secretly describing her. Who knew what had been going on, and with whom, while they'd been separated *this* time? Who knew what kind of a smart-ass bastard this Nick Wilde really was? Maybe he'd think it would be funny to come in here and start talking to Barry about Zelda, pretending he was talking about somebody else . . .

"She's forty-one," Nick told him. Eileen's birthday had been in April. Nick had treated her to an elegant dinner at Paul's to celebrate it. Nick showed Barry her picture on his phone.

"Nice," Barry said with more appreciation than he felt. She was all right, not bad-looking for as old as she was. He felt a wave of relief. This guy that worked with Zelda, whom she said she'd *dated* for a while – Barry could never get her to admit whether or not she'd ever slept with him – he wasn't talking about Zelda at all. Apparently, he really did want some advice.

341

"So what's the problem?"

Feigning an exaggerated concern that he might be overheard, Nick glanced up and down the bar, then leaned closer to Barry and whispered, "We haven't . . . you know. We haven't . . . *been intimate* yet."

Barry's eyebrows went up, but still he communicated only mild surprise. *He's quite the mellow dude*, Nick observed. Barry sipped his beer before replying, then finally opined, "Maybe she doesn't like you."

Nick smiled, winked at his companion. "No, that's not it."

Nick's confidence was absolute. He knew for a fact that Eileen liked him. He was also damn near positive why she hesitated to commit to him. It had to do with the fixation she'd once had on Adrian, the fixation she'd transferred to his son.

Surely she must realize that such a thing could never be? Nick had said to himself enough times. *Christ, what would people say?*

But in his darker moments, Nick knew that it *could be.* The minds of Adrian's womenfolk were as open as the great outdoors, and after all the miracles that had occurred to return him to them, they surely could not be concerned with what he chose to do behind closed doors, and with whom. And whatever Randi might think . . . Nobody cared about that.

And Adrian . . .

Nick thought that the only thing that had kept Adrian from seducing Eileen – or, more accurately, the only thing that had kept Adrian from allowing Eileen to seduce innocent, boyish, uneducated Leo – was that he'd not as yet felt the whim to do so. And maybe because he felt some whiff of loyalty to Nick.

Regardless of Adrian's participation so far, Eileen was obviously drawn to the boy that looked so much like the man she'd desired so much, twenty years ago. Nick was convinced that this improper attraction was the reason that Eileen would not allow herself to become fully involved with him.

But Leo was out of town for the weekend. Nick hoped he came back with a cute little girlfriend, with whom he'd then commence to spend all his time.

Nick was in a good mood, looking forward to seeing Eileen, and his second martini was only adding to his lightheartedness.

He said to Barry, "No. I know she likes me. She's tells me that all the time."

Barry studied him for a moment. "How serious are you about this chick? Is this just a hit-it-and-quit-it thing for you? Or do you plan on sticking around with her?"

Nick's smile faltered. He'd been just messing around, killing time, asking Zelda's game-character-looking husband for romantic advice, as if there was a snowball's chance in hell that he'd ever take it. But Barry had brought up a valid question. What were his intentions toward Eileen, for the long run? If he could convince her to step up and *consummate* their friendship, as he sincerely wanted her to do, then that would turn it into something more than just a friendship, now wouldn't it? If Nick could finally talk Eileen into sleeping with him, then what?

"I like her very much," he told Barry sincerely.

Nick sometimes thought he could love Eileen, but he wouldn't allow himself to do so, because she wouldn't allow him to do so, either. Something – and Nick was convinced that it was the unconcealable yen that she had for his apparently nineteen-year-old cousin – something made her keep Nick at arm's length. But if they could have a normal, man-woman relationship . . .

"I'd stick around," he said.

"Ask her to marry you, then," Barry suggested.

"What?" Nick asked in astonishment.

Again, Barry's expression was mild. "How old are you, Nick? Thirty-eight? Forty?"

Nick fought a feeling of offense. Did he look older than he was? "I'll be thirty-six in December."

"And you've never been married, right? What about your lady?"

"I've never been married," Nick told him. "She's been married twice. She's got a grown daughter."

"So she's a couple years older than you, on her own now. You're a lifelong bachelor." Barry nodded thoughtfully. "Maybe she figures you're just with her to see what you can get. Maybe she doesn't like that."

He sipped his beer again. "I'm telling you, ask her to marry you. She's no spring chicken. Maybe she figures that her time is running out to find someone who's gonna stick around with her for the time she's got left. Maybe she doesn't want to waste it messing around with someone who's just out for a good time. Maybe she's looking for a little security. Maybe she wants a promise, a guarantee, before she agrees to give it up. I'm telling you – ask her to marry you.

"You don't have to go through with it, of course. But just the suggestion . . . I bet that'll make her a little friendlier to you. Hell, if she thinks you want to settle down with her, she might even figure that she *owes* it to you."

Out of the mouths of babes, Nick thought in stupefied amazement. He realized that young Barry could very well be on to something here. Eileen was forty-one – seriously, what profit was there in it for her to be just hopping into bed with Nick, of behaving like some twenty-five-year-old tramp (like his sweet friend Juliana)? Just because Nick took her to the movies and dinner – that was all meaningless. Just because they were both single, that it was obvious that they liked each other – was that any reason to just nail some guy?

Eileen was calm and sober and successful – all the qualities that Nick admired, but had never been able to find in a woman. These traits didn't lend themselves to casual, no strings attached sex, now did they? Maybe the act had to *mean something* to Eileen – maybe she wanted it to be accompanied by some kind of commitment – or else, why bother?

I'll be goddamned! Nick said to himself. *The kid's right.*

He slapped Zelda's husband on the back. "I want to thank you, Barry. I think you've opened my eyes. I think you are one hundred percent correct."

Barry paused with his beer halfway to his mouth. He smiled faintly at the older man's compliment. "Like I say, you don't really have to marry her. Just give her a little feeling of security. You say that she likes you. Maybe that's all she needs."

"I will certainly take it under advisement, my friend. Thanks."

Zelda entered the bar and gave her husband a big noisy hug and a sloppy kiss on the cheek. Apparently things *were* looking up between them. She said hello to Nick, then after a few minutes of conversation, Zelda led her brilliant young husband out of the bar.

Nick took out his phone and Googled *engagement rings.*

ONE HUNDRED THREE

Adrian looked at Carmen's dwindling supply of poker chips. "Here. Let me lend you some money." He placed three stacks of his chips onto her side of the table. "But I gotta tell you, the juice is running now. If you don't start winning, you're gonna owe me some large change."

Carmen giggled. "Juice?"

"Interest." Leo told her about some high stakes poker movie he'd seen, full of loan-sharks and gangsters, and always, throughout, huge sums of money and staggering rates of interest. "It's like three hundred percent or something. Compounded daily. So, if you don't start winning pretty soon, you're gonna have to sign your car over to me when we get back home."

Carmen thought that his faux threat of extortion was clever. She didn't fail to notice that Leo had not offered *trade* as an out for her imaginary debt, even in jest. Carmen liked that.

"Okay," Leo continued. "Let's make this interesting. Jacks or better to open. How about red fours and black twos are wild."

Again Carmen giggled. "All right."

One-eyed Jacks, the man with the axe, suicide king.

Adrian had never had so much fun playing poker, not in two lifetimes. And he didn't even make a dime.

ONE HUNDRED FOUR

Carmen and Leo stayed up all night, talking, laughing, telling stories, playing cards, making snacks, getting to know each other. It had been completely, surprisingly enjoyable, different, exciting – for both of them.

But when the sky started to lighten in the east, Carmen had an attack of the yawns. It was a purely physical reaction: she'd been awake for nearly twenty-four hours. She felt neither tired nor sleepy. She felt alive and aware, maybe even a little tingly.

Leo Wilde was so much fun. He was attractive and charming, witty, funny, attentive, complimentary. He was . . . *Respectful. That's the word. He clearly likes me, and we're having such a good time together, but that doesn't erase the fact that we've just met. I've been awake for twice as long as I've known him. It wouldn't be* respectful *for him to make any kind of intimate suggestion so soon . . .*

Carmen marveled at how refreshing, how unusual Leo's behavior was. She'd only been on the front lines, in the trenches, of the battle between the sexes for a few short years, but already, she was disillusioned with the way men and women were expected to behave with one another in the modern world, especially when they'd just met. She reflected, not for the first time, that perhaps the forgotten tenets of old-timey morality had some value. Perhaps the stern mothers and fathers of yesteryear had been on to something.

Maybe these ancient strictures still had their uses. Carmen pondered the theory that perhaps it was better – it was so much better, so far! – to get to know a person before you just automatically leapt into bed with him. Laughter and conversation allowed you to find out if you were compatible with this stranger, if you actually *liked* him. Everybody was compatible between the sheets; everyone liked what took place there. But the discovery of commonalities, shared interests – finding out about that stuff took a little time.

You might be down to nail some guy based on his looks alone, but if you weren't compatible with him on any other plane, you'd still have to deal with those disparities, usually sooner rather than later. Usually you had to deal with them the next morning. When no outside-of-bed compatibility existed, most people dealt with it by just taking off.

Another wasted night, followed by another couple of days spent kicking yourself for doing something you shouldn't have done. What was the profit in it? *Sure, he was cute, but he was really a reprehensible human being. By the end of breakfast, I discovered that I couldn't stand to be in the same room with him for another second. So why did I sleep with him in the first place? Oh, yeah. He was cute.*

It could be an ugly, self-hatred inducing game.

Maybe there wouldn't be so many broken marriages, so many hate-filled, disastrous, failed relationships if people took a page out of great-grandma's book and got to know each other first . . .

Carmen reckoned that she'd definitely like to kiss Leo, to run her fingers through his long hair – that would definitely be a first. Clint wore his hair close-cropped, like a Marine. It was silky, like velvet . . .

Clint who? Carmen asked herself with a little inward grin. He hadn't crossed her mind once the entire night, until just that moment. She certainly couldn't concern herself with him now. Carmen again forgot that Clint even stalked the earth. She returned to thinking about how she'd like to run her fingers through Leo's black hair, how she'd like him to take her in his muscled arms and kiss her . . .

But in addition to all the commonplace, hormone-driven musings of youth that ran through her mind, Carmen also wanted to just talk to Leo some more, to hear his voice, to laugh at his jokes. Carmen wanted to further contemplate the things he told her about himself. She wanted to hear more of his opinions about life in general. Carmen also found that she wanted to tell Leo more about herself, she wanted to reveal to him her own observations on events past and those that were transpiring presently in the big world outside of this cozy little kitchen on the Colorado River.

Carmen's enjoyment of their bonhomie made her realize that she might like to share a future with Leo, with lots of interesting and thought-provoking discussions and analyses along the way. He was cute, that was undeniable, but Carmen enjoyed so much more the rapport that they'd developed.

The antique philosophy of getting to know a person first was certainly working for her. This affection that she felt for Leo would surely outlast the momentary, anonymous pleasures of a quick roll in the hay between strangers.

Carmen wanted to just keep on talking to Leo, but her physiology had other ideas.

We're just meat and chemicals, her Biology prof had said once. *What a piece of work is a man! How noble in reason! How infinite in faculty!*

All that's just an illusion, he'd continued with a grin. *All the intellect, all the reason in the world can't overcome the inescapable reality – ya gotta eat when you're hungry, sleep when you're tired. No amount of philosophy can alter those requirements.*

Carmen yawned again. Her body was tired, no matter how much her mind wanted to continue to learn about Leo. No amount of philosophy could alter the requirement: she had to get some rest.

Leo was delighted at how Carmen was fighting sleep, just so she could keep talking to him. He'd noticed the onslaught of a little drowsiness himself, but had put it down to the warm, relaxed feeling engendered by her excellent company. Then she'd started to yawn, and he'd picked it up, too. They still had two days and another possibility-filled night ahead of them. It was time for a nap.

Leo rose, stretched – *with all that gorgeous black hair, he makes me think of a jaguar, ready to pad off into the jungle,* Carmen thought appreciatively.

"Come on," he said and offered his hand. Carmen took it without hesitation, and continued to hold it while they walked down the short hall, out of the kitchen to the living room. Carmen liked holding his hand, but . . .

She almost had time to mourn that the magical spell of their absorbing night of conversation was now going to be broken. She almost had time to reluctantly embrace reality, disappointment: fascinating Leo *was* going to make a play for her already, regardless of the fact that they'd just met. The thought had almost formed in her mind that Leo was just like all the other guys. *What else did I really expect?*

But before any of these depressing ideas could achieve any concrete cognitive traction in Carmen's mind, Leo said, "The one on the left was always my room when we stayed here as a kid." He gestured with his free hand at the closed door across the living room. "The one on the other side has big windows – lets in a lot of sun. Not the best for early morning siestas. The one over there is attached to the bathroom on one side." Leo paused, smiled blankly at her. "Your choice."

It was subtle, almost imperceptible – if Carmen didn't like him already, she wouldn't have even detected it – but since she did like him, Carmen realized the Leo was offering her the choice of *all three* rooms. She could have the bright one, the one with the bath . . . Or, if she so desired, she could join him in his room.

It was the most flawless proposition Carmen had ever heard. If she chose to sleep by herself, it wouldn't seem like she was turning him down cold, because he hadn't laced his offer with a sly tone of voice. He hadn't plied her with a smoky, come-hither smile as he spoke.

Leo had not in any way communicated that he *expected* Carmen to join him. From his upbeat tone and his blank, friendly smile, it was understood that if Carmen took one of the other rooms, their fun friendship would continue exactly as it had up to that point. No battlements had been stormed and defended, no attacking army repelled.

No decision had to be reached at that very moment, because no black and white, *will you* or *won't you* question had been posed. No if-then-else path had to be taken on the flowchart of their brief association right this minute. Carmen could choose to . . . Or she could choose not to, and either way, nothing would change in Leo's attitude toward her. Nothing would be any different from how he had thought about her, how he had treated her a few seconds ago, when they'd been in the kitchen, laughing and joking and getting to know each other. They *could* become lovers, but they didn't *have* to, and if they didn't, they would still be friends.

Leo's words were just that awesomely, subtly, open-ended.

The youthful fire in her blood, the simmering attraction that she had felt for him all along, prompted Carmen: *go on to his room with him.* She wanted to kiss him, she wanted to feel his skin beneath her fingertips . . .

But a more poetic part of her made Carmen pause. She had so enjoyed what they'd shared so far. She didn't want to relinquish this new and different, almost magical feeling. It was a wondrous new experience to appreciate a man for who he *was,* for what he thought and said, to feel a clean affection and fondness for him. It was so much better than simply liking how he looked, wondering what he could *do.*

Sex was sex. Leo was sexy, and Carmen imagined that he would be great and all, and a part of her sincerely wanted to find out. But she wanted to hang on to this warm affection she felt for him for a little while longer, and a quick tumble would undoubtedly dissipate the feeling. Carmen had discovered that she *liked* Leo, in a manner that she'd never experienced before. She wanted to enjoy that joyful, almost child-like sensation of liking him for a little while longer, before she consented to *loving* him in the more commonplace, expected, routine physical way.

"I'll take the one with the bathroom," she said.

"Great." Not a shred of resentment, not an iota of pouting disappointment colored Leo's voice or expression. "If the bed's not made, there should be sheets in the bottom drawer of the dresser, and a blanket in the closet." He squeezed her hand, then released it, and smiled. "Good night, Carmen. Good morning. I'll see you in a couple hours. Sweet dreams."

Leo turned and strolled across the living room. He opened the door to his room and entered, without a backward glance. He didn't stop and wave at her, didn't hesitate in the doorway and shoot her a little hopeful glance to indicate that it wasn't too late for her to change her mind. Leo didn't even turn around, instead closing the door gently behind him with his foot.

Carmen went into the room she'd chosen, quickly made the bed and crawled between the cool, crisp sheets. She sighed in relief, still reveling in her *like* of Leo. Had he asked her to join him after she had chosen not to, Carmen thought she would've given in. He was cute and sexy and funny, and she very much wanted to . . .

Carmen rolled over and hugged the pillow to her. She was glad that Leo hadn't asked her to sleep with him yet. She closed her eyes, and smiled to herself, imagining what it would be like . . . But it was all right that it wasn't happening right this minute. Carmen was immensely enjoying this newfound feeling of fondness for the adorable young man that she'd just met. It had a subtle, more intoxicating effect than just plain old run of the mill lust.

The lust was there, too, but Carmen liked the idea that it hadn't been necessary to act on it right away. The anticipation of what might happen tomorrow or the next day, or next week, provided an additional layer of heat to the warm and tingly sensations that she was already feeling.

Carmen had not experienced this brand of cheerful anticipation before, even though she'd never failed to make any of her beaux wait in the past. The requisite time had never been less than three dates. Not three *days,* but three outings – three dinners and three movies, or two dinners and a concert, or a concert and a movie and a day at the beach. This delay had never been to allow Carmen to make up her mind, or to allow her to get to know the guy better, or to delve into the possibility of compatibility. She'd arrived at a decision within a few moments of meeting him. If it was a thumbs down, she'd politely decline any opening salvo along the lines of *Hey, we should have coffee sometime . . .*

If Carmen felt an attraction, she'd accept his invitation to coffee or dinner, and then she'd make him wait for three more dates before she allowed him to act. The verdict had already been pronounced in Carmen's mind. The wait was just calculation, the societally accepted manner by which a young woman communicated to a new suitor that she was a mature and sober adult, and not a horny slut who could be had for a Carmel Macchiato from Starbucks or a Scotch on the rocks at Mickey's.

It was all part of the dance, part of the game, designed to engender a modicum of respect in the dude. Men didn't value anything that they achieved too easily: if he won the lottery, he wasn't going to soberly sock the money away for a rainy day. He was going to blow it – easy come easy go. If a girl gave in too easily, he'd place no value on her surrender. Men liked a woman better when they had to expend a little effort, spend a little time and money on her first.

Yet it's all the same in the dark, eventually, Carmen mused. Long before she agreed to go out on that fourth date, she'd already decided that he was going to get lucky. It was all part and parcel of the game.

After that first night with him, Carmen would then decide if the whole package was worth pursuing. Was he any good? And if so, could she stand to talk to him? Did he chew with his mouth closed?

If his foibles and eccentricities were tolerable, Carmen would continue to see him. She liked men, liked going out with them, telling them about the things that had happened in her day, listening to the things that had happened in theirs. She enjoyed their bodies, their strong arms around her. She enjoyed all the other intimacies as well.

But sooner or later, they inevitably began to annoy her. Ticks and mannerisms that had been tolerable at first became glaring: this one didn't *always* chew with his mouth closed; that one argued on the phone with his mother entirely too often; another one didn't clean his apartment well or frequently enough.

Even Clint, whom she'd been seeing for quite some time, had suddenly become snappish and short-tempered to her lately. Maybe he'd always been that way – he'd always been impatient and quick to anger – but Carmen had never before noticed that his pique had extended to her. She'd liked Clint quite a bit. Over the months of their relationship, she'd discovered several things that they had in common. She couldn't recall a single one of them at the moment, however, and in the final analysis, whatever those small compatibilities had been, they hadn't been sufficient to overcome the larger annoyances.

Carmen was done with Clint. She'd go over to his place as soon as she returned to Riverside. She was no coward. She wouldn't dream of dumping him over the phone or via a text. She'd go to his apartment and calmly tell him that things just weren't working out. She'd always be fond of him, they could still be friends – these stock lines were also part of the script of the game, and Carmen knew them well.

Had she not met Leo, she might've considered offering Clint a good-bye, consolation-prize style quickie, just for old times' sake, just to show him that there were no hard feelings. It wasn't him after all, it was her . . .

None of the calculated machinations of *making him wait* had occurred to Carmen as she'd stood in the air-conditioned living room of Leo's riverfront hideaway, debating whether she should just go ahead and give in, if she should just discard the grimy, tattered rulebook entitled *What Had To Be Done To Ensure His Respect,* and just go with the subtle, insistent desire she'd for him. They were both adults, after all.

Carmen realized that, while she would've been disappointed if Leo had asked her, maybe that disappointment wouldn't have stopped her. She would've seen that Leo wasn't really unique, that the unusual, friendly, playful time that they'd spent together hadn't signified a different, better way to approach a member of the opposite sex, after all. The effect of Leo's boyish, no-pressure charm on her hadn't really meant that she liked him better, differently, hopefully, girlishly. Nor had it meant that he'd liked her any differently than any other girl that his fine looks had no doubt snagged for him.

If Leo would've straight up asked her, Carmen would've been disappointed – it would've meant that no kind of magical camaraderie, innocent affection, and just plain ol' friendly fun had actually existed between them, as she'd thought it had. Nope. It had all been just an unusually well-executed ploy on his part, the same song, second verse – no uplifting, refreshing friendship, no childlike affection – it was all just the same old plan, aiming at the same old result: to get her in bed with him.

Carmen thought again that she probably would've gone for it, disillusionment or no. Leo was cute, they were out of town. It still would've been a thrilling, naughty adventure. And if he didn't call her again after they returned to the avenues of polite society, Carmen would have been neither surprised nor disappointed. She'd engaged is a few one night stands in her life. They were fun for what they were, like shots of tequila: a quick, pleasurable high, invariably followed by a sickish-feeling hangover the next morning.

Carmen smiled in the brightening room. She joyfully squeezed the pillow; she wiggled in delight. Leo *hadn't* flat out asked her to sleep with him. The ticklish joy of liking him, of believing that he liked her, sang in her blood.

Maybe he *was* different. Maybe this could lead to some kind of . . . Something that would last, something that wouldn't be over abruptly when the desire waned, when she could no longer ignore what she'd known all along – she'd only been with this guy because he occupied her time, gave her something to do on a Friday night; because he kept her from sitting all by herself, watching television in a darkened room, like her mother and grandmother did.

Maybe this child-like affection that she felt for Leo . . . Maybe she wouldn't eventually dump him when the sex grew stale, when the glaring conflicts in their personalities that she'd tried to ignore became too much to tolerate.

Maybe this could turn into something. Maybe this was . . .

Carmen drifted off into a contended, dreamless sleep, with that last thought accompanying her all the way: *maybe this was love.*

ONE HUNDRED FIVE

Unlike the peacefully comfortable young woman in the other room, Adrian Wilde could not sleep. It was not an entirely unpleasant insomnia, and Adrian recognized the cure.

Carmen.

He'd seen that she was going to decide to sleep by herself before she said it. It had been one of the first solid flashes of precognition that he'd experienced since his return: that weird doubling of time, like frames of celluloid jammed in a projector.

She's gonna turn me down.

Since he'd seen it coming, Adrian had been able to disguise his dumbfounded surprise. Now he reclined upon the unmade bed and stared at the ceiling of the rapidly brightening room. And he ruminated.

She turned me down.

Adrian didn't quite know how to wrap his head around that. To say that he'd never been turned down was a statement akin to Will Rogers's famous quote: *I never met a man I didn't like.* Adrian had never met a girl that hadn't liked *him.* Of course, that wasn't precisely true. There was a world full of women that were immune to him. The achievement of the local black-haired, blue-eyed, white boy was not every one's raison d'être. Adrian just wasn't everybody's type.

But he qualified as desirable to a hefty section of the population. He was fine and confident and he played the guitar, and these qualities had put him at the top of enough lists that he'd never had to consciously sally forth and look for a girl. They'd always come to him, sometimes in groups, such as when Urban Equinox played a party.

Like a smorgasbord of feminine pulchritude, the choices had always set themselves out before him: big, tall, and small; blonde, brunette, redhead. Adrian never had cause to wonder what they were serving at the restaurant down the street, because the delectables that came to him were always more than sufficient.

After his band finished a set, it was like he was the *It* in the center of a game of Blind Man's Bluff. A crowd of willing girls surrounded him, just dying to be caught. The lucky one he picked then got be his *It,* at least for the rest of the night.

"Eenie, meenie, miney, mo. *You.* I'll take you," was the sum total of the effort Adrian had ever had to expend to enjoy female companionship for the evening. If Adrian was of a mind to make a suggestion, it had never fallen upon ears that weren't already aware of him, that weren't already interested.

And he'd believed that it was a similar situation with Carmen. Had she not agreed to go out of town with him, just like that? That had to signify that she was at least a little bit interested.

Adrian had continued to feel that *little bit interested* vibe from her all night. Sometimes it would flare in intensity: as they'd laughed and conversed, for a split-second every now and again, Carmen had been thinking about how much she *really* liked him.

But these momentary flashes of desire that Adrian sensed from Carmen, like solar flares in intensity, were still only gradations of mood. Her precise thoughts, the words she said to herself, remained hidden from him.

She turned me down.

Adrian didn't reflect on this occurrence with any kind of resentment, only a sort of dumb surprise, because it had never happened to him before. He was like a little kid that opened the can that said *Peanut Brittle* and got the springy snake instead – for the very first time. An adult would be surprised, sure, but an adult had seen the trick before. Adrian's surprise was absolute, like the kid's: he'd never seen a springy snake come out of a can of peanut brittle before. He'd never been turned down. He had not a clue that such events occurred.

In the span of his unnatural, fortunate existence, scores of girls had made a play for Adrian. In terms of statistical numbers, he'd actually passed on the vast majority of them, especially in his first incarnation, when he'd made a conscious effort not to be a heartbreaker. But once Adrian had made up his mind, it was on. If the cute chickie with the big brown eyes smiled at him and he decided to smile back? The evening had always then unfolded unerringly to the specifications that he desired. There'd never been any surprises. Never. Not once. None of them had ever changed their minds at the last minute. Like Lola, whatever Adrian wanted, Adrian got.

It wasn't like I made a deliberate pass at Carmen, he rationalized to himself. The next obvious thought immediately followed: *And why was that?*

That was the $64,000 question, was it not? That was the crux of the matter, the reason he couldn't sleep. *Why didn't I just make the suggestion?*

He'd seen that she was going to choose a room all to herself, but at the same instant, he'd also felt that spike in her interest again. She was thinking about it, considering it . . .

All Adrian would have had to do was make the offer.

Why had he not done so? He most assuredly wanted Carmen, most definitely, indubitably. The ferocity of this particular desire was an unaccustomed feeling to him. It was a solid need, it had form, shape. It was a desire with teeth, with strength. A persistent, thrumming goad in his mind.

Sex had never been the end-all and be-all for Adrian. It was an amusing way to spend the afternoon, or the evening, or sometimes even the weekend, but it had never been something that he *had to have.* If the mood struck him and a partner was on hand, he'd proceed. But Adrian had never gone out on the prowl for girls. Desire had never been a monkey on his back. He'd never been a slave to it.

But this *itch* that he felt for Carmen . . . That was the only word for it: an *itch.* Adrian didn't use the term in a derogatory or demeaning manner. He didn't think *itch,* as in a small or insignificant thing. Quite the opposite: the extraordinary, insistent yen that he'd developed for Carmen – and in such an extraordinarily short period of time – it was neither small nor insignificant. It demanded his attention. It refused to be ignored, like that maddening mosquito bite on your elbow. It itches so badly that you cannot focus your mind upon anything else until you scratch it.

Adrian *sincerely* wanted her. So why had he not asked?

In strictly technical terms, the asking had never actually fallen to Adrian. His question – *Hey, do ya wanna . . . ?* had in reality always been a confirmation. He'd read the smiling girl's thought: *I wonder if Adrian would be down to . . .* If he was, he couldn't just say he was. He couldn't just answer her as if she'd spoken her curiosity aloud.

That had only happened once, his very first time, when AnneMarie had thought: *I wonder if you'd like to go back to your room with me for a minute, so I can give you a special birthday surprise?*

Adrian had immediately replied to her unexpressed question: "Yes," he'd said. "Yes, I most certainly would."

But Adrian couldn't just go around replying to girls' unsaid thoughts as if they were regular, spoken-out-load conversation. That would just freak them out. So he'd always made it seem like he was asking, when in reality he was actually just agreeing.

But Adrian *wanted* to ask Carmen. He wasn't getting anything more than sporadic blips on the radar to indicate that she was interested in him, so for the first time ever, Adrian was willing, nay, he *needed* to be the one asking the question. She was so bright, so pretty. She vibrated with an electric sexiness of the most subtle, sublime kind. She was captivating. By ways and means unfathomable, beyond Adrian's ken, Carmen had captivated *him*. It was a first.

Adrian put his hands behind his head and considered the ceiling. He played out a little scenario in his mind, how it would go: he'd ask her and she'd say yes. Then Adrian imagined in detail what it would be like to touch Carmen, to kiss her, to feel her surrender . . .

He frowned. How had this chick managed to get inside his head like this? He'd never wasted time wondering, fantasizing about what some girl would be like. He'd always just proceeded to find out.

So why had he not just gone ahead and asked *this* chick, *this* time? Why the hell not?

The novel idea that he hadn't asked Carmen because of a fear of rejection occurred to Adrian for a laughable split-second. No, that wasn't it. Not unaware of his flawless track record, Adrian smugly thought, *I can't be afraid of something I've never experienced, now can I?* No one had ever turned him down, and he was pretty damn sure that Carmen wouldn't have turned him down either.

He frowned again. *So why didn't I ask her?*

The answer eluded him. But tomorrow, or at least this afternoon, was another day. Maybe he'd ask her then.

ONE HUNDRED SIX

After tossing and turning for an hour or so, Adrian gave up on sleep. He tiptoed out of the house and walked down the driveway to the little private dock, dove off the end with a barely perceptible splash. The water was warm, like blood, even in September. Adrian had always been able to think more clearly when he was in the water.

He floated on his back and once again the picture of Carmen swam into his mind. It seemed like he'd become incapable of thinking of anything else. He hadn't yet known her for twenty-four hours, but like some kind of fast-reproducing virus, the thought of her had devoured all other ideas, blotted out all other meditations from his mind.

Just what the hell is this? Adrian asked himself. *Sure, she's cute and all, but so what? Her mom's cute, too. But it's effortless for me to put Eileen out of my mind . . . or anybody else.*

But not Carmen. He tried to analyze this never before encountered situation. How had it come to pass that she so thoroughly dominated his mind? What was it about her that made her *irresistible* to him?

Now there was a word. *Irresistible.* That was the most apt description, in a nutshell. His mind was unable to escape the thought of Carmen: it was unable to *resist* her. Adrian had never had any trouble resisting a girl before. If he wasn't interested, he wasn't interested, and no amount of come-hither looks or whispered propositions would sway him.

But Carmen had not done anything even remotely along those lines, now had she? Not at all, no, siree! It wasn't as if she'd offered Adrian a suggestion that he could've in turn resisted. Not even vaguely. She'd just gone on along and taken a nap by herself.

Adrian climbed up onto the dock and dove off again.

Perhaps *irresistible* wasn't the most accurate word then, although it was close. The thought of Carmen, his desire for her – he was *unable to resist* those. But a better word to describe Carmen herself would be . . . *undeniable.*

She'd gotten into his mind somehow, and it was impossible to get her out. This incomprehensible desire that he'd developed for her, seemingly out of nowhere, *could not be denied.* It was *undeniable.*

But that wasn't entirely accurate either . . .

"Fuck it," Adrian said aloud. Irresistible, undeniable. Whatever. The word didn't matter. The whole concept didn't matter.

So, yeah, I've got a little extra yen for this one particular girl. She's beautiful, sexy. She's irresistible, undeniable.

This point had been established. Yet still the most important question remained unanswered. If it was taken as a true fact that Adrian had a sincere and abiding desire to see Carmen undressed and to commence to committing all sorts of enjoyable consenting-adult-type acts with her, then *why in the hell had he not just asked her?*

Seriously. The golden opportunity was there. He saw her say no, before she actually did so, but at the same time he'd felt that spurt of desire in her. Yet he'd failed to offer the customary, ratifying confirmation to that. He should've described the rooms as he had done, then, after saying, "Your choice," he should've said, "Would you like to join me?"

Maybe he'd just been too ambiguous, too vague in his initial statement. Maybe she hadn't realized that he was offering her a choice of where to sleep that included sleeping with him. Adrian shook his head. No. Carmen had known that she'd been offered the opportunity. He'd felt her debate it for a second.

If I would've flat-out asked her, she would've gone for it. It hadn't been fear of rejection that had stopped him – he *knew* Carmen would've gone for it. So, why hadn't he asked her?

Adrian shook his head, unhappy with himself. It was confusing and a trifle distressing to be unable to identify his own motivations.

He ran through it all again in his head.

Carmen was a pretty girl; exceptionally pretty. The idea had struck: ask this exceptionally pretty girl if she'd like to get the hell out of Dodge. The inspiration for this idea was as clear to Adrian as was the summer sun: he wanted to be alone with her, so they could do what comes naturally. Adrian's thing with Carmen's mother had made his own place off-limits – the risk of discovery was entirely too great – so there wasn't any other private place available at the moment.

The legendary Wilde luck had held: Carmen had agreed to accompany him to Arizona.

After their ride up, after their arrival, that's when Adrian's previously single-minded motivations began to go wonky. They'd hit it off right away, laughing and talking – at the grocery store, cooking dinner, cleaning up after dinner, playing cards – they'd hit it off right away and had continued to hit it off all goddamned night. The opportunities had therefore been manifold, yet Adrian had not acted.

Well, this is all just bullshit, he said to himself, as he vaulted out of the water again. He sat on the side of the dock and dangled his feet over the side. The situation was simple and commonplace enough. There was a pretty girl inside an otherwise empty house. Adrian sincerely desired to spend what remained of the weekend in bed with her. Said desire had become annoying, actually.

So the next time I see her, I'm gonna suggest it.

It wasn't a complicated scheme or even a difficult one. Adrian had never been denied, and he knew that his perfect record wouldn't fall now. Carmen wouldn't deny him either. He couldn't fathom the source of his hesitation, so he'd just cease to hesitate. He'd wasted too much time already.

Talking a girl into bed was a skill at which Adrian excelled, and it was time to put this never-fail talent to work. There wasn't anything different or special about Carmen. She was a nice girl, and beautiful, too, but Adrian knew that all he had to do was ask, and he told himself that he was going to do just that, at the very next opportune moment.

He'd just give Carmen that never-miss, killer smile, and put his cards right down on the table. He'd say, *Hey, baby, wanna –*

The sound of the glass door to the house sliding shut was clearly audible on the still morning air, and it startled Adrian out of his time-to-stop-messing-around-and-get-laid pep talk to himself.

Carmen was walking down the driveway toward the water, and even though she wasn't yet close enough to see it, Adrian smiled at her anyway. He waved. She waved back.

She was wearing a black, one-piece swimsuit, and a gauzy, cover-up skirt that reached almost to the ground. Over this ensemble, she'd thrown a large, white, long-sleeved, collared shirt. The outfit was simple, modest. But Adrian's determination to have her – maybe right here on the dock; there wasn't anybody around – was redoubled, as if Carmen had been wearing stilettos and the tiniest of bikinis.

But as she got closer, when Adrian could see her cheerful smile and her sparkling tan eyes, when he gleaned from her expression how happy she was to see him, how much she just plain *liked* him – the ego, the *selfishness* of his desire for her was humbled. The hard, sharp, prodding demand of it softened. The glaringly lit, graphic vision he'd entertained became fuzzier, dimmer . . . *romantic.*

Carmen walked out onto the dock. Adrian stood, and as she smiled at him and looked up into his eyes, his fiery, demanding need to possess her – and as soon as goddamned possible – lessened, although it didn't fade entirely. That maddening itch still remained, but it had become faint.

Its former prominence was taken over by the simple joy that Adrian found from beholding her smile, from anticipating her words. There was just something about Carmen, some intangible, appealing quality that exceeded the sum of her parts.

His desire was still there, but Adrian discovered that he greatly enjoyed just looking at her. He still wanted her, but realized that he liked more about Carmen than just her body. He remembered her stories, her thoughts from the night before, and this review of the fun they'd had (without having to jump into the sack together) put a leash and muzzle on Adrian's unaccustomed lust.

He knew that he could never be so coarse as to just proposition lovely, intelligent Carmen in some vulgar way. Even if he said it in a playful manner – some girls responded favorably to that – it was what they wanted, after all, so why beat around the bush about it? No, Adrian couldn't ever talk to Carmen like that. He still wanted to ask her, but it would have to be in some tender, thoughtful way, when the time was right . . .

"Are you hungry?" Carmen asked.

Adrian said that he was, and after a moment of hesitation, he took her hand. It was a far cry from throwing her down right there on the rough wood, as he'd been contemplating just moments before, but it was nice.

Adrian knew that if he had suggested just such a thing, Carmen would've agreed. At most, she might've insisted that they go back into the house. She liked him enough, and he was not unaware of his own charm. His ego was placated by knowing that he *could do it,* that it could be achieved at his whim.

But his imagination was fired by the idea that there could be something else besides just sex between them. He *could do it,* but suddenly, there was no longer a *need* to do it, right this minute.

If it didn't happen here in Parker, that was okay. It would happen sometime, but . . . Adrian was suddenly no longer in a big mad rush to consummate things, because he recognized that he wanted Carmen to stick around. There would be time for all of that later.

For right now . . . *Adrian liked her.*

ONE HUNDRED SEVEN

Adrian and Carmen sat at the old, sun-grayed picnic table on the patio and ate leftover pork-cilantro tacos and continued the odyssey of getting to know each other.

Carmen sat facing toward the house. Adrian sat across from her, looking out toward the water. Will and Rob's big old six-seater runabout, covered with a faded blue tarp, sat on a little slab of concrete beside the driveway, a little to the right of his line of sight. He talked and listened to his charming companion, but his attention kept being drawn back to the boat.

Each time, his mind made a note of some irrelevant detail about it. This time it was that the sticker on trailer license was the wrong color: its registration was long expired.

But we wouldn't need to go out on the road . . .

". . . something with computers?"

Adrian looked blankly at Carmen. Realizing she'd lost his attention for a moment – Carmen was able to interpret a few of his expressions already – she repeated herself.

"My mom says Nick does something with computers?"

"He's a software engineer. They help people organize their small businesses."

Nick – I owe it all to him. Adrian reminded himself again to thank Nick immediately upon their return to town, and to dump Eileen, if for no other reason than that Nick wanted her.

Adrian looked at the boat and trailer again. *The tires are good . . .*

He realized that Carmen had again spoken, and he'd again missed it. He smiled at her. "I'm sorry. This is driving me crazy. It's probably . . . But I won't know unless I look."

He got up, walked over to the boat, and lifted the corner of the tarp. He was delighted to discover a 2011 registration sticker. "Well, I'll be damned!" Carmen was still seated at the picnic table. He called to her, "How does a boat ride sound?"

Adrian didn't wait for an answer. He released the tie-downs holding the tarp in place and slid it off onto the ground. He vaulted gracefully into the boat, then reclined elegantly in the driver's seat and smiled at her.

Carmen strolled over to him. "How are you going to get it into the water?"

"O, ye of little faith," Leo replied. He hopped back over the side of the boat. "Fear not."

He dashed into the house and fetched his phone. When he came back out, Carmen heard him say, "Hello, Sissy. This is Leo Wilde. I wonder if you could help me out. Do you know anyone that could run out here and drop Rob and Will's runabout into the water for me? I don't have a trailer hitch."

Leo listened.

He winked at Carmen. "Thanks, Sissy! Could you ask him to bring a set of jumper cables? And maybe a gas tank and some gas? The registration is current, but I don't know how long it's been sitting."

Pause.

"You don't say? Well, that's awfully nice of you. It's not like any of us ever come out here anymore."

Pause.

"I'd like to hope so." Leo smiled at Carmen. "Okay. See you soon."

Carmen waited for the news.

"Apparently, Nick's mom pays Sissy to keep the boat up, too. That's why it's got a current sticker. Sissy's son puts it in the water and runs it up and down the river a couple times a month, just to keep everything in good condition."

"But you said Nick's parents don't use the place anymore. So why would they bother –"

"I dunno. Nostalgia for the old days, maybe? Maybe Will wants the boat ready in case he ever comes out again, but then he just never does." Leo shrugged, then grinned at Carmen. "I think it's kismet. It has to be fate guiding Nick's mom's hand – she didn't know why she had to keep the old scow running, she just knew she had to – it was so it would be available for us."

Carmen grinned back at him. "Is that how fate works?"

"Maybe."

But probably not in this case. Adrian recalled that the formidable Mrs. William Wilde ran the operations of her household like the most niggling of micromanagers. She never delegated a single responsibility.

The Wildes had always employed a groundskeeper, a housekeeper and a maid and a cook. They'd a tax man and a lawyer on retainer, but it had always been Marta who'd kept meticulous track of all the family's household income and outlay. From when he was a kid, Adrian remembered seeing her sitting at a desk in the den of the Wilde manse, wearing an unbecoming pair of half-specs, interrogating Doctor Wilde about European vacation plans and payment of Arizona property taxes. Adrian had always speculated that Marta might've made an excellent accountant, if it had ever been necessary for her to find any sort of employment whatsoever.

She enjoyed bestowing extravagant tips at Christmas time to those employees that had pleased her during the year: the gardener that had caused the roses to thrive was rewarded handsomely; there was always an extra hundred or sometimes two in the Wilde's Christmas card to Mr. Johnson, Nick and Bobby's music tutor.

No, it hadn't been fate that had guided Marta's hand to pay this particular local to look after their seldom used house and boat in Arizona. It was because she was a self-important, entitled snob: Sissy had been good friends with her husband and his brother and his cousin back in the day, and Marta no doubt took great relish in paying her to look after their valuable but carelessly neglected interests, as if she was nothing more than another one of the Wilde servants.

Or maybe it *was* fate.

Adrian knew that Carmen would find a boat ride fun and entertaining, and when they came back this afternoon . . . He imagined making dinner for her tonight, gazing at her across the softly candle-lit table – Adrian's vision of romantic precursors was really quite clichéd – and then he'd take her gently in his arms, tell her how much he liked her. He'd kiss her tenderly . . .

And a boat ride was the perfect forerunner to all that.

ONE HUNDRED EIGHT

Eileen met Nick at Mickey's promptly at six o'clock on Friday night. Her arrival was so prompt, she told Nick, because she, too, had ducked out of the office a few minutes early, dashed home, then hurried back to the bar to meet him.

Nick greeted her effusively, wrapping her up in a big bear hug, picking her up off of her feet and spinning her around joyfully. It was as if he hadn't seen her in weeks. Eileen asked what she'd done to deserve the long-lost friend's welcome.

"I'm just glad to see you, that's all," Nick replied with a mischievous grin. He looked at his watch. "What d'ya say to Paul's? I got us an early reservation, just under the wire. We have to hurry."

Eileen nodded. Paul's was the most expensive restaurant in town, and it wouldn't do to be late for their reservations.

"Is there some special occasion?" she asked.

"No, not particularly. I just felt like taking you someplace nice tonight." Nick threw a twenty onto the bar and took her hand.

This Friday had turned out to be an odd one for Eileen. First she'd left work at lunchtime, on a whim. Her workload had been light all morning, and her mood had been the same. Why the hell not use a couple hours of the vast chunk of vacation time she'd accumulated, being such a conscientious and diligent employee? Why the hell not? Eileen thought that she'd just go out and visit her friends on Parcay Street for a quick minute, then visit Leo for a not so quick, many minutes.

She'd texted him, and he'd agreed to the assignation. Leo always agreed: for a young man, he was almost as much of a shut-in as his relatives, or so it seemed to Eileen. He never seemed to go anywhere – he just sat around the house, played his guitar and waited for Nick to join him after work, so that they could jam in the garage. And after Nick went home, Leo entertained Eileen a couple of times a week . . .

But apparently Leo's calendar was not as open as Eileen had imagined. Apparently Leo had *some* other interests, because one of them had unexpectedly called him out of town. Eileen had been a trifle disappointed about that. She wasn't going to get to see him as she'd planned, and a suspicion had crept into her mind that maybe he'd at last met a girl his own age.

Eileen had once again reviewed the secrecy, the impossibility of their – she couldn't really call it a relationship, now could she? She came to the conclusion that whatever would happen, would happen.

Now Nick was behaving like *he* was nineteen, giggling and smiling and holding her hand as they walked from the parking lot into the ritzy restaurant. He continued to act strangely throughout the meal: he frequently smiled slyly at her, he seemed distracted, but in a happy way, as if he had news he was just bursting to tell her. He drank too much.

"Did you get a promotion or something?" Eileen asked, returning his devious smile. She couldn't help it – his good mood was infectious.

"No, no promotion." Nick drained his drink and signaled one of the snooty waiters for another one. "To tell you the truth, I've kinda . . . I've kinda got something cooking. A surprise."

Eileen frowned. She hated surprises. The last surprise she'd weathered was finding out that the guy that she'd loved twenty years ago, the guy that she'd just grown the gumption to go out and find again, was dead. The crushing of the incredible anticipation that she'd felt at the thought of seeing Adrian again – that had been a devastating surprise.

But that's not really the last surprise I had, Eileen corrected herself. *The last surprise I had was the discovery that I've got a hidden streak of wildness, of badness . . .*

Who would've thought that middle-aged, hard-working, twice-divorced Eileen Artus – she'd discarded both Allan and George's last names – would just go right ahead and have an affair with a nineteen-year-old *boy?* And for no other reason than because he looked so much like his daddy that she couldn't get him out of her mind? And because he was down for it? It was crazy, it was sinful, it was wrong . . .

Eileen pushed those thoughts away. What she had with Leo was crazy, but it was neither sinful nor wrong. He was a consenting adult, albeit a young one, and his consent was spectacular . . . It wasn't wrong, it was just . . . it just wasn't quite right. It was their little secret.

Eileen stopped thinking about Leo and concentrated on Nick. "What kind of surprise?"

"If you promise to let me make brunch for you tomorrow, I'll tell you then. Say eleven o'clock?"

"All right," Eileen agreed slowly. She speculated that maybe he'd made arrangements to take her on that trip to San Francisco that they were always talking about. Other than something like that, some fun plans for travel together, Eileen didn't have a clue what kind of a surprise he could have planned.

"Great!" Nick said, with far too much enthusiasm.

After dinner, he took Eileen directly back to her car, still parked at Mickey's. He reminded her to be at his apartment at eleven o'clock sharp the next day, and gave her a brotherly peck on the cheek. Then he jumped into his Accord, waved, and drove quickly away.

Eileen was left standing in the parking lot with her car keys in her hand, nonplussed. What a bizarre day it had turned out to be!

ONE HUNDRED NINE

Nick hopped onto the 91 Freeway and headed out to the Galleria at Tyler. He had just enough time to hit the Robbins Brothers before they closed, if he hustled a little bit. The guy on the phone had said that they had a large inventory of engagement rings in stock, to fit every budget. It would've been better if Nick already knew his intended's ring size, the guy had said, but it wasn't anything that couldn't be worked around.

Just make an educated guess, the salesman had suggested, naturally assuming that Nick was familiar with Eileen's fingers, that he'd held them, perhaps kissed them, that he'd no doubt squeezed them in moments of passionate embrace . . . it was 2011, for Christ's sake.

Regardless, the man had assured Nick, if the ring he chose turned out to be too large or too small, the bride-to-be could always come back in and they would size it for her, free of charge.

Nick giggled. His *intended.* The *bride-to-be. Hot damn, Link, if you're not the cleverest kid I've ever met . . .*

Sissy showed up at the Wilde vacation house personally, in an old shop truck. Beat-up and faded, it reminded Adrian of the one Ian had owned. He reflected that he'd had a lot of laughs in that old pickup, going to and from the water with his Dad and his Uncle Rob when he was a kid, and then dragging *One Wilde Ride* to Lake Elsinore with Bobby, after he was old enough to drive.

Sissy expertly hooked Will and Rob's ancient runabout onto the trailer hitch, backed it down the driveway, and dropped it into the water for Leo and his girlfriend.

The boat fired up on the first turn of the key. Leo smiled at Sissy. "That's awesome," he said.

"I told you. My son and Freddie take it out a couple times a month, just to make sure everything still works." She paused, then said, "I always liked your grandpa's little boat better than this one, though. I suppose your grandma sold it after he passed?"

"No, we've still got it."

"One Wilde Ride." Sissy's eyes twinkled. "The hours, the *days,* I spent waterskiing with your grandpa, Leo! It was so much fun! You'll have to rent a truck and bring it, the next time you guys come up here. I'd love to see it again."

"It's a date," Leo said, and winked at Carmen. He offered his hand to her, helped her into the boat. He said to Sissy, "I'll just tie up here overnight. Can I call you tomorrow to pull her back out?"

"I've got a better idea. If you'll ride me over to the marina, you can keep the truck overnight. Just bring it back to the shop when you're done with it."

"Thanks, Sissy! That's so nice of you!" Leo exclaimed, genuinely touched.

"Oh, it's nothing," she replied with a dismissive wave of her hand. Sissy murmured wistfully, "In another life, I always wished that Ian and I . . ." Then she quickly shook her head and smiled at Ian's grandson again. "It's the least I can do. Your grandpa and I were great friends, and Rob, too. You're practically family."

Sissy pulled the trailer out of the water and parked it up the driveway, just a little bit. She didn't want the kid to have to back it up too far to get it back under the big boat. He was just a youngster, and she didn't know how accomplished he was at such maneuvers.

Sissy untied the lines and hopped into the boat. Leo backed it up and turned them out of their secluded cove and into the chop of the Colorado River.

ONE HUNDRED ELEVEN

Just about the time that Leo and Carmen were heading out for a fun day on the water in Parker, back in Riverside, Nick and Eileen were sitting down to brunch.

Nick served chilaquiles with fried eggs over tomatillo salsa, crunchy tortilla chips and rotisserie chicken. As always, Eileen marveled at his culinary prowess.

"How did you ever learn to cook like this?" she exclaimed. The dish was delightful, a subtle melding of spiciness, color and texture.

"Esmeralda," Nick said with a wicked grin. "She was our housekeeper when I was a kid. Taught me everything I know." Everything he knew about *what*, and if it involved more than just Mexican cuisine, was left unsaid.

At the mention of the Wilde family housekeeper, Eileen was again reminded that Nick came from money. She recalled that his father and grandfather, and his uncle, too, were all doctors. Leo's grandfather had been a schoolteacher; his great-grandfather, a college professor. The Wilde clan was quite a few steps up on the socio-economic ladder from plain old Eileen Artus, title officer, with two failed marriages, one to an ex-convict. She wondered vaguely for a moment if Nick's continued pursuit of her was some kind of idle slumming . . . But that was just silly. Nick liked her. They were both too old to be worried about social status.

His frenetic mood continued. Eileen sensed an anticipation in the air. Nick seemed nervous, hopeful; maybe even a little bit *hysterically* hopeful. He cleared away the brunch dishes, insisting that Eileen stay seated at the kitchen table and not help him. He brought out a pitcher of mimosas, poured her a glass, as well as one for himself. Before Eileen had time to do more than sample hers, Nick quickly downed his own and refilled his glass.

Then, before Eileen could quite grasp what was going on, Nick had dropped to one knee and was holding up a little midnight blue velvet box. There was a diamond ring in it.

She heard the words: "Will you marry me?" But they had no meaning to her. The whole scene was common enough. Eileen had experienced it twice her own self.

But this just couldn't be happening. Nick couldn't be . . . No, it was just too ridiculous. They didn't even know each other. They'd only kissed with any kind of passion that one time. Nick had never even looked hopefully at her regarding such things again.

"Are you serious?"

Nick's happy smile faltered. "Yes, I'm serious."

He hadn't thought far enough ahead to consider what Eileen might say to his proposal, but *Are you serious?* was not the first thing he would've expected.

"But we hardly know each other, Nick."

"It's going on a year now, Eileen. I . . . I love you." Saying it out loud didn't make it true, but Nick thought that he *could* love her. It was just so strange – he'd never dated a woman for going on a year, without having slept with her. At least once, for God's sake . . .

Nick knew that he could love Eileen – he loved everything that he knew about her – he knew he could love her if they could just start behaving like adults . . .

Nick mouthed the next, down-on-one-knee, proposal cliché. "I want to spend the rest of my life with you."

Did that sound as ridiculous to Eileen as it did to him? But it was true enough.

Nick suddenly felt ludicrous. He felt positively comical. He'd listened to a kid who didn't know half as much about life, not nearly half as much about women as Nick himself did. He'd gone right ahead and taken his silly, adolescent advice. *Ask her to marry you,* Link had said. *Maybe she just wants a feeling of security,* he'd said.

Eileen had security enough. She wasn't holding out because she thought Nick was just out for a good time, or anything as puritanically juvenile as that. She was holding out because . . .

Quite without realizing that she did it, Eileen glanced over her shoulder at the shelf beside the empty space on the wall above Nick's computer, where the picture of Adrian and his band reposed.

This was just crazy. Nick couldn't want to marry her. Confusion enveloped Eileen like a mist. She liked Nick. He was a lot of fun, he was cute, he was sexy, he was clever, intelligent. And maybe she could love him someday, but Leo . . .

When Eileen glanced back at Nick, his face was clouded, angry. He snapped the box shut and tossed it carelessly, roughly, onto the kitchen table. He rose from bended knee and flopped down into the chair across from her. "Do you know where he is right now?"

"Who?"

"Adrian." Nick gritted his teeth in anger at himself, at her. *"Leo.* Do you know where he is right now, what he's doing?"

The denial leapt instantly to Eileen's lips. "Why would I know where –"

"He's with a girl. Some girl he just met, that he just picked up. He took her up to our vacation house in Arizona, for a weekend of fun in the sun and all the nookie that she's undoubtedly willing to give him."

So it was true. *I guessed right.*

Nick glared at her broodingly. The angry hurt glowed in his pale green eyes.

Eileen had no right to hurt Nick. He was a good guy, and he'd put up with her acting like a shy, virginal schoolgirl for almost an entire year, without so much as a single complaint. She had to soothe away that hurt. She had to say something.

"I'm really flattered, Nick."

Now if that didn't sound like a cliché, Eileen had never heard a cliché. She hurried to say something more original.

"I'm just so surprised." That wasn't very original either. "I like you Nick, I really do. This is just so sudden . . ." Eileen willed herself not to look at Adrian's picture again. "I need to think about it. That's not too much to ask, is it? You've got to admit that it's unexpected."

"I've been thinking about it for a long time," Nick lied.

Asking her to marry him had just seemed like a novel idea. Cute, original. Clever. For Christ's sake, all he really wanted to do was get closer to her, and he'd been willing to make this absurd proposal in order to do that. Nick thought it was only what he had coming, this sensation of stupid, dumbfounded rejection that he now felt. That's what he got for listening to some idiot kid.

Eileen didn't want him. She didn't want to be married to him, she didn't want to go to bed with him. All she wanted was Adrian, all she wanted was Leo . . .

"Give me a minute to think about it," Eileen requested, with more pleading than she had intended.

It was really a great idea. The chances of meeting another guy as nice, as sweet and sexy as Nick, the chances of meeting someone with whom she shared such compatibility – *I'm forty-one years old, for crying out loud* – the chances of finding any kind of happiness, any kind of surcease from loneliness, were getting to be slim and none. But . . .

See u on Monday?

"Let me think about it until tomorrow night."

Let me think about it until Leo gets back . . .

"All right," Nick said expressionlessly. "That's fair enough."

373

ONE HUNDRED TWELVE

A watery film of tension permeated the rest of the afternoon. The ghost of Nick's proposal and the spirit of what Eileen's answer would be clanked and moaned just below the surface of pleasant conversation. They talked less than usual, and the sparse words were about unimportant things. Subjects that were studiously avoided included Leo, Arizona, the past, the present, and most assuredly, the future.

Nick suggested that they go see a movie, and with relief, Eileen assented. She wouldn't have to not talk to him in a dark theater. They wouldn't have to continue to not discuss his question, nor the reasons for her hesitation in answering.

They caught a matinee of *Apollo 18,* but the ominous discovery of lost cosmonauts on the moon passed Eileen by. She was considering her own life: its comedies, its tragedies. Its possibilities.

Eileen admitted to herself that she was currently getting to have her cake and eat it too, in the most spectacular of ways. The whole situation seemed as if it was nothing but a dream, when she wasn't actually with her young lover. When she was alone, it had no more meaning, no more relevance, than one of the warm, languorous fantasies that Eileen had daydreamt of Adrian when she was twenty.

And when she and Leo were together, it was like she was twenty again, and it was like he was Adrian, and it was like every one of those long ago fantasies was coming true.

Yet even when she touched him, kissed him, ran his soft, feathery black hair through her eager fingers, there was still a quality of unreality about it all to Eileen. None of it was concrete, reliable. There was no we've-got-a-future-together sense to it. Even when they were together, it was still all just a dream.

Eileen wasn't twenty, although Leo was – that reality was inescapable. And Leo wasn't Adrian, no matter how much he looked like him. And they were never going to live happily ever after.

But Nick was real. He'd come completely off the wall with this proposal of marriage. *Unexpected* didn't begin to describe it. No question that had ever been put to Eileen had even remotely surprised her as much as Nick Wilde asking her, *Will you marry me?*

I don't even know you, Eileen thought, as she ignored the paranoia of the mythical astronauts on the screen. But she'd been sure that she'd known Allan and George, had staked large chunks of her life and happiness upon her confidence in that knowledge. Yet she'd been mistaken both times.

What Eileen knew of Nick, she liked. He was neither a dangerous tough guy nor a preening egotist. He was tough enough, confident enough, but there was more to him than these one-dimensional characteristics. His proposal was preposterous, but it was real.

Eileen could accept it. They could wed, they could make a life together. This thing with Leo was just a dream, and if Eileen didn't wake herself up from it soon, if she didn't start living in reality . . . If she didn't start acting her age, then the opportunity for a happy life with a real man that actually had some feelings for her – all that was going to pass her by, as surely as the opportunity to be with Adrian had slipped through her fingers, all those years ago.

When she wasn't with Leo, he was just a dream . . .

But he wasn't just a dream. He was a living, breathing, incredibly sexy young man. Lying beside Leo was like attaining a fluffy, heavenly cloud. It was like making love to an angel. One tender kiss from his flawless, cherubic mouth, and Eileen was transported to paradise.

But possessing him was also committing the most exquisite sin. It was rolling around between the hot sheets with the most impish, most brilliant, most clever of cloven-hooved devils.

Leo was good, and divinely so. But he could also be superbly, breathtakingly *bad*.

Eileen couldn't make any life-altering, irrevocable decisions until she saw him again. She had told Nick that she'd give him an answer on Monday, and so she would.

After she saw impeccable young Leo, just one more time.

ONE HUNDRED THIRTEEN

Leo and Carmen didn't take Sissy back to the marina and drop her off, after all. The boat needed fuel, and she directed them to the nearest, cheapest place that sold it. Then she showed them all the cool sights along the river, the ones that only a lifetime local knew about.

Adrian had not spent a great deal of time in Parker as a kid. It was a trip that required a great deal of preparation to undertake: there was packing and planning; Rob's schedule had to be consulted; there was the long drive from Riverside. The Wilde crew had come to Parker, but their visits had been few when Adrian was young.

And when he and Bobby were old enough to take the boat out on their own, they'd been ensorcelled by their music. Adrian knew Lake Elsinore like the back of his hand, but the majority of the time he and his cousin had spent on the water had come about as a spur of the moment thing. Broken strings, blown tubes, songwriter's block – these kinds of occurrences had usually been the sole impetus for a *Fuck this, let's go skiing* adventure. And the lake was so much closer.

So Adrian was unaware of the good beaches and secret coves on Parker's stretch of the Colorado, but Sissy knew them all, and she handled the big boat like she'd been born to it, because of course, she had been. Letting Sissy drive also afforded Leo and Carmen the opportunity to sit side by side on the curving back seat. It allowed them to sit with their thighs pressed together, holding hands, laughing and smiling into each other's eyes, trying to make themselves heard over the roar of the outboard. It wasn't as if Leo could whisper sweet nothings into her ear, even if they had been alone.

Sissy and Leo switched off the task of piloting, and a few times, they even gave Carmen a chance to steer the runabout, to open up its powerful motor and run full out up the river.

Leo could see that Sissy was having fun. She told them many an entertaining story about a yesteryear crammed full of skiing and boating adventures with Ian and Rob.

There was the one about how the three of them had crashed a drunken frat party at this beach, how Ian and Rob had then proceeded to fill the boat up with girls – Sissy had to keep telling the drunker ones to *Sit down!* Ian and Rob had snatched them from directly under the college boys' noses and whisked them away for other adventures, dropping a pouting Sissy off at the marina beforehand.

The propeller on the outboard had hit a hidden log upon approach to that cozy cove. Ian and Rob had sheared a pin and had to be towed back to the house. Will had been furious about that, but Ian had just laughed at him, because Sissy had no trouble at all making the necessary repairs. The big boat was again ready for adventure before the sun set.

Sissy looked at Leo curiously every now and then, her smile contented and nostalgic. The good-looking nineteen-year-old whom he appeared to be brought to Sissy's mind no pictures of long dead Adrian Wilde, and that was refreshing to him for a change. Adrian had inherited his mother's black hair, but he'd had Ian's dark blue eyes, and it was a trait that had also been passed on to his grandson. When she looked at Leo, Sissy didn't remember Adrian – she hadn't known Adrian. Instead, she was happily, wistfully reminded of Ian, the man that she'd unrequitedly loved for a few summers a million years ago – or so she confessed to Leo and Carmen.

Sissy told the young people about the great crush she'd had on Ian in the late sixties, how she'd pestered him and flirted with him, how she'd risked her father's ire and pursued him all over the river, whenever he and his cousins were in town. Without a trace of rancor or resentment, she told Leo and Carmen that Ian had always refused her. She was too young. It was just not to be. She told them that it was not without a teenager's maudlin melancholy that she'd resigned herself to the fact that Ian would never be anything more than a friendly big brother to her. But oh, the fun they'd had skiing!

Adrian was amazed at the complete lack of bitterness in Sissy's long-ago acceptance that Ian Wilde would never be hers. She'd obviously loved him, but she'd been realistic. Ian was her friend, and she aimed to enjoy that to its utmost, and ignore the little pricks of jealousy that had no doubt plagued her when she saw him with other girls, and eventually with a wife and child. Ian's feelings for her were never going to change. Since it was all she was ever going to get, Sissy had decided that being friends with him was good enough.

Adrian contrasted Sissy's mature realism to his AnTeen's dark malevolence. The witch had desired his father, too, but surely no more than had the bouncy, self-assured river rat teen that Sissy had once been. But AnTeen had not been able to accept this most common reality of life: the man she loved, loved someone else. It was something that Sissy had been able to overcome, and she'd gone on to marry, have children and grandchildren. She'd lived a full, joyous life, and now her memories of Ian Wilde were happy, if a trace wistful. They brought her no pain.

Unlike AnTeen, whose obsession had twisted her, filled her with acrimony and a thirst for revenge. Her inability to lay down her torch had left her vicious, a bitter old witch with not one thing to show for a life spent waiting for a man that would never, ever come to her. It was not like Ian had ever said or done anything to encourage her to hang onto the fruitless hope, Adrian knew. The feeling of victimization to which Nadine had clung had all been a product of her own stubbornness, her own self-pity. Adrian hoped that she'd been able to get over it by now.

ONE HUNDRED FOURTEEN

Even though three could have undoubtedly been construed as a crowd, the fun day they spent with Sissy on the river left Leo and Carmen feeling even closer. As the sun began to set, they finally dropped their kind benefactor off at the marina, thanking her profusely for the local's tour she'd given them.

Again, Sissy demurred with a wave of her hand. It was nothing, she assured them. "It's fun to play hooky from the shop every now and then. And I couldn't have asked for better company."

Adrian tied the boat up at his family's private dock, and Carmen and Leo held hands and smiled at each other as they walked slowly up to the house. A calmness had settled over both of them. They knew it was going to happen tonight, but the affection that had grown up between them took the edge off of what otherwise would have just been an urgent, anonymous desire.

The time was right. Carmen forgot about the calculation of three-dates-first-to-ensure-his-respect. Leo already respected her. He *liked* her, past just a common desire to sleep with her.

Adrian wanted this girl, but he also wanted to continue with her, to see her smiles and hear her opinions. Although he didn't actually see it, not with the precognitive eye that fate had gifted him, Adrian still predicted that their first time would be slow and tender, filled with giggles and affection, in addition to grand passion. He lazily looked forward to it, without the normal, demanding determination to *just get on with it.*

They shared a delightful dinner, and in preparation for what they both knew was to come, they dimmed the lights and settled in on the couch to watch a movie. The anticipation was like a warm blanket on Adrian's skin as he put his arm around the beautiful young woman cuddled up next to him. He laughed to himself: *or maybe I'm just sunburned . . .*

As the opening credits faded and the film began, Adrian thought that he'd just lean closer to Carmen, kiss her cheek, her mouth . . .

ONE HUNDRED FIFTEEN

Adrian realized that it was daytime.

He was awake, lying on his back, but he didn't open his eyes. He smiled in contentment and recalled the night he'd spent with Carmen. There was a dreamlike quality to his recollections: he again saw her sparkling eyes, her lovely smile, felt the warmth of her hand in his . . .

But the memories of the hunger at last sated, the cries and shivers, the ecstasies of physical culmination, were strangely absent. Yet still Adrian smiled. His right hand touched something soft and firm beside him. He would only have to open his eyes and turn to her, and he could again experience the passion they'd shared . . .

Adrian turned his head, opened his eyes, and came face to face with the back of the couch. He looked around in confusion, and discovered that he was in the living room, had been asleep there. He was not in his room, not naked in his bed with his new lover. Instead, he was fully clothed, in the same pair of shorts and tank top he'd worn the day before. His new lover was gone.

Adrian sat up, feeling stiff and uncomfortable. The slight sunburn he'd acquired the day before made his skin feel hot and a little raw.

Just what was going on here?

Before he had time to think on it any further, Carmen came down the hall from the kitchen. She was carrying a tray with two sandwiches on little plates, two glasses of milk. She set it on the coffee table in front of him, and Adrian flashed to all the lunches that his aunts and his mother had prepared for him as a child. It had been one of their favorite tasks, another excuse to shower affection on their beloved Capo, the most important, exceptional little boy in their lives . . .

Adrian shook his head. He blinked. His eyes felt sandy. After their thrilling first night together, he and Carmen should be enjoying aphrodisiacs, chocolate-covered strawberries – Adrian had slipped a package into their cart at the market – not having sandwiches and milk like schoolchildren. They should be sharing affectionate glances, tender touches, contended sighs. They should be doing it all over again . . .

Just what had happened last night? Adrian remembered the spellbinding anticipation, his plan to at last lean over and kiss her . . .

"It's about time you woke up," Carmen said with a giggle.

She could've added some smart-ass remark, like *I didn't realize my company was so boring,* or something equally as sarcastic, but she didn't. Even so, with dejected chagrin, Adrian grasped what had happened. He'd been awake since Friday morning, and all the excitement and desire engendered by the evening he'd spent with Carmen, laughing, talking, playing cards, hadn't allowed him a wink of sleep that night.

Then they'd spent all day Saturday bouncing around on the water, enjoying Sissy's excellent company. He and Carmen had returned, had dinner, settled in on the couch . . .

But even Adrian's anticipation of making love to Carmen hadn't been enough to stave off the inescapable fact that he was exhausted. There'd been no night of passion with the beautiful blonde. Whatever he thought he remembered, he'd only dreamt it. Adrian Wilde, ladies' man, had fallen asleep, right here on the couch.

"I'm sorry," he told her, hangdog. He had not been so sorry for anything that'd occurred since he'd returned from the oblivion of the other side.

"It's okay, Leo," Carmen said brightly. She plopped down beside him, took his hand, squeezed it. "I'm not going anywhere. Eat your lunch."

Lunch? "What time is it?"

Carmen released his hand and picked up her phone from the coffee table. "It's twelve-thirty." She looked at him earnestly. "I've had such a good time, but we should really be starting back home soon. You've still gotta take Sissy's truck back . . . It's a long drive. I have an early class tomorrow."

Carmen squeezed his hand again to underline her words. She'd had a wonderful time. She wasn't blowing him off, just because he'd fallen asleep like an old man, and made her miss what had been shaping up to be an awesome evening.

The thought that Carmen was disappointed, that she was through with him, hadn't entered Adrian's mind. Everything was the same between them – happy, affectionate, promise-filled. Time had just run out. Life was intervening. There would be another chance.

"Eat your sandwich," Carmen prompted again.

Adrian picked it up, took a bite. It was peanut butter and jelly, and again he was remembered of his extraordinarily privileged and enjoyable childhood.

"We'll pack up and get on the road as soon as we're done eating," he assured Carmen. She smiled, and Adrian thought that his life would only continue to be enjoyable. They'd have another chance.

ONE HUNDRED SIXTEEN

The configuration of Leo's little car, with its bucket seats and center console, precluded Carmen from sitting close to him on the ride home. Adrian again missed Ian's old pick-up with its bench seat, perfect for long, snuggly drives. But still Carmen managed to show her friendly affection by patting him on the shoulder frequently, by smiling and giggling with him.

A small portion of Adrian's arrogance and cynicism returned. The devil popped up and perched upon his shoulder, and proceeded to reflect that Leo didn't have to rush right home and righteously, abruptly break things off with Eileen, seeing how nothing of any kind of an even remotely physical nature had transpired between him and her daughter. The trip had been impulsive, but Leo had not sinned.

He was *friends* with Eileen, was he not? They were friends with benefits, as the saying went, yet he still remained only the most platonic of friends with Carmen. There was no need for a big tearful break-up scene. Not quite yet.

Adrian listened patiently to the shady little demon that comprised an inescapable part of his fearless personality. But he also felt a small, sharp knifing of guilt. Even though nothing had happened between Leo and Carmen – the whole just taking off on a whim with another woman deal was still kind of a shitty thing to have pulled on Eileen. If she knew, she'd be jealous, and while Adrian had never himself ever experienced even a whiff of jealousy, he knew that Eileen would feel it.

And who knew better than Adrian what jealousy could do to people? He'd seen it in Nick's eyes, a lifetime ago, whenever he'd look and at Randi and Gil. He'd seen it in Nick's eyes again, that day when he'd been playfully attempting to teach Eileen how to play the guitar. Nick had not appreciated Leo's seemingly innocent closeness to this women he coveted, their easy, comfortable smiles. Nick would *sincerely* not appreciate it, his jealousy would come to a boil, if he found out that not one single other thing innocent had transpired between Leo and Eileen all summer . . .

Nick was a civilized human being. He was capable of holding his jealousy in check. But Adrian could not fail to recall Gil, whose rage – over what had been nothing more than a meaningless roll in the sack to Adrian – had driven him to homicide. And AnTeen, whose lifelong bitterness over that which she simply could not have had driven her to goad Gil into it.

"O, beware, my lord, of jealousy," Adrian had heard his father tell his Uncle Rob with a grin once. *"It is the green-eyed monster . . ."* They'd been discussing Rob's plan to date two nurses at that same time, who worked on the same floor at the hospital. Ian had wondered about the danger of such a plan. "One of them's liable to stab you . . ."

Adrian speculated as to what form Eileen's jealousy might take, how it might affect her, what it might drive her to. It wasn't like Leo knew her very well. It wasn't as if they'd ever sat around for a weekend and discussed current events, political opinions, hopes and dreams and aspirations, as he and Carmen had done.

Would Eileen's jealousy turn her bitter and vengeful, as it had turned AnTeen? *Heaven has no rage like love to hatred turned, nor hell a fury like a woman scorned.* Adrian remembered his eighteenth birthday party, when AnTeen had recited those words to him, seemingly apropos of nothing. But they'd been significant to her.

The hourglass of Adrian's first life had been almost out of sand by then. AnTeen had already spent half her life in seething hatred at Daina and her son, all as a result of her unhinged jealousy. That jealousy had led her to be an accomplice to Adrian's murder. His own jealousy had led Gil to *become* his murderer.

In a moment of paranoia, Adrian imagined Eileen siccing Allan on him in her rage, when she found out why he was breaking it off with her. *This horrible, reprobate musician has sullied our innocent child!* she'd say to her ex-husband. *Are you going to allow that?* It was one possible reaction on Eileen's part, once it became apparent that Leo would no longer be sullying her anymore.

Adrian pushed that crazy scenario away. Surely Eileen wouldn't lose her mind when Leo ended it. They'd never spoken of commitments. It had never been anything more than a fun, secret, physical thing between them.

But still . . . Adrian realized that he was skating on thin ice, dog paddling in shark-infested waters, walking a tightrope – all the clichés fit. Apparently, he had not learned anything by being dead, had not learned anything by being a cautious, watchful kid for seventeen years.

Leap and the net will appear. God hates a coward. These had always been fearless, confident, just-slightly-shady Adrian Wilde's mantras. Adherence to them had gotten him in hot water before. They'd gotten him *dead.*

So, yeah, the devil on his shoulder said. *Maybe it's just as well that nothing happened with Carmen. You can just keep on keepin' on with Eileen. No reason to end it just yet.*

But the angel on Adrian's other shoulder just smiled serenely. Something *had* happened with Carmen. He'd discovered that he longed to spend more time with her. He wasn't even put out that the spur of the moment weekend had turned out to be a sexual bust. There would be time, it would happen soon enough . . .

And then there was Adrian's startling realization of the overwhelming debt of gratitude that he owed to his cousin.

He had to end it with Eileen, and it had to be sooner rather than later.

ONE HUNDRED SEVENTEEN

Mercifully, Eileen's car was absent from the driveway when Adrian and Carmen arrived at her house. Adrian hoped that she was off somewhere with Nick. He hoped that his cousin had finally stepped up and made some kind of move. He hoped that Eileen had given in, and that they were even now over at his apartment, being in love.

Leo walked Carmen to the door, like they were high school sweethearts, still in high school.

"Can I call you later?" he even asked.

Carmen nodded. They gazed into each other's eyes, and Adrian Wilde, never shy, at last took the opportunity that she offered. He kissed her for the first time, slowly, languidly, and Carmen felt a flow of electrical warmth flood her to the ends of her fingertips. Adrian felt it too, and continued to kiss her, softly, tenderly, affectionately.

When they both felt the stirring of a stronger passion, Adrian broke the kiss. He thought that if he didn't stop now, he wouldn't be able to stop, and there was no place for them to go right at the moment. He didn't want to despoil the magic of everything they'd shared with some kind of quick adolescent grope against the wall of the porch. He sensed that Carmen wouldn't have stopped him. Her desire was as plain as his in her kiss.

But now was not the time. Adrian would see to it that they next time he saw Carmen, it would be when they could be alone, with no fear of interruption.

"I'll call you later," he promised, and bid her farewell.

ONE HUNDRED EIGHTEEN

The devil materialized on Adrian's shoulder again as he drove home. *All right,* he said. *You want to call it quits with Eileen, because you suddenly think you owe Nick, and you think you're in love with her daughter. That's all good.*

Adrian blinked in astonishment. Was he in love with Carmen? After spending just an enjoyable two days and two no-sex nights with her? Adrian's intellect denied it. Carmen was just a pretty girl, but there was nothing special about her . . .

The purer side of his nature disagreed. *She's just a girl that you can't get out of your mind. You can't wait to talk to her again. You want to call her the minute you get home.*

"No, you hang up first," Adrian said aloud and grinned to himself.

You can't wait to see her again, the angel on his shoulder said. *You just wanna see her eyes, her smile, hear her voice. You don't even care that the two of you haven't –*

And that's where Eileen comes in, the devil said in a sly whisper. *You want to end it with her and that's all honorable and shit. But why not send her off with a bang, give her something to remember you by? You know she'd love it. It would take the sting out of the break-up for her, and it would sure take the edge off for you . . .*

Adrian was appalled at his own wickedness, and dismissed both angel and devil, although he soon allowed the goodness in his nature free rein again. He did want to see Carmen again, and as soon as possible. And it didn't really matter if they didn't have sex right away, although that would certainly be great . . .

The afternoon was hot, even for mid-September, and Adrian had a touch of sunburn from Arizona. So he started a cool bath and scooped himself out a bowl of ice cream, and ate it while the tub filled. He liked being alone, after the exciting, surprising, whirlwind weekend he'd spent with the enticing, captivating blonde.

Being alone, he could concentrate on thoughts of her, of continuing to get to know her, and kissing her, and maybe making love to her soon, and whether or not all these fabulous feelings he was experiencing might just be love. He could clear his mind of all extraneous realities: his aunts and his mom; crazy Randi and her bitter best friend; Leo's middle-aged lover; his covetous cousin, whom he again reminded himself to thank at the first opportunity.

Adrian didn't want to think of any of them, didn't want to think of dealing with them. All that would come soon enough.

Adrian ate his ice cream and relaxed in the cool water. Then he decided to take a nap. He'd deal with his relatives tomorrow. He'd thank Nick and talk to Eileen. Tomorrow. For right now, he just wanted to rest and think about Carmen. He turned off his phone and went to sleep.

ONE HUNDRED NINETEEN

Carmen couldn't rest. She took a shower and flopped onto her bed. She was tired, but elated.

She'd had *such a good time* with Leo! He was so smart and cute and sexy, and she thought it was comical that he'd fallen asleep at just the wrong moment. But that was okay. It only showed that he was relaxed around her. They were already friends, and they had the rest of their lives to become more than friends . . .

Eileen and Carmen's grandmother were not at home. Sunday was grocery day, so Carmen figured that was probably where they were. But even though she had the big silent house all to herself, she couldn't sleep. She got out of bed and got dressed again. She made herself a snack.

Carmen turned on the television, but not a single thing being broadcast that afternoon intrigued her. The internet was the same. The familiar cute-cat videos were still cute and funny, but they failed to hold her interest, and world events seemed plodding and contrived at the moment.

Carmen felt distracted. An odd kind of loneliness seemed to descend upon her. She was inordinately glad to see her mother and grandmother – *the whole matriarchy* – when they returned from the store, and set about helping them put away the groceries with gusto.

But when Eileen mentioned Carmen's utterly forgotten boyfriend, a strange despondency again struck her. "You're not thinking about moving in with Clint, are you, Carmen? I haven't seen you all weekend!"

"No, Mom. I'll never move in with Clint."

"Trouble in paradise?" Eileen asked nonchalantly.

Carmen nodded and shook her head at the same time, a gesture she'd unknowingly picked up from Leo. She didn't want to talk about Clint. He was nothing but a memory to her now.

Clint was her past, although he was still operating under the assumption that he was a part of her present, and maybe even her future. Carmen had texted once, after she and Leo had arrived at the charming house on the river, told him that she was sick.

Clint had texted back that he hoped she'd feel better soon, and had not texted again. Carmen hoped that whatever, *whoever,* it was that was keeping him busy would continue to do so, especially after she delivered the *It's not you, it's me* speech.

Carmen wanted to tell her mother that she and Clint were through, and wanted to tell her that she'd just spent the most wonderful weekend imaginable with Eileen's friend's charming grandson. Carmen wanted to tell her mother that she might be falling in love with Leo . . .

But she also didn't feel quite up to putting all these thoughts and emotions into words at the moment.

The oddly joyful feelings engendered by the reunion with her mother and grandmother soon faded, and again Carmen felt a strange sadness, an ambiguous emptiness, as if some invisible hole had opened up in her world, right in front of her. Inexplicably, Carmen felt like something was absent in her life.

But what? *Something . . . some undefinable thing. It was here, but now it's gone . . .*

The weird melancholy lingered for a few more moments. When she at last recognized its cause, its source, its cure, Carmen brightened. She gave her mother and grandmother a kiss on the cheek.

"I've got a few errands to run before class tomorrow," she told them. "I'll see you guys later."

ONE HUNDRED TWENTY

Adrian's nap was brief but refreshing. He'd already slept half the day away in Arizona, after all. He went out to the living room and turned on the TV, flipped through the channels. There was nothing on. He picked up his Charvel and strummed it idly, but he didn't even bother plugging it into its little amp. After a minute, he set it back on its stand again.

Adrian paced back and forth in his living room a few times, then flopped down on the couch. He felt as though he wanted to do something, go somewhere, see somebody, but nothing in particular appealed to him. The thought of *What am I gonna do about Eileen?* tried to impress itself on his mind again, but he dismissed it. That was a problem for tomorrow. He'd told her that he'd see her on Monday, and Monday would be here soon enough. He'd worry about it then.

The sun had already set – *maybe it'll cool off a little bit,* Adrian thought – when his doorbell rang. He felt a flash of annoyance. His phone was still on the little table beside his bed. He'd shut it off – wasn't that the modern day equivalent of a *Do Not Disturb* sign? Did it not indicate that he wanted to be left alone?

But was that what he wanted? To be alone? Adrian wasn't sure. He felt out of sorts, *at odds and ends,* as his aunts always said. Maybe he should welcome a visitor. Maybe some conversation would help to even out his strange mood.

Adrian opened the door and blinked in pleased surprise. It was Carmen.

"I . . . I missed you," she said softly. "I had to . . . see you."

Adrian discovered that he'd missed her, too, that Carmen's absence was the reason that all the bowls of ice cream and cool baths and quick naps had failed to content him. He'd spent such a short amount of time with this beautiful young woman, yet it seemed like he'd spent his entire life with her. They'd only been apart for a few hours, yet Adrian had felt out of sorts because Carmen wasn't there with him.

Adrian opened his arms and she rushed into them. She threw her own arms around his neck and kissed him breathlessly, as if they'd been separated for weeks. As if they were already lovers, and this was a homecoming . . .

Adrian broke their kiss just long enough to close and lock the front door. Then he picked Carmen up as if she were his bride and carried her to his bed.

The direct *genuineness* of their encounter surprised and delighted them both.

With all others, there'd always been a vestige of something else, an undercurrent other than simple desire. The idea that one or the other was being tricked or deceived in some small way, the possibility that one was getting something over on the other, the ugly thought that it was indeed a *battle* of the sexes, and when they got up and got dressed afterward, there would be a clear winner and a clear loser – these propositions had always marred sex for both of them in the past, to a greater or lesser degree.

Carmen had always believed that the men she'd agreed to sleep with had wanted her for nothing else, and she'd always known in the back of her mind that she'd wanted them for nothing else. Adrian had always known that women wanted him far more than he'd ever want them. In his first incarnation, he'd sometimes harbored a trace of guilt about that. Nowadays, it was just all part of the game to him. But with Carmen, there was need to be false, no need to play any manner of game.

They fell together to quench a need that overwhelmed them equally. They could no longer ignore their desire, could put it off not another second. At first, it was a burning, selfish thing, the way that Carmen wanted Leo and Adrian wanted Carmen, but it then quickly grew into a generous aspiration. They each sought to drown themselves in the pleasure to be found in the taking, but soon there was an irresistible craving to please the other person. Adrian wanted to possess Carmen, but he also wanted to impress her. Carmen wanted to devour Leo, but she also wanted him to be enthralled.

It was passionate and ecstatic, flawless. It was giggly and fun. It was right. It was perfect. It was love.

ONE HUNDRED TWENTY-ONE

Carmen missed her Monday morning class. She missed all her classes that day, because she and Leo didn't leave the house. Empires might've ended, governments been toppled by strident revolution; they would not have noticed. There was no world outside of the little house on Parcay Street that day. They made love and took showers together, they made snacks and laughed and giggled and talked. They said, *I love you,* and both of them knew it was true, beyond a shadow of a doubt.

But the real world and Carmen's sense of responsibility reasserted themselves a little before six o'clock that evening.

"I can't miss my study group," she told Leo, hastening to find her clothing, her purse, her forgotten cellphone. "It's for Women's Issues." Carmen rolled her eyes and Leo grinned. "The assignment is to create a magazine that doesn't include all the tiresome stereotypes that we've been fed all our lives, about what it means to be a modern woman.

"No Cosmo style pandering to the ideal that we're just men's playthings," she intoned, not believing a word of it. "No *Ten Things Guys Crave in Bed* or *Twenty-five Sex Positions That'll Make Him Cry,* or anything like that." Carmen unexpectedly grabbed Leo, and he jumped. She smiled. "But nothing militantly feminist and serious either. No abortion diatribes, a la *Our Bodies, Ourselves.*"

Leo had not a clue what she was talking about, so he just smiled.

"Just something fun and informative and fair." Carmen grinned. "We have just about not much, so far. I have to go."

Leo grabbed her hand. "But you'll come back?"

"You can count on it."

Adrian threw on his shorts and a shirt and walked her to the door. He kissed her quickly. Carmen was in a hurry.

"I'll be back in a couple of hours."

Carmen turned the lock on the door and opened it. Eileen was standing on the porch, her finger poised halfway to the doorbell.

Mild surprise colored Carmen's features, but she didn't have time to talk to her mother at the moment, so the story that had led to her momentous, life-altering meeting with the man with whom she now found herself in love sprang immediately to her mind.

"You got my text then?" There had of course, been no text.

Eileen shook her head. She was so surprised to find her daughter coming out of Leo's house that she was struck dumb.

"I asked if you wanted to go to the movies. You know, do something different on a Monday night." Carmen willed herself not to turn around and look at Leo. He was certainly something different, and she planned to be doing him for the rest of her life, if there was a God.

"I didn't get any answer," Carmen continued, "so I drove out here to look for you. I didn't know what house you were at – but since there's only two, I just knocked on the first door. This charming young man –" Carmen now turned and looked innocently at him, "said he knows you. He said that you might be at his mother's house –"

"My aunts' house," Leo corrected.

"He said that you might be at his aunts' house. He was just going to show me the way, but then I remembered that I have to go to study group, or we're all going to flunk. So, we'll have to go to the movies some other time, Mom." Carmen kissed Eileen quickly on the cheek, and skipped past her out the door. "I'll see you later!"

Eileen watched Carmen cross the yard and hop into her car. Eileen had hidden her own car up the street, as she always did, and hadn't noticed Carmen's little white Toyota parked in Leo's driveway. Carmen backed out, and waved to her mother as she drove past the house. Eileen waved back. When her daughter pulled out onto Jurupa Road, Eileen turned back and looked at Leo. Silently, expectantly. It was Monday, and she was here to see him, just as he'd suggested in his text on Friday.

"Would you like to come in?"

ONE HUNDRED TWENTY-TWO

Eileen wanted to ask Leo where he'd been all weekend, what he'd been doing, and with whom. But she couldn't think of a way to phrase it that didn't make her sound like a desperate, jealous old harridan.

Besides, he was so damned cute . . .

Eileen wanted to kiss Leo. She'd ask him all the cold, hard, sure-to-be-disappointing questions after she kissed him. She would ask him . . . later.

Eileen closed the distance between them. She put her arms around his neck.

Go for it! the devil whispered in Adrian's ear. *Make it a good one, one she'll remember you by, my son, seeing as how this is the last time you're ever gonna kiss her . . .*

Adrian complied. He kissed Eileen slowly and tenderly, but without any passion. When she seemed to want more, he stopped. He sighed.

"We have to talk, Eileen."

Here it comes.

Eileen smiled ruefully. "I thought as much. Nick told me that you met someone."

Adrian blinked in surprise. *Goddamned, jealous, petty Nick!*

But then Adrian retracted his curse. Maybe his cousin had done him a favor. Eileen wasn't crying. She wasn't furious. Maybe whatever Nick had told her had softened the blow somehow. But she was still waiting for an explanation.

Adrian sighed again. "Throughout my entire life . . ." *Throughout all my lives . . .* "I've understood the concept of true love, Eileen. You might say I can sense it. *Read it.* But I don't feel it. I've never been in love. But sometimes knowing that someone loves you is enough. I could tell how you felt about me, from the moment we met." *It was the same as it was twenty years ago . . .*

"So I gave in to it. I kissed you, because you wanted me to. And everything else . . ." Leo shook his head. "Maybe it wasn't the smartest thing for me to do. I knew a girl once . . . Giving in to her love got me killed."

Eileen blinked. *What an odd way to put it.* He was obviously referring to some failed relationship, one that had clearly ended badly for him. *Giving in to her love got me killed . . .*

"So, I did this for you, Eileen," Leo was saying. "Because you loved me." He sighed yet again.

"But I discovered something this weekend. The kind of thing that we have – it's great and important and fun, don't get me wrong – but it's not love. Love is more than . . . what we have." The words tumbled quickly from Leo now. "We'll always be friends, Eileen, but I . . . We can't do this anymore. Carmen and I –"

"Carmen?"

"I just met her on Friday. It was like she said. She showed up here, looking for you, to go to the movies. It was love at first sight, Eileen, just like my parents . . ." Leo shook his head again. "Like my *grandparents* had."

The recollection of Daina's stories of the joy that she'd shared with her husband crowded out the outrageous revelation that Leo had just dropped in her lap, that he thought he was in love with *her daughter,* just because he'd spent one weekend with her . . .

How in the hell had that happened? *It was love at first sight . . .*

There was a rushing in her Eileen's ears, like a freight train. Oh, my god, Leo was ending it, what was she going to do without Leo . . .

The rushing abruptly stopped. What was she doing *with* Leo? It was all just a selfish extravagance, a naughty decadence. She was more than twenty years older than him. It was a depravity that ignored two decades.

If Eileen examined her feelings dispassionately, she was forced to admit that Leo was the equivalent of walking, talking, breathing pornography to her. She loved the effects that looking at him produced, but she'd be mortified beyond all belief if anybody ever found out that she'd been looking. Not to mention everything else. The thing between them was so awesome because it was forbidden. But that didn't make it love.

On the other hand, Eileen had often imagined that Nick would be a lot of fun, too, and they could walk down the street hand in hand, arm in arm, and people wouldn't turn around and stare at them. People wouldn't wonder if they were a disturbingly affectionate mother and son.

Nick was no Adrian Wilde, but it the naked light of day, *neither was Leo.* If Eileen stripped away the decades-old fantasies of things with Adrian that never were and now could never be, the impossibilities that had prompted her involvement with Leo, all she was left with was a dirty little secret.

Now Leo wanted out. He was offering Eileen an out. And Nick was waiting for her.

Eileen paused for another moment, waiting to see what emotions would come. Would she feel betrayed, sad, angry, bitter? To her astonishment, the only feeling that washed over Eileen was relief. As the old song said, she'd *been driving with her eyes closed.* She'd only narrowly missed hitting something – *but that's the way it goes*

"You're right, Leo," Eileen said at last. "It wasn't love, but you helped me to experience something that I never had. *"*

He heard her thought: *Adrian* . . .

Eileen sighed and patted him on the shoulder, almost maternally. "What we have now is a secret. From Carmen."

Adrian spoke her next thought, before Eileen could get it out of her mouth: "And from Nick, too."

ONE HUNDRED TWENTY-THREE

Once back in her car, Eileen texted Nick. *I've come 2 a decision. Do u want 2 hear it?*

Nick was sitting in his living room. The television was on, ignored. He read Eileen's message and wondered if she could really be so callous as to turn his heartfelt proposal of marriage down via text, like a haughty high school cheerleader.

Yes. I wanna hear it.

He didn't really, but the ridiculous proposal had been put into the air, and now Nick had no other choice but to stand by and watch Eileen shoot it down. *Pew, pew, pew.* Nick was unsure whether or not he could live down that embarrassment, and he didn't think he'd be seeing Eileen anymore after tonight.

I'll b at ur place – say an hour?

Ok.

Eileen grinned to herself. It really wasn't very nice to make Nick wait, to make him wonder for a whole hour. But it was fun for her, and once she told him yes, then the wait would make it seem all the sweeter.

She took a last look at Leo's house as she drove by. Eileen sighed, remembered what fun they'd had. *God, he was fantastic. But it wasn't real, none of it.*

"It was great, Leo," she said aloud. "I'll see ya around."

Eileen went home and took a shower. She powdered and primped and preened a little bit in front of the mirror: tonight was gonna be Nick's lucky night. She felt positively giddy with excitement, like some turn-of-the-century virgin bride on her wedding night.

Nick wanted to marry her. How insane was that? What she could have with Nick wouldn't be just a *thing,* like she'd had with Leo. It was going to be a real, proper relationship. Eileen wasn't sure if she was ready to marry Nick quite yet. Like that virgin bride, she didn't know if they were compatible behind closed doors. But also like that bride, she was excited to find out. And since it was 2011, not 1911, taking the giant plunge into marriage (for the third time!) wasn't required to find out.

As Eileen was walking out the door, Carmen returned from her study group. Her mother noted the sparkle in her tan eyes, her smile, the bounce in her step. Eileen smiled to herself because she knew the source of her daughter's good mood. She was in love. With sexy, talented, good, *bad* Leo Wilde.

Eileen arranged her face into a frown of parental offense. "When were you going to tell me about you and Leo?" she asked imperiously.

What about Clint? also sprung to Eileen's mind, but Clint was no doubt a memory already. Carmen had spent the weekend with Leo, so she'd undoubtedly already given her sour boyfriend the old heave-ho. There was no reason to bring him up.

Carmen smiled. "I figured you'd be wondering what I was doing there. It was just like I said. I wanted to go to the movies with you."

"Leo said that was on Friday."

Carmen's grin widened. "Yes. Yes, it was. But I didn't have time to tell you right then, Mom. I had to get to study group." Carmen giggled. "You want to hear about it now?"

"Leo told me. It was love at first sight."

Carmen's eyes further lit up, in pleased surprise. "Is that what he said?"

Eileen nodded. "Is that how it was for you, too?"

Carmen seemed to debate for a moment. Then she agreed. "Yes. I've never met anyone like him. He's just so . . ."

He is most assuredly just so, Eileen thought. She gave Carmen a hug. "Well, congratulations, honey. And good luck. Leo's always seemed like a kind, thoughtful young man to me." *That's right. Just a kind, thoughtful young man.* "He's always so helpful to his aunts and his grandma."

"Thanks, Mom."

Carmen paused and they looked at each other for a silent moment. Eileen sensed that a new door was opening in her daughter's life, and she could see Leo standing there on the threshold, welcoming Carmen, encouraging her to step through it. Carmen had not a clue that her mother had just shut a similar door in her own life, and that the same person had been standing on the other side of it.

Carmen said, "I've gotta go. I said I'd go back out and see him."

"You have fun." *Don't do anything I wouldn't do,* Eileen thought and almost giggled out loud. "I won't wait up."

ONE HUNDRED TWENTY-FOUR

Nick opened the door to his apartment, looking like a whipped pup. Eileen was pleased to see an unmistakable gleam of hope in his pale green eyes, nonetheless.

Wordlessly, she wrapped her arms around his neck and kissed him. Nick responded eagerly. That tiny hope he'd felt converted itself immediately to passion from the catalyst of her kiss.

Eileen discovered that being with Nick was as good – no, it was *better* than being with his cousin, because it was real. It was not just some dark, pornographic fantasy.

Eileen had loved the *idea* of Leo, because he was the embodiment of the *idea* of Adrian. But she had not loved Leo himself, any more than she'd ever had the opportunity to love Adrian. The woman and the boy had nothing in common. They could've never been partners in life, never equals. Too many years would've always stood in the way.

Eileen knew that she could love Nick. Hell, she loved him a little bit already, she realized, now that all that other sordid business with Leo was over. Eileen was not sorry that she'd done it. Now that it was over, now that it had ended so seamlessly, she felt no regret, no shame in her heart that she'd taken a nineteen-year-old boy for a lover. For a season, loving Leo had filled a void in her life. Eileen had loved Adrian once. She'd desired him as she'd never desired another man, and getting to love his son had satisfied all of her burning fantasies. It had brought closure to her dreams of Adrian, now lost irrevocably.

Eileen knew that Leo could never have loved her, not past a physical thing, and that would have quickly become stale. But Nick – Nick must truly love her, to go all the way out on a limb and ask her to marry him. Eileen still didn't want to rush into that right away, but she could see a real future with Nick. Everything was looking up.

ONE HUNDRED TWENTY-FIVE

After dying and being reborn, after unknowingly living as a shy, mistreated boy for seventeen years, after again coming back to himself, Adrian Wilde had finally found the love that he'd always known existed. Just like his mother and father had been, from the moment they met, he and Carmen became inseparable. Before the next week was out, she'd moved into Leo's house on Parcay Street. She had discovered that she just couldn't bear to sleep without him there beside her.

By the 15th of October, Adrian had come to the conclusion that he wanted some kind of permanent symbol of their love, something that showed the world that their union was the product of destiny. He became quite frustrated with his station. To his family, he was more than just a grown man. He was a powerful warlock. He'd traveled the astral spheres, although he remembered nothing of his time spent there. He'd crossed over and back again. But to his beloved and to the world outside of Parcay Street, he was only a nineteen-year-old boy.

Leo was still just too young to get married. It would be comical. He wouldn't even be able to buy his new bride a drink on their honeymoon, not for more than another year and a half.

Leo discussed their situation with Carmen. There was nothing he didn't talk about with her, save for the two secrets that he'd vowed to take to his grave a second time: the summer of unspeakable pleasures that he'd encompassed with her mother, and the fact that he was not a nineteen-year-old kid at all, but Adrian Wilde returned from the abyss.

Carmen was willing to marry Leo. Her conviction was absolute, just like Daina's had been for Ian, and Nadine's too, in her own stubborn, twisted way: there would never be another man for Carmen but Leo Adrian Wilde. That they'd be together until death did them part was second nature to her, but she did agree that all the trappings of a wedding seemed a little silly right at the moment.

"It was a teenage wedding and the old folks wished them well," Carmen sang to him with a giggle, off-key as always. He smiled and kissed her.

Adrian cursed a world that worshipped youth but didn't trust it. Not only could he not yet buy his woman a drink, he couldn't even rent a hotel room if they went out of town for their honeymoon. Leo Wilde didn't have a credit card with which to make a reservation at that hotel, he didn't even have a checking account. He'd never even had a job, except for his short stint bagging groceries at Hilltop Market, when he'd needed cash to purchase his first car. He wasn't enrolled in college. He was a kid, barely more than a child in all aspects, except for his mind and his will and his personality. He was an indolent, guitar-strumming *boy.*

Yet still Adrian longed to make some kind of commitment to Carmen, to consecrate their love in some concrete, palpable manner. Uncharacteristically, he suddenly cared how the world judged them. He wanted to make an honest woman of Carmen. It pained him to think that people would see her as just a careless young woman, living in sin with an unemployed musician, that people would view their fated love as nothing more than just two kids shacking up, playing house.

This desire for permanence, for continuance with one woman, was a new thing for Adrian Wilde. He recognized it as love, what his mother and father had possessed, the thing for which he'd searched through two lifetimes. The cards never lied. His previous lifestyle, his old way of thinking, had indeed been swept away, just that easily, just that completely, in the blink of Carmen's lovely tan eyes. Adrian was no longer a ladies' man. He gave not a thought to any other, except for his one and only lady.

But secular marriage seemed comical to Adrian at the moment, owing to Leo's youth. It would again seem that he was only a boy trying to appear grown up, a child reaching for a man's responsibilities. A religious ceremony was out, also. Neither Leo nor Carmen belonged to any church, and after calling around, Adrian discovered that the established religions were as suspicious of a boy in a hurry to get married as were those hotels and car-rental agencies that wouldn't accept a cash down payment from a kid with no visible means of support: there must be some reason for the rush, and they didn't think that his eagerness made him a good risk. He was too young to engage in custom with the grown-up world, and no local pastors wanted to bless the union of two kids that must be in trouble, especially when they didn't even belong to their faith.

Aunt Penny frowned at the very idea. "Their polished wooden pews are full of a Sunday, Capo. They have enough sheep to worship the God that they have created in their own image, so they have no qualms about shutting the holy doors in your face. Why would you seek a blessing from that kind of worn-out, sanctimonious patriarchy, anyway? You don't ascribe to their narrow-minded tenets."

"Not in the least," Bellona added.

"Because you know better," Daina added.

"Yet I still have to live in my culture," Adrian said irritability. "I want something to show the world –"

"How silly love has made you, my dear," Penny said with a rare, indulgent smile. "Since when has the judgment of the world ever mattered to Adrian Robert Wilde?"

"It's just a piece of paper, Capo," Bellona said.

"That's what Carmen says," Adrian replied. "She has no problem with waiting until Leo's twenty-one, 'til we can go on a honeymoon as adults." He frowned. "But the Magna Carta was just a piece of paper, too, and the Declaration of Independence. Mom and Dad's marriage license. My death certificate. All just ink on chopped up trees, but each –"

"The Magna Carta was written on vellum, Adrian," Bellona said. "A little more durable than –"

"Yet each established a moment in time, made a statement," Adrian insisted. "This event occurred, and the world is forever changed because of it."

Penny and Bellona and Daina blinked silently, nonplussed. Adrian was, as the colloquialism termed it, *as serious as a heart attack* in his desire to create some sort of permanent monument to his love for Carmen. He was single-minded about it. And when Adrian made up his mind, on the rare occasion when he really *cared* about something, his formidable will would not be turned aside.

"Forget about churches and contracts, my boy," Penny said. "We will join your soul and spirit to Carmen's via the old traditions. You can sign man's contract and go on your European honeymoon when man says you have reached your majority, when you can get into man's debt and all the other claptrap associated with being an adult. But for the time being . . . What the universal forces bring together, no man may put asunder!"

Adrian continued to frown. "Carmen doesn't know about our ways."

"You're going to have to tell her sometime, Adrian," Bellona said softly, putting a quiet emphasis on his name, underlining the inescapable fact that he wasn't *Leo* Wilde, just a shy, regular kid. He was *Adrian* Wilde, accomplished warlock, magician, speaker of spells, teller of fortunes, celebrant of the mysteries of the ancient craft.

"The old ways are the fabric of your being, Capo," Penny added. "You cannot separate them from yourself. Carmen wouldn't want you to attempt such a fruitless, foolish sacrifice.

"While it's true that what we are might come as a shock to her, her love for you will overcome the societal stereotypes that she's been taught. Show her the purity of our ways, Adrian, the truth, the destiny. She'll accept that you belong to them."

"You really have no choice," Bellona added, with a trace of arrogance. "You are what you are, my boy. You are of the ancient blood, and nothing in the universe, not even your love for this girl, can change that. If her love is true, she'll accept it. And if she cannot, then it just goes to show that her love isn't –"

"Fate brought us together," Adrian said firmly. "Carmen loves me."

"Then you have nothing to fear," Penny said, a light of challenge sparking in her clear, gray eyes. "I say we undertake the ancient joining ritual. You people can always *get married* later."

"All right," Adrian replied, accepting the challenge.

"How about on Hallowe'en?" Daina suggested. "The day I met Ian . . ."

Hallowe'en was soon: barely two weeks away. But Adrian desired to wait no longer, and besides, he felt that there was something right about the choice of that date. It smacked of just the historical significance he sought, the pinning down of a moment in time that would stand for all eternity. His parents' love had begun on the mystical Sabbat – it would be the perfect time to join his soul with Carmen's.

"All right," he repeated. "I'll explain . . . *us* to her. Today."

ONE HUNDRED TWENTY-SIX

Carmen returned to the house later that afternoon with Eileen. Carmen's mom said hi and smiled maternally at Leo, just the greeting that would be expected of a woman seeing the pleasant young man to whom her daughter was engaged. No trace of untoward appreciation or longing remained in Eileen's expression, because none remained in her heart. The secret of what had been for a season was buried forever.

Eileen was Nick Wilde's woman now – sexy, green-eyed, fun-loving Nick. She glanced down at the sparkling diamond on her finger and smiled to herself. She could ask for nothing more. After a lifetime of annoyances, of struggles, of ups and downs, of heartbreak (when she learned that Adrian was dead), everything was at last stable and happy for Eileen.

She bid her daughter farewell and left to join Penny and Bellona and Daina for an early supper.

Leo was sitting at the kitchen table, shuffling a deck of cards. He nodded at the chair across from him. Carmen sat, and looked at him expectantly.

Leo shuffled the cards one last time, then randomly cut them, holding up the deck so that Carmen could see the card to which he'd cut, but he could not. The first time it was the ace of hearts. He shuffled again and cut again: the ace of clubs. Then the ace of diamonds, and finally the ace of spades.

Leo grinned. *"I cry out for magic,"* he sang in a fair imitation of Ronnie James Dio. *"I feel it dancing in the night."*

Carmen grinned back. "That's not magic. It's just a trick."

Leo's eyebrows went up. "You think so?" He hovered his hand of the deck for a moment, then tapped it decisively. "Now you try it."

Carmen continued to smile curiously at him. She cut the deck at the ace of hearts. She blinked in surprise. She cut again, and it was the ace of clubs. Then the ace of diamonds, and finally the ace of spades. Leo took the deck from her and smiled mysteriously.

"I don't know how you did that. But it still has to be some kind of a –"

"So you're saying that you don't believe in magic?" Leo shuffled the cards again. He set them down and tapped the deck again. This time the four aces were all together at the top.

"Meeting you was magical," Carmen allowed. She reached across the table and covered one of his busy hands with hers. "But these are just tricks."

"Meeting you was fate." Leo set down the deck of cards and took both of her hands in his. "That's what I'm asking you, Carmen. Do you believe in fate? Do you believe there are forces outside of our five senses that play a part in our lives? Do you believe that we can see and understand these forces, wield them to our own purposes sometimes, if we know how to look? Do you believe in magic?"

Here was one of the reasons Carmen loved Leo. He came off the wall with the weirdest topics sometimes. They never failed to give her pause, make her think.

"You mean *real magic?* Not like card tricks and sleight-of-hand, or pulling a rabbit out of a hat? You're asking me if I think that curses and devil worshippers really exist?"

Leo frowned. He released her hands and started shuffling the cards again. This was just the direction in which Adrian did not want the conversation to go.

"Satanism attempts to raise the physical above the spiritual," he said with a patient sigh. "Their practices center more around instant gratification that any kind of –"

"If I sacrifice this virgin to Satan, then he'll grant me that promotion and the corner office!" Carmen said in gleeful derision.

Leo smiled faintly. "Exactly. The physical over the spiritual. The give and take of a transaction –"

"A devil's bargain!" Carmen supplied.

This is not going well, Adrian thought. *Not well at all.*

He tried again. "There is not some greedy central figure lording it over our existence, requiring contracts and sacrifices before reward is meted out, like the Satanists would have us believe. Sometimes boons are granted, if the words and the thoughts and the rituals are right. But sometimes all the wishing in the world will not cause a millimeter in deviation from a prophesied path."

The thought occurred to Adrian that he could have Leo tell his dad's story as an example, at least partially, to demonstrate the reality of divination. He could describe how it'd been foretold, when Daina was just a child, that the boy she'd bear to her one true love would die upon reaching his majority. And damned if it didn't go just like that.

But Adrian decided against it, because even if it did prove that sometimes the future could indeed be seen, it was a depressing story.

Fatherless Leo could tell his beloved that it'd been prophesied that Adrian Wilde would die, and he did die. But then he couldn't reveal the glorious denouement of Adrian's triumphant return. The uplifting, incredible truth could not be revealed to her.

Added to that was the myth of the car accident, instead of the truth of homicide. Adrian just didn't want to go into any of it at the moment. He wanted to assimilate Carmen slowly into his world, not immerse her in all of its supernatural mysteries all at once. It was just as his aunts had said: witchcraft was a part of him. He had to make Carmen aware of his beliefs, but he didn't have to make her believe them.

When Carmen didn't say anything, Adrian tried another angle. "Do you believe in God, Carmen? The Father, the Son, and the Holy Spirit?" When she blinked in surprise, he added, "That kind of thing?" He waited for her to respond.

"Well, yes . . . of course. I believe in God," she stammered after a moment.

"Yet you don't belong to a church. You don't follow any particular *religion.*"

The subject seemed to fluster Carmen. In the incredibly short period of time that they'd known each other, they'd talked a great deal. They'd explored feelings and opinions, memories and perceptions. But one of the subjects that they'd not even touched upon was religion.

Do you believe in God?

Carmen had never thought too much about the existence of a higher power, and she'd certainly never given too much reflection to what His influence might be in her life. She'd never had cause to pray fervently for anything. *God helps those who help themselves,* was about all her mother had ever said on the subject.

And when Allan had made a mention of Jesus in a letter, from his early days of incarceration, Eileen had drily quoted George Orwell: *"Religion is the last refuge of a scoundrel."* Allan's piety had not lasted, and the subject of God hadn't come up again.

But now Carmen felt a small tremor of fear. Was Leo religious? Why was he asking her about a belief in God now? They'd declared their love for each other almost from the first moment. They'd been together barely a month, and had already talked about marriage. Carmen knew Leo wanted to get married, but he wanted to be an adult when he did it. That was still two years away . . .

407

Is he having second thoughts? Carmen wondered. Or, since there was plenty of time before he turned twenty-one, had Leo decided to go over every possible thing that could lead to discord between them?

Do you believe in God?

Carmen followed along with the theory of evolution, basically understood the Big Bang. Maybe there had been some conscious guidance to all of that. It was possible, but not probable, and regardless, the truth of creation was unknowable, so she hadn't really thought about it.

Carmen certainly believed in Leo and her love for him more than she believed in God. She suddenly felt like an unprepared student who'd been called upon in class.

What does he want me to say?

"No. No church. No particular religion," she repeated back to him, to give herself another moment to think. "Mom didn't have time to waste sitting around in a church on a Sunday morning."

Carmen dared a little smile, and to her relief, Leo smiled back. "I guess I'd just call myself a Christian, if someone asked me what religion I am."

"Are you, though?" Leo narrowed his eyes, and again Carmen felt nervous. Why was he making such a big deal about this? "Would you say you're a Christian because you hold Christian beliefs, or because it's the only faith with which you're even vaguely familiar? Would you say you're a Christian because you don't know anything about being a Muslim or a Buddhist or a Zoroastrian or a Jew?"

"A Zoro –?"

"It's an ancient Iranian faith."

Carmen's eyes widened. "You're not a Zoro . . .?"

Leo laughed. "No. You can't convert to Zoroastrianism. You have to be born into it."

Carmen reflected that perhaps it really did take a lifetime to get to know a person. She thought she knew Leo thoroughly. Although their time together had been short, it had been intense. But here he was, surprising her. Who would've thought that her sexy long-haired musician knew anything about some obscure Middle Eastern religion? Who would've thought he knew anything about religion at all?

He'd never mentioned it before. Again Carmen was tense. Was this going to be some make or break point to their relationship all of a sudden, coming completely out of nowhere?

But that was just ridiculous. The thing about their brief relationship with which Carmen was the most comfortable was the ability to talk to Leo about anything. So she just asked the obvious question, the one that he was skirting around for some reason.

"So, if you're not a Zoro-whatever, what are you?"

Leo's smile was immediate, wicked; Carmen's favorite.

"Well, I'm certainly not a Christian. Not by a long stretch." Uncertainty clouded Carmen's light-brown eyes at this declaration, so Leo continued quickly. "It's not precisely a religion, not as you think of Christianity or Judaism. It's a set of beliefs which reach back through European history to the cradles of civilization. Mesopotamia, Egypt, Greece. We've borrowed from more mainstream faiths over the eons, and they've borrowed from us.

"It's a tradition that combines a knowledge of the natural world – remedies and potions and poisons – with an understanding of the unseen forces that guide the universe."

"So you're a Wiccan?"

Adrian winced. "No. Wicca's only been around since the 50s. The *1950s*. It's a derivation of nineteenth century occultism, coupled with its adherents' misguided belief that they are the survivors and descendants, the keepers and passers-on of the mystic knowledge, if you will, of an utterly non-existent European witch-cult, the innocent members of which were once burnt at the stake. No such organized pagan religion ever existed, nor was it harassed by the church. Accusations of witchcraft and executions for it were politically motivated. That's a historical fact.

"Wicca, Neopaganism, whichever of the labels that they choose to put onto themselves . . ." Leo stopped, then abruptly continued. "My Aunt Lily owns an occult bookstore. She sells candles and robes and pentacles and incense to all the new believers. She tells me that the majority of them use their *faith* as an excuse for late night orgies in the woods." When Carmen blinked in disbelief, Leo shrugged. "That's what I've heard, anyway.

"The Wiccans believe that they can trace their rituals back to some widespread Mother Goddess cult, which was brutally and almost completely suppressed by patriarchal Christianity. Except that's all bullshit, Carmen. There was never a cult of maiden, mother, and crone. The founders of Wicca *made that shit up.*

"Crowley spoke of the Archetypal Mother, the Womb of All, the Great Yoni, because he was attempting to try out as many of them as he could." Carmen looked at Leo in mild surprise. He grinned. "There was never a Great Mother Cult, Carmen. The Great Mother is nothing without the Great Father."

Again he grinned. "Not in the sense of the great overseeing god, the man with the white beard, grandfatherly, making sure you say your prayers at night. Not the Christian, Our Father who art in Heaven.

"That we are all derived from woman had always been recognized, from Neolithic stone figurines, through Hathor and Isis and Demeter, Inanna, Brigid; Mary, mother of Jesus. But always was she in concert with the male deity, young and virile. Ready to go, if you will. He represents the potency that, combined with the lushness of the female, leads to creation: Cernunnos and Osiris and Pan and Priapus.

"There is not one without the other. Our Eastern friends call them Yin and Yang. The duality of life – light and dark, fire and water, male and female – each is meaningless without the other."

Adrian shook his head, realizing that he had told Carmen nothing that he'd set out to tell her, about himself, about the arts he practiced. He'd given her a smug diatribe on the artificiality of Wicca, an opinion that was derived from listening to his superior womenfolk through two lifetimes. According to them, Wicca was not the enlightened path. It was a contrived belief system, worth nothing more than a roll in the bushes with a stranger by the light of the full moon. Wiccans were dabblers, dilettantes, poseurs, while Penny and Bellona and Lily, Daina and AnTeen, Randi and himself followed the true ways.

But Adrian had failed to communicate to Carmen just what it was they should be called. What it was they *were.*

He sighed a third time. "You remember how you told me, right up front, that your dad's an ex-convict? Because you didn't want me to be surprised or shocked about it later?" They'd discussed the whole phenomenon, just as they discussed everything.

"What I'm trying to tell you is akin to that. Maybe I should've told you sooner, but it's never been worth explaining to each and every chick I ever met at a party . . ." Adrian paused. He was letting himself show again. Leo had never met too many chicks. He'd just had the one girlfriend.

"But I love you, Carmen. So it's time to tell you the awful truth." Leo grinned, letting her know ahead of time that the truth really wasn't so awful after all, at least not to him.

"I'm neither a Satanist nor a Wiccan, but because of Hollywood stereotypes . . . It's because of Hollywood stereotypes that I even have to make the statement that I am neither of these things.

"But because we burn candles and say prayers and wear robes . . . Not always black ones, mind you. They're colored according to the ritual. But because of these similarities . . .

"My mother . . ." Adrian was thinking of Daina, but his statement also applied to Randi, Leo's mother. "My mother and her friend Nadine, and my grandmother, and my aunts . . . Especially my aunts . . . We all practice witchcraft, Carmen. Not Wicca, Christ save me, but plain old witchcraft.

"It's a family tradition. Not from the Wilde side of the family . . . Dad and Grandpa never went in for it, but I was initiated at an early age." Adrian decided to gloss over Leo's father's participation and include him as a non-believer, along with Ian. In truth, Ian had always more or less *wanted* to believe, because he'd seen enough evidence of the universal forces at work in his life. And at that last, he had certainly believed. But Leo's father and grandfather were both dead. There was no need to talk about what they'd known.

When Carmen didn't speak, he took her hand again and turned it over. "I can read your palm . . ." Leo caressed it lightly with his thumb and Carmen shivered. "I can read your future in a Tarot deck, although it's always best to have an uninterested third party read your cards, lest your interpretation be skewed toward what you *want* to see . . ."

"So you knew ahead of time that we would meet?" Carmen asked skeptically. "You knew everything that was going to happen before it actually did?"

Leo leaned forward in his chair and gazed seriously at her, blue eyes aglow. "I didn't *see* anything about you and me specifically, Carmen. It doesn't work like that." *Not all the time, anyway.*

"I just had a feeling that something was coming. Something life-changing. Aunt Penny read my cards, but that was all she could get either. A big change was coming . . . And then I met you."

Carmen still seemed to be concerned as to whether or not she'd been had in some way, if she'd been tricked. "Did you give me a love potion or something?"

Adrian couldn't tell whether she was serious or not. Like all the women that had ever been important to him – his mother and his aunts and even AnTeen – Adrian couldn't read Carmen's thoughts.

411

He could get a flash of emotion, a mood, but that was all. Now, he couldn't tell if she was believing and accepting that he was a witch, or if she was just having him on about the whole thing.

Leo shook his head. "It's just like the Genie in *Aladdin – I can't make anybody fall in love with anybody else."* He smiled wickedly at her, and Carmen again shivered. "I could give you a little something to make the dreams you have of me a little sweeter, more . . . lifelike. But I can't induce you to dream of me. Your dreams are a product of your own desires and imagination.

"I can sprinkle an aphrodisiac onto your food to make you want me a little bit more, and make you enjoy it a little bit more, once you get me . . . But you had to want me on your own."

Carmen still did not seem entirely convinced. "Did you do any of that?"

"No," Leo replied. Adrian let his arrogance show; he'd certainly earned it. "I didn't have to."

He leaned across the table and kissed her, and Carmen realized it was true. There was witchcraft enough in his kiss, in his touch. Anything else was unnecessary.

"It's just like what they say about alcohol: *what's on a drunk man's breath is on a sober man's mind.* No one can be mystically compelled to act against their will. That's just more Hollywood bullshit.

"I'm telling you about this for two reasons," Leo continued. "First of all, I cannot keep anything a secret from you, Carmen." Except for those two very real, very large secrets. "And it isn't a secretive thing, regardless. It's *part of the fabric of my being,* as my Aunt Penny says.

"I practice mostly *solitaire,* but occasionally join them. We say prayers, burn candles, perform rituals to banish evil forces and invoke helpful ones. We make wishes. There is no monotone chanting, no anonymous sex in the woods with either boys or girls, and I have never attended a human sacrifice."

Unless you count Gil, Adrian thought. *And if you count him, I did more than attend. I was the celebrant on that one . . .*

"I'm telling you so you can have further insight into why I am who I am."

Although the truth of that would probably never be told, either. The intricacies and implications of *The Incantations of Thoth* were better left unexamined, unrevealed.

"It's not like I'd ever expect you to . . . Let me put it this way. Are you familiar with the term *transubstantiation?*"

Carmen blinked. "For an uneducated long-hair, you sure know some big words." It was a joke between them. Leo possessed not a shred of guilt about his indifference to higher education.

"It's never a waste of time to understand other people's beliefs, even if you don't believe them yourself," Leo replied. "When the Catholic priest holds up the wafer and says, 'This is my body, which is for you; do this in remembrance of me,' the church teaches that by means mysterious and holy, the bread, and the wine, too, *are actually transformed into the body and blood of Christ.* They are not meant as mere symbols. They are transformed, *transubstantiated.*

"Now," Leo continued with a grin, "if I were a Catholic, I might believe this to be true. But as I am a fair and thinking individual, I couldn't expect you to believe it to be true. As a thinking individual, I would have to admit that it's a pretty damned far-fetched proposition, especially to someone not raised as a Catholic. I couldn't expect you to believe, but maybe, since you love me, I could ask you to accept *that I believe.*

"And so it is with my family and me, Carmen. You don't have to believe. You just have to accept that we do. And you surely don't have to participate . . ."

Leo grinned brilliantly. "Except for this one little ceremony that I have in mind. That's the second reason that I'm telling you about all this. As soon as I turn twenty-one and can take you on a proper honeymoon, we'll get married. *Sign man's contract,* as Aunt Penny says.

"But in the meantime, there is a ceremony that I'd like you to undertake with me. It's intended to join my soul to yours, Carmen. For all eternity, or at least that's what we believe. What d'ya say?"

"I love you, Leo. I want to be with you forever. That's all I need to believe. If you want a ceremony to celebrate what I already know, I am perfectly willing to go along with it."

"So two weeks or so's not too soon? On Hallowe'en?"

Hallowe'en? How witchy is that? He's certainly serious about all this . . .

"Not too soon at all."

ONE HUNDRED TWENTY-SEVEN

Adrian called Daina to tell her the happy news, and scant minutes later, his phone buzzed. It was Randi.

"I wonder if you could come over here for a minute, *son,*" she said testily. "It's important. But I won't keep you from your domestic bliss for long."

"All right," Adrian said slowly. "I'll be right there." Leo said to Carmen, "That was my mom."

A tiny shadow crossed Carmen's face. She hadn't had too much interaction with Leo's mom, nor with the handsome, silent woman that lived with her across the street. They made Carmen uncomfortable. They'd only stared curiously at her when Leo introduced her, and a curt *pleased to meet you* was all the conversation that they'd suffered to share with her. In the intervening weeks, if she saw them outside, Carmen had waved to them and they'd waved back, unsmiling.

Now that she knew they considered themselves witches . . . Carmen smiled to herself. *Maybe they don't bestow smiles upon unbelievers . . .*

"She needs me to come over there and see her for a minute," Leo said. Adrian picked up Carmen's distaste at the thought of Leo's mom. He smiled. "You don't have to come. I'll be right back."

Carmen smiled gratefully. "I'll be right here."

Leo kissed her affectionately and left the house.

Adrian wondered just what the hell Randi wanted. Now that she was besties with AnTeen, she seldom visited with Penny and Bellona and Daina anymore, so he'd managed to avoid her all summer.

It was just as well: the singular phenomenon of *my lover became my son, and could very well become my lover again, because no one around here would give a good goddamn about it* had sent Randi halfway around the bend. Then the certainty that Eileen was availing herself of that action – Nick might have suspected, but Adrian knew that Randi *knew*, just as Penny and Bellona and Daina knew – those clandestine goings-on had almost sent her the rest of the way around it. That was the main reason that he'd avoided her all summer.

Yet Adrian felt no guilt about Randi's fragile state of mind. We all had our crosses to bear. And AnTeen was there with Randi now to help her accept hers.

Adrian walked into the house without knocking. It was as much his house as it was Randi's: he was blood to the women who held title to it. Hell, it might even be his name. Or maybe his aunts were waiting until Leo turned twenty-one. One more detail pointing up that he was chronologically just a kid.

Adrian didn't know what he was expecting from Randi, but a joyful smile and a motherly hug had certainly not even been on the list.

"Congratulations!" Randi cried. "Daina just called to tell us that you and Cathy are going to be joined!"

"Carmen," Adrian corrected.

Randi was positively perky. All trace of distracted insanity was gone, or at least held in check. Adrian believed that perhaps she'd finally gotten a hold of herself. He'd obviously broken things off with Eileen: generational alliances had righted themselves properly once more. Randi seemed genuinely happy that Adrian, masquerading as her nineteen-year-old son, had pledged himself to a girl his own age.

Nadine stepped forward and offered her hand. She knew better than to attempt to hug the person upon whom, for all intents and purposes, she'd once put out a hit.

"Congratulations," she said, and Adrian shook her hand. "I asked Randi to call you over here, because I'd like to bury the hatchet, Adrian."

AnTeen considered him coolly. Adrian had never been able to read her, past that palpable darkness. It still existed there; he could still feel it. But it seemed cooler now, like her gaze. Coagulated, like hardened tar. He figured that maybe after all these years – he did the math in his head – what was AnTeen, now, sixty-three? Maybe the darkness was a permanent part of her now, like a scar, old and forgotten. It no longer seemed like a wound to Adrian, fresh and throbbing.

So he listened to her words.

"I'd like to apologize for any ill feelings that my past . . . *mischief* may have engendered between us."

No hard feelings, huh? Allan had said, after he'd sold Adrian out to the cops twenty years ago. *You're fucking with the wrong guitar player, Fat Boy,* Adrian had thought at the time, and his thought was similar as concerned AnTeen's apology now.

"No hard feelings," he told her.

415

"I wanted to tell you that I wish you and your girl all the happiness in the universe. You must send her over here to us. She must be prepared –"

"I'm not trying to convert her, AnTeen. I just told her about our beliefs today. She doesn't need any preparation." *Especially not from you.*

"I wasn't referring to an initiation into the old ways, *Leo*," AnTeen replied with a little giggle. She glanced at Randi, who also giggled. "What you choose to reveal to her of the arts . . . Why, that's all up to you. What I meant was – you need to send her to us, so we can prepare her, as we would any young woman about to get married. I'm sure she's not going to tell her mother about this particular ceremony . . ."

"Her mother wouldn't understand," Randi commented.

"I'm sure Cathy would like some other women to laugh and giggle with –"

"Her name's Carmen."

"Of course. I'm sure *Carmen* would like some other women to laugh and giggle with, to help her pick out a dress to wear, and shoes, and all those girlish things. We're a little old for her, but she should have someone to help her. It's a monumental step in a young woman's life, regardless of her beliefs. You haven't given her much time to make ready."

Adrian didn't necessarily trust AnTeen, but he couldn't see any reason why she'd want to harm him anymore, either. Ian was gone. There was nothing left to covet, no further reason to hate.

Perhaps it was never too late for a person to turn over a new leaf, even a bitter, black-hearted old witch like his AnTeen. Carmen's happiness was taking nothing away from her, or Randi either, and Adrian knew that women liked to see other women succeed, as long as they lost nothing themselves in the deal.

And the old women would undoubtedly enjoy playing dress-up with a fresh young girl. They'd pride themselves on setting Carmen upon the path correctly, as they saw it, properly decked out for this important ceremony.

"I'll tell her to come over and see you in the morning," Adrian said.

"Oh, that's great!" Randi gushed, and hugged him again. "We'll have so much fun! A new adventure!"

"Indeed," Nadine agreed.

ONE HUNDRED TWENTY-EIGHT

But in the two weeks prior to the ceremony, Nadine and Randi did provide Carmen with an initiation into the old ways, after a fashion. Nadine explained that when a regular marriage was unfeasible – as in their case, when the world didn't quite recognize Leo as an adult yet, or in ancient times when a couple might not want the eye of the church upon them for some reason – a joining of souls ceremony might be performed.

"And there was that first night thing," Randi added.

When Carmen blinked in confusion, Nadine supplied: *"Jus primae noctis* or *droit du seigneur. The right of the lord.* It was a practice that allowed the medieval gentry to sleep with the daughters of the serfs." When Carmen still looked confused, Nadine said, "Didn't you see *Braveheart?"*

Carmen shook her head.

"It doesn't matter," Nadine dismissed the ancient custom with a wave of her hand. It certainly didn't apply in Carmen's case. "Suffice it to say that there have always been ceremonies for secret marriages. As you are aware, there is nothing legally binding here. No licenses, no contracts, no records kept. But you and Leo will be bound heart and soul, in the eyes of those who follow the craft."

"If it will make him happy . . ." Carmen said with a smile. "Tell me more."

So Nadine and Randi regaled Leo's bride-to-be with the old legends of the great loves of the gods and heroes and heroines of yore. They explained the meanings behind the talismans and symbols, the herbs and flowers, the importance of the four directions, the fire and water and earth and air. This was supposed to bring luck, good fortune. That was supposed to ensure fertility.

Carmen giggled. "I'm not sure I'm ready for fertility just yet."

"No?" Nadine said with a grandmotherly smile. "It's the purpose of the joining."

"Eventually," Randi added.

"And the Wilde genes make for some beautiful babies. Adrian and Leo inherited Ian's blue eyes . . ." Nadine smiled at Randi, including her. Regardless of the supernatural machinations of *The Incantations of Thoth,* Randi's blood ran in Leo's veins, as much as Adrian's. "And Leo inherited Randi's black hair, which he also got from Adrian, by way of Daina. A dynasty of splendor . . ."

Randi grinned. "Or maybe your baby would have green eyes, like from Nick's side of the family. I understand that trait goes back to his grandfather, who was brothers with Adrian's grandfather."

"Perhaps," Nadine mused. "And you are a beauty, yourself, Carmen. Any child born to you and our Leo couldn't help but also be beautiful."

Carmen smiled shyly, acknowledging the compliment. "I think I'd like to finish school first."

"Of course, dear!" Nadine gave Carmen a little hug. "You have your whole lives ahead of you!"

ONE HUNDRED TWENTY-NINE

Penny frowned at Adrian.

"I'm not sure I approve of your choice of witches, Capo."

"What are you talking about?"

"Nadine and Randi . . . Why would you not have Bell and me, or your mother, instruct Carmen in the old ways? Or even Lily?"

Adrian realized that his aunt was miffed. It'd been she and her sister and Lily that welcomed Randi into the fold when she was just a girl. Then Nadine had snatched their protégé away late in life. Penny had perhaps seen the opportunity for a new convert in Carmen, and now it seemed to her that Adrian had turned his beloved over to Nadine, also, without so much as a consultation with his aunts and mother. Witches that'd eternally had his best interests at heart, that had never sought to harm him. Witches that were blood to him.

The beldame's reaction surprised Adrian. "They're not *instructing* her, Aunt Penny. They're not leading her blindfolded into the covenstead's casting circle, or giving her a magical name and terming her *dedicant*.

"No one's trying to convert Carmen to the mysteries. Not yet. If she wants to join us later, then certainly she'll learn the ways at your knee. But for right now, AnTeen and Randi are just helping her pick out a dress. Telling about her what all the herbs and berries and pentacles represent. Knocking down the culturally-ingrained Satanism vibe." Adrian grinned.

Penny shared a glance with her sister, and in its silence, they recalled Nadine's hatreds, her curses, her murderous actions . . .

But Bellona believed in redemption. "It's nice of them to show Carmen the ways, even perfunctorily, I suppose. Randi is of her mother's years, and perhaps it gives Nadine a chance to do something wholesome, for a change. And Carmen might be more comfortable hearing about simple charms and good-luck rituals from them, instead of withered old crones like us."

Penny frowned for another moment, then reluctantly smiled. "It's not like they need attempt to teach her curses and spells to ensorcell your spirit, now do they, Capo? Carmen did that quite on her own, did she not?"

Adrian smiled. "That never works anyway, does it? If it did, then AnTeen would've captured Dad, and Leo would actually be her grandson. After a fashion."

"You blaspheme, Adrian," Bellona said seriously. "It's unseemly to ridicule the desires of others, especially when fate chose not to answer them."

"It's all water under the bridge now, my dearest," Adrian replied, and gave his frowning aunt a hug. "AnTeen is looking to the future now. All her thwarted yearnings . . . All that's in the past. I think she's found a measure of kindness for Carmen that she never had for the rest of us."

"Reply hazy, try again," Penny said, her dourness returning somewhat. "In the same book where it's written of repentance and redemption, one may also find the old saws about ducks that walk and quack like ducks, and the impossibility of tigers changing their stripes."

"I do believe you've become a cynic in your unnaturally old age, Aunt Penny!" Adrian exclaimed. "Why would AnTeen want to harm Carmen? Or me? Or even Leo, through Carmen? Despite what we all know to be true, Leo is still her best friend's son.

"You're seeing old grudges as alive and well, but I say they've turned to dust by this late date. AnTeen is just showing kindness to a young girl, righteously helping to set her on the path to happiness with a warlock of the craft."

"It strikes me as unusual that you'd choose that word, Adrian. From that same book of truth, we are advised to forgive, but never to forget. Once upon a time, Nadine *righteously* believed, and with all her heart, that we'd conspired to steal Ian from her —"

"I'll hear no more of it," Adrian said quietly. "I believe AnTeen's vengeful days are behind her. It feels so strange that I, of all people, feel it necessary to defend her, but I don't think she means me any harm anymore."

"Your future, and Carmen's, may well be riding on this hunch," Penny insisted.

Adrian shrugged. "I think you give AnTeen entirely too much credit, Aunt Penny. She's not imbued with any great power to influence Carmen, or anything else. She's just a bitter old witch, and maybe now she sees a chance to relieve herself of some of that bitterness by befriending Leo's chosen. Besides, it's not as if Carmen has pledged herself to the old ways, and picked AnTeen to be her mentor. I don't think there's anything evil that AnTeen could accomplish in the short time that's left before the ceremony."

ONE HUNDRED THIRTY

It was really a little dramatic, a little Hollywood-witchy, to be conducting what amounted to a pagan wedding on Hallowe'en. Samhain was traditionally a somber Sabbat, not one for new beginnings. It marked the end of the harvest season, the beginning of the dark, cold days of winter. Spirits of the dead hovered, and it was once deemed necessary to disguise oneself to avoid them. It was once believed that those same restless dead needed to be propitiated with food and drink to assure that the faithful would make it through the lifeless, cold season until spring.

But the early purposes of the Sabbat had been forgotten in the modern world, even though the ladies of Parcay Street hadn't forgotten them. Propitiating the dead had turned into trick-or-treating for children, and disguising oneself to avoid one's deceased kin on a dark winter road had turned into an excuse for adults to dress up as pirates and naughty nurses. And besides, this was Riverside, California and the deepest chills of winter would never materialize. Plus, it was the only even vaguely supernatural holiday of which Carmen was aware. Since her beloved claimed to be a witch, Hallowe'en seemed the appropriate day on which to be reciting vows with him.

Randi and Nadine chose a red peasant blouse and matching, flowing skirt for Carmen; they sewed herbs for luck and fertility into its hem. They told the bride-to-be that the portrait of chastity and ignorance and obedience to her husband, symbolized by the traditional white, was unnecessary in the ceremony that was to take place. It was laughable in fact: Carmen was a grown woman, vibrant and alive. The red of her gown symbolized the passion and knowledge of her irrepressible womanhood. At least that's what the old witches told her.

Carmen already knew that the non-traditional color of her attire would not be the least of the odd aspects to the unusual ceremony, which was at last nigh.

She'd been separated from Leo since the morning before, had slept on the couch at Randi's house. Nor had she seen him all day. Just before sunset, Nadine gave Carmen a funnel of scented rice paper filled with herbs, and told her it was for a ritual bath.

"Just throw the whole thing into the tub," she instructed, "paper and all. It'll dissolve."

Carmen donned her red clothes, applied her make-up. When she went out into the living room, Nadine placed a wreath of myrtle leaves in her hair. Nadine then decamped, leaving Carmen alone with Randi.

As mother of the groom, Randi's role was one of honor, and she filled it with only minimal giggling.

"These are for luck, and fertility." She presented Carmen with a handful of dates and a piece of sesame and honey cake and waited patiently while she ate them.

Then they went outside and paused in the street. Nadine, Daina, Penny and Bellona each approached from one of the four points of the compass. They hugged the bride-to-be and wished her well.

The mother of the groom led the procession across the dark street, and up the lighted path. Carmen followed, trailed by the other women. *I mustn't think of them as a* coven, she told herself. *Leo would say that's too Hollywood.*

The deck was dim, lit only by a few fitful torches. Carmen understood the significance of the many flowers and herbs that festooned the railings, all symbols of luck and good fortune and hoped-for fertility for the young couple. The light from the crescent moon showed Carmen that Leo's Aunt Lily would be officiating. She was wearing a dark purple gown, o'ertopped with a cape of a slightly lighter shade of lavender, and Carmen thought, *Well, she's certainly witchy enough.*

There was a large table before Lily. Arranged at the cardinal points were various accoutrements necessary for the ritual. In the center was a flagon of bluish oil and a black, velvet, drawstring bag. The groom stood in front of the table and faced his bride and the other ladies as they came up onto the deck.

Leo wore black: shiny patent-leather shoes, snug-fitting pants, a loose, long-sleeved shirt that laced at the neck. The light from the moon glanced fitfully off of his black hair; it glowed in his dark blue eyes. When he smiled at Carmen, she felt light-headed. Her groom was breathtaking.

Lily also smiled. She gestured for Carmen to come forward. "Enter the sacred circle, young woman."

Carmen did as she was bid. She stood beside Leo. They faced Lily and she joined their hands.

"It is with great joy that I stand here today to join the lives and souls of Leo and Carmen before this company. A lifetime of practice and devotion to the unseen forces of the universe imbue me with the pride and the confidence to invoke this blessing on their behalf.

"In the not too distant future, Leo and Carmen will stand before another officiant. And when he intones, 'By the power invested in me by the great State of California, I now pronounce you man and wife,' he will join them together in the manner of mankind. He will acknowledge their love by means of a contract. He will join them in name, in property, bidding them to honor and obey, to forsake all others, at least in the legal sense."

The assembled witches tittered.

"At that ceremony, all of their family will serve as witnesses. They will rejoice at Leo and Carmen's joining under man's laws. But only those of the blood are present tonight. Only those initiated in the ways of the spheres that guide our destinies bear witness and rejoice at this joining. Man's laws and contracts are oft times entered into foolishly, carelessly, for all are aware that man's contracts can be easily broken, easily tossed aside. There is a different kind of brotherhood that serves to assist in the severing of the ties wrought by mankind. They're called lawyers."

Again the ladies of Parcay Street tittered.

"But the bonds you're about to undertake here tonight are unbreakable. In addition to those members of the blood that are here to bear witness and give blessing, the vast forces of the universe, of fate, all that has always been and will ever be, are invoked to witness and bless your union. That they approve – we know that in our hearts by your very desire to perform this ritual.

"Time will pass. Fortune may smile, or trials may come. No matter what you encounter together, your lives are hereby forever joined, not merely as husband and wife, but as friends, lovers, confidants. Your union will be the staff upon which to lean in trying times, the rock upon which to rest in weariness. Together will you walk the path, from this day forward.

"Behold, the symbol of this joining."

From the round table in between herself and the happy couple, Lily took the black bag, and held it up for the small assemblage of women to see.

"From the realm of the physical, the north, I invoke health, a happy, centered home, and the blessing of fertility." On one corner of the table was a tiny, round loaf of bread, beside a small pile of salt, and one of soil. Lily broke off a small corner of the loaf and put it into the bag, then sprinkled some of the salt and soil atop it.

"From the east, the sphere of air and the mind . . ." Lily tied a feather to the drawstring, and rang a silver bell. "For wisdom, clear communication between you, and the broadening of your intellects."

"From the south, the place of action, symbol of creativity, harmony, vitality and sensuality . . ." Lily struck a match and lit a candle placed on the southern quadrant of the table. She passed the bag above the flame.

"And finally, from the west, the eternal waters, the guarantor of understanding, emotional support, intuition, and friendship." Lily's long fingernails were lacquered a pale, sky blue. She dipped them into the chalice on the west side of the table, and sprinkled the droplets into the bag. She paused, then with a resolute tug, she closed it. She set it down in the middle of the table, then picked up the flagon of oil.

Lily again stuck her enamelled fingertip into the flagon, then anointed Carmen's forehead and then Leo's with a droplet of the fragrant oil. "From the spiritual realm, the very center of the universe, I invoke balance, wholeness, integrity, and growth in the true ways."

With a flourish, Lily swept the velvet bag from the table. She wrapped the string around Carmen and Leo's joined hands, leaving it to dangle between them.

"With a free and unconstrained soul, as freely as God has given me life, I invoke the unseen powers to join you together. Where there has been cold, you have brought warmth to each other. Where your lives held only darkness, now there is light. Your miracle lies in the path you have chosen together. May the true magic of love guide you to navigate it successfully, all the days of your lives."

Leo and Carmen together spoke the words that they'd memorized separately. "We pledge before this assembled company that we shall ever belong to each other, from this day forward. Let us make of our two lives, one life."

Then Leo said, "I give you all I am and all I am to become. Take this ring, and with it my promise of faith, patience and love, for the rest of my life."

Carmen took the ring from him and placed it on her finger. "What have I to give you, Leo? The promise to take you as my only love from this day forward, to stand by your side, to listen when you speak, to comfort you when you cry, and to join your laughter with my own. Take this ring, and be my own."

Leo took the ring Carmen offered him. While Adrian had insisted that Carmen have her own ring – Daina still wore the symbol of her eternal union with Ian – the ring that Carmen gave to Leo had been Ian's own.

"Now are your lives, your spirits, your souls, forever entwined," Lily said. "Wherever you go, you will go together. Whatever you face, neither will face it alone. For good or ill, in happiness or sadness, come riches or poverty, now are you eternally bound, for this life and all others. Love has given you wings, and your journey begins today. Wherever the wind may carry you, you will be as you stand today, side by side."

Lily took the bag from around their hands, and laying her own hands on each of their shoulders, she gently prompted them to turn and face those gathered behind them. She held the bag of their blessings aloft, and cried, "I give you – Leo and Carmen – united! May their days together be long, and may those days be seasoned with love, understanding and respect."

ONE HUNDRED THIRTY-ONE

The rest of 2011 passed quickly.

Carmen threw a small birthday party for Nadine on November 12th, in gratitude for her help in preparing her for the joining ceremony with her beloved.

Penny and Bellona's deck was a hive of activity and familial joy on Thanksgiving. The whole clan was there: Bobby and Tracy, Nick and Eileen, Randi and Nadine, Leo and Carmen and Daina. Just one big, happy family, with not a single secret apparent amongst them to mar their enjoyment of the feast.

Carmen and Leo enjoyed an intimate Christmas together, and Urban Equinox was in full vigor on New Year's Eve, seeing 2011 out with their accustomed bang.

Leo turned twenty on April 8th, 2012, and again the band played.

Carmen was not aware that May 1st marked the Sabbat of Beltane in the wheel of the pagan year. She'd not delved any further into the mysteries of the craft since her soul had been joined with Leo's for all eternity. It wasn't that she was uninterested. It was just that she was too busy with school, and too joyous in making her life with Leo, to be spending very much time hearkening to the idle ramblings of the witches that comprised his family.

May Day fell on a Monday in 2012, and when her classes concluded for the afternoon, Carmen sought Leo at his aunts' house. She founded him in the little clearing there, piling up wood. He smiled at her and gave her a fond kiss.

"I have to talk to you, Leo," Carmen told him.

As always, Adrian could read nothing but a mood from his woman – a slight agitation this time – but he couldn't tell if it was bad news or good news on her mind.

"Give me just a few more minutes," he told her.

She nodded and went up the steps to the deck. There she found Daina and Penny and Bellona, sitting at the little table, as always. Daina told her that Leo's efforts were to enable his womenfolk to enjoy a modest bonfire to mark the Sabbat later that evening. The ashes would then be sprinkled onto Penny and Bellona's garden to ensure a bountiful harvest. Prayers would be said, and special rituals enacted, to protect them from the fairies and other spirits that tended to cause mischief on this Sabbat, as on Hallowe'en.

"It is the day to greet spring with optimism," Bellona said. She gestured at the bouquet of various yellow-hued flowers in the center of the table. "The yellow embodies the fire, and the potency and fertility of the waxing, springtime sun."

Carmen was standing beside the table, listening to the old woman's explanations. Penny studied her closely, taking in all the details of Carmen's loveliness: the slight flush to her cheeks, the round fullness of her figure. She realized at once. "Speak not to our Carmen of fertility charms, Bell. She needs none."

Carmen blinked at her in utter surprise.

"Do you already know, dear?" Penny said with a smile. "Or am I telling tales out of school?"

"I took the test today. It said —"

Bellona also saw the signs, now that she looked for them. She clapped her hands together in glee. "Congratulations, Carmen! How wonderful! Have you told Leo yet?"

"No, not yet. Like I said, I just took the test a little while ago."

Daina was not as perceptive as her aunts. "Tell Leo what?" she asked. "What kind of test?"

"Carmen's pregnant, dear," Bellona said, as if it was the most obvious thing in the world, now that she'd noticed it.

Daina remembered the night that she discovered the wedding ring in Ian's pocket. She'd told herself that she didn't love him, that she couldn't marry him . . . She'd tried to fight the inevitability of the prophecy. She'd not even realized that she was already pregnant with her doomed son on that night. Penny and Bellona had had to point it out to her.

Daina hadn't even realized when she was pregnant herself, and she saw no difference in Carmen's appearance. Daina would have to hear some confirming words from the young woman to believe the news. Daina looked at her expectantly.

Carmen nodded. "There were two lines in the little window . . ."

There was a heartbeat of silence, then all three of them began talking at once, hugging Carmen and patting her, exclaiming over the joyous news. There would soon be another Wilde in the world.

ONE HUNDRED THIRTY-TWO

Leo no longer cared about the silliness inherent in someone his age getting married. He would now soon be a man, even in the eyes of the world, despite only being twenty. He'd soon be a father. He got Nick on the phone, and within moments was talking to Nick's mother.

Marta was an old hand at planning weddings, and she was thrilled to be asked to make the arrangements for Leo and Carmen's.

"I haven't planned a wedding since Bobby and Tracy!" she exclaimed. "And Nick continues to take his sweet time . . ."

Nick and Eileen had announced their engagement, but no date for the actual nuptials had as yet been set.

"You know, Leo . . ." Marta whispered conspiratorially to him on the phone, "Your grandmother found herself in a similar situation. As I did myself. Nowadays, young women don't feel as though they have to get married when . . . when these things happen. There is little shame in being an unwed mother these days."

Marta put the shame back into *unwed mother* just by the tone she used to speak the words.

"Are you kids sure that you want to take this step?"

Leo hesitated. What should he call Nick's mother? Though Adrian remembered Marta well, this was the first conversation that Leo had ever had with her. Her sons were grown, each had his own house, his own life, and young Leo had never had cause to visit the ancestral Wilde manse. He'd never spoken to Nick's father, either, nor had he spoken more than a few words to Nick's Uncle Rob. The twin orthopedists and Will's wife had been a generation removed from Adrian, and two from Leo. They were distant relatives.

"Yes, we're sure . . . *Aunt Marta,"* Leo finally said.

He could tell she was pleased with the appellation. Marta Wilde displayed all her emotions without equivocation, through her tone of voice. "Send me the bride," she said joyfully. "I'll have everything prepared in about a month or so. Under the circumstances, we mustn't waste any time."

ONE HUNDRED THIRTY –THREE

True to her word, Marta made all the arrangements and bookings. She decided that Leo and Carmen must have the quintessential June wedding. It could take place on no other day than Saturday, June 9th, 2012, at precisely one o'clock in the afternoon. No other date would suffice.

Marta was forced to exercise her formidable powers of persuasion upon the management of the country club. She reminded them that the Wilde family had patronized their establishment for decades. Since the hoary old days of the 1940s, Professor Jameson and his brother Doctor Felix had drank cocktails, smoked cigars, played golf, and paid the hefty membership fees there.

This history lesson was necessary because the wedding of some nouveau riche newcomer's daughter was already scheduled for Leo and Carmen's golden Saturday. But at a few words from Mrs. William Wilde, the other couple's ceremony was bumped (and unceremoniously) to the following weekend.

Carmen enjoyed the excitement of the millions of decisions she had to make, with Marta's help: the invitations, the colors and the flowers, the cake, the food. She asked Nick to book the band, and was thrilled when he talked Mickey's house band, Rolling Blackout, into taking the gig. Carmen had enjoyed their sound on many a Saturday night while she'd been dating Clint, and she particularly liked their good-looking singer, Wes Thomerville. She thought that Leo might come to resemble Wes a little bit, once he got into his thirties.

Marta also helped with Carmen's dress selection, mostly because Eileen hadn't had a formal gown for either of her weddings, and was at a loss as to what to choose. Eileen was also a little nonplussed with the budget Leo had afforded his bride for the ceremony. She at last discovered the primary reason that he continued to be an indolent musician, even in the face of impending fatherhood: Leo had plenty of money.

But despite all the glitz and glamour, despite the unspeakable extravagance that was going into her grand, country club wedding, Carmen valued the little ceremony that she and Leo had undertaken by the light of the October moon far more. Just as Lily had said, this June ceremony was for the world, to join their names and their assets, to assure that their baby would be born into the proper, upstanding social setting. While she didn't count herself as a believer, the little pagan ceremony meant more to Carmen than any official matrimonial contract ever would, despite the lavish setting, the band, the food, the liquor, the extensive guest list.

Leo was a believer, and he believed that the little bag that still hung from the corner of their headboard, and the words that had accompanied it, had linked his soul to Carmen's forever. And because Leo believed it, Carmen cherished that brief, torchlit ritual far more than the big wedding that was to come. Despite the expense, their country club wedding was just man's contract, designed to bind them until death did them part. The other ceremony had bound them for all eternity.

ONE HUNDRED THIRTY-FOUR

Adrian was ecstatic that he'd soon be a dad, and long-held priorities shifted in Carmen's mind at the idea that she'd soon by a mom. The prospect of the exciting world of land use law – Carmen had taken a page from Eileen's career choice book – no longer seemed so exciting. She was currently enrolled in classes for the summer semester, but was undecided if she'd go back in the fall. The baby was due in January, and by then, she'd be a different person, with different priorities. It would be time to care for her baby then. School could wait, as could a career.

Leo, on the other hand, was suddenly awash in the need to assume adult responsibilities, after they returned from their brief honeymoon in San Francisco. This need didn't stretch so far as to compel him to go to college – Adrian would never go to college – but he did run out and look for a job. He didn't need the money, but he also didn't want the powers-that-be to put *Unemployed* under *Occupation* on his kid's birth certificate. So he trotted out into the big wide world and acquired the first job for which he applied, selling guitars at Guitar Center. Adrian was inordinately proud of himself – he'd been two people, but he'd held few jobs. He planned to keep it only until his baby arrived. Then he planned to be a hands-on dad.

Carmen was again immersed in the charms and talismans of witchcraft. All the ladies of Parcay Street wanted to ensure the health and happiness of the latest Wilde offspring, and they offered advice to the mother-to-be, and said mysterious words over her growing belly, gave her charms to wear, and herbs to put under her pillow whilst she slept. They came in pairs: Nadine and Randi, or Penny and Bellona, or Daina and Penny or Nadine and Bellona, and they also visited her individually. Leo just nodded and smiled. Rituals for a mother-to-be were unknown to him, but his womenfolk were steeped in the craft.

During her seventh month, Carmen picked up a copy of *Rosemary's Baby* from Penny and Bellona's vast library. The tale was ominous and horrifying – Rosemary had been impregnated by Satan, with the assistance of a coven of witches that lived in her building, and her selfish, ambitious husband. But the story amused Carmen, even though she couldn't help but draw the inescapable comparison between Minnie Castevet and Penny, Bellona, Daina, Randi and Nadine. Minnie brought Rosemary potions to drink and talismans to wear, as did Leo's witchy womenfolk, but the talismans they gave to Carmen didn't stink, and the potions caused her no pain.

Despite the witchcraft that positively permeated her pregnancy, Carmen felt only love from the ladies of Parcay Street. She wasn't carrying Satan's child, she was carrying Leo's, and since his relatives wanted to see the baby thrive and grow, they called on their supernatural beliefs to ensure its health. Carmen of course believed none of it, but the wearing of a few pentacles and charms was harmless, as were the words Randi and Nadine said over her fat belly. And the delicious herbal portions never failed to make her feel fit and refreshed. Carmen believed her complete lack of morning sickness was a direct result of these concoctions.

Throughout her pregnancy, whenever the topic of delivery was brought up, no at-home, midwife nonsense was ever discussed, however. Carmen had a fine obstetrician. Bellona had Googled his credentials. Carmen would give birth in a hospital, as had Daina and Randi. If any complications arose, the witches of Parcay Street trusted in modern medicine to alleviate them.

ONE HUNDRED THIRTY-FIVE

Carmen went through all the classical steps to delivery, like something out of a sitcom, right down to *Honey, it's time.* David Nicholas Wilde made his entrance onto the stage of life on Sunday, January 15th, 2013, at 1:37 in the afternoon. He gave his mother very little trouble in being born, and his father none at all.

Allan Coleman had left the state the previous year, before Carmen had even met Leo. She hadn't talked to him since, so he was unaware that she was wed, unaware that he was a grandfather. Carmen was not sure if he even still lived, but she didn't miss him. He'd either come back and she'd give him all the joyful news, or he wouldn't. Allan had never been a big part of her life.

Carmen's grandmother and Eileen and Nick had sat around in the waiting room through Carmen's brief delivery, so they were the first ones in to congratulate the new mother and jubilant father, the very second that visitors were permitted. There were hugs and tears and well-wishes, reminisces of Eileen's birth from Mrs. Artus, and tales of Carmen's birth from Eileen.

Baby David's mother's side of the family (and Nick) peeked in the nursery window at him for a moment, then departed. Carmen was to be released the following day. They'd all be seeing little David soon enough.

Tracy and Bobby also popped in for a quick look-see at the new arrival.

Penny and Bellona didn't feel it necessary to visit the hospital at all. Their thoughts echoed the Artus branch of the family: they'd be seeing the baby soon enough. In addition, they were getting on in years, and barely ever left Parcay Street anymore, not even to do the shopping. Since they'd once again embraced Nadine and Randi into the fold, Randi did their shopping for them.

Daina and Randi and Nadine also took a laid back approach to visiting the happy mother and child. There was no reason to rush to the hospital, to stand around in the hallways, to pace the waiting room, while the historic event was taking place. No need to pounce upon the exhausted new mother, the moment she was put into a room. They waited until the day after David's birth to visit. Like a hotel, check out time was eleven, so the three witches arrived about nine o'clock. They planned to congratulate Carmen, take a peek at David, slap Leo on the back, and then return home and prepare everything for the arrival of the heir apparent.

ONE HUNDRED THIRTY-SIX

Randi and Nadine stood in the hallway and gazed fondly at the newest Wilde to enter this vale of tears.

Daina was still saying a few words to Leo and Carmen, but she soon joined them. She scanned the rows of clear plastic boxes for a black-haired, blue-eyed babe. To her consternation, however, Daina could glean not a single familiar feature upon any of the faces of the brand new lives contained therein. She looked the babies over a second time, then a third. An expression of utter embarrassment wreathed her own features.

"'Deen!" Daina whispered fiercely. "Which one is he?"

Nadine pushed down the hatred that she'd felt for this woman for the better part of her adult life, and smiled. "Right there." She pointed to the box directly in front of them. Nadine watched Daina's expression, and reveled in the surprised disappointment that seized it for a split-second.

"Oh . . ." Daina said, erasing the distress from her voice as quickly as she did from her face. "He's got blonde hair."

Randi grinned. "He's got no hair."

"He's got a little," Daina disagreed. "You just can't see it very well because it's . . . blonde."

"You sound surprised, Daina," Nadine chirped, entirely too cheerfully.

Daina looked at her former best friend quickly, making sure to make her expression surprised, and not disappointed. "I guess I am." She looked back at the baby and giggled nervously. "It doesn't matter though, does it? As long as he's got ten fingers and toes." Daina paused, then mostly to herself she murmured, "I guess I expected him to have black hair, like . . ."

"Like his father," Randi finished for her.

"And like you," Daina said defensively. "And Adrian, and me."

Nadine sighed theatrically. "Genes are tricky things, Daina. You expected our David to inherit black hair from his closest male relatives? Both of Leo's parents had black hair, but Adrian inherited his from the female side, from you. Ian's hair was brown." *That beautiful, rich, chocolate brown . . .*

"But Adrian inherited his blue eyes from Ian. And so did Leo," Daina countered. "From the male side."

"Yet you and Randi also have blue eyes," Nadine pointed out. But the women's blue was of a lighter shade. No one who'd ever known Ian could've failed to recognize that his son and grandson had inherited their eye color from him, regardless of their mother's genes.

"David has obviously inherited his blonde hair from his mother," Randi postulated. "It might darken up as he gets older . . ." She grinned at Nadine. "But I doubt it."

Nadine grinned back at Randi. They were entirely too happy, and Daina wondered vaguely if they were on something. She knew that Nadine had become a big fan of what she termed *relaxation potions,* since she'd taken up residence with Randi. And throughout Carmen's pregnancy, the two of them seemed to imbibe on a quite regular basis. Some days, they'd seemed positively slap-happy with mirth.

"So maybe David's also inherited Ian's blue eyes," Nadine suggested. "We'll just have to stand here and wait 'til he wakes up to find out. In fact, that's just what Randi and I have been waiting to see."

Nadine was inescapably reminded of the day in 1970 when she'd stood outside another nursery and gazed at another baby. This hospital where Carmen delivered her bundle of joy hadn't even been constructed then.

Nadine had found newborn Adrian Wilde to be ugly, like a little, black-haired monkey: he looked just like Daina. But when he opened his eyes, Ian had been unmistakable in him. After a moment, Nadine had been forced to look away from the little person that probably couldn't even see her, because it'd been too much like gazing into his father's beloved, dark, cobalt-blue eyes.

Adrian should've been hers. But since he was Daina's, hatred for him had settled onto Nadine then. It was a different kind of monkey, and its influence on Nadine's thoughts and actions had abated little in the ensuing decades.

Now Nadine stood with Adrian's loathed mother, and with his one-time-and-one-time-only lover, the vessel of his rebirth. They waited for his son, *for Leo's son,* to awaken.

After a short time, the newborn smiled, perhaps having his first dream, then opened his eyes. As doting relatives always believe, he seemed to look directly at them.

Daina frowned in unconcealable disbelief. "Why he's got . . . he's got green eyes!"

Randi leaned closer to the window. "So he does!" She grinned at Nadine. "Like Nick!"

"No," Daina disagreed. She was suddenly put in mind of Nick's father, Will, her one-time lover, from a million years ago, from before Ian, before Adrian. Her six weeks' boyfriend, Will Wilde, from before her life had truly begun. Will had beautiful, pale green eyes, the color of creamy jade. He'd passed the attractive trait onto his sons.

Ian had inherited his own stunning blue eyes from his mother, and he might've carried the gene for green eyes from Jameson. He might've passed it on to Adrian, and Adrian might've passed it to Leo, *recessively,* or whatever the word was . . . genetics had never been Daina's long suit. But this dark shade of green that David possessed – Daina reckoned that it must've come from Randi's side of the family or more probably from Carmen's. No one in Daina's clan had ever had green eyes, and the color of David's was not a shade possessed by any other Wilde of her acquaintance, and she knew all of them.

"In what seems like another lifetime," Nadine said sagely, "I dated an ophthalmologist."

"An ophtha –?"

"An eye doctor, Randi," Nadine told her with a touch of irritation. Then she smiled again. "It was in Paris . . . I waxed poetic about his profession. Oh, the kaleidoscopic spectrum of colors of the human iris that he got to see! From the blackest browns, the clearest hazels, the tans, the emeralds, the pale jade greens. The blues, from the palest powders, through the skies, to the darkest porcelains . . ."

Like Ian's and Adrian's and Leo's, but unlike David's . . .

Daina and Randi waited for Nadine to get to the point.

She sighed. "But my eye doctor wasn't much of a romantic, for a Parisian. He shot down all my lyrical meanderings. He said, '*Pour un médecin, les yeux viennent dans deux couleurs seulement. Bleu et brun.*'"

Again, Randi and Daina waited, this time for Nadine to translate. Neither had been world travelers, as she'd been. She might've been speaking Swahili for all they knew.

"It means, 'To a doctor, eyes come in only two colors. Blue and brown.' I said that such a thing was patently ridiculous – all the gradations, that were neither brown nor blue – the tans, the hazels, the greens . . . but he shook his head. 'Green is an illusion,' he told me. 'It's actually a shading of brown or a shading of blue. There is only blue and brown.'"

Randi gazed at the baby again. "Carmen has tan eyes. They're so pretty, so unusual."

"Brown," Nadine said.

"And Adrian . . ." Randi put her hand over her mouth, like a contrite schoolgirl. "Leo has –"

"Leo has blue eyes," Daina said in amazement. "From Adrian. From Ian . . ."

"Apparently Leo's dark blue mixed with Carmen's light brown has produced David's beautiful shade of dark green!" Randi clapped her hands together gleefully.

"Maybe they'll blue up or brown up more when he gets older," Nadine opined. "Maybe you'll be able to see his parents in him more . . . *later.*"

"Or maybe not," Randi said. "Sometimes kids don't look exactly like their parents. Maybe he'll be more than just the genes he inherited, the little squiggly things for hair color and eye color. Maybe David Wilde is just gonna be a new individual . . ."

Nadine laughed heartily. "He's already an individual, Randi, like no other little boy ever born. Whoever he was in his last incarnation . . ." Nadine's eyes sparkled with delight. "He's got five initiated grandmothers of the blood, now. We know who he will be in this life."

"David Nicholas Wilde." Randi also smiled merrily. "Newborn warlock!"

"He'll grow into a man of unparalleled consequence under our tutelage," Nadine continued, eyes ablaze. "A man of mystical power, of majesty, of vengeance . . . A force of nature . . ."

"A force to be reckoned with!" Randi added triumphantly.

To her amazement, Daina watched them give each other an exuberant high-five. The sound of their palms smacking together reverberated down the hall. Two or three babies in the nursery began to cry. But not David. He just seemed to smile at them.

"Well . . ." Daina said uncertainly. "We'll all be here to guide him on his . . . unique path."

Though nonplussed a little by Randi and Nadine's fervent love and commitment to the newest member of the Wilde clan, after a moment, Daina also smiled.

****

Also by LM Foster

A Passing Resemblance
Contrariwise – A Tale of Twins
Corvino
Crypsis
Duck Feet
Peter's Sisters

Two Green Keys:
Two Green Keys
Adapted for the Screen

One Wilde Ride Trilogy:
Part One: It Might Have Been
Part Two: An Exceptional Boy
Part Three: What Should Never Be

Stars and Guitars:
Talk To a Movie Star
Where The Guitars Play

Tom and Wiley:
This Carnival of Strange
Wiley Royce
Generally Recognized as Safe
Wiley Royce Versus The Martians